CRIM
HITS HOM

CRIME
HITS HOME

A COLLECTION OF STORIES FROM CRIME FICTION'S TOP AUTHORS

EDITED BY
S.J. ROZAN

NAOMI HIRAHARA	WALTER MOSLEY
DAVID BART	TORI ELDRIDGE
SARA PARETSKY	ELLEN HART
SUSAN BREEN	G. MIKI HAYDEN
GARY PHILLIPS	JONATHAN SANTLOFER
NEIL S. PLAKCY	JONATHAN STONE
RENEE JAMES	OVIDIA YU
CONNIE JOHNSON HAMBLEY	BONNIE HEARN HILL
GABINO IGLESIAS	STEVE LISKOW
A.P. JAMISON	S.J. ROZAN

HANOVER
SQUARE
PRESS

HANOVER
SQUARE
PRESS™

ISBN-13: 978-1-335-42579-9

Hanover Square Press
22 Adelaide St. West, 41st Floor
Toronto, Ontario M5H 4E3, Canada
HanoverSqPress.com
BookClubbish.com

Printed in U.S.A.

CRIME
HITS HOME

CONTENTS

INTRODUCTION

Home is the place where, when you have to go there, they have to take you in.

—Robert Frost

Everyone comes from someplace. Everyone lives someplace. Everyone feels safe, feels at home, someplace. These three places may all be the same; or maybe not.

Some people have found a home and are content where they are. Some feel trapped where they are and yearn to leave to find a home. Some have left and yearn to go back home.

Everyone also has a group they feel they belong to, a tribe that's theirs. For some this is family, blood relatives; for others, coworkers. Or people of the same skin color. People of the same religion. The same gender identity, the same politics, the same love of millinery or *Minecraft* or the Mets.

Safe at home—that feeling you get when you're in your living room, your team's stadium, at your family's Sunday dinner.

Your local café, or bar, or church, synagogue, temple, mosque. Walking down the streets of your city, your village.

But even here, in this safest of places, sometimes

CRIME HITS HOME

What happens then?

In this volume, twenty writers consider this question. They've tackled the subject from varied angles, using varied tools: microscopes and telescopes; maps, time, and memory. Some of the stories are dark, some funny; some proceed inexorably to tragic outcomes, others to triumphant ones. Protagonists range from children to elders, ex-cons to family members to hired assassins. Settings are cities, suburbs, islands, ranches, and swamps. Nothing ties these stories together except the sense of home— and a strong tie it is.

This book was conceived pre-pandemic, before most of us became far more intimate with our homes—at least, their physical manifestation as the places where we live—than we ever thought we'd be. Now, when the worst of the pandemic seems behind us and we're starting to venture out, it may be a good time to ask again: What happens when CRIME HITS HOME?

We invite you to allow the stories here to guide you as you contemplate this question.

S.J. Rozan
New York, NY
July 2021

GRAND GARDEN

NAOMI HIRAHARA

"Five cents."

"Pardon me?"

"Five cents, mister." I jumped in to help my mother.

The mustached patron wore a blinding white suit with a navy blue string tie fastened around the collar of a striped shirt. His straw hat was tipped to shield his pale splotchy face from the Southern California sun. Grasping his elbow was a proper madam with a bouffant hairstyle and a long pink flowing dress. Over her shoulder she balanced a pastel yellow parasol, long tassels hanging off of its edges.

Okāsan lowered her eyes, ashamed that she could not be understood. The obi around her waist was tight around her kimono. Because she was so padded, only my father and I knew that she was pregnant. My father insisted that she continue to work because most visitors to the Grand Garden in Pasadena, California, expected to see a Japanese woman in a kimono.

The patron placed two nickels on our wooden counter. My

mother slowly picked up one coin at a time, placing them into
the far left compartment of the money box that the owner had
provided for us. My mother was a woman of few words, which
made me pay attention to her every time she spoke.

"What an enchanting place," the madam said, admiring the
moon bridge over our goldfish pond beside a pathway lined
with cherry blossom trees. "I never knew this existed." A high
fence hid the public from our world. Our garden was flanked
by young pine trees, their branches extended like arms reaching
out for help. Down in a valley was a dark brown Japanese-style
wooden house. "Does anyone live there?" she asked, loosening
the grip on her umbrella.

By this time, my father had arrived from trimming one of
the pine trees. "We do," he said proudly, his pruning shears in
one hand.

"Really?" The couple were fascinated by my father's figure,
wearing a cotton yukata with a sash tied below his slightly protruding belly. Unlike my mother, my father loved to talk and
spoke both English and Japanese fluently, making him a perfect
ambassador for the garden.

After he turned to take them to the moon bridge, we could
hear his regular spiel. He and five other Japanese men had built
the house from scratch on this block just south of downtown
Pasadena at the turn of the twentieth century. Absolutely no
nails were used in its construction. My father himself had carved
the decorative rectangular wood panels that were affixed above
our sliding doors.

The woman cooed. Okāsan had again won over our patrons.

I had lived in Grand Garden my whole life up to then. I didn't
realize how odd our home was until perhaps my seventh year.
We had a gong hanging from a stand in front of our house, and
whenever the milkman would make his delivery, he would hit
it with a stick that was attached to the frame by a thin rope.

He didn't have to do that, but I think that he got a thrill from making a sound that reverberated through the pine and cherry blossom trees and down the streets of Fair Oaks and California, which were lined with parked Model T's.

There were only a handful of Nisei children in my school. One was the son of a laundryman in downtown Pasadena, a few blocks north. The business took up the first floor of his building; in the back were Japanese women, their faces flushed from the heat, bent over ironing boards that flipped out from the wall. The smell of starch permeated the crowded room and after a while, beads of sweat collected on my forehead from the heat and humidity.

A few of the laundry workers folded the billows of bleached bedsheets that would be delivered to the area's luxury hotels. Kentaro lived upstairs in rooms carpeted by rugs from East India and slept in an actual bed. My other friend, George, lived behind their nursery in a wood-framed building that had planks on the floor. George's family also had a Japanese garden, but it was a small one, a point of pride for his father but no one else in the family.

Both Kentaro and George knew about my living situation at Grand Garden but never asked about it. They certainly never came by. We all wanted to fit into our grammar schoolmates' circle. Grand Garden only confirmed the perception of how foreign we were.

In terms of our white classmates I avoided telling them any personal details. "We live downtown," I'd say and they assumed that I lived in a brick building like Kentaro's family laundry storefront.

I hoped that my classmates would never visit Grand Garden and for the most part, I had nothing to be worried about. Our visitors were usually older couples or high school girls seeking to take special portraits. Every March we'd have our Cherry Blossom Festival and my father insisted that I get dressed in an indigo-colored kimono and straw zori and bow to the guests from the landing around our house. When I was five, it had been like pretend play. But standing in front of white faces five years later, I felt like an animal on display at a zoo. Alongside my mother, who repeatedly bowed in her kimono, I waved my limp wrist unenthusiastically. It was as if I was shooing away flies rather than being a good ambassador.

I lifted my head and then spied someone I knew—a classmate, Nicholas Buchanan, who looked as bored as could be, but then his eyes met mine and his expression changed to confusion and then delight. He was with his three younger brothers and pulled at their elbows and shoulders. He pointed at me, his mouth moving fast. He doubled over in laughter and his siblings followed suit. The inside of my mouth felt dry and pasty. I felt like vomiting.

After the program was over, my mother was called to greet guests at the front of the garden. I attempted to retreat back into our house, but Nicholas stood in my way on the landing that surrounded the first floor. He was tall with thick brown hair that could not be tamed.

"Do you live here?" he asserted more than questioned.

I wanted to deny my connection to the house and even the entire entity of Grand Garden, but how could I explain my costume and familiarity with the premises? I wanted to beg for him not to tell anyone, but I couldn't be that direct.

While on the landing, he searched through the crowd for his brothers. Unable to locate them, he turned his attention back to me. "Take me to your room," he ordered.

"Visitors aren't allowed up there."

"But my father paid a nickel for all of us to come in here." Nicholas took a few steps toward me. He was at least a head taller than me and his breath smelled like licorice.

I wanted to push him away but I knew that Mr. Buchanan was a respected community member. He served on the board of the Tournament of Roses Parade. He could cause trouble for my family. I felt that I had no choice but to relent.

"You'll have to take off your shoes," I told him as we reached the genkan where we left our shoes neatly in pairs.

He reluctantly agreed and slipped off his boots without undoing the shoelaces. His socks were filthy and holey. I found the miserable state of his socks strange as the Buchanans were supposedly well-to-do.

He whipped through the bottom floor, not finding anything of interest. The tearoom on the corner was open to all. A recessed tokonoma displayed a flower arrangement with camellias and pine that my mother had created. The middle room, where we ate, was virtually empty, aside from a low table and three zabuton on the tatami mats. The kitchen was virtually all linoleum, an uncomfortable place that no one, even my mother, wanted to spend too much time in.

We marched up the wooden stairs, Nicholas's heavy footsteps sounding strange to my ears.

Upstairs were two rooms—a living room and a sleeping room. Like the bottom level, the floor was covered with rectangular tatami mats.

"It smells funny in here," he said as he entered the bare room where my parents and I slept.

I sniffed and didn't notice anything out of the ordinary.

"Do you sleep on the floor?"

I barely nodded. Oh, how I wished that I had an iron bed frame like all my other friends had.

I pointed to the wide sliding doors on the other side of the room and Nicholas pulled open one of them to reveal folded padded mattresses that we lay on the floor each night.

Nicholas returned to the living area, which was separated from the sleeping area with a shoji screen, paper squares painstakingly glued on a light wood frame. The paper wore out after time, and once every three years, my father would dedicate a weekend to replacing the paper squares. Against the opposite wall was another recessed tokonoma, where my father rotated various sumi-e ink screen paintings. For this season, the featured painting was of a daruma with bulging eyes. He had no arms and legs; they had atrophied from disuse while the daruma stared at a blank wall and meditated nonstop for several years.

Next to the tokonoma was a wooden tansu, where my mother stored our undergarments, smaller pieces of clothing and toiletries in its many small square drawers. Nicholas ignored its contents because the item on top of the tansu, an impressive samurai sword resting on a wooden stand, was much more enticing. That katana had been given to my father by a neighborhood antiques dealer in exchange for some woodworking repairs he had done. The sword was from the 1600s, when Japan had been completely closed to outsiders.

"Don't play with that." I was going to add that the blade was sharp, but he had already taken the katana from its stand. He slipped off the scabbard, which was made of lightweight wood and wrapped with a red decorative cord. Nicholas's dirty fingers took hold of the long grip, making clumsy swipes. He obviously did not expect that the sword would be so heavy.

I stood frozen for a moment. My father had forbidden me to touch the katana. When I was younger I was fixated on the sweeping curve of the covered blade and the round tsuba, the guard between the blade and the handle. Now, without permission, my classmate had taken hold of the sacred artifact. I was both offended and envious of his brashness. I wished that I wasn't so restrained. Why, in fact, did I have to ask permission to touch something in my own home?

As Nicholas adjusted to the weight of the blade, his movements became more aggressive. He even brandished the sword my way, missing the long sleeve of my kimono by only inches. As I retreated, he pulled back his elbow and stabbed one of the paper squares in the shoji screen. RIIIIP, the tearing sound was horrendous and I almost blacked out before I focused on the damage. The torn paper hung down, allowing sunlight to stream through its hole.

"What have you done!" I screamed. Nicholas could tell from the desperation of my voice that he had done something seriously wrong. He immediately dropped the blade onto the tatami mat and ran down the stairs back into the garden. I went to the balcony and watched him as he zigzagged through elegantly dressed women and men, past the wooden tower holding an ancient bronze bell and through a line of shedding cherry blossom trees, a carpet of pink petals on the dirt path.

My hands shook as I slipped the blade back into its scabbard and returned the sword back on its stand. It no longer held any allure for me. All I knew was that I had to repair what it had wrecked.

I spent the rest of the afternoon attempting to fix the torn shoji screen with some paper I used for schoolwork and leftover rice gruel. What resulted was worse than the initial damage itself.

My mother returned to the house and began to prepare our dinner. My appetite had completely diminished. In fact, just the thought of food made me feel queasy. The sun was going down and I prayed that the darkness would overtake our house to win me at least a night of reprieve. Yet the atrocity did not escape my father's eyes. Despite being puffed up from the success of the day's festivities, he was prepared as usual to see any kind of imperfection in me and our house.

"Who did this?" my father bellowed, pointing to the damaged square, the paper obviously mismatched and the rice gruel creating unsightly bumps on the wood frame.

His question was rhetorical because who else could have done such a thing? No outsiders were allowed into our house without an official invitation.

The thrashing came, hard and quick with a bamboo stick. Afterwards, my mother cleaned my back with soap and water and spread the healing sap of an aloe vera plant onto my wounds.

That night the Santa Ana winds blew through San Gabriel Valley and I dreamt that somehow our house would completely fall apart. I pictured the second floor where we slept collapsing onto the first, destroying the tearoom below. But the next morning the house remained standing and the trees below lay bare of any pink blossoms. It was as if the garden knew the festivities had ended.

The next Monday I was on the schoolyard with the other Nisei boys when Nicholas, wearing suspenders over his white shirt, burst into our circle.

"My brothers want to go into your Japanese house."

I said nothing at first. Scabs had already started to form on my back from my father's thrashing.

"Did you hear me, we will be coming to your Japanese house today."

"You'll have to pay a nickel each to get in," I told him.

Nicholas's shirttail stuck out from his pants. "You don't want the whole class to know that you live in a Jap house, do you?"

There, he had made the ultimate threat. If the secret of my residence became public, I imagined boys breaking into the garden, throwing rocks at the house and climbing up the bell tower. My family and I would be tormented on a regular basis. I was now beholden to Nicholas until he became bored with my curious living situation.

"After school. We'll meet you there," he stated.

After Nicholas left to join his brothers, both Kentaro and George looked wounded. How could I have let our white classmate invade my world?

Nicholas had made good on his word. When I rushed home, he and his three brothers were already waiting on the corner outside the garden. My mother always sat at the entrance to collect nickels from visitors but often had to take bathroom breaks, especially during her pregnancy. I instructed the boys to watch for me to replace her. They would only have a few minutes to sneak inside.

As soon as my mother left her station, the boys crept in as if they were on a spy mission. I felt like I was a double agent and my stomach felt heavy as if I had swallowed a metal weight.

When my mother returned from the ladies' room, she studied my face. She must have noticed that I was distressed but said nothing. She was used to being in pain and was training me to weather my emotional storms like she had when she arrived in America.

As soon as I was released from my duties, I ran through the bare cherry tree pathway, past the goldfish pond.

The Buchanan boys had already taken their place on the landing of the house, making slashes with their hands, ready to transform into what they heard about the samurai and Japanese warriors.

"You'll need to take your shoes off if you're coming inside," I told them and left my boots in front of our genkan.

"I'm not doing that," Nicholas declared.

"I'm not either," said the second brother and of course, the two younger ones followed suit.

All four boys came traipsing into the house, tracking clumps of mud on the tatami mats. I was mortified and shut my brain from thinking about what Papa was going to do to me after he discovered the mess resulting from the Buchanan boys' trespass.

The littlest brother climbed on top of our low dinner table, while the Number Two Buchanan took his position in the downstairs tokonoma, almost stepping into my mother's flower arrangement. He then emerged, his arms outstretched as if he were Frankenstein's monster coming to life. I, on the other hand, rushed back and forth from one brother to another, saying, "Get off of there. Don't touch. Be careful." I was woefully outnumbered. I didn't stand a chance.

"It's up here!" Nicholas stomped up the stairs and I knew what he was after. The katana. He had told them about the sword.

The other boys scrambled to follow but I was able to beat them to the second floor.

Nicholas had already unsheathed the sword and was holding it up in victory. He greeted us with a maniacal grin and his brothers were first frozen in awe before clamoring to have their turn with the weapon.

"No! Stop!" I shouted. What if one of them damaged more than our shoji screen? I imagined the prized daruma painting slashed in half.

Nicholas kept the katana out of reach from his brothers and ran from one side of the room to the other. I needed to disarm him, whatever it took. I was able to get my sweaty hands over his on the grip. He thrashed back and forth and we both fell onto the tatami floor. "Let go!" I screamed, faintly hearing the cheering of the Buchanan boys around us.

I wrestled with him for control and was able to get on my knees. I thrust the sword forward and then the resistance ended. Nicholas's body withered like a rag doll, blood spurting from his neck. I had almost severed his head from his body.

The brothers, who had been so boisterous and bold just minutes ago, started shrieking, sounding like tortured puppies.

I could not move. I watched the blood soak through the tatami—first one mat, a second one and then three. Nicholas's eyes and mouth remained open in an expression of astonishment.

The police arrived in seemingly minutes. My father and mother were on the scene beforehand, but I don't remember how they responded. My wrists were handcuffed behind my body—dangling so loose that I could have easily gotten free from the restraints.

The owner of Grand Garden assisted my father in hiring an attorney to represent me. I never saw my father during my incarceration at the Pasadena jail. All messages were relayed through my lawyer, a young man who sported long sideburns that made him look much smarter than he was.

At our first meeting, a few days after my arrest, my attorney spoke very slowly as if I wouldn't be able to understand him. I didn't correct him. In fact, I hardly said anything at all.

"You're going to have to help me, Harold. The case is really stacked against you." He slid a copy of the Pasadena daily newspaper on the table toward me.

The lead headline read, CRAZED NIPPONESE BOY BE-HEADS CLASSMATE WITH A SAMURAI SWORD.

I stared at the headline, at first not knowing that the story was about me. Its absurdity hit me hard and soon I was laughing like I had never laughed before.

The lawyer shook his head, as if I was a lost cause.

It didn't surprise me that none of the Buchanan boys would testify truthfully about what really happened. That they had trespassed into my house and that Nicholas had been the one to unsheath the katana. They probably wanted to protect their eldest brother's legacy or maybe in their young minds, I had been the terrible villain described in the newspaper.

My lawyer negotiated a deal with the district attorney. He told me that anger toward me had fomented throughout Pasadena and there was no way a jury would not convict me of first-degree murder.

"You're just lucky that they just opened up a juvenile hall for delinquents in Boyle Heights. Otherwise, you'd be locked up with hardened criminals," he said.

Before I was transported to juvenile hall, my mother came to visit me by herself. She had dark bags under her eyes, which made her look much older than twenty-six years. She was so big now that her obi could not hide her pregnancy. "Be a good boy, Harold-*chan*," she finally said. I figured out later that was her way to say goodbye.

I've been in juvenile detention for eight years now and I may possibly be moved to an adult prison. I've stayed in the same cell, but roommates have come and gone. The rumors about me have spread and become more fantastic as time has passed.

I can kill with my hands, my kicks are lethal. "He knows jiu-jitsu," I heard one boy whisper to another.

We have two bunk beds, but the boy assigned to the bed underneath me sleeps with the other boy in the other bottom bunk. No one dares challenge or speak to me. They think that I cannot speak English, which I use to my advantage. I think of myself like the daruma, staring at the bare walls. Someday perhaps I will lose use of my arms and legs and my eyeballs will bulge out their sockets.

The only person who writes me from time to time is Kentaro, who is now getting ready to graduate from the local high school in Pasadena. I've heard from him that my sister is doing well, but I've never met her. My parents made a new life for her and themselves in San Francisco. They've changed their last names. They are now working at a Japanese garden in Golden Gate Park, where patrons leave five cents to enter and my sister wears a kimono every spring for the Cherry Blossom Festival.

THE WORLD'S OLDEST LIVING DETECTIVE

DAVID BART

You live this long you end up with regrets; definitely more than Sinatra's "too few to mention." But one thing I don't regret is breaking the law in the Senator Portnoy case. Must be forty years ago now.

I was fresh off physical therapy for a gunshot wound, my fifth anniversary as a homicide detective in the Albuquerque PD, the injury incurred while attempting to arrest a suspected serial killer. Did manage to return fire as I fell, putting the guy down before he could turn his gun on his latest victim, a UNM coed he'd kidnapped three days earlier...can still remember the transformative look in her eyes: abject terror to grateful relief.

The mayor pinned a medal on my hospital gown, flashbulbs going off, questions shouted by reporters; the police commissioner promised a modest disability pension for my shattered knee—enough for a car payment and a bottle of vodka—and the governor directed the secretary of state to fast-track a PI ticket.

So, for the next thirty years I sleuthed the hell out of Albuquerque, Santa Fe, Rio Rancho, Las Cruces—pretty much all of New Mexico. The Portnoy case even took me up to Idaho.

But that was then and this is— Now I'm in a retirement home in the Northeast Heights of Albuquerque, Pilar Menendez checking my blood pressure and oxygen level, mentioning how since I'd been both a cop and a longtime private detective perhaps I could look into the disappearance of Ripley, the home's resident cat. A garden variety tabby: grayish brown with stripes and spots, and even older than I am if you figure feline to human years. Rip hangs out in my room a lot, demanding treats I keep well stocked in a bottom drawer of my dresser. Thinks I'm a mark.

"He'll show up," I tell Pilar. "It's only been a few hours."

Though I am a tad worried. Missing his daily treats is beyond unusual and I feel the old urge to check things out, sniff around—investigate. At a slower pace and no doubt limited effectiveness.

"Loved the article about you in the *Journal*—you're famous! Oldest detective, wow!"

Pilar. One of the nurses here at the acceptably tidy, but marginally run-down Desert Hills Home for Seniors near Tramway and Academy Boulevard. Tramway's a boulevard too, runs along the foothills of the Sandia Mountains at the eastern edge of the city. The home is pretty much like its two hundred residents; long in tooth, short on rejuvenation.

"How's the knee today?" she asks, smiling warmly.

"Not too bad," I lie.

Don't like to complain; though I'm happy to bitch about the food, which isn't fit for human consumption. Grated carrots suspended in watery lime Jell-O? I wouldn't eat that crap in the first grade and I'm not gonna eat it now, eighty years later.

Pilar pats my arm. "It's important to keep your mind active, Ethan. You're good at figuring stuff out, thinking things through—after nappy why not ask around about Ripley?"

After *nappy*? You know you're old when they talk to you like you're a little kid.

But after she left, I did as suggested—took a nappy.

Course, I don't usually sleep all the way down while it's daylight…feels more like floating on a lazy river, the here and now of my present existence soon overwhelmed by memories of an often exciting past.

And as the green odor of new-mown grass wafts through my open window, hazy images of that long-ago Portnoy case begin to form a separate reality…

"I want the bitch found, Brock, she's a goddamn thief," the little man said, talking to my back because I was looking out my second-story office window, trying to figure how I could cut this guy loose without pissing off the police chief who'd sent him to me.

New Mexico State Senator Larry Portnoy: five-foot-whatever, wearing owlish black-framed glasses that, though stylish, did little to ameliorate the tragedy of his sparse comb-over—Danny DeVito without the charm.

The Albuquerque Old Town square was below my office window, a lengthy drought having yellowed the foot-traffic patterns across the pale green lawn. The smell of freshly cut grass was more imagined than olfactory, windows closed tight so I wouldn't, as my old man often said, "Air-condition the whole goddamn neighborhood."

I turned to face my tiny, but hugely annoying client.

"Her name's Marcy Lannister. Stole some videotapes out of my car," he said.

To describe his squinty dark eyes as a weasel's would be cliché; let's just go with nearsighted ferret and be done with it.

"And don't bother with her parents, she's not there," he said.

I took three limping steps to the moderately abused credenza that the steroid twins, Jorge and Deshawn, had delivered last week from the Salvation Army store. Picked up a bottle of Grey

Goose from among its potable companions and filled a plastic motel glass about halfway—okay, maybe two-thirds. Pulled an ice tray out of the tiny fridge, twisted it over the drink and I was in business.

My short client exclaimed: "Christ, Brock, it's too early for booze." *Well, of course it's too early. I drink because it's too late.*

My cop career had disappeared forever in the rearview and this sleuthing gig was beginning to feel like a major mistake… my knee hurt even after three surgeries and a titanium replacement that didn't work right. Still need a cane.

So, a little nip takes the edge off.

Just after midnight I'm awakened by nature's call and limp to the bathroom, wait for my ancient body to decide if it's gonna do something…hours later, seemingly, I make my way back to bed, scanning the dimly lit bedroom for a familiar dark shape: namely, a slumbering feline.

I can make out the recliner, a dresser, little table and two chairs, my bed…but no cat.

Where the hell is he? Worrying about Ripley keeps me from sleep and when I finally doze off it's just in time for my bladder to awaken me and I do the whole damn thing again.

"So where do you think Marcy Lannister might be?" I asked Senator Portnoy, rattling ice cubes around in my glass of vodka because it bugged him.

A look of sly predation informed the little man's features, an expression politicians are probably born with. "I don't give a rat's ass about *her*, Brock, just want the video."

Porta Potty, as I then nicknamed Senator Portnoy, scratched out a check, rose to his full diminutiveness and handed it over. "Twenty-five hundred. Get the tapes in one or two days and you can keep it all, and I'll cover verifiable expenses."

My fee was two hundred fifty dollars a day, plus travel expenses, and he'd just made me an offer I couldn't refuse—*hot damn*—ten days' per diem up-front for what would be no more than a two-day job.

He left, his unpleasantness lingering like a toxic cloud, as I again gazed out my second-story picture window, past the square to the nearly two-hundred-year-old church, San Felipe de Neri. A herd of pink tourists and their sugar-hyped kids were careening into each other along the sidewalk like quarks colliding in a particle accelerator.

That comparison came to mind due to a recent client, a physicist from Los Alamos, who'd claimed "they" were out to get him. *They* weren't, but his wife was…and then it got complicated.

I raised my plastic glass of vodka/rocks in a toast to the mob of teeming humanity below. Life in the fast lane.

Out in the hallway, no cat in sight, just a corpulent biped clutching his squeaky walker, trudging down the green-and-maroon carpet.

"You seen Ripley, Shapiro?" I say in a raised voice.

"Who?" Feigning ignorance.

"You know who, you old pirate—you seen the cat or not?"

I always get a hit of something wrong about Shapiro, like I knew him back in the life, someone unlawful. Course, I've known a lot of A-holes and miscreants, might just look like one of them.

"Oh, you mean that mangy cat," he says.

Why do I call Shapiro a pirate? He claims to have sailed a fifty-foot schooner around the world for the last twenty years, coming home for his final days. But his regional accent doesn't fit the Southwest; more like Atlantic seaboard, saying things like "wicked smaht." Figure he's a pirate of some kind.

"I saw the little crapper yesterday when they were mowing lawns," he grumbles.

"Where?"

Big sigh, attempts a look of exasperation—not easy when your face is rigid from Botox injections and maybe a little knife-work. I figure he's one of those guys who always wants to look younger. Probably has a tangle of gold chains in his dresser, shiny disco shirts and bell-bottom trousers.

"How the hell do I know?" Shapiro says. "I can't remember where I put my friggin' slippers this morning." Heads off, leaning out over the walker, shuffling barefoot down the hall toward the rec room to watch Judge Judy harshly pontificate from within the wall-mounted TV.

After spending the day talking with most of the other residents I reluctantly conclude that Ripley has run off and it bums me out, so I have dinner early—sans the carrot/lime Jell-O they're always trying to palm off.

After I'm settled back in my digs, cannabis lotion rubbed deep into the scar tissue of my knee, someone knocks.

"Enter."

Pilar comes in with a balding guy wearing light blue scrubs, white sneakers and a dark scowl.

"This is Bradley Jacobs, just started today. Physical therapist from Santa Fe—thought he could maybe work on getting your knee more flexible."

No eye contact from the guy; just keeps nursing the scowl.

"Ethan Brock, pet detective," I say, reaching my hand out, which he takes reluctantly, quickly letting go.

What, doesn't like touching old people?

Pilar explains my "pet detective" remark: "Ethan's looking into Ripley's disappearance."

Jacobs shrugs, says to Pilar, "Well, if he can't find it you can always get another cat." She looks down at the floor, shaking her head.

I'd just turned forty-six and I'm celebrating in Idaho?

Other passengers in the Boise airport concourse glanced

warily at me as I gimped and grumbled along, irritated with myself for listening to Portnoy. He'd told me not to bother with Marcy's folks and so I'd begun the investigation back in Santa Fe interviewing Portnoy's staff at the Roundhouse in Santa Fe, the appropriately circular building where New Mexico legislators argue over who's the most important.

No leads from that, so I'd driven over to busy St. Francis Drive to chat with residents at Marcy's condo complex.

Another dry hole.

But Marcy's self-described drinking buddy, Siobhan McShane, who lived in an adjacent condo, caught me up in the parking lot as I was leaving. "I just talked to Marcy and she wanted me to tell you she's at her parents' in Boise, wants to talk to you about your dumbass client."

"What's the number up there?" I asked.

She motioned me to follow her back into the condo complex, saying over her shoulder, "You know, Marcy really liked Portnoy."

I gasped, hand to my chest. "Seriously?"

Siobhan grinned, nodding her head. "I know, right?"

I used her phone to call Marcy, who asked me to come up to talk in person. Booked a seat on Southwest, drove down to Albuquerque Sunport, arriving just in time to catch my flight.

Landed in Boise late afternoon…

Found my way to the Lannister house, located inside a plush community whose gate was left open during business hours for deliveries and to admit the occasional out-of-state PI. Old-growth trees shaded razor-cut lawns that were greener than freshly minted thousand-dollar bills.

At the front door an explosive mother shouldered aside a Guatemalan maid and threatened me with cops if I didn't remove myself from the premises. "Told that little son of a bitch, Portnoy, Marcy's not here!"

But she *was* there, stepping around her ranting mother to

usher me inside to a cavernous room resembling a furniture showroom: leather couches and chairs sprouted alongside artful floor lamps to form an archipelago of conversation islands… exotic coffee tables fashioned from glass-topped broken chunks of marble statues or wind-twisted stumps of thistle-cone pine created an ambiance of wealth.

I couldn't have been more intimidated if a butler had appeared and asked me to shower. "She's protective," Marcy said about her mother, returning from somewhere and handing me a mug of aromatic coffee, which I accepted after resting my cane against the arm of a handmade natural leather couch the approximate size of an aircraft carrier.

Protective? A mama bear is protective; Mrs. Lannister was medieval.

Marcy was a petite twenty-four-year-old blonde with impossibly large, Keene-type green eyes; could've been cast as a really cute extraterrestrial on *Star Trek*.

Though I'm fairly certain there'd never been a pregnant extraterrestrial on the show.

I can't sleep and so I limp to the bathroom…

Back in bed I keep thinking: What is it about Shapiro? I mean, the guy feels wrong.

Larger question: Why do I care? Answer: I'm an over-the-hill sleuth whose mind wanders in search of misplaced thoughts… maybe I should stop thinking about the past and— Just try to get a…good night's…

Marcy played the videotape I'd been hired to retrieve.

State senators and representatives doing tasteless skits, accompanied by past administration officials from DC ridiculing voters, mocking their naiveté, confident that no matter what was said or done their clueless sheep could be herded into the voting booths.

She shut off the tape player. "That's what he's worried about, that and—"

"Raping my daughter!" the mother interjected, barging into the room. "Impregnating her, refusing to take responsibility— what do you think of *that*, Mr. Private Investigator?"

Mama Bear had been listening in the hall.

Before I could reply Marcy said, "You know it wasn't rape, Mother." Her big Keene eyes teared up, in sympathetic concert with her sad expression.

Mama bear sighed, shaking her head. "You are a *child*—he's a forty-five-year-old *married* man."

Marcy looked over to me, eyes brimming as she shrugged. "He gave me a greasy roll of hundred-dollar bills, practically tossed it at me—two grand *cash*, so there's no record. He told me to get rid of...*it*."

"I stole the tape, not Marcy," the mother said in a triumphant tone. Wait, what?

"You stole it?" I said. "Portnoy thinks it was Marcy."

"Well, he's an idiot. If you can be a *stupid* narcissist."

I thought about this new information...couldn't make sense of it, seemed to lack motivation. "Why did you steal it?" I asked her.

She sighed heavily, took a seat in an oversize leather chair. "Well, I planned to give it to the networks and ruin his lame career."

I frowned. "He said it was stolen a couple weeks ago—what were you waiting for?" I said, but then figured it out. "Black-mail."

Marcy's mother looked a little sheepish, something I wouldn't have thought was in her repertoire of facial expressions. "Don't care about getting money from him, but merely ruining his rep-utation didn't feel like enough pain...figured coughing up a half a million dollars on top of it would sting pretty bad."

Sting? Five hundred thousand dollars would put him in agony.

In contrast to my ill opinion of Portnoy I liked the two women; the mother for being so fiercely protective and I guess you could say enterprising in a slightly larcenous way, and Marcy, so badly wronged, yet still surprisingly nice.

Before leaving I handed Marcy a glossy business card and she said, "You gave me two," handing the extra one back with a smile so melancholy I had to blink a couple times.

Southwest Airlines got me to Albuquerque via a red-eye flight in just over two hours and I called Portnoy from my office, told him I didn't get the tapes, but he could pay the Lannisters for them, grinning to myself as he sputtered some fairly creative, though filthy, language… I finally tired of it and hung up.

I wake with a start…thinking I can hear Ripley's rattling purr I reach over to touch him, but he's not there.

It's predawn outside my slightly open window; no longer the smell of cut grass, just the cool promise of rain on a freshening breeze…moths are thumping the window glass for reasons known only to moths; probably the sound I'd mistaken for Ripley's rattling purr.

A soft knock on the door. "Come in."

Pilar enters, does her thing with the blood pressure monitor and oxygen gadget, asking, "How you doing on Ripley's disappearance?"

"Nobody's seen him and I can't get around good enough to check out the neighborhood."

She squints at me for a couple beats. "Makes me sad," she finally says, shaking her head. Here's the thing: with just a few words a woman can, unintentionally or purposefully, carve you up like a Thanksgiving turkey.

In the psychobabble class I never took, it might've been called emasculation.

I call after her as she hurries out the door. "I promise, I'll keep looking into it."

That afternoon, after lathering cannabis cream on my knee, I gimp around the grounds of Desert Hills, intent on my purpose...but still feel weird, living in a home for old people; it seems so... I mean, I know I'm old but— So, here's the thing: in my shaving mirror I see myself basically unchanged, only thirty-five/forty years old, except for long, shaggy white hair giving me an aging biker look. Weird thing is when I look at photographs taken of me recently I see an octogenarian: slightly bent, deep wrinkles, clearly past his time. So, why the difference? Why's looking in a mirror not the same as seeing yourself in a photo? Trick of the brain? Denial? Wishful thinking?

Whatever. And this is way off topic, but I'm wondering was it really all that wrong what I did back then on the Portnoy case? I mean it'd sure felt like the right thing to do.

I limp on past the shed where the landscaping crew stores mowers and other implements, the wind blowing so hard through the trees I can barely hear the heavy traffic on our nearby thoroughfare... I make my way down past the circular drive at the entrance, stand there at Academy Boulevard, traffic whizzing by, the drivers not even noticing the old white-haired dude alongside the road, leaning on his cane, looking left and right.

No Ripley.

But cats are unpredictable, right? Sometimes they just move on. Thing is, Pilar's angst is contagious and I feel compelled to find out what happened to that treat-loving little critter.

Do I love that old cat? Let's be adults, eh?

Shapiro's in the rec room when I return to the main building— quickly turns away to pretend he's gazing out the window at a darkening western sky. Rain's a comin', as my immigrant grandmother used to say. She made the best strudel and was always right about the weather.

I squint at Shapiro, thinking: hell, I wouldn't be surprised if he'd done harm to Ripley—there's just something about that guy, something sneaky.

★ ★ ★

Marcy Lannister and her mother had both been shot poolside outside their home up in Boise. The cops found my business card in Marcy's purse at the scene and Albuquerque detective Harlan Culver had been asked to interview me on behalf of the Boise PD.

He arrived at my Old Town office just before noon, looked around the spare little room and asked, "Why you doing this crap, Brock? You were a good cop back in the day, it's embarrassing to see you like this."

I poured myself a drink, not offering anything to the detective because he'd pissed me off and I'm sometimes petty. Not often, sometimes.

Okay, often.

"How 'bout you, Culver, still on the take?"

And back and forth like that for a while, finally dropping the cop banter to reminisce about famous old busts, Culver admitting that some of my investigations were still considered high art around the cop shop.

Then down to business.

"Thirty-eight caliber, hollow-point slugs," he said. "One shot hit the daughter in the leg, second shot killed the mother as she shielded her kid; they'd been sunning on chaise lounges next to their swimming pool."

Mrs. Lannister had been a mama bear indeed. A good mother. I said, "Let me guess—shooter got the video from the house?"

He frowned. "What video?"

My turn to shrug. "Something Marcy said, not sure really." Felt a bit nauseous at having to honor PI-client privilege on behalf of Portnoy. "How is she?"

Culver sighed. "Trauma-induced labor, docs delivered the baby, but it's okay."

I sighed. "Did she identify the shooter?"

"Ski mask, but she thought it might be your client. Trouble is, Portnoy's got an airtight alibi."

★ ★ ★

The rain's coming down hard, wind howling around the residence.

Shapiro's grinning. "So, Brock, I just read in the *Albuquerque Journal* about you being the 'World's Oldest Living Detective.'"

I shrugged with admirable humility.

His grin turned malicious. "They found an older PI in London. Bet that stung, eh?" My license is still in active status, despite my decrepitude, and that's why a "cub" reporter—if that's still a thing—came out and interviewed me, wrote an article.

Then a London supermarket tabloid named Clive Chidderston as the world's oldest living detective, frequently mocked for wearing a deerstalker hat like Sherlock Holmes. The rag claimed Chidderston was "mental." Of course their papers are trashy nonsense; ninety-one-year-old Chidderston had died a few months before they even ran the story.

I was sure that Senator Portnoy was the shooter. That he'd killed Mrs. Lannister as she tried to shield her wounded daughter and unborn grandchild.

Portnoy's child.

I hadn't believed in the concept of pure evil until then.

When I asked, repeatedly, the cops maintained that Portnoy had a solid alibi. I figured his considerable political weight had trumped justice; amazing what politicians and bureaucrats can get away with just by offering thirty pieces of silver.

Portnoy answered on the fourth ring. "You know what time it is, Brock?"

"Shut up and listen, asshole. I know you did it and I'm going to prove it." The son of a bitch hung up on *me* this time.

"Mr. Brock," someone calls from behind me.

I turn and look across the cracked shuffleboard courts, still glistening from the rain though it'd stopped an hour ago. Bradley Jacobs, the new orderly, stands behind a wheelchair with randy ol' Maggie Troutman in it, the once pretty woman waggling her still-black eyebrows at me. Always wanting me to "cuddle" with her.

Jacobs, all of a sudden friendly, says, "I think I saw that cat run across the street and into that apartment complex. After I'm done, I could take you over there in a wheelchair."

Newberry Heights Apartments. A labyrinth of twenty buildings adjacent to Desert Hills. Deep and treacherous concrete arroyos run through the adults-only complex. Good place to have an accident.

I shrug. "Maybe later." And I head back inside, a chill gathering the skin at the back of my neck.

Portnoy showed up at my Old Town office, spouting accusations. "You been following me," was one of them.

I hadn't been, but I smiled enigmatically, just to be a dick.

"Best watch your back, cripple," he shouted, knocking my cane from where I'd hooked it on the edge of my desk.

He stormed out and I retrieved the cane, stood at my window and looked down at the Old Town square…a little red-haired boy was crying over the ice cream cone he'd dropped in the gutter alongside the old church. Senator Portnoy's chauffeured black town car pulled out from that curb into light traffic and I thought: he has to pay.

A month later Portnoy was found dead in his hot tub, his wife and two daughters out of town visiting grandparents. He'd been electrocuted by a defective underwater light socket.

"Attempts to resuscitate proved unhelpful," Detective Culver told me over the phone, chuckling.

I really missed cop humor.

The third morning since Rip's disappearance I'm awakened by an odd sensation; realize my left arm and left side of my face are numb. Coming in through the slightly ajar window is a strange sound, forlorn and at some distance... I figure my hearing has been damaged by what must've been a stroke.

I jerkily push to a sitting position using my right arm, press the call button.

A nurse who is not Pilar comes in, amends my self-diagnosis of a stroke to a "transient ischemic attack," a TIA—of course they're the same thing, but scientific types like to be specific.

At Lovelace Hospital, after an MRI and other tests, I'm told, "Bit of therapy and you'll be fine."

That next night I awaken to light from the hall spilling into my room and then the door slowly closes...

"I know you killed him, Brock," the intruder whispers from my bedside, holding up a syringe dripping clear solution onto the sheet.

"What the hell, Jacobs?" I demand. "Killed who?"

"The name's *Portnoy*, asshole. You know, it would've been nice to have had a father."

Roughly grabs my weakened arm, jabs the needle in, but before he can push the plunger, I scoop my cane off the headboard where I hang it and whack him alongside his head, dropping him, as I had that serial killer all those years ago who'd ruined my knee.

When he awakens, his hands tied—had a hell of a time doing that with one arm—I explain the reality of my history with his father. Since his mother never said anything good—and plenty bad—about Portnoy, he grudgingly believes me. I untie him and Bradley leaves my room, saddened by what I'd told him, but understanding the motive behind it.

Early next morning I grab two cereal bowls, a sack of treats and a fresh bottle of Evian from the fridge, drop myself into the wheelchair and roll out into the hall...immediately feel like crap, stop to rest.

Pilar hurries out from behind the nurse's station and asks me what the hell I'm doing. "Push me, *chica*, and I'll show you."

On our way to the front door I see Shapiro going down the other hallway and I ask Pilar to get my sunglasses. "Eyes are sensitive after my cataract surgery last year."

"*Hey*, Shapiro," I call out after she's gone, using my old stop-or-I'll-shoot cop voice.

His glare is impotent due to his tight Botox features.

I grin. "Checked you out, *Boston* boy. You best get a better attitude when talking to me, or do I give Whitey's goons a call?"

An old buddy at APD had run Shapiro's fingerprints through the system for me. Sean O'Hara, Shapiro's real name, is believed to be in witness protection after ratting out Whitey Bulger. The seaboard mob was still after him and those Irish lads don't care how old you are; if they find you, you're soon moldering in a landfill...at least it's that way in the movies.

I figure Shapiro/O'Hara will be cloyingly amiable from now on. "I'll expect at least one of those Boston cream pies you get sent your way every month."

He scowls, then quickly nods. Turns and heads on down the hall.

Pilar comes back, hands over my sunglasses and we head outside into a bright New Mexico day. I point the way, ignoring her pleas to explain what we're doing.

I'd remembered the smell of mowed lawns on the day Ripley disappeared and when Pilar rolls me down to the toolshed I open the creaky wood door and the cat *streaks* out—abruptly stops at the bowls I'd brought, gulps down the water, eats all the treats.

The old cat must've gotten itself locked in, the lawn guys leaving, not scheduled to return for two weeks. I figured this was where the distant sound had come from that I'd heard in my room the morning of my stroke.

Pilar bends down, grasps my robe lapel in an interesting way and pulls me forward a bit to kiss me on the cheek. "Ethan Brock, you are not only the world's oldest, you are the world's *greatest* living detective."

★ ★ ★

Curiosity is the curse of the private eye. It can put you in moral jeopardy.

I'd checked out Portnoy's lethal hot tub after his death and noticed droplets of candle wax near the control panel; could've meant anything, but after examining them closer this is what I figured:

The sealed glass cover had been removed from the underwater light socket, then carefully cracked with slight pressure, water-repellent wax dripped onto the glass, sealing the cracks, holding the glass together while also insulating it until Portnoy filled the tub with hot water and it'd slowly melted, allowing contact with the electric circuitry.

Investigators believed the glass cover had been merely faulty, the senator's death an accident. Nothing to see here.

So, how'd I break the law in the Portnoy case?

By being an after-the-fact accomplice to murder. I didn't tell the cops about the thumbprint I found in one of the droplets of wax, a print with a lateral scar identical to the print Marcy left on the extra glossy business card she'd handed back to me up in Boise. I'd stuck it into the back of my card holder, unwittingly preserving material evidence.

Marcy had rigged the hot tub, avenging her protective mother.

When the cops interviewed an elderly neighbor, he'd told them he'd glimpsed what looked like a girl in a hoodie, limping through the backyard of the Portnoy house the morning before the "accident." The cops attributed the sighting to the widely known fact that Portnoy had numerous dalliances and so the young woman had no doubt been one of them.

And that worked for me.

Ripley jumps into my lap, curls up and falls sleep as I stroke his head, avoiding his ears because it bugs him when you touch them. I gaze out over the grounds at what is home sweet home, Pilar pushing me toward the residence, happily humming an old Beatles tune.

Am I the greatest living detective?

Okay, let's be humble here... I'm not the greatest, but maybe the oldest, since Clive Chidderston, of London, England, has gone to his great reward.

"Hey, Pilar?" I say, scratching Rip's neck. "Think you could order me a deerstalker hat online?"

LITTLE HOUSE IN THE BIG WOODS

SARA PARETSKY

She had found the house when she wandered away from the group meeting on the beach. When Rev. Kanba wasn't with them, the meetings went on forever, without focus and without resolution. Ana used to say, *Shouldn't we wait for Rev. Olive?* or *Isn't that something only the Reverend can decide?* But she'd been mocked for being a weakling. *We won't be at university forever; we have to learn to think for ourselves. That's what Reverend Olive is training us to do.*

Ana climbed the sand hills above the lake, walked along the ridge at the top. She felt a kind of freedom that she wasn't used to—no one telling her what to do, or criticizing her for what she said, and she danced along the ridge high above the others, blowing kisses, making grand speeches that the gulls and sandpipers heard. She twirled too many times without looking down, caught her foot in a tree root and fell down the other side of the hill from the lake.

All these years later, she could still remember how humiliated she'd felt—as if her moment of joy were something that had to be punished.

She'd landed in a dense part of a forest that covered the east side of the hills. Her arms and legs were scratched by the bushes that had stopped her fall. After sitting for a bit, bracing herself for the mockery of anyone who'd followed her, she felt safe and got up.

She wasn't ready to face the group again; she followed a track through the trees, but it petered out after about four hundred yards. She stood, indecisive: push through the undergrowth, to see if the track continued on the other side, or admit defeat and rejoin the group. And then she saw that the track ended at the remains of a house, so weatherworn that it had blended into the landscape. The house had been built into the hill, and the back walls and chimney still stood. It was only the front that was missing.

She was sitting on a boulder, imagining the family that might have lived here, when Lance Bleeker suddenly appeared.

"You were right to wander off," he said. "The meeting was a bore. Bloviators one and all."

Lance was one of the cool guys, not someone who ever engaged with Ana. He was a team leader, one of the people who Rev. Olive relied on to present their message at student union meetings. Ana felt awkward with him now, alone in this abandoned house, but he was looking at the remains of the house, not at her.

"You know, this would be a wonderful getaway place. We could fix this up. It just needs the interior walls recovered, a new floor."

"And a front wall," Ana said.

"That, too," he agreed.

He sat cross-legged on the dirt floor and used a stick to sketch out a plan for the house. His father was a builder; Lance had worked construction jobs in the summer, he could get supplies, they could make it a project. And somehow, Ana ended up taking off her clothes and laying them flat on the floor next to his, and having sex. First time, yes, no protection, yes, lucky—yes, no pregnancy, no bad diseases.

They'd rebuilt the house, coming to the country on weekends. Others in the group helped out occasionally—the university had a conference center in the national park that abutted the lake there. Rev. Olive liked to hold retreats two or three times during each term, and she became enthusiastic about the house as a place where the group could bring sleeping bags and spend the night instead of camping on the beach—the conference center didn't have sleeping rooms.

No one owned the house. The last owners had been forced to leave when the area became a national park. The rangers must have known what they were doing, but no one interfered with them. Drywall covered the bare studs. A chemical toilet. A woodburning stove, inserted into the fireplace. Lance hooked up a water tank and an outdoor shower.

For about five months, Ana lived what seemed like a dream life, a blissful life, Lance's lover, weekends with him in the woods. On Friday nights ten or fifteen of the mission's core would show up. There'd be a potluck, and guitars and singing. Even though the males paid lip service to tearing down gender roles, Ana and the other women ended up doing the dishes in water heated over that woodstove.

Ana's lip curled in memory. *What a chump you always were!*

"Everything changes; nothing remains still." A line from Plato she still remembered.

Rev. Olive preached action. She was passionate about social justice, or injustice, and thought the university needed to take a stand against atrocities in South and Central America. She encouraged students to bear witness at the School of the Americas, cheered when someone was arrested. She sent Grace and Ben to Nicaragua to document atrocities committed by the Somoza government. They were arrested, and released after three months in a jungle prison only because Grace's father—CEO of one of the multinationals Rev. Olive had her disciples picket—paid the Contras three quarters of a million dollars in ransom.

The university censured Rev. Olive and ordered her to stop sending the students she worked with into danger. Rev. Olive said she sent no one, but she couldn't stop students from volunteering.

Ana was deeply moved by the witness her fellow disciples bore and longed for her chance to be on the front lines. She immersed herself in Spanish and in liberation theology. She wrote an impassioned letter to the university president, defending Rev. Olive's commitment to justice.

Lance was breaking away from the group. "Haven't you noticed that Olive is never on the front lines when the police arrive? If she goes to Nicaragua, she stays with friends inside the US Embassy compound in Managua. I hear she entertains government officials."

"Only to try to get them to let our team go in as impartial observers," Ana cried hotly.

"You are deluded, Anastasia. Your father has made you susceptible to—hero worship, to put it politely. You don't think for yourself, you need a strong personality to think for you. You thought you were breaking away from your father when you joined the church and became one of Olive's disciples, but you were trading one bullying cult leader for another."

Her father had named her Anastasia, because his own grandmother had been a cousin of one of the Romanov princess's tutors. Her father wanted her to emulate the princess, who was raised to cook, sew and clean in addition to learning languages and other schoolbook subjects. Ana hated the name and was bitter with Lance for using it, over her objections, ashamed of herself for telling him about it.

"If you'd stop being a good little Anastasia, I'd call you Ana," he said.

"And so you are just another bully," she said. "You have your definition of a good little Ana, my father had his, I suppose even Rev. Olive has hers, but hers, at least, ties me to the greater good of the world."

Lance ended the affair with Ana—he walked away. He walked away from theology and justice to study business, and became an intern in Grace's father's business. Ana thought perhaps he was in love with Grace, and lived in daily fear of hearing they were going to marry.

Lance didn't leave the group entirely, but when he came, it was to persuade others into leaving.

Rev. Olive smiled sadly. "Lance, if I left the university today, you'd jump in like a kangaroo to take charge of this group. You only oppose me because you can't stand to be subordinate to anyone, and you especially can't be subordinate to a woman. Don't worry, Lancelot—I pray for you every night, and one of these days, the Holy Spirit will enter your heart again."

As university chaplain, Olive had a budget from the school to cover her duties on campus, but for her social justice work, she solicited money from foundations. Organizations that supported free press or opposed South American juntas were eager for her to speak to their annual meetings. No one knew for sure how much money she raised, but rumors were that it was in excess of ten million.

"The Ford Foundation gave her a quarter million dollars for refugee resettlement work. How many refugees has she resettled?" Lance demanded.

Ana thought it was her duty to uphold Rev. Olive. Ana herself had found housing for a Guatemalan family, and she occasionally spent the night in the house in the woods so that visitors from Daniel Ortega's Sandinista movement could stay in her apartment near the university campus.

The arguments between Olive and Lance became more frequent, and much louder. And then came the night of the blowup. The last time she ever saw either Lance or Rev. Olive.

From the distance of thirty years, from the perspective of "sadder but wiser," she knew Lance had been right, that she attached herself to strong personalities.

Her father had been one of those—the kind that gets called "larger than life" by those who know them only in their public sphere. Inside his personal sphere, his gravitational pull was so intense it was hard to build escape velocity.

He hadn't led a cult, exactly, but he had an inner circle of employees at his firm—Fred Brochu, Engineering—who were dedicated to him and responded quickly to his whims. He also had a fierce temper, and didn't take kindly to contradiction. Ana's mother, tiring of his intensity, had drifted off to the West Coast. The two never divorced, but she also never tried to stay connected to Ana, the couple's only child.

Ana took over running the house for Fred. He oversaw her homework, her school essays. He chose the university where she studied. It was an urban campus, not far from where his engineering labs were, and he descended often, like Zeus from Olympus, to check up on the classes she was taking, the friends she was making. Friends! A handful of women in her dorm who she sometimes studied with.

Fred had outlined her curriculum for her, and her feeble acts of rebellion had withered under his sarcasm.

That was why she had started attending services at the Episcopal church. Her father was thoroughly anti-religious, and it disgusted him that she fell for "bells and smells." He'd even sent a deprogrammer to try to convince her that she'd been brainwashed and needed to return to reason. But Rev. Olive was more than a match for any deprogrammer, or angry father. Watching her treat Fred with a contemptuous amusement had sealed

Ana's devotion to her, even though Lance told her, as their relationship crumbled, that she was changing one bully for another.

Olive Kanba was one of the earliest women to be ordained in the Episcopal Church. She had the kind of personality Ana imagined Joan of Arc possessed—Joan's ardent spirit, inflamed by her mission, by her voices, rousing thousands of young French people to follow her into battle. Olive had a voice like a cello, deep, rich, full of emotion. Her voice alone could inspire a crowd, and when her voice spoke words of preaching truth to power, she roused her disciples to action.

Olive's battle was against totalitarian forces, and against the American government's support of such forces. Young people who yearned for a great cause, something bigger than they were—Civil Rights, anti-war, women's rights—found in her the leadership they needed.

Ana was baptized by her. It was an exhilarating day. She felt as though the heavens had opened above her as they had for Jesus and that the Holy Spirit had truly descended on her. Olive had embraced her, and taken her back to her home for dinner with Grace, Ben and a few of the other most committed disciples.

As her relationship with Lance disintegrated, and as he kept attacking Rev. Olive, Ana clung more tightly to the priest. She also clung to the cabin in the hills. That wasn't in the hopes that Lance would come back, but because it felt like her own space: even though Lance had done the lion's share of restoring it, it was Ana who discovered it.

The weekend before the fall term started, Olive had led a retreat at the conference center for new students interested in the social justice mission. Ana had participated in the retreat, to answer questions, although she'd refused to speak. ("Don't sulk, dear Ana," Olive had said. "It's my fault you were sent on a mission you weren't ready for." Ana smiled, ducked her head—techniques she'd mastered with Fred to avoid conflict.)

Lance had been there, trying to tell the students to be careful about getting involved in a program where they might be captured and held in a Nicaraguan jungle prison.

Olive said, "Lance feels strongly about our work, but if you ask him, you'll find he's never been to Nicaragua, never endured any hardship greater than sleeping on an air mattress in our cabin in the hills, never seen a jungle, let alone a prison. If you want to learn about the risks and rewards of our work, talk to Ana or Ben or Grace."

That night, there'd been an explosion at the conference center. The noise woke Ana, sleeping alone in her cabin. She'd pulled on her clothes and hiked to the top of the ridge. Looked down and saw the conference center in flames. There were no cell phones then, no way to call for help from the park rangers. Ana had scrambled down the hill to the beach, helped start a bucket brigade, ferrying water from the lake to the fire. A late-night boater had spotted the flames and notified the Coast Guard, but by the time help arrived, the conference center was gutted.

At first, the police, and then the FBI, thought Olive might have been killed in the explosion, but they didn't find any bodies. Ana told the cops about the fight she overheard between Olive and Lance. Other members of the group had already talked about it, after all. Lance had been shouting that he would report Olive to the IRS. No one knew what Olive had said—they'd all heard her laugh but if Lance had provoked her to rage, she was too sophisticated a fighter to reveal it.

"Everyone said you were the student the Rev. Kanba trusted most. She would stay in this cabin with you, right?"

Ana had shifted uncomfortably. "She sometimes stayed here, if she didn't feel like driving back to the city at the end of the day. The conference center doesn't have sleeping rooms. But trusted the most? I don't think so. I only ever went on one mission to Nicaragua for her, and the people there seemed disappointed that it was me and not one of the others, or Rev. Olive herself."

It had been a difficult trip. The Spanish Ana had been learning from tapes hadn't prepared her for actual spoken Spanish in live situations, and she'd felt herself on the outside of—everything. Politics, the humor, sex, music, food, planning. The youth who drove her to the airport had stuck his hand inside her jeans and pinched her labia when he dropped her off. Then he handed her a box wrapped in striped paper for Olive—her favorite Nicaraguan *galleta*—and said, "I see why they sent a child on this mission. Come back when you're an adult."

Ana had given the box to Olive but hadn't told her anything about the trip. The experience at the airport caused enough revulsion in her that she stopped studying Spanish.

Despite reports of Olive's embezzlement, most of the foundation money she'd received wasn't in her own bank accounts or in her university chaplain's account. The FBI looked for offshore accounts, although those are notoriously hard to find. Local police and feds searched the cabin, Ana's dorm room back at the university, and even searched her father's house, looking for some trace of the money.

Her father had predictably erupted like a thousand volcanoes. He told his daughter it served her right, getting tangled up in religion, thinking she was smart enough to stand up to a devious fox like Olive Kanba.

All kinds of lurid stories began circulating—that she had orgies with her students of both sexes; she'd been smuggling cocaine into the States in hollowed-out prayer books; the money she'd raised had gone to Daniel Ortega and the Sandinista movement. Some people claimed that the fight she'd had with Lance the day the conference center blew up had been staged: the two were living on a yacht in the Caribbean, sailing lazily from port to port.

Like the FBI, reporters thought Ana must surely know where Olive and Lance had gone, and whether it had been together or separately.

After a time, the furor died down. Ana dropped out of school and went to New York. She found a job as a personal assistant to a magazine editor, quit when she realized she was falling back into the familiar rut of being the admiring, overworked underling, and took a job as a data-entry clerk in an anonymous company. There had been something soothing, healing, about getting up every day to do something mindless with thirty other women in an anonymous room. A paycheck every two weeks, a few acquaintances to go for a drink or to a movie with.

For a while, she'd continued to go to church, but the bells and smells stopped having any meaning for her. Instead, she attended lectures on ancient Egypt and Mesopotamia at the Metropolitan Museum, or at some of the local universities. People who were long dead seemed more tolerable than the living. She was thirty when she began taking classes for a degree. She learned classical Arabic, learned how to read cuneiform, had started going on digs, graduated, and ended up in Pennsylvania, working for a prestigious antiquities museum there.

Cataloging pottery shards, deciphering inscriptions, had the same soothing quality as the data entry work she'd done. She made a few friends, had a few lovers, but after Olive, she remained guarded in her approach to the world.

Ana had not returned to the Midwest, until the day a derecho swept across the hilltop above her cabin. A thousand trees were uprooted. And when the rangers began sawing them up and carting off the brush, they found the skeleton.

Missing Crusader's Body Found!

Rev. Olive, Maverick Woman Priest, Discovered in the Dunes!

Old Mystery Solved!

Those were a sample of the headlines Ana saw when she logged into her Twitter account. "Olive, back from the dead?" Ana murmured to herself. "I've been wondering when you'd show."

She braced herself for reporters, or for questions from coworkers. Even though her name appeared in some of the background reports, no one seemed to connect her to the undergraduate who'd been part of Olive Kanba's inner circle.

A week later, the headlines reappeared, even more startling: that hadn't been Olive under the tree, but a man, perhaps in his early twenties. Dental records had been found that matched the skeleton's. It was Lance Bleeker. A week after that, Ana had a call from an FBI agent. They'd appreciate it if she'd return to the Midwest to answer some questions about the dead man.

Natalie Simon had been a new-minted field agent when the conference center blew up. Women had been with the Bureau for fifteen years by then, but hostility to women still ran deep among the more senior men. Among most of the men, if she were honest. She'd been assigned to the Rev. Olive case. Besides fetching coffee for senior agents, and listening to the clever jokes they made about women priests cavorting with parishioners, Natalie combed endless pages of bank statements and wire transfers between the States and Managua, looking for something that would signal where Olive had gone, or at least where the money had gone. Natalie wanted to prove herself, she wanted to shut up the men in her unit; she hoped for that tantalizing break that would lead her to Lance and Olive.

When the case was moved to the cold case file, Natalie still looked at it from time to time. She was sure Olive would surface somewhere, under some name. Olive thrived on adulation and attention—she couldn't live in the shadows. Every time she caught wind of a woman with power and a following, she'd track her down, try to match her with the identifying details she had for Olive.

After the first decade passed without any sign of the woman, Natalie figured she must have died in the blast. No trace of human remains had been found, but that was based on local cop findings. By the time the Bureau came along, the crime scene was hopelessly compromised.

When the derecho turned up those old bones, Natalie had instantly moved in with a forensic team. She was so sure she was going to find Olive—she was flabbergasted that the dead body was Lance Bleeker. She had a team explore the entire area, from the lake to the little cabin in the hillside, using ground-penetrating radar. She was a special agent in charge these days, and while she had to argue her budget with her division head, she did that after she deployed the forensic team. She was sure she'd find Olive buried nearby, but the only other big skeletons they turned up belonged to coyotes and deer.

Natalie reshuffled her thoughts. She went back and reread all the old interviews. Grace and Ben had talked about an affair between Lance and Ana that went sour. And so Natalie found the museum in Pennsylvania where Ana was working, and summoned her to Chicago.

The FBI building on West Roosevelt hadn't existed when Ana left the city all those years earlier. Back then, Natalie Simon had interviewed her in a cramped room in the Federal building, and then traveled with her to the incident site to walk her through her actions on the night of the explosion. Natalie and another woman, solemnly dressed in protective gear, had searched the little cabin, looking for—Ana didn't know what.

Now Ana sat in an interview room with a new young agent, while Natalie watched through the one-way glass.

"You must have been very angry with Lance," the agent said.

"Why?" Ana asked.

"He broke up with you, left you."

Ana shook her head. "Lance thought Olive was exploiting me—my naivete, I should say. He thought she was embezzling funds that were supposed to go to refugee assistance. He left me because I wouldn't agree with him. The criticisms troubled me, because I wasn't sure whom to believe, but they didn't make me angry."

The interview went down the road for a few more minutes, but Ana had nothing else to say about her feelings for—or against—Lance. The agent switched to the actual burial of his body.

"You know a lot about digging, don't you?"

"There are many kinds of digging," Ana replied. "What kind do you want to know about?"

"You're an archeologist; you're used to digging trenches, if I have the terminology right."

"I'm used to sifting through dirt and sand, looking for tablets and shards. I don't have the skill set necessary for digging a trench."

She gave a lengthy lecture on the decisions about when to dig and where, and what kinds of tools to use. Natalie, watching, was annoyed with her young agent for not stopping the lecture. He did, finally, and asked the crucial question:

"But did you have the skill set necessary for digging the hole where Lance Bleeker was buried?"

"I haven't seen the hole," Ana said. "I don't know what tools or skills would have been required to create it."

"Come on, Ana—"

"Ms. Brochu to you, young man."

"Ms. Brochu. A hole in the ground. You could dig that, couldn't you?"

Ana hunched a shoulder. "It depends on the soil. Hard-packed? Dirt? Sand? Rocky? Filled with roots?"

"You spent a lot of time at the university's lakefront conference center. You know the soil there—that soil."

"If Lance had been buried on the beach, in the sand—no, digging a deep hole in sand is very difficult. But going up the hill, you start encountering a network of roots from plants and trees that know how to seize the soil in order to survive. That would be difficult as well. I couldn't do it, no."

After a time, when Ana's calm was maddeningly undisturbed, the young agent asked her about the quarrel between Lance and Olive. Ana explained that she hadn't overheard it.

"At one point they were arguing about stones. What does that tell you?"

Ana spread her hands—helpless ignorance.

"Some people say that Rev. Kanba was converting money she received into precious stones."

"I never heard anyone say that," Ana said.

"But is it possible?"

"Anything is possible. You're asking what I know, and I know nothing about that."

"So it wouldn't surprise you to learn they were arguing over whether she had turned money into diamonds?"

"She was a priest," Ana said. "She could turn wine into blood, but I don't think she could turn money into diamonds. She liked to express herself with rough language, trying to shock people into paying attention. She might have been accusing Lance of not having the stones to do the hard work that her missions required."

The agent paused, unable to come up with a meaningful response. Natalie gave a wry smile behind the glass. She turned on the mike so she could speak into the room from behind the glass.

"Let's talk about the trip Ana—Ms. Brochu—made to Nicaragua for Rev. Kanba. Whom did you meet there, and what did you talk about?"

Ana flinched at the sound but said, "Are you a ghost, Ms. Simon, trying to distress me by speaking out of the ether? I never did know the names of the people I met. I had been studying Spanish, and Rev. Olive thought I was ready for a mission, but it was embarrassing: they spoke too fast, and with too much slang, for me to understand anything they were saying. After three days in some back rooms in Managua, the Nicaraguans realized I couldn't help them and sent me home."

"Did they give you anything to take to Rev. Kanba?"

Ana paused, eyes narrowed, looking back over the distance of time. "A box of cookies—a Nicaraguan specialty that they said she was partial to."

"What was actually in the box?" Natalie asked.

Ana shook her head. "It was wrapped, some kind of striped paper, festive-looking. I didn't try to unwrap it. I gave the box to Olive. That's all I can tell you about it—she didn't open it in front of me."

Finally, after eight hours of questioning, they let her go, although Natalie said she wanted Ana to go with her to the cabin in the woods in the morning.

The little house was in surprisingly good shape after all these years. The park rangers must have done some minimal repairs. Otherwise, it would surely have ended up as derelict as when she first stumbled on it thirty-five years earlier. The door was swollen, and took the effort of both women together to pull it open, but inside, except for the dust, the one-room house looked the same.

Natalie opened the stove door and sifted through the ashes. She looked behind the stove, surveyed holes between the logs that formed the back and two sides of the house, lifted the mattress from the bed and inspected all the seams, looking for tears and repairs.

"If you had found a box of diamonds, what would you have done with it?" Natalie asked Ana.

"It depends on where I found it," Ana said. "If it looked like stolen property, I'd give it to the police. If it seemed as though somebody had lost it, I'd try to locate them."

"And if you couldn't find the owner?" Natalie said.

"I'd make a list of my favorite charities and divide the jewels among them."

"Are you pretending to be a saint? Or is this what you would really do?"

"I'm not a saint," Ana said. "But I'm a person without many desires. The money I earn covers my needs with more left over. A box of diamonds would be a tiresome responsibility. I'd have to worry about keeping them safe from thieves and swindlers."

"Your father didn't leave you his company, did he?" Natalie said.

"No. He divided it among his most loyal employees. I don't have any engineering skills; it would have been inappropriate for me to inherit the firm."

Natalie prowled some more, checking the outside, although what she could possibly hope to find after all this time was impossible to say. Ana sat cross-legged on the floor, only occasionally watching Natalie's performance, mostly staring into space.

"What happened to Olive?" Natalie said abruptly.

"The FBI has vast resources that I don't," Ana said. "You know how my father left his estate; you probably know what I earn in a year, and the last time I was able to go to a dig in Iraq. If you don't know where she is, no one does."

"Guess," Natalie said.

"Does that mean you know, and can tell me if I'm getting warm?" Ana asked.

"It means I have no idea but hope that someone who knew her well could imagine a scenario I haven't thought of."

Ana shook her head again. "Olive needed an audience. Every time I read about a woman with a vast internet following, I look at her pictures, trying to see if she might be Olive. That's my only guess. Also, of course, she might have had plastic surgery, changed her face in a way that I wouldn't recognize today. She might be dead, in some location no one has seen. You searched this area again when you found Lance, I understand, and didn't find any other human skeletons. Olive could be dead in Nicaragua."

"Why do you say that?" Natalie demanded sharply.

"If she killed Lance, she'd have run away, and the one remote place she knew people was Nicaragua. I'm just guessing—I haven't heard from her. And I expect you've been monitoring my mail, so you'd know if she'd been in touch."

Natalie bit her lip. Of course she'd been monitoring Ana's mail, electronic and paper. No one from Olive's mission had been in touch with Ana. They'd found some old mail between Olive and one of Daniel Ortega's lieutenants—she was complaining that they'd double-crossed her. Was that what had happened to the money?

Ben and Grace were sure Olive was getting the Sandinistas to convert cash into diamonds. They kept half and gave her half. But Ortega's people could just as easily have kept all the stones for themselves. Or Lance had found them and hidden them where not even the FBI's most skilled searchers could find them.

"Who killed Lance?" Natalie said. "You were there, weren't you?"

"I was *here*," Ana said. "Olive and Lance had been sniping at each other all afternoon. I was tired of it. I went for a walk in the woods until the light began to fail; I made my own supper here in the cabin. I read by the light of our lantern—battery-operated, it gave a good amount of light. I went to sleep around ten and woke when the building blew up. I went to see what happened, and ran down to help put out the fire."

"Who blew up the building?" Natalie said.

"I don't know. Lance's father was in the building business—he could have given Lance dynamite."

"And Lance blew up the center to keep Olive from indoctrinating more students?"

"I don't know. You're asking me to speculate about events that I didn't witness."

"Isn't that what you do for a living?" Natalie asked. "Speculate about events you didn't witness?"

Ana smiled. "Usually there are clues in the pottery and the inscriptions, but you're right; it's guesswork."

Natalie finally left, frustrated. She drove Ana back to the city, dropped her at the B & B where she was staying.

Ana picked up some supplies and drove back to the cabin. One last night here, in her safe place, before returning to Philadelphia. She built a fire in the stove—it was the end of summer; nights in the woods were chilly.

The water tank she and Lance had installed was full of water, but the hose to the shower was clogged with leaves and pine needles. Ana cleaned those out and filled buckets with water to heat on the stove. The cabin was dirty, not just from the detritus of time, but the fingerprint grease various cops had used covered every surface. Ana scrubbed the walls, the little table, the two chairs. She shook out the bedding, but it was too grimy to put back on the bed. She had a sleeping bag in her car; she brought it in and spread it on the mattress.

She lay down, not taking off her clothes, dozing but not really sleeping. It was two when the door opened.

"I've been waiting for you to come back." The voice was hoarse, harsh, unrecognizable.

Ana sat up. "I knew if you were anywhere in the area you wouldn't be able to stay away. What happened to your voice?"

"My voice—Lance ruined my voice. He slashed my throat with a carving knife. My vocal cords—I had a dozen surgeries but nothing could give me back my voice."

"You must have changed your name," Ana said. "Otherwise surely the FBI would be interviewing you."

"I changed my name," Olive said. "And then I couldn't get a job as a priest, not unless I went through the charade of seminary and ordination under a new name. I run an employment agency in Valparaiso, but it's not the same."

"I saw you, you know," Ana said. "I watched you fighting with Lance on top of the ridge."

The noise of the explosion had woken her. She'd scrambled into her clothes, grabbed the powerful flashlight by the cabin door and rushed into the night. The flames from the beach outlined the pair fighting on top of the ridge. Lance fell. Olive beat his head, over and over, and then rolled his body to the hollow under the tree. Ana saw her stuff the body into the hole, saw her dig up a small bush and stuff it into the opening.

"If you'd gone for help, instead of staying to kill Lance and dispose of his body, maybe they could have saved your vocal cords," Ana said. She spoke in the same calm, unemotional tone she'd used throughout her FBI interrogation.

"You were watching, and you wouldn't help me. You were a conniving bitch from day one, and I didn't know it. I thought you were an eager ingenue, hanging on my every word, but you had your eye on the main chance from the start. You stole the diamonds. I want them back. What did you do with them?"

"I did nothing with them," Ana said. "I never had them. The Nicaraguans told me I was a child, and that you should have sent an adult to them. They clearly didn't think I could be trusted with diamonds."

"They should have been in that box of cookies," Olive insisted. "All I found were pineapple cookies, and I hate pineapple."

"Mr. Ortega's assistant told me pineapple was your favorite. I guess they didn't know you well."

In an access of rage, Olive picked up the grimy bedsheet from the corner where Ana had put it. She opened the stove and set fire to it, touched it to the cabin wall, trying to set the dry wood alight.

Ana picked up one of the buckets of water and flung it over the flames, over Olive.

"It's enough, Olive. It's done. It's time for you to leave, to go back to your employment bureau and make the most of the time you have left."

Ana thought Olive might try to attack her. The priest looked wildly around the cabin, as if trying to spot a weapon, but after a moment, she left. Ana went to the door, shining her flashlight on Olive, watching until she disappeared over the top of the ridge.

If the youth at the Managua airport hadn't stuck his hand into her body, she would never have opened the parcel. They thought she was a child, someone who would ask no questions. Inside the airport, she saw similar boxes, wrapped in striped paper—*cajetas*—gift boxes with special Nicaraguan cookies or cakes inside.

She took the carton the youth had given her into the women's toilet and opened it. Under a layer of pineapple sweets, she found fourteen stones, in different shapes and colors. She supposed they were diamonds.

She imagined herself going through customs at O'Hare, being stopped by customs officials—perhaps tipped off by Ortega himself to double-cross Olive, or perhaps because she looked so young and naive. What she'd said to Natalie yesterday was true—she had no desire for valuable rocks. She kept one, as a souvenir, but the others she left in the box, which she dropped in the nearest trash bin on her way out. She bought a box of pineapple sweets from a gift stall, wrapped in the same gay striped paper as the one she'd been given.

Olive had met her flight, had wrapped her with solicitude, but Ana saw the greed in her face when she took the box. She'd dropped Ana at her South Side apartment, said she'd get details of the trip later in the day, and driven off at high speed.

Ana lifted the stove from the fireplace. The brick she'd remortared came away after some delicate prying with a dental pick.

The stone was still there, covered now in dirt. She had kept one stone back, not intending ever to sell it, but wanting some proof to herself that she hadn't imagined the events of her youth. She held it now in front of the fire, admiring the way the crystal cut the light, refracted it, reflected it.

Ana replaced the brick, put the stove back over it. In the dark, she hiked up to the top of the ridge, down to the beach. She cocked her arm back, threw the stone as far as she could. The crashing of the waves on the sand covered the sound of the diamond dropping into the water.

BANANA ISLAND

SUSAN BREEN

Three bedrooms. Two of them with closets. One with a view of Long Island City's most popular parking garage. Standing Room Only kitchen. One-and-a-half baths. Front lawn iced with concrete, except for a square foot of soil from which erupts a fragile mimosa tree. For all this, someone has just offered Marly Bingham two million dollars.

She found the offer in her mailbox, typed up on a lawyer's stationery, the paper of better quality than the thread count of her sheets.

Marly would have laughed if she could find something about two million dollars to laugh about. But she can't. It's a serious number. A number that forces you to act. To reconsider your life, your home, your family. All because a bunch of entitled corporate types have suddenly discovered that Long Island City is only a three-minute subway ride to midtown Manhattan. No matter how much money you spend in Long Island City, it's only a quarter of what you'd pay in Manhattan, and you can rip it all down and start over.

She's not selling. She refuses to be blasted out of her life.

But the rest of her family is problematic. They've been getting letters too, and they're tempted. Her grandmother wants to move to Scottsdale and her youngest cousin wants to go to Vegas. Two uncles have already absconded to Boca. Every time there's a family gathering it's like a frigging plague hit. You don't know who's going to be gone. Marly's doing what she can to hold the family together, but she's not the important one. She's the orphan, the outsider. It's her cousin Aaron who will decide everything, and Aaron's on the fence.

She's going to see him later that afternoon at her grandmother's birthday party.

But meanwhile there's Danjuma. Who's calling her now, as he does every day at about noon. And at four and at seven.

Marly doesn't answer right away because there's no harm to letting him wait, and it's not like he's going to go away. Predators don't surrender.

Instead she goes into her kitchen and pours herself some coffee from the drip pot. Puts it into the IRS mug she got at the office party last year. Gulps some of it down, and looks at the air plant in the corner. Strange, awkward plants that don't need soil to thrive. They look prehistoric. They frighten her and excite her, like just about everything else in her life.

When she finishes her coffee, she goes into the living room and settles down on her gray couch. White wall behind her. Her Zebra phone is specially adapted so that Danjuma can't trace it. It's still ringing.

"Did you get another offer?" Danjuma asks, as soon as his face appears on her screen. He has a sincere face. Dark-skinned, broad smile. He always wears a buttoned-up shirt with a tie.

Marly's been telling him about the offers on her house, hoping to provoke him into making his play. At some point he's going to ask her for money. This is what he does. He strikes up friendships with vulnerable women on dating message boards. He pretends to love them, he listens to them, and then at some point he asks for money. Just a small amount at first. He tells them he's got a son in the hospital who needs $2,000 for an operation and he can't pay it because his money is trapped in a bank. Something like that. Next thing you know, the women have lost everything.

Marly's met a number of his victims. Trusting women who were desperate for love. Who knew, on some level, that they were being seduced, but were so desperate they were willing to take the risk. She understands them. Her own parents were gamblers, lost absolutely everything at a casino and wound up dying in a car crash when Marly was just eighteen. She was left all alone, with nothing but this house, and she would have lost that if her cousin Aaron hadn't stepped in to help her. She understands better than anyone that there are people in this world who can be destroyed by false hope, and she's sworn to defend them. That's why she's a scam baiter.

Her job is to talk to Danjuma, because if he's talking to her he's not hurting anyone else.

That's it. And sometimes she's able to trap the scammers, get them arrested or get them in trouble.

She's been quite successful in her field. Has a reputation for being ruthless. She's known in the community as Safari Girl, for a trick she once played on one of the scammers. But this bait with Danjuma has been going on for months. He hasn't asked for money yet. She's not sure what he's about, and so she keeps trying to tempt him with information about real estate.

"The offer was for two million dollars," she says.

"That's crazy. Are you going to tell Aaron? The party's this afternoon, right?"

"I'm not telling Aaron. He'll get upset and he's upset enough."

"Why would a man be mad about being offered money?"

"He's mad because he's having to make a difficult choice." Aaron has been offered even more money than she has, because his house is larger and closer to the subway.

"I don't understand. I would take the money right away." Danjuma speaks English, but it's a different form of English than what Marly knows. There seems to be more air in his mouth, and he clicks his *t*'s when he's excited, which he almost always is when he talks about money. He becomes almost incomprehensible.

"That's because you think money's more important than anything," Marly observes.

"I've seen people starve because they didn't have money. It's important."

"We're not starving. We have a nice life. With us it's about wanting more. We don't need it." She feels her voice choking up. "Why do I need two living rooms? Or two cinema rooms?"

"Ah," he croons, "you've been looking at the ads, haven't you? You've been looking at the ads for Banana Island."

"How can I not look when you talk about it all the time?" she says, but she's smiling. She can't help herself.

This is Danjuma's obsession, to live on Banana Island. He wants Marly to live there too. He wants her whole family to live there. He thinks it is the most wonderful place in the world. A man-made island in the shape of a banana off the coast of Lagos. He's never actually been there because it's very exclusive and you can only get onto it by crossing a long and narrow bridge across the Lagos Lagoon and then giving the security guard a password, which changes every day. But he's seen pictures. It's where the Nigerian billionaires live. It's full of sleek high-rises with elevators and electricity and saunas and maids' quarters and Jacuzzis and green, carefully manicured grass. Though people don't walk on the grass. They're too wealthy for that. They have drivers.

You can buy a nice place on Banana Island for 700,000,000 naira, which works out to two million dollars. This is all Danjuma dreams about and it is the one thing about him that Marly believes is not a lie. For that reason, she loves talking to him about it. Because when she talks to him about Banana Island, she can almost believe he's her friend. Instead of a man who wants to destroy her.

Her grandmother's birthday party is at a small restaurant that has no sign out front. You don't go there unless you know it's there, and you don't get seated unless you know the owner. There's sawdust on the floor, black-and-white photos on the wall and a bullet hole by the far window, remnant of a time in the 1920s when the mob ruled Long Island City. Marly's family occupies a large table in the center of the room. Her four cousins have obviously been arguing. They're big men with red faces, but at the sight of Marly they shut up.

Her entire family peers at her as though they can't get her into focus, and for just a moment Marly falters. She smooths down her blue dress, which is just a little bit too tight. She should buy a new one, but she hates shopping, though now she wishes she had. She feels like a spotlight's on her.

These are the people she loves most in the world, and yet she always feels so strange around them. She's the one who didn't go into the family manufacturing business but instead took this strange job chasing down Nigerian scam artists. She's the one who hasn't married, who has the parents who died in a crash, though no one is really sure whether the crash was an accident or suicide. Turns out her parents had a lot of gambling debts come due soon after. She's the obligation, and no matter how much she loves her family, she's afraid that none of them really like her. She also suspects that if they sell their homes, she'll never see them again.

But then Aaron stands up. Big Aaron. He strides over to her with his gap-toothed grin.

They used to call him The Pumpkin. He squeezes her in a

hug. "Hey, Marly," he whispers. "Don't worry. It's all coming together."

"Really? But how?"

"Can't talk about it now. Later. Right?"

And just like that everything shifts in her mind. Her anxiety about her house floats away and she sees her family, waving at her, and Aaron's wife, Serena, beckoning for her to come over.

"How you?" Marly asks, when she sits down next to Serena. The chair creaks underneath her.

"Splendid," Serena says, and she is, actually. She's stunning. Aaron met her on the subway a couple of years ago. She's an artist and has shows in venues in Manhattan. She specializes in collages with nails and fasteners and staples. Homely objects, she calls her creations. Marly considers herself a homely object, so she's always appreciated Serena's work. Always felt she had a special relationship with her. Serena actually gave her one of her collages as a present some years ago, and Marly knows for a fact that it was valued at $15,000. She hung it in her bedroom, which she suspects is weird, but she couldn't put it in her kitchen and the living room has to stay bland so that Danjuma can't pick up any clues about her.

Serena also happens to be the most moisturized person Marly's ever met. She smells like she just walked off a beach on a tropical island. Tonight she wears a black dress that has cutouts, so that bits of her fair skin peek out all over the place. She has straight black hair with bangs. She blinks her eyes in a way that makes Marly think of porcelain dolls. Marly never played with dolls, but she'd have played with Serena, which is a really weird notion. Do other people have these thoughts? She doesn't think she's gay, but she's not really sure. People in her family don't talk about such things. Not in a way that would make you want to be one.

"Why were you late? Talking to that Nigerian of yours."

"I don't know that I'd put it like that, but yes. Danjuma."

Her grandmother is sitting on the other side of Marly, but

she's not completely conscious. Wouldn't be a birthday party if Grandma didn't drink herself into a stupor. But Marly kisses her soft cheek, and turns her attention back to Serena, who is signaling the waiter for another drink.

"Scotch?"

"Please."

"And I'll have another old-fashioned. So what do you and this Nigerian talk about?"

The restaurant smells of prime rib. That's what they always get at these parties. Huge slabs of beef and roasted potatoes and Yorkshire pudding and fried Brussels sprouts and creamed spinach. Marly reaches for a roll from the basket in front of her. She suspects they buy them at Stop & Shop and microwave them, but they're still very tasty and she loves the way the butter melts into the dough and seeps through it. She could eat the whole basket, but decides not to. Not while she's sitting next to Serena.

"What does anybody talk about?" Marly says. "Well, actually, we spend a lot of time talking about Banana Island."

Serena nods. "That's supposed to be nice."

Marly's stunned. "You've heard of it?"

"Of course. It's very fancy. I knew someone who lived there. He bought one of my collages, actually. Worked for one of those big Nigerian communications companies." She pulls out her phone and begins scrolling through it. "'Adebiyi,'" she reads, nodding her head. "That's his name."

"What a small world."

"He's very rich," Serena says. "When he was in New York, he lived in a penthouse on Central Park West. He had the entire floor. Had to be worth upward of thirty million dollars. He was a dangerous man. He wanted to marry me, but then I met your cousin, and I fell in love."

She puts her hand on Marly's, and the sensation is so powerful that Marly jumps, to her embarrassment. She hadn't seen it coming. Usually she can prepare herself for Serena's touch.

Her face heats up. She suspects she looks like one of Serena's collages, all red and effusive and molten. Growing up all the kids, and her cousins, called her Manly.

"I don't mean to tease you about your Nigerian," Serena goes on. "I really do admire the work you do. It just seems so dangerous to me. I hope there aren't gangs of them in New York, trying to hunt you down."

Serena's hand is so creamy. Marly's own skin is red and rough, like her cousins. The Binghams are all big people. They are lumbering, loud people.

She wants to move her hand away from Serena's, but she doesn't want to either. That's when Marly notices the bruise on Serena's wrist.

"What's that from?"

Serena holds up her hand as though studying a painting. "Oh nothing. I tripped. You know how clumsy I am."

"You're not clumsy at all," Marly cries out, more loudly than she intended. Her grandmother snorts awake for a moment, then recloses her eyes. "You move beautifully," Marly whispers.

Serena shrugs. Picks up one of the rolls and begins to massage one of the little pieces of dough.

"Is it Aaron? Is he hurting you? He can't do that!"

Marly starts to rise, but Serena tugs her down. "Don't make a scene, Marly. Things are tense enough as they are. You know Aaron. He's got a temper, but I can handle him."

"It doesn't look like you can." Certainly Aaron has a temper. She's seen him fight. He's been banned from Yankee Stadium because he once jumped onto the field to punch an umpire. She refuses to drive in a car with him because if he gets angry at someone on the road, he loses all control. But not with Serena. He adores Serena.

"I have to talk to him."

"Please, don't." Something in Serena's eyes stops her. Is it fear?

She can't read it. All she's ever seen in Serena's eyes is confidence and amusement. "Not now."

The one true thing Marly knows is that once things start to go bad, they get worse. She sees that with people who get scammed. After a certain point, even though they know they're being scammed, they can't pull out. They've gone too far. They'd rather be destroyed than admit what idiots they were. They keep holding on to hope even if it's destroying them.

But she wavers.

She knows what she should do. But to take on Aaron would be to destroy the family, and it's not only that. She does think Serena can take care of herself and she loves Serena and doesn't want to go against her. And she's a coward. That's what Marly realizes as she walks back into her house after the dinner's over. Her cousin is beating his wife and she's done nothing, because she's a coward, just like her parents. They had gambling debts and so they killed themselves, leaving Marly alone to deal with the fallout. The accident was never officially designated a suicide, but she's always known. She's always remembered the last time she saw her father, when he hugged her and told her that he loved her. He gave her his watch. Asked her to have it fixed. She keeps it in her drawer upstairs, though she never looks at it.

The phone is ringing when Marly walks into her living room, and for the first time in their relationship, she's actually looking forward to talking to Danjuma. She trusts him, in a weird way. Maybe because she knows who he is. Her opinion of him is completely unfiltered. She snaps the phone off the couch. It's warm, must have been ringing for a while.

"What's wrong, Marly? Is it your grandmother?"

"No," she says, oddly touched that he knows so quickly that she's upset. "My grandmother's fine, but my cousin's in trouble."

"Aaron?"

"Yes, I think he's hurting Serena. Well, I'm sure of it, and she doesn't want me to get involved."

He's silent. Outside the wind howls. It's a cold February night. A dim green glow from the Citicorp building settles over everything. This was the construction that started the revitalization of Long Island City. Not surprising that its light seeps into everything.

"She's right. Do not get involved with this. You should sell the house and leave them behind."

"I'm not going to do that. Anyway, she needs me. I can make an anonymous call to the police, but I think it's better if I talk to Aaron. Maybe I could persuade him to get help."

"Don't be stupid, Marly. He could attack you."

"She knows about Banana Island. She knows someone who lives there." That distracts him.

"Who?"

"I forget his name. It started with an A."

"Abiyo?"

"I don't know."

"She has a lot of money?"

Marly shuts up. What is she doing? The next thing you know she'll steer Danjuma to Serena. What's wrong with her? She clenches her fists. She looks out the window, out at the little mimosa tree flapping around in the wind, at the parking garage, which has a line out front, at one of the best bakeries in Long Island City. Almond-filled croissants, and at that moment a bullet cracks through the window.

The wall behind her screams.

Marly flings herself off the couch, which causes her phone to skid across the floor. She's got to cover it up. She cannot have Danjuma seeing where she lives. Her curtains are open. He can see outside. She inches over, flips over the phone, blinding it, all the while Danjuma is shouting her name.

"Marly, Marly, are you all right?"

She gets to her feet, staggers slightly. There's blood on her hand. She charges out the front door, looking for the shooter.

Some people walk by, but she doesn't know them. Her neighbor's house is closed up. Scaffolding's on the outside. Mr. Ferguson's moved to Scottsdale with his wife. They'd sent Marly a postcard. She runs down the road, looking for something.

Someone. Her cousin. Or maybe a Nigerian, someone from a gang that's here to take revenge on her. Impossible to tell in the mix of people outside her house. No one is running. She pushes to the end of the block. Looks to her left, and sees the New York City skyline.

She's freezing. She's only wearing the blue dress she had on at her grandmother's party.

Her shoes are crushing her toes together.

She heads back to her house. Danjuma's still calling her name.

Cold air is blowing through the shattered window. She has some cardboard in the kitchen, but she doesn't want to stand in front of the window to repair it. She's anticipating the next shot.

"It sounded like a Beretta," Danjuma says.

"How can you tell?" The Beretta is her family gun. They all have them. She has one upstairs. She has a cousin who became a police officer just so that he could get a special police officer Beretta. He's now in California, working in personal security for a Hollywood star.

"I was in the army. I fought in the Battle of Konduga." This is a new bit of information, though it could be a lie. "Show me the bullet," he demands.

Marly feels drowsy. Suddenly she thinks she sees her father walk through the door. He was a noisy man, and he'd always grab her up in his arms and swing her around. She has a picture of him teaching her how to roller-skate, right on the sidewalk in front of her house. She wears a polka-dot dress. He's crouched alongside her, beaming, wearing a fedora. She still has the skates. But she doesn't have the fedora. He was wearing that when he died.

"Marly, pay attention to me."

She looks into the phone. Danjuma's face fills the screen. It's as though he's trying to press his face to New York. His eyes are large and bloodshot. If she didn't know he was a criminal, she might think he was sincerely worried.

"I've got to go see Aaron."

"Are you crazy? He'll kill you. Call the police."

"I have to see him. I owe him that much."

"Bring your gun then."

"I'm not going to shoot him." She can still hear his heartbeat from when he hugged her after her parents died.

"You are being stupid," he cries out. That is Danjuma's most damning insult. There is no flaw so appalling as stupidity. That is how he justifies what he does, because his victims are stupid. If they were not stupid they would not let him trick them, and so it is not his fault. There is a part of Marly that has always agreed with him on this point, though she would never tell him that. She's listened to the victims' stories and there have been times she's wanted to shake them and say couldn't you see? A man calls you from Nigeria and tells you he wants your bank account number. Wouldn't that raise a warning flag?

But in this moment, as she prepares to leave her house, it occurs to her that there are worse sins than stupidity and one of them is to strand those who you love. Serena is at that house with Aaron. If he's mad enough to shoot at Marly, who's to say what he might do to Serena.

If she calls the police it will end in violence, but maybe she can calm things down. "I've got to go."

"Take me with you."

"What?"

"Put your phone in your pocket. I can listen for you. I can help you analyze people's voices. I can tell if someone's telling a lie."

"That's ridiculous."

"I might be able to help."

His voice was so tempting. She feels so alone. If she stops to think about what's happening, it's terrifying. Her cousin, the person who has protected her all these years, who was the person who told her that her parents were dead, who helped her save her house, might now be trying to kill her. Because he's angry about being pressured into not selling? Because he's worried she'll call the police on Serena? Because he seethes with anger. The earth moves beneath her feet. The sensation that life can change in an instant.

She walks out onto the sidewalk, holding the Zebra phone in her hands. It feels heavy, a bomb. But there's nothing unusual about holding a phone in your hands while you walk around Long Island City.

She knows the route to Aaron's house without even seeing it. The reverberation of the train that draws her in his direction, the sweet smell of the Greek bakery, the clinking of the wine bars, the men standing outside the hashish stores, even in this weather. Over everything the lights of Manhattan, so close you could almost feel like you could walk across the river and be there.

A couple bump into her. "Bitch," one of them whispers, and moves on.

Aaron's house is a three-story white building with lots of trim. Pillars by the front door. Iron railings round the side. Every narrow window curtained. Easily the best maintained house on the street. At one time, Aaron rented out the bedrooms, but Serena put a stop to that. She had no intention of being a landlady.

Marly climbs the stairs and rings the bell. Serena answers so quickly it was as though she'd been waiting for her. She wears black silk pajamas and black slippers. She has on no makeup, which makes her look both more beautiful and more damaged. When she moves, Marly can see another bruise under her sleeve.

"Oh baby," Serena says. "What happened to you?"

"I need to see Aaron."

"You've got blood on your forehead. Let me clean it."

"Where is he?"

Serena shakes her head. "You don't want to get involved with this."

Marly's sure he's in the basement. That's where he always goes when he's upset, or that's what Aaron used to do. The house is so changed from what it was that she can't be sure. Where there was once a narrow hallway, there's now a large entryway. All the carpet's been ripped up and replaced with light oak. There's a giant succulent of a chandelier overhead. Only the narrow stairway to the right is the same, a stairway so steep it's like a fire ladder. They used to ride mattresses down those stairs.

She should have brought a weapon. Danjuma was right about that. She's put the phone in her pocket. Suddenly Marly appreciates the danger she's in.

She could grab Serena and run. They could just get out of there. If Aaron's in the basement, they have time to escape and they could go anywhere. That's the beautiful thing. She has a couple of thousand dollars in her bank account, and her house. Two million dollars. She could go anywhere with Serena with that.

She laughs.

Danjuma asks her if she's okay. She puts her hand over the phone to quiet him, but she doesn't think Serena's noticed.

She could actually go to Banana Island. Serena would love that. They could buy one of those vast complexes that overlook the Lagos Lagoon. She thinks of all that white wall space that Serena could fill with her paintings. Marly could find an online job. She doesn't think the IRS would still employ her if she lived in Nigeria but she could work as a consultant. Or she could completely change what she does. Maybe she could teach.

For just a moment she's seriously tempted to grab Serena and run out the front door, but she can't do it without checking on Aaron. She remembers the way he came to tell her that her parents were dead, how he visited her every afternoon, how he comforted her. She can't just go running off with his wife unless she's sure he's a murderer.

She heads toward the basement. "Marly, don't go there," Serena says.

"It's okay. He's not going to hurt me."

"No," Serena says, fluttering behind her, but Marly pushes on, through the kitchen, which is stunning in how different it looks. Used to be a cramped space with red walls and dark wood cabinets, but now it gleams with sleek white doors and wood floors. It looks like something out of a magazine. There are flights of candles on the counter and everything smells of vanilla.

The door to the basement is at the far end of the kitchen. Marly heads toward the door, flings it open and starts down the steps.

Here at least everything is familiar. So Aaron has not let Serena get her hands on this. It's as dark and musty as it ever was. Marly runs down the steps. She wants to see him, has to know what's going on, needs to see his face, but when she gets to the bottom, the room's empty.

There's the Ping Pong table, the pool table, the little refrigerator that she knows will be stocked with Sam Adams. There are the posters from their childhood, including one of some movie star with a bottle that's downright obscene. But no Aaron, unless he's hiding, which would be unlike him. He is not a man who hides. In fact, he's not a man who would shoot you through a window. He'd look at you and pull the trigger.

Maybe the bathroom.

That's when Danjuma speaks. "Marly, are you alone."

She jumps. She'd forgotten he was in her pocket. "I must be. I don't see Aaron anywhere."

"You have to get out of there now. You're in danger."

"I don't think so. I don't see him."

"It's her voice, Marly. She means you harm. She's lying. I can hear it."

"What are you talking about?"

That's when she hears Serena walking down the stairs. Automatically Marly turns toward her, smiling, which is when she sees Serena is holding a Beretta.

"Talking to your Nigerian?"

"What are you doing, Serena?"

"Pass me your phone." She points one slippered foot to the floor and indicates where Marly should slide it.

"Run, Marly, run," Danjuma shouts, but Serena picks up the phone, laughs and then launches it against the wall. Danjuma's voice gurgles and dies.

"Doesn't it bother you," Serena asks, "to be so ridiculous."

"Where's Aaron?"

"Walking around with some Nigerian in your pocket. Talking to him like he's going to help you. Sitting in that house of yours talking to him and thinking that there's something so special about it that you shouldn't sell it for two million dollars."

Marly's backing away from her when she notices her cousin lying on the floor, behind the pool table.

"Mooning around about me, and wearing that dress. You can see your stomach!"

Aaron's been shot once, in the head. He looks surprised. She hadn't realized the dead could be so expressive. So strange to feel no heartbeat. She has been hearing his heartbeat in her mind since the day she leaned her head against his chest and he told her about her parents. It's been the rhythm of her life and now it's gone.

"You're such a goddamned loser," Serena shrieks.

"You were the one who shot at me through the window. You knew I'd come here."

"You're fairly predictable," Serena says. "Think of the most stupid thing a person can do and then wait, and you'll do it."

Marly feels blindsided. This is what scam victims talk about when she interviews them. That sudden shift when reality changes. That moment when you realize you've been looking at life through the wrong lens. She feels her face contorting. She suspects she looks ridiculous, like a fish gasping for air.

"I begged him to sell the house. I never lied about who I was. I told him from the moment I met him that I didn't want to live here and he promised we wouldn't, but then he began changing. Talking about community and family. And what about me? What about what he promised me?"

When they find her body, the police will figure she and Aaron had some sort of shoot-out. Serena will be there saying that Aaron beat her and Marly ran to her defense. It would be nice to think someone would dig deeper, but she's seen with her parents that there are some deaths that are never wrapped up.

She feels so tired.

Marly's hit with a wave of sympathy for her father she's never felt before. All those years of being angry at him, and now she understands that he was just a man who had to deal with too much. Something dark swallowed him up. She feels the darkness on the edge of her vision, but she just cannot let it take over. She has to fight this. Oddly enough, it's Danjuma she thinks of in that moment. That he would be disappointed if she surrenders.

She'll run toward the basement door. It will force Serena to shoot her in the back, which will at least raise some questions. Maybe.

On the count of three. One. Two. Marly clenches her hands, starts toward the door, and at that moment it slams open and a pack of police officers push through.

Four police officers run past. Marly drops to the floor. Feels the heat of a bullet go by.

Hears Serena scream.

★ ★ ★

It's almost dawn by the time Marly makes her way back to her house. She stayed with Aaron's body until the coroner came and took him away. Serena's gone to jail.

From her concrete front lawn, Marly can hear the phone ringing inside her house, which is odd. The Zebra phone that Danjuma calls on has been destroyed. No one calls her on her regular phone, and certainly not at dawn, but that's the one that's ringing and Danjuma's face fills the screen.

"How did you get this number?"

She's still in the blue dress she wore to her grandmother's party, though now it's dirty from crawling around Aaron's basement floor. And of course some cold air is blowing on her stomach.

"Are you okay?" Danjuma asks, and she realizes in that moment that he's known about her all along. All the private information she's so carefully hidden from him.

He knew exactly where Aaron lived. "You called the police?"

"Yes, I knew she wanted to hurt you. I saved your life."

"But what did you do?"

"I called the police."

"From Nigeria?"

"They were not inclined to believe me but I gave them so much information, they had to act."

Marly sits down on the gray couch, where she's sat for hours and hours listening to Danjuma talk, planning ways to trap him.

"Why haven't you asked me for money?"

Danjuma smiles. She knows that smile so well. She's spent months looking at it, at the little scar under his lip, the slight stubble of beard, the white teeth that erupt from his dark red gums.

"It's not my job," he says.

"I would have thought it was your only job."

"No," he says. "My job was to keep you talking. As long as you were talking to me, you could not be capturing anyone else."

"You're a scam baiter, but in reverse?"

"You have quite a reputation here, Marly. We wanted to keep you out of commission for a bit."

"I guess it worked."

Blindsided. Her immediate instinct is to call Serena. She would find it all so wonderfully ridiculous. That Marly has spent months talking to a man to stop him from hurting anybody and all the while he's been talking to her to stop her from helping anybody. Does that make them even?

"She was not a good woman," Danjuma says. So he knows that too, Marly thinks. But of course he does. He's a man who makes his living by playing on women's romantic fantasies. Of course he knows how Marly's sympathies lie.

"No," Marly says. "But I loved her."

Danjuma shrugs. She turns off the phone. She should feel depressed, but Marly feels surprisingly happy. The future unfolds. A new life. An honest life. She can choose whatever life she wants. Especially because soon, she'll have two million dollars in her bank account.

FLIP TOP

GARY PHILLIPS

Aunt Millie's house on Field Avenue looked different from the outside. For one the rosebushes were gone. Since moving away from Los Angeles, Cully Graham had only been back here twice in this century. He shut the rental's motor off and got out.

"Cully, child, is that you?"

"Yes, ma'am." He went over to his aunt Ruth, Millie's younger sister. She used a cane but was rather spry. Her son, his first cousin Robert Porter, opened his arms wide.

"What's going on, showtime?"

They hugged. "If I had your hand, I'd throw mine in, Bobby." Cousin Bobby was a big man, linebacker size and some two inches taller than Graham. He'd been a star football player at nearby Dorsey High and received a sports scholarship to UCLA. He'd even made the pros, fifth-round draft pick for the Colts, but only lasted three seasons, dogged by injuries. He'd disappeared for a while after that, swallowed up by drugs and despair.

They laughed and parted. He then bent to give his aunt a hug as well.

"How you doing, Aunt Ruth?"

"Well, not so bad for an old lady I suppose. You know Millie was suffering so much toward the end, it's a blessing our Lord finally took her home." She patted his back as they embraced. When he stepped back, she regarded him. "I see some snow starting up top. How's that wife of yours and the boys?"

"Everybody's doing fine. They of course send their love. Gerald's on his way to Howard."

She beamed at that. "Majoring in math?"

"He is."

"Good, good," she said. "He always had a head for them numbers like you did. Why you didn't become a math professor or send rockets to the moon I don't know."

"Mm-hmm."

"Boy, don't you be patronizing me." She tapped his arm playfully.

"Yeah, Cul," his cousin added, smiling.

Between them, he and his cousin walked her toward the house as other friends and family got out of their cars. Some had gone to the funeral and others were arriving now for the repast. Arriving from two doors down was Mrs. Matsamura also using a cane. Age had hunched her over.

"Go help Christine, would you, Bobby?"

"Of course." He went over to Mrs. Matsamura.

Inside the modest house a sizable grouping of adults and children stood in the living room, talking and sipping on juice or seltzer in cups. In the breakfast nook off the kitchen catered fried chicken, short ribs, greens and several other savory offerings were laid out in rectangular foil tubs along with serving spoons. A stack of paper plates and whatnot were on a side table. Several people were already eating.

Graham ladled out a helping of macaroni and cheese to go along with the greens and chicken he'd placed on his plate.

"Sure good to see you, Cully. Even under these circumstances."

"You too, Mrs. Matsamura." He put his plate aside and they hugged as well.

"I'm sure going to miss me and Millie having our tea together."

"Of course, yes." The two had been neighbors since his aunt had moved into this house in LA's Crenshaw District in the 1960s. Back then the area was composed of Nisei, second-generation Japanese Americans like Mrs. Matsamura and Black people like his aunt whose folks had migrated from the South before and after World War II. Mrs. Matsamura was born in the late forties. She had an older brother who'd been a child at Manzanar, one of the internment camps here in California the government had sent the JAs to during that war. Graham had fond memories as a kid of first being repulsed then loving to eat rice topped with natto, the fermented soybeans and chopped green onions she'd introduced to him.

"Excuse me a second," he said to the older woman as they talked. His smartphone was chiming. Recognizing the number, he answered, turning away from her slightly.

"Yes, Herb?" he said to his manager on the other end. He listened for several moments then said, "How about we borrow the Goldhofer from the Imex job and send it over to the center so they can use it? Stan over there is running ahead of schedule so it shouldn't be a problem." He listened some more. "Right, okay, good, thanks for calling." He tapped off and put his phone away.

"Problems?" Mrs. Matsamura asked.

"No, the usual."

They resumed catching up. Eventually Graham took his plate into the backyard where his cousin was talking to another man

and a woman. Cousin Bobby had finished his plate and tossed
it into a recycling bin.

"Hey, Willie Lee," Graham greeted the other man. He was
wiry, in his late fifties in a sharkskin suit and snap-brim hat,
and smoking a cigarette. It was as if he'd stepped out of a men's
fashion ad in a 1970s issue of *Ebony* magazine. The two shook
hands vigorously.

"Good to see you, Claudia." He gave the woman a kiss on
the cheek.

"You too, Cully. Sorry about Aunt Millie. Long time, huh?"
She squeezed his upper arm. Claudia McIntyre wore black and
a large hat, part of her face in shadow. She was two years older
than Graham. Willie Lee was her uncle through marriage. They
too were cousins but further removed.

Graham looked past her at the large backyard area. It was a
wide expanse of lawn with a few trees at the rear, all of it bordered by a combination cinder-block wall and chain-link fence.

"I remember when we built our clubhouse back here," he
said. He'd grown up in a cramped apartment. How he treasured
hanging out in this yard for hours. Just laying on his back and
staring up at the sky.

"Justice Guard headquarters," his cousin piped in.

As youngsters they'd been influenced by the Marvel comics
they read and passed around to each other. This desire to right
wrongs was coupled with a nascent understanding of the causes
of the Rodney King riots in 1992. A real-life conflagration like
something the Sons of the Serpent would instigate. But comics
hadn't informed them about the unrest. Their interpretations
were derived from snatches of adult conversations and hearing
gangsta rap older teenagers in their lives were blasting back in
the day. The three and a few other friends had formed their super
group. To not only thrash super villains like the Red Skull or
Dr. Doom, but to regulate fools, including the whack ass po-lice.

Cousin Bobby chuckled, recalling, "Some came and went but we was always the fantastic five."

"Ricky and Devon," McIntyre said, mentioning the other two he meant.

"Yeah," Graham said. "Ricky was Power Pulse, master of magnetism like Magneto." He ate more of his food.

"And damn if he didn't become an electrical engineer," McIntyre said. She and Ricky Cooks had been sweethearts in their late teens.

"Who was Devon in our group?" Cousin Bobby wondered aloud.

McIntyre frowned trying to dredge up the memory. "I can't remember."

"Mr. Amazing," Graham said.

"Shit, that's right." She gaped at him, taking in a breath.

"What?" Willie Lee said, noticing her reaction.

"Devon became a big-time slanger," she said. "Started as a lookout and worked his way up. Mr. Amazing became his drug dealer nickname too."

"Hard mutha." Cousin Bobby had a grim look on his face.

"Crack?" Willie Lee asked.

"No, this was the '90s. He started with coke, the powder, then it was meth and pills, oxies and doxies," McIntyre said.

"That some white boy shit," Willie Lee observed.

Cousin Bobby said, "Mr. Amazing was nothing if not enterprising. He had it going on not only out here but in Cincinnati, down into Kentucky and parts of Florida too."

"Damn. He still around?" the uncle asked. "In the joint?"

"The game got him," Cousin Bobby declared. "He's in the graveyard. Had hisself a fly funeral. Tricked out lowriders and luxury cars fo' blocks deep leading into Inglewood Cemetery."

"Figures." Willie Lee fired up another cigarette. "Live by the sword and whatnot." He wandered away, smoking, waving at a man in a turtleneck.

"Zip, zap," a kid in a buttoned-up starched shirt said as he chased another child into the backyard from the kitchen. "I got you with my ray gun, you're frozen." He looked to be about eight and was pointing a blunt object at the other one a year or so younger it appeared.

"No I had my force field up," the second kid protested.

"Naw you didn't."

Laughing, they ran past then circled back around the three. A woman in her thirties came to the house's rear doorway. "Terry, you and Alex get back in here and say hello to your cousin Bernice from Kansas City."

"Mom," one of them protested.

"Today, young man."

"Okay," he drawled. Head down he and the other one marched back toward the house. He was holding the squarish black object at his side. Just as he crested the back steps trailing the other one, he unlimbered what was in his hand, flipping the top open, grinning at the thing.

"Cul, you still got that classic Mustang you bought from Pops Rayford?" Cousin Bobby said.

The car he was talking about was what he'd left town in. "Had to sell it," Graham said, distracted, watching the kid go into the house.

"Aw man, that's too bad."

"Yeah. But working on the car every weekend became more chore than joy."

"I hear you," his cousin said. "Crawling up under a ride at our age ain't like when we was in our twenties or thirties even."

"Next you'll be talking about your prostates," McIntyre remarked.

They chuckled, Graham looking toward the house. He said, "Be right back, gonna get something to drink." He went inside, setting his plate on the kitchen counter along with a few others. More mourners were in here and he had to worm his way through them to get back into the dining room.

"Where'd you get that?" the mother asked her son Terry holding the flip-top phone.

"Found it."

"Where?"

"Over there," his brother Alex said, pointing toward the living room past the archway. "Behind that," he added, though it was unclear where specifically he meant.

"That was Millie's, wasn't it?" Aunt Ruth said, having walked into the room through the archway. She looked over at Graham. "You and Bobby got her that in case she fell again."

"That's right," he said, eyes on the phone which was at least two decades old.

Back then in the late 1990s Aunt Millie was still driving. When she'd return from the grocery store, she'd put her purchases in one of those collapsible carts to take the goods from her trunk to the house. Once she'd fallen but hadn't broken anything as she'd landed on the lawn. Thereafter her nephews at Aunt Ruth's urgings had bought her the phone and programmed in several numbers like an ambulance service Aunt Millie could call at the touch of a button. In that way their aunt, who didn't want to have one of those "I've fallen and can't get up" doohickies for old people, still felt independent.

"She'd finally lost it for good and we figured it had accidentally been thrown out," Aunt Ruth said. After that, her sister convinced her to get an alert bracelet like she had.

"Give it to auntie," the woman told her son.

The kid frowned. "It's mine."

"No it isn't, honey, it belongs to her."

Aunt Ruth gestured and said, "I don't care. Let him keep it."

"You sure that's okay?" The woman had her hand on Terry's shoulder.

"What am I going to do with it?"

The mother bent toward her son. "Say thank you."

"Thank you," he dutifully replied. Off he and his brother went, returning to their escapades as space pirates.

"Who is that, Aunt Ruth?" Graham asked, indicating Terry's mother.

"That's Cissy, Clarence's daughter from his second marriage." His face clouded.

"Clarence from the Daniels side of the family," she illuminated.

Vaguely he understood the connection. "She live out here?"

"No," she drawled. "Hey, Cissy," she called out, "don't you still live in Houston?"

"Yes, you want to come visit?"

"Cully asked."

"Oh?" she said, stepping closer.

Put on the spot, Graham had to come up with an excuse. "I was just asking auntie 'cause I couldn't remember."

She was staring at him. "I don't think we've seen each other since Little Ocee died."

"See what I mean?" he deflected. But now he had to stay and talk when in fact he needed to get that phone from her son. Particularly as she and her boys would probably be leaving town in the next day or so.

As the two chatted, Graham tried to keep track of Terry and Alex. But having the energy of children their age, they hardly remained in one place any length of time.

"And when Morris lost his leg in the car accident, that was when I went to Texas to help Rita," Cissy Daniels was saying. He'd also learned she'd taken back her family name after the divorce from her husband who ran away to be in a cult.

"Did y'all drive out here for the funeral?"

She gave him a lopsided grin. "I guess it's been awhile since your kids were small. Have those two knotheads torture me all the way here. Please."

He grinned. "You guys flying back tomorrow?"

"Yes. We're staying at Aunt Ruth's building tonight."

"Right," he said, nodding. Aunt Ruth owned income property, an eleven-unit apartment complex further into the 'hood.

Later as the gathered began to leave, Graham stood on the lawn in front of the house. Terry and Alex and another kid their age were there as well.

He walked over to them. "Hey, you still have that old phone you found?"

The brothers looked at him quizzically.

"What phone?" Terry said.

"That thing that opens up," he pantomimed.

The brothers looked at each other then back at him. "I don't know," Alex said.

"How about I pay you for it?" He showed them a twenty.

"Momma's got money," the older Terry said.

"But this would be yours. You know, for candy and ice cream."

"She said don't take money from strangers," Alex said, cocking his head as if to perceive Graham's true nature.

"Stranger danger," Terry insisted.

"You guys saw me talking to your mother. We're family."

"No we're not," Terry said.

"I mean we're related."

"What's related mean?" Alex said.

Graham was about to try and explain but the three ran off.

"Shit," he said, watching them go. Not long afterward the two brothers got in a car with their mother and another woman he didn't know. Damned if Alex wasn't playing with the phone, continually flipping the top open then closed. The four drove off, the unknown woman at the wheel.

Back in the house, he went over to his cousin. He tapped him on his arm, indicating he wanted to talk to him alone. They stood off to one side.

"I need you to get that phone for me." Bobby managed his mother's apartments. He would have to have a passkey, Graham reasoned.

"What?"

"The one the kids found."

"Why?"

"I'll pay you a hundred for it. Five hundred."

"What's this about, Cul?"

"I just need to get that phone."

"So you'll pay me five hundred to go over there and what, tell her Mom wants the phone now?"

"It would be better if you could sneak in. But that should do it."

The big man folded his arms. "If it's worth five hundred, then it's worth a thousand to you."

"Fine." He pointed at him. "You deliver the phone first, then you get paid."

"But you ain't told me why."

"Insurance."

"What, Aunt Millie have a policy?"

"That's not the kind of insurance I mean."

His cousin shook his head. "Naw, this is too shady and I don't want to be in the middle of it. But I tell you what, you pay me the five hundred and I loan you the keys. You get caught, I'll swear to Mom you stole them from me. 'Cause I ain't losing my job over whatever bullshit this is about, Cul."

"Deal."

Graham waited until evening to drive over to his aunt's building. It was a two-story dingbat structure of modest-sized apartments with compact balconies. From what he'd been told, Daniels and her two children were staying on the second floor in a vacant two-bedroom. There was a security gate and he let himself in using one of the two keys he'd received from his cousin. The other was the passkey. It was past ten at night. His threadbare plan depended on the mother being tired out from her trip and dealing with those youngsters. He figured once she got them quieted down and in bed, she'd kick back with a glass of wine and fall asleep herself. At least that's how he remembered it from the time when his kids were small.

He crossed the concrete courtyard adorned with earthen islands at either end from which anemic palm trees sprouted. He went up the stairs toward the back and onto the breezeway. Checking the metal numbers tacked to the doors, he arrived at Apartment 10. He paused, doing his best to slow his heart beating in his ears. Behind him a door clicked open and he turned his head sideways. The door closed.

Graham was cognizant now of a low thrum, a rhythmic thudding coming from within the apartment. Music that seemed to be a blend of fusion and old world African. There was a window looking out onto the breezeway, the curtains drawn but gapped. He crouched down and crept forward to chance taking a look. Peering inside he looked into the front room. There were two candles burning, dispensing flickering light. Daniels and the other woman sat on the couch. Daniels was lengthwise on the couch, leaning back as the other woman he'd seen her leaving with earlier massaged her feet. There was a squat bottle of cognac and two glasses on the coffee table as well. Were they lovers? Simply good friends? Who knew but he did care that they were awake. The door behind him opened again. This time a flashlight's beam was on him.

"You some kind of pervert?" a female voice said. That she was old was easy to hear in its timbre.

"Ma'am, this is a private matter," Graham hissed.

"Private my wrinkled ass." She had a Creole accent.

He rose, hurrying toward where the woman looked out, the door held on the chain. "Keep your goddamn voice down."

"Don't you tell me what to do. I've got grandmaman's gris-gris to deal with punks like you."

He was leaning his face toward her, her light shining on him from below his chin. It made him seem like an old-time movie villain. "Be quiet and get back inside, will you?"

She held her fist palm up and opening it, blew powder into his face and his nose.

Graham reared back, hacking and coughing. Now the door to Apartment 10 was opening and he ran off, back toward the stairway, sneezing.

"What's going on?" he heard Daniels say.

"Peeping Tom," the old lady said. "He was bent down at your window about to dingle hisself," she huffed.

He made it back outside, stepping off the curb.

"Watch it, asshole," a driver yelled at him, honking and weaving around Graham in the roadway.

He tumbled onto the asphalt. A new set of oncoming headlights got him up. Half running and stumbling, his eyes tearing and throat burning, he banged into the side of his car parked across the street. He got inside, figuring it was best to retreat in case the police were summoned. He drove away. Trying to clear his vision, Graham clipped his outside mirror against the same on a parked car, breaking that one off and shattering the glass of his. On he went. Not far from the apartments he had to pull over and get out. His stomach gurgling, he felt as if he might vomit its contents. Instead, when he bent over coughing, blood and bile filed his mouth. He spat several times. Straightening up, he wiped his lips with the back of his hand. He was sweating profusely. It was as if all of a sudden he'd come down with the flu or food poisoning.

"The hell did she do to me?" he muttered.

Graham got back in his car and using his phone to find a location, he drove to a 7-Eleven and bought some coffee and aspirin. Sitting back in the car behind the steering wheel in the parking lot, he took two aspirin chased by a slug of tepid coffee. A stooped-over homeless man with a greasy tattered blanket wrapped around him shuffled by his windshield on the walkway. He stopped before getting past and swiveled toward Graham. His face revealed under the fluorescents of the store's eaves was that of Mr. Amazing, Devon Teekens. Long-dead Devon Teekens.

Graham gasped. The homeless man continued walking. His hands stuck to the steering wheel, he couldn't move but he had to move. Graham got out of the car and caught up with the homeless man, latching on to his upper arm.

"Hey," he said.

"Wha?" the destitute man said, turning toward him. He was old, brown skin gone gray and ruination prominent in his milky eyes.

"Never mind," Graham said, letting him go. He bent over retching again but this time it was only dry heaves.

Graham returned to his hotel suite near the airport. He sat on the edge of the bed, lying down on his back, feet on the floor. In a half sleep he and Teekens fought, the room's disarray and broken furniture testament to their struggle. Both were younger and stronger, each bloodying the other. Teekens was high on his own product. The drug dealer was bold but reckless. Graham was fueled by a righteous fervor. At one point he got behind Teekens, his arm around the other's windpipe. As he arched backward, Teekens tried to get free, his hands seeking purchase. The cell phone Graham had on his belt in a holder came away in Teekens's hand. He wrenched loose and stumbled to his knees. Teekens flipped the top open, frantically tapping at buttons.

"He's trying to kill me, Cully Graham is murdering me," he yelled into it.

Graham brought the metal base of an overturned lamp down on Teekens's head, toppling him over. He struck him again, crushing his skull and killing him.

In the present in his hotel room, Graham started awake, blinking into the dark. Looking over at the clock, he noted it was 2:13 in the morning. His head hurt. No matter whatever the hell the cut-rate witchy woman had peppered him with, he had to get that phone. He drove back to Aunt Ruth's apartments. All was quiet on the street. He entered again and cautiously ascended the stairs.

He snuck past the conjure woman's place to Apartment 10. The curtains were still gapped but there was nothing to be seen in the interior blackness. Ear to the hollow core door, he could discern no movement on the other side. Inserting his key, he turned the lock slowly, his hand turning the knob. The door came open but its travel was limited due to the chain being fastened. He'd prepared for that. Earlier he'd gone to a hardware store and bought a pair of heavy-duty wire cutters. Conversely the chain's links were not of a heavy gauge. He snipped through these and eased inside. Closing the door quietly behind him, he stood in the front room listening. He'd also bought a small flashlight and put it on. He used its tight beam to scan the room in the hopes the kids had left the phone in here. He didn't see it. Graham got down on his stomach to shine the light under the coffee table and the couch but no phone.

Back on his feet, the carpeting muffled his footfalls as he went into the kitchenette. On the table in there was an empty pizza box and other signs of their dinner. The sink faucet dripped and the refrigerator hummed. Still no phone. Down the hallway he went.

The first bedroom door a little further on was to his left, ajar. Listening at the crack, he heard light snoring. He was pretty sure that was an adult in there. The other bedroom door was closed. He turned this knob slowly too, opening the door. The hinges creaked and he stopped. For several moments he stood there holding his breath. Satisfied he hadn't disturbed anyone's slumber, Graham eased the door open wider, a sixteenth of an inch at a time. Finally the crack was enough for him to step sideways into the bedroom.

He put the light on and quickly extinguished it. He'd done that to get a brief glimpse of the room. The two youngsters, Terry and Alex, were asleep in the one bed. The youngest one had his head toward the foot of the bed. Stepping across to the far wall, he let the shade up to allow in moonlight. On all fours, he powered on the flashlight again, clamping it between his teeth as he searched the floor.

"Hi," said a small voice. It was the younger one.

"Hey, Alex," he said in a friendly low voice, "you remember me from today?"

"Uh-huh. Watchu doin'?"

"Shhh, don't wake up your brother. You remember that phone you guys had?"

"Phone?"

"The ray gun."

"The ray gun?"

"You know where it is?"

"Uh-huh."

Learning earlier that money was not a motivator, Graham had come prepared for this as well. From a plastic bag he had with him he extracted a tricked-out toy truck with big wheels and towering exhaust pipes. Alex grinned.

"Is that mine?"

"If you give me the ray gun."

The kid stared at him. Graham couldn't decipher his thinking. Then he went under the covers and came back out, holding the flip phone. Tentatively he held it forward. Graham handed him the truck. The kid didn't hand over the phone.

"I thought we had a deal, Alex," he whispered. He resisted grabbing the thing from the kid. When Teekens had tapped the phone, he'd managed to call Aunt Millie's preset number.

"Must be it picked up one of those police shows by the radio waves," she'd told him. His aunt had been listening to the message when he'd "just happened" to come over to visit a week after killing Teekens. She'd played it for him, the sound going in and out. He heard Teekens say his name but that part was in a low register. Aunt Millie's hearing wasn't so good and she hadn't made out the name clearly.

"Alex, come on," he said, forcing himself back to now.

"I want another truck."

"I don't have another one with me. But I'll get you one in the morning."

The kid retreated back under the covers with the phone and the truck. Terry stirred.

Loudly Alex reiterated from beneath the blanker, "I want another truck. I want two trucks."

The time for negotiations was over. He rose and putting the flashlight on, snatched the blanket and sheet off the kids. A shocked Alex glared up at him behind the light. Terry woke up.

"Hey," he said, reacting to the light on him and his brother.

"Mom," Alex blurted. "Mom," he repeated, louder.

Graham took the phone and ran from the room. Daniels was coming out of the other bedroom and he knocked her over. He kept going as she yelled.

"Boys, you all right?"

Out on the breezeway lights came on inside apartments. Down the stairs he raced to skirt across the concrete apron. He reached the security gate and pushed the crash bar. The gate swung outward and he rushed out so fast he got tangled up with his feet and fell onto the walkway. He had his hands out to break his fall, skinning his palms in the process. Upright again he got to his car and drove away. In his hotel room he pried the back off the phone to remove the SIM card and flush it down the toilet then destroy the phone. Only there was no such module in the phone.

Glaring at the flip top Graham turned his head at the sound

of a soft knock at the door. "Cul, it's me, Bobby," his cousin said from the other side.

Graham had mentioned to him where he was staying. He opened the door. He was surprised his aunt was standing next to his cousin.

"Ain't you gonna ask us in?" he said jauntily. They both entered and took a seat on the couch. "Got the phone, huh?" Cousin Bobby grinned.

He wasn't sure what to say. His aunt spoke.

"The phone was found when the hospital bed was moved in for Millie a few months ago," his aunt said. "Things had to be rearranged, you see."

"Just 'cause I was curious, I got one of those apps to fetch the info off of them old phones," his cousin said. "Kinda shocked at what I heard. Guess the message got downloaded to the phone which they could do back then." He shook a finger at him. "That's what you were worried about. And you were right to be."

After he'd heard the message all those years ago his aunt put the phone in the pocket of her housecoat. He'd returned the next day to wipe it clean. Only by then she'd gone to the store and had misplaced the damn thing, which she would do from time to time. He of course helped her search for the phone, even looking in the trash, but couldn't find it. Another search a few days later was also unsuccessful. Soon weeks went by and given the police hadn't come for him, he hoped the phone was gone for good.

"Yeah," he said dryly. He sat down heavily in a chair.

"We thought on it for a spell as to what to do," Cousin Bobby said. "Then, well, Aunt Millie passed away and it all came into focus you could say."

"Put me through my paces," Graham said flatly.

Cousin Bobby shrugged. "Couldn't lay this on you at the gathering. And anyway, Mom said we should see how bad you wanted it."

"They said Devon had moving boxes full of money around," Aunt Millie enthused.

"Like Freeway Rick and Harry O back in the day," Cousin Bobby added, naming two legendary South Central crack kingpins.

His aunt said, "But you always had a head on your shoulders, Cully. You didn't spend that money of his on hoochies or flashy cars. No, not you. You used that money to get a leg up, leading to you starting that construction equipment company of yours."

"That's not why I…" he began but trailed off.

"I know, man," his cousin said quietly. "He'd hooked your old lady, made her an addict, turning tricks. One day she'd OD'd and up and died. Goddamn shame. You had every right to take his life."

"Every right," his aunt echoed. "You been doing right since then, including a scholarship you started for wayward youth. You gave back, Cully, yes you did."

He waited.

She leaned forward on her cane. "But us'in is family, Cully. Those apartments Bobby tends to seem to require more upkeep than what they bring in. And what with you scaring Cissy half to death, calling us and we had to put her and the boys at my house, clearly the security over there has to be updated."

"Speak on it, mama," Cousin Bobby testified.

"And, child, social security got those threadbare cost of living raises." She shook her head from side to side. "Government act like it's their money. Mm-hmm."

"How much?" Graham said.

Cousin Bobby threw his arms wide. "I'm sure between the three of us, we can come to an understanding. Like an annual tithing, something like that." He looked at his mother and the two laughed.

So did Graham.

OYSTER CREEK

NEIL S. PLAKCY

My phone rang early on Tuesday morning. I was groggy, but the attorneys who often used my services as a private investigator had my home number, and I felt bound to answer because business was slow that spring of 1968.

A syrupy-voiced Southern gal asked if I'd take a collect call from my father, and I agreed. It struck me anew what a cheap bastard he was, and had always been.

"George?" he asked.

"Yes, Pop. What's up?"

"It's your mother. She's dead. Funeral this Friday at St. Agnes Church. Eleven in the morning."

"What? What happened?"

"She was walking home after dark last night. Someone hit her driving 'round the bend at Oyster Creek. Knocked her clear off the road."

"Do the cops know who did it?"

My dad made a sound like spitting. "You know what cops are like. You gonna come up here for the funeral?"

"My bank account is tight. I'll have to drive and sleep in the car on the way."

"Be careful, son. Your mom gone, you're all I got."

He hung up.

If he'd had a motto, my father's would have been "use as few words as possible."

It was my mother who had read to me as a child, nursery rhymes and stories about monkeys and elephants, and one about a mole and a rat who got in a boat together and rode off down a river, through the willows that grew along the bank.

Stories like that told me it was possible to get out of my small town, where everyone knew everyone else's business. It was probably that river boat that motivated me to join the Navy, that and growing up in tidal Maryland, where the fingers of the Chesapeake Bay infiltrated the land and promised the connection to a wider world, if you could just paddle far enough.

I called the three attorneys who fed me work and let them know my circumstances. All offered their condolences and told me to get back in touch when I returned. I hesitated before making the next call, to a gentleman I had been seeing for the last few months. We had been intimate, but we were still in the process of getting close.

"It's George," I said, when his secretary rang the call through. "My momma was run over last night walking home and I have to drive to Maryland for her funeral."

"Oh, I'm so sorry," he said. "If it helps, imagine me by your side at the funeral." He was that kind of a charming fellow, and I wondered sometimes what he was doing with a lunk like me.

"I just might."

I let my landlord know I'd be gone, then set out in my 1958 lime-green Chevrolet Bel Air. My first day was a long, slow slog along US 1 to Jacksonville, passing the surfing beaches at

Cocoa and the space station at Cape Canaveral. When the roadway curved west past acres of orange groves, I stopped for gas and bought a big bag of sweet oranges. I nibbled on them for miles, the juice dribbling down my chin.

And all the way, I wondered who had run down my mother on that bad turn past Oyster Creek. A local? An out-of-towner?

There wasn't much reason for someone who didn't live in Wright's Head to pass through. The main road was Route 50, which ran from Annapolis to Salisbury, but we were miles off that, and our local roads all dead-ended at one of the many inlets along our porous shore.

I made it across the Georgia state line before exhaustion overtook me, and I slept in my car by the beach. In the morning I took a swim and a long run to stretch out my muscles, then paused at a truck stop for a shower and breakfast.

I was in the land of segregated schools and water fountains. I kept my voice polite and neutral, letting my natural Mason-Dixon line accent come through. Listening to country music stations helped with that, and it seemed like every place I passed through was obsessed with Elvis's newest, "A Little Less Conversation."

I left spring behind as I drove farther north. The flowers that sprouted along the highway through Georgia and South Carolina pulled back into the ground and the temperature grew cooler.

Pushing hard, I made it all the way to the Virginia border by nightfall, focusing on the drive and on the speed limit rather than on what awaited me back in Wright's Head. It was forty degrees by the time I decided I would treat myself to a Holiday Inn rather than spend another night in the car with the temperatures so low.

I resisted stopping in bars or taverns along the way, and ate in the most wholesome diners I could find. I didn't need the temptation of men who wanted to meet me in dark corners—I had my boyfriend back in Miami for that. I wanted to get to

Wright's Head, pay my respects, find out who killed my mother, and get home.

Thursday morning I cut across the fields and through the small towns of Maryland to Annapolis, where Route 50 led across the bridge and then south to the banks of the Choptank River.

I could tell I was getting close when the horizon changed. There was nothing ahead of me but emptiness, a flat landscape, and endless sky. Elvis was still with me, though.

I pulled up in the driveway of the house where I'd grown up, a single-story clapboard building that dated from the 1800s, complete with outdated plumbing. My father's weathered truck sat in front of the garage, which I knew from experience was too full of broken-down tools and half-empty bags of lime and lawn fertilizer to accommodate any vehicle.

I had long ago lost my key to the front door, so I rang the bell. I heard my father's heavy footsteps. "Whatever you're after, I don't want it," he said. The door swung open.

"Hey, Pop."

We stood there awkwardly for a minute, and then he stepped back. "You might as well come on in."

I followed him into the living room. My mother had always kept it neat, but now that she was gone my father hadn't picked up the slack. A crumpled newspaper rested on the couch and empty beer bottles were scattered on the floor next to his Naugahyde recliner.

I dropped my Navy bag on the floor, folded up the paper, and sat down. "What happened?"

"She took to cleaning for Ethel Grace," he said. "Walking home from her house Monday evening, somebody run her over on the road."

There was a lot there to parse. The last time I spoke to my mother was Christmas, and she was still working at the chicken plant. She was proud of the holiday bonus she'd received. Why had she left that job to become a cleaning woman?

The Graces were the most prominent family in Wright's Head. They lived in a big Federal-style house on Main Street, and their backyard ran down to the Chesapeake. Mrs. Grace was a bossy, bony woman, as far from my gentle, rotund mother as you could get. Sure, my mom could keep a clean house—but what would have put her into Mrs. Grace's orbit?

"You want a beer?" my father asked.

"Sure."

He sat down in his recliner. "Good. Then get one for me while you're at it."

I got up and grabbed a handful of empty bottles, dumped them in the trash, opened a pair of fresh ones.

"How'd she come to work for Mrs. Grace?" I asked. "I thought she was happy at the chicken plant."

"Ran into her at the five-and-dime one day. Got to talking. Came home that day all fired up to go work there. Money was better, so didn't bother me."

"What do the police say?"

"About what?"

"About who ran her down, Pop. It's a crime. They've got to investigate."

"They come and talk to me. I told them she was a fool to get mixed up with people thought they were better'n us."

I drained my beer and heaved myself off the sofa. "I'm going to go talk to them."

"Don't go causing trouble, George."

"My mother's dead, Pop. I want to know who killed her and see they get punished."

I stalked out of the house and down to the street. Wright's Head is the kind of small town where if you have a good arm, you could pitch a ball from one end to the other.

I had a good arm, back in the day.

I walked one block down to Main Street, turned left, and strode toward the combination police station, city hall, and post office. As I walked, I looked at every car I passed. A couple of Fords and Buicks in driveways, Chevrolets and Lincolns, even a Volkswagen bug parked along the street.

None of them had any damage that made it look like they'd run someone over. And none sported brand-new fenders, either. Mostly they were dust-spackled and salt-water rusted. The fancier, newer ones were blemished by Wallace for President stickers on otherwise pristine bumpers.

Miss Marva Delaney, who had been my elementary school teacher before they closed the school and started busing us, sat at the desk in the police station lobby. "George Clay," she said. "As I live and breathe."

"Hello, Miss Marva. You working here now?"

She nodded. "I was so sorry to hear about your mama. She was a good woman."

"She was. She didn't deserve to die like she did. I want to talk to whoever's investigating the case."

"We don't really have what you would call an investigator," she said. "We don't get much crime here in Wright's Head. You'd have to talk to the chief."

I looked up at the wall, where a photo of the chief of police had pride of place. Harmon Judd. Really?

Harmon was four years older than I was, and he had been the town bully. He picked on the little kids, the couple of Black kids, anybody who was younger or weaker than he was. When I was ten years old he tried to take my lunch money from me and I punched him in the stomach so hard he fell down and hit his head on the dirt.

He left me alone after that. But I still didn't like him and didn't trust him.

Miss Marva picked up the phone and dialed a number, and I

heard it ring in a back room. "Chief Judd? George Clay is here to talk to you about his mother."

She listened for a minute. "I told him that, Chief. But I think you owe him the courtesy of a conversation."

That old schoolteacher was still inside Miss Marva. She hung up the phone and said, "Second door on the right."

I walked past her. The second door was closed, so I knocked politely.

"Come on in." There was no welcome in his voice, only res-ignation.

"Hello, Harmon."

"Hello, George. Sorry about your mama. Like I told Miss Marva, there isn't nothing I can tell you."

I could have sat down across from him, but I chose to stand. Harmon had gone to fat, but I hadn't. I had kept my muscles up manhandling drunks a few nights a week at a men's bar in Miami. I knew I could stare him down.

"Tell me what happened."

He sighed deeply. "It was Monday night. Your mama had been up at the Graces', cleaning, and she left just as dark was falling, say five o'clock. Ethel Grace stood at the doorway and said goodbye, watched her walk down to the street and turn toward home."

I nodded.

"Six-fifteen, Ernestine Maupin was driving down Front Street by the bend at Oyster Creek, and her headlights picked up a person by the side of the road. She got out to see who it was."

I pictured the scene in my head. The road was real close to the water there, with a swamp on the other side where we used to search for oysters at low tide, so there were no houses.

"Ernestine went up to the Millers', the first house on the right, and used their phone to call us. Half-hysterical, she was. Dick Miller had to give her a shot of brandy to calm her nerves."

I just stood there.

"Call went up to the EMTs at Cambridge, and they sent someone down. I got there about the same time, recognized that it was your mama. She was too late for any help. I went out to the Millers' and talked to Ernestine, and then spoke to your Pop, then to Mrs. Grace."

He shrugged. "That's all I can tell you."

I didn't know what else to say, so I said, "Thank you," and I turned around and walked out.

I walked out of the station, down Main Street, and followed the smell of salt water toward the bay. I kept looking at cars for damage. When I passed anyone on the street, the question *Did you kill my mother?* bubbled at my lips.

Though I had grown up there, I had been gone for years, and new people had moved in. My mother might have been a low-class stranger to them, a woman whose life was unimportant.

Main Street curved a bit, following the landscape, and then the vast expanse of water spread out in front of me, glittering in the late-afternoon light. A couple of sailboats moored close to land, a freighter far off moving sluggishly across the horizon, trailing a ribbon of smoke.

The Chesapeake had been a huge part of my life growing up. My father fished there, my friends and I swam there. I remembered standing on the shore watching storms gather force over the water until they swept over me. I knew of fishermen who had died in those storms, kids who had drowned in that water.

And yet there was something so peaceful about it. I had my own little corner of sand, isolated by beach grass and sea grapes, where I'd sit and watch the tide come in and go out. Sometimes I'd spend hours there, to get away from my father's yelling and the weird feelings I started to have as a teenager.

The bend at Oyster Creek was a notoriously dangerous place. There had been at least three accidents there when I was growing up. Usually someone with too much liquor in him missed the turn and ended up in the bay or the swamp. And yet my memories of the place had been happy ones, wading through the ankle-deep water, looking for oysters with Maria Della Bella, who folks called my girlfriend when we were little. Once I found a tiny pearl in one, and I handed it to Maria and told her I'd marry her someday.

That hadn't worked out.

I kept going until I got to the bend. The Main Street sidewalk ended, and there were no streetlights. A careless driver could have come around the corner, hugging too tight toward the swamp, and run right into my mother.

I crossed the street and walked on the sand. The beach was narrow there, but I kept going, until I found that old safe place I had. I sat down there, my knees pulled up to me, and for the first time I allowed myself to cry.

I cried for my mother's sweet nature, for her good-night kisses, for the smell of her lavender perfume. For the times I spent with her as a child making homemade applesauce, when she carefully peeled, cored, and sliced the red delicious that grew on the tree in our backyard, and let me mash them to a pulp with an old-fashioned mortar and pestle. For the tears on her face when I graduated from high school, the first in our family to do so.

For her stoicism when I left for the Navy, as if she knew I was never coming back. On the way home, I looked at cars once more, searching for dented bumpers the way Maria and I had foraged for pearls in the oysters we pulled from the creek.

By the time I got back to the house my father had drunk himself to sleep. I found a box of macaroni and cheese in the cabinet, the kind I had loved as a kid, and made myself a pot, along with another beer. It didn't taste anywhere near as good as I remembered.

The next morning I had to make sure my father took a bath, dressed in his one suit. I even had to tie his tie for him, because his fingers were too shaky. For a moment I stopped to look at him.

His weathered skin testified to a life on the water, and his blue eyes, rimmed red, were cloudy. I remembered as a boy how eager I'd been to see him come sailing toward shore on his old fishing boat, how I'd rushed down the dock to help him unload his catch, even though I was probably more in the way than I was helpful.

He had been good to my mother and me, in his way. There was always food on the table, even if sometimes it was only the trash fish he couldn't sell. My mother knew a dozen ways to cook potatoes, and the three of us would sit at dinner, quietly, because my father spent so much time alone on his boat that he had forgotten how to make conversation.

I saw my face in his, the same wide brow and square jaw. I had inherited his broad shoulders and stocky build, but my muscles came from the gym, not from hauling nets and carrying buckets of bait.

There was sadness in him, too, and I wondered if that was simply the death of the only woman in his life, or if the weight of his long, angry years had finally caught up with him.

"Ready to go, Pop?"

He nodded, and we walked over to St. Agnes.

Father Peter was still in charge, a lot older and grayer than I remembered. He told my father and me what a good woman my mother had been, and that she would live on in Christ, her redeemer and her savior.

I didn't believe any of it, but it was nice of him to say.

Then the funeral director came in. "Would you like to say goodbye to Mrs. Clay?" My father shook his head.

"I would," I said.

They say sometimes the dead appear to be sleeping, but there in the coffin my mother looked dead. They had put too much makeup on her, to cover a bruise on her right cheek, and her hair had been styled in a bouffant such as she never wore. The dress my father had given them wasn't even her nicest one for church; it was a simple yellow shift she wore on Saturdays for shopping.

I couldn't bring myself to say goodbye. She was already gone.

When I went into the chapel, I was surprised to see more than twenty-five people there.

Wright's Head had only had a couple of hundred residents when I was a kid, and I knew that many of those I went to school with had moved on.

I noticed Mrs. Grace at the back of the church, looking uncomfortable. Of course, the Graces worshipped at the Highway to Heaven Apostolic Church up in Cambridge. I had heard her husband once call Catholics "mackerel-snappers" because we would not eat meat during Lent.

It always struck me as a silly term because everyone in town ate Spanish mackerel and king mackerel, caught fresh in Chesapeake Bay.

Father Peter said the same things to the mourners that he had said to my father and me. He didn't mention the circumstances of my mother's death. As he spoke I looked around at the faces, mostly familiar, even if I didn't know the names. People in Wright's Head tended to have a weather-beaten, life-beaten look to them. None of them looked guilty, though some kept their heads down looking at their prayer books instead of meeting my glance. Had I become that much of a stranger? Or was someone hiding something?

Mrs. Grace left right after the service, as the men from the funeral home grasped the handles of the coffin and lifted my mother. My father and I trailed behind them, to the cemetery behind the church, where a grave awaited.

Most of the people from the funeral followed us and waited until after we had all recited the Lord's Prayer, and the priest had blessed us, to trickle away. Several, though, stopped to offer their condolences.

The first few were women who had worked with my mother at the chicken plant. They were cautious, avoiding my father and speaking only to me, and in each case I was sure there was something they were not saying.

Had something happened at the plant to cause my mother to leave? She wasn't the kind to complain or speak up. When the third woman introduced herself as a coworker, I took the initiative. "Is something wrong at the plant? A reason why my mother left?"

She looked startled. "No. Everything's the same. She just wanted...more."

She left quickly, and Daniel Piechowski, who had stayed in Wright's Harbor to fish with his father, stepped up. "Sorry for your loss," he said, in the stilted way of people unfamiliar with death. "Your mom made the best peanut-butter cookies."

"She did," I replied. "Thank you for coming."

Eddie Zephyr, who I'd had a crush on as a teenager, was next. He was the quarterback for the football team when I was a linebacker, and I'd scared myself by stealing glances at his naked body in the locker room after games. He was tall, blond, and handsome, and he had left Wright's Head for the University of Maryland on a full football scholarship. "You back in town now?" I asked, after he'd said his bit.

"I busted my knee junior year at Maryland," he said. "Came home and married Carrie Burton. I sell some real estate, notarize paperwork for people. Let me know if you need to do anything with your father's house."

"Do anything?"

He shrugged. "Sell it, rent it out." He pulled a card from his jacket pocket. "Take care of yourself, George. You were a good teammate."

I thanked him for that, and moved on through a few more people from town. I felt like they all had something to tell me, but no one would. Why would Eddie assume my father would sell his house? What, and move to Miami with me?

The last to step up was Maria Della Bella. Our childhood

friendship had led me to take her to the senior prom but all I could manage was to kiss her chastely on the cheek when the night was over. She came over and put her arm in mine. "You must be very sad," she said.

"Shocked is more like it."

Maria had taken over the small grocery her parents ran. "What are people saying?" I asked her, hoping she'd know the thing that no one else seemed willing to tell me.

"The usual. The town should pave the sidewalk around the bend, add a couple of streetlights."

"That's all? Was there something going on at the chicken plant? Did she have a fight with someone in town?"

"I don't like to gossip," Maria said. "I know how harmful that can be."

Maria was always a statuesque girl, tall and busty before anyone else in our class. No other boy would take her to the prom because she had a reputation as being "fast." I asked her because I thought she was pretty and that she'd appreciate a boy with manners who wouldn't expect anything of her.

I was plenty naïve, let me tell you.

We walked through the cemetery, back toward the church. "There were rumors," she said finally.

I ran quickly through what I expected Maria to say, so I wouldn't be surprised. My father was a drunk, and other fishermen were careful about hiring him, only when they couldn't find anyone else. Perhaps my mother had tried to organize a union at the chicken plant, or was lobbying for better treatment for the Black women who worked there, who she had told me made less money than the white women, and had to use a toilet clear on the other side of the plant.

But Maria blindsided me anyway.

"Rumors about your mother and Mrs. Grace."

I stopped. "What kind of rumors?"

"Well, you know Mrs. Grace had a perfectly good Black

woman who cleaned for her family for years. Betty, I think her name is. She come to the store now and then to pick up an item Mrs. Grace forgot."

I still didn't understand.

Maria squeezed my arm. "People said that your mom and Mrs. Grace were friendly. That's why Mrs. Grace let Betty go and hired her."

"Because it's better to have a friendly white woman clean your house?"

Maria frowned and stared at me, and then the penny dropped. "You think my mom and Mrs. Grace were—romantic? But Mrs. Grace is just an old stick."

Maria laughed. "Oh, honey, the sap still flows when the branch is withered."

I felt myself blushing. Damnedest thing, after being in the Navy all those years, knowing myself what two men could get up to, the thought of two women together embarrassed me.

Especially my mother. Moments of affection between my parents had always been rare, though I assumed they had loved each other, and I was living proof that they'd had sex together once.

"I thought you ought to know," Maria continued. "Maybe it would give you some comfort."

"To know what? That she cheated on my father?"

"No, honey. That she was…like you."

I was certainly slow on the uptake that morning. "Did you know? About me?"

She smiled. "Well, I wasn't sure back then. But then I figured it out."

"Wish you had told me. I didn't understand myself until I was years into the Navy."

She squeezed my arm. "We all take our time becoming who we are meant to be," she said. "It just took your momma a little longer than most."

I had some experience watching men in love. No matter how

they tried to hide it, there was a glow that came from inside them. An unaccustomed shyness around the object of their affection. If you watched closely you might spot a shared look, the way a quickened heartbeat might lead to a show of interest pressed against slacks.

But women were different, weren't they? The only lesbians I knew in Miami were tough girls, with close-cropped hair and an affinity for men's clothes. I didn't know any who looked or acted like my mother, or Ethel Grace.

Maria kissed my cheek. "I've got to get back to the grocery. Weekend coming, people need to stock up."

I clasped her hand. "Thank you. For everything." She smiled, then turned away.

My father had long since left the church, so I walked toward home by myself.

Somewhere along the way I made a turn I wasn't expecting, and I ended up at the Grace house on Main Street. I had to know if this rumor was true. Had I missed something in my own mother?

I rang the bell, expecting that the Black maid, Betty, would be back. But instead it was Mrs. Grace herself who answered.

She was still wearing the black dress she had worn to the funeral, with a white lace collar and cuffs. "I thought you might come by."

She stepped back to let me in, and the expanse of Chesapeake Bay shimmering through the series of French doors surprised me. "It's a beautiful view, isn't it?" she asked. "I don't think I could breathe if I didn't have this view before me every day."

We walked into the living room together. "Can I offer you something? Coffee? A soda?"

I realized how hot and sweaty I'd gotten on the walk in spite of the chill. "A glass of iced tea would be nice, if you have some," I said.

"Certainly. You have a seat there and look out at the water. Your mother so loved that view, too."

I stared at the relentless motion of the bay. It was early afternoon, and the sun had begun its descent. Clouds hung low over the horizon but shards of sunlight cracked through, each wave cap glittering like the pearls Maria and I had hoped to find in Oyster Creek.

Mrs. Grace came back with two crystal tumblers of cold iced tea, and coasters for the table. She sat across from me in a wing chair, with a low coffee table between us. "Your mother was a lovely woman, George. A sweet soul trapped in a loveless marriage. I'm sure I don't need to tell you your father is a brute."

"He is," I said neutrally.

"I felt so terrible for her, working in the chicken plant, coming home to him, you gone, no joy in her life. I thought I could at least share this view with her."

"Is that all you shared?"

My voice was harsher than I expected, and harsher than Mrs. Grace deserved. But she placed her tumbler on the table and said, "We had a deep and abiding friendship."

"See, that's what I don't understand," I said. "How did you even know my mother? You didn't have anything in common."

"There is something in this world that brings souls together," she said quietly. "I found my soul mate in her."

Suddenly, something broke inside me. I thought of the boyfriend I had left back in Miami. Was he my soul mate? Or just a man I had sex with? I honestly didn't know, and I realized I was so glad my mother had found someone in this world who cared for her in a way that my father clearly couldn't.

"I bought her a dress," Mrs. Grace said, almost as if I wasn't there. "I was in Annapolis and I saw this blue-green dress in the window of a store, the very color of that water out there when the sun shines on it. She didn't want to accept it from me, but

I pleaded with her. She said she'd wear it home that night, that your father wouldn't even notice."

She looked directly at me. "He didn't. She wore that dress most times when she came to see me, and he never once said anything about it."

"Was she wearing it the night she was killed?"

Mrs. Grace nodded. "That was the one comfort I had. That at least she had a little bit of me with her at the end."

I finished my tea and put the crystal tumbler down carefully on the coaster, then stood. "Thank you for talking with me. It's good to know that my mother had someone who cared for her."

"She loved you, George. She told me that many times she'd have left your father if not for you. She couldn't leave you behind, and couldn't see how she could take you with her if she left."

I felt tears pricking at the edges of my eyes, so I walked quickly to the front door, and then outside.

On the walk home, I wondered how many people in Wright's Head knew about my mother and Mrs. Grace. Would people simply say, "They're an unusual pair, bless their hearts"? Was that the secret I had read in the faces of the mourners?

Or would they speak meanly, and make veiled threats? Did someone run my mother down like a dog because she had fallen in love?

I walked home slowly. I ought to leave that afternoon to return to Miami. I could not work, either as a private eye or as a bouncer, if I was out of town.

Yet I felt tied to Wright's Head. I couldn't leave until I knew who had killed my mother. When I got home, my father was drunk, passed out in his recliner. I cleaned up the beer bottles and thought about what I ought to do. I needed to get out of town before my anger burst through, a heat that I had inherited from him and had struggled my whole life to control.

I was hungry, too, for a real meal. Nothing I could make myself. Nothing I could get in Wright's Head. Instead I drove to a steak house in Annapolis I had been to once, on a trip home from the Navy. I had a Caesar salad, a porterhouse steak, medium rare, a huge baked potato loaded with butter and sour cream and bacon bits. A slab of chocolate cake.

I drank two beers with dinner, but didn't feel any effect. Nothing like the release I had hoped. I was still angry when I drove back to my father's house, and found him fast asleep in his recliner, holding a framed picture of his wedding to my mother.

I was plagued by violent dreams, storms on the Chesapeake, the time I had gotten separated from my mother while we were in Annapolis shopping for school clothes.

I woke early in the morning, just after dawn, and went for a long run around the outskirts of town, past chicken farms and country antique places for the tourists. The smell of wood smoke and chicken excrement mingled with the salt air.

By the time I got back, I was exhausted and sweaty. I leaned against my father's truck to catch my breath.

That's when I saw it.

A scrap of blue cloth, the color of the Chesapeake on a sunny day, caught behind the fender. You wouldn't see it unless you were slumped the way I was; otherwise it was hidden by the metal. His fender had sustained plenty of dents over his many drunken drives. Who would notice one dent more?

Somewhere deep inside, I had always known that my parents' marriage would end badly. I had hoped that he would drink himself to death, or crash his truck when he was over the limit.

Never this way, though.

And I had allowed it to happen. I had deserted my mother in her pain and sorrow, and gone off to travel the world and have sex with men and settle myself in the sunshine and tawdry shadows of Miami.

I could not let this pass. I owed that much to her.

I walked down to the police station, chilled in my sweaty

T-shirt and shorts, and waited in the parking lot for Harmon Judd to arrive. I told him what I had found and he drove me back to the house, where he inspected the truck himself.

"You're sure you want to do this, George?" he asked, when he was satisfied. He had seen my mother's body in its torn blue dress; he knew the truth without me having to lay it out for him.

"Hang the bastard," I said.

I waited outside until Judd radioed for a patrolman to back him up, then went up to the front door and knocked. When my father didn't answer, he walked inside.

I waited for some yelling, for an argument, but there was none. Judd walked outside with my father in handcuffs and I made sure he saw my face, and knew what I had done.

Then I drove back to Miami.

STALKING ADOLF

RENEE JAMES

My dream becomes a black wall surrounded by darkness so impenetrable I can only sense where the wall ends and something else begins. The first time this vision consumed my slumber it scared me awake, but I'm used to it now. I focus on the wall, intent on seeing the first movements within it, wondering why there's enough light to see the movement, but nothing else.

On cue, the black wall begins flexing and undulating as if it had an elastic skin and a family of pythons was trapped in its midst, looking for a way out. As I watch, the wall stretches into the shape of a huge human form. It's at least six-six and built like an NFL tackle. Its mouth opens and closes in silent fury, and its meaty fists thrash at the black wall, stretching it to impossible extremes, like an overfilled balloon. In a couple of pounding heartbeats, the wall will fail and the crazed mutant on the other side will crash into my space and rip my brain to shreds. These images used to wake me from my sleep, trembling and moaning, but not anymore. They are still horrific, but familiar.

What wakes me is the sound of a floorboard creaking. Sound isn't part of this particular dream. Sound is in the waking world, and there are only two places in my flat where the floors creak. One is the back entry, the other is at the entrance to Tiffany's room.

My skin crawls as if an army of cockroaches were creeping across my body. My eyes open wide. My breath comes in gulps. I allow myself to hope the squeak is just Tiffany getting up to pee in the middle of the night. I'd even settle for it being an illicit lover, sneaking into the house to deflower my teenage daughter, whose goals for the summer are to get high and get laid, like her friends. A hormone-driven teenage boy would be easy enough to subdue.

But it's not Tiffany going to the bathroom, or a lover stealing into her room in the dark of night. I know it without looking. I get up and grasp the two-pound ball-peen hammer at my bedside, and with sickening assurance, my mind fills with the image of the huge man in the wall of my dreams. I know who he is. I know what he looks like in the bright light of day, all tattoos and muscles and sneering antagonism. He's my pet Nazi, one of the thousands of right-wing crazies who have celebrated the rise of fascism in America by beating and killing minorities for sport.

Adolf is here in the dark of night in my private space because he's finished with the subtle acts of intimidation, like following Tiffany and me to and from work and loitering outside my café. He's here because it's time to destroy us.

I heft the hammer like a tomahawk and force my mind to focus. I would rather cower in the corner than face the terror on the other side of the door, and if it wasn't for Tiffany, I probably would. My body is shaking so violently I have trouble getting my hand on the knob of my bedroom door. When I finally manage to grasp it, I don't allow myself to procrastinate. I swing open the door and rush into the living room, screaming my war scream, hoping to land a debilitating blow on the Nazi before he can disable me and have his way with my daughter. My war scream is pathetic. I sound like a damsel in distress, which

I am, but it seems to work. A large man darts into the shadows, just out of my vision, in the direction of the front door. I hear the door open and close before I get there. I look out the front window just in time to see his form retreat in the gloaming of the street lamps. I watch him disappear, my breath coming in pants, like I'd just run a marathon. He could have killed Tiffany and me tonight, but he chose not to. He's playing with us, the cat torturing the mouse before crushing its spine.

Tiffany is standing behind me, her hip cocked in that smug pose teenage girls like to strike. She's staring at me like I'm bat shit crazy. She obviously missed the part where the Nazi was just outside her door.

"Are you out of your mind, *Dad*?" she asks. If her sarcasm was an alcoholic beverage, there'd be enough for both of us to get a buzz on. She calls me "Dad" to deliberately misgender me. I was the man who sired her sixteen years ago, but I've been a woman almost all her life, a fact for which she will never forgive me. It gives her something in common with Adolf, my pet Nazi, whose murderous hatred of me is based solely on the fact that I'm a transgender woman. We've never met. I've never kicked his dog or stolen his car.

"We had an intruder," I tell Tiffany.

"Sure we did," she says, that haughty smirk still on her face.

I'm too tired to argue with her. "Go to bed," I tell her. "Lock your door and your windows."

"Right." She shakes her head in disgust and goes back in her room. I check the locks on the doors and windows, and brace the entry doors by lodging chairs against them, then go back to bed myself. I keep my door open and the ball-peen hammer at my side. Tomorrow, I will deposit my disbelieving daughter with friends and try to find a solution to my Nazi problem.

Getting Tiffany to a safe place turns out to be painless, even though she wasn't willing to go back to Mom's. Mom, it turns out, is boring—as awful in her way as I am in mine. On the other hand, staying with one of my transgender friends is fine. Ophelia is cool, and Tiffany doesn't have anything against other trans people, just me.

Disguising myself as a man is even easier, disgustingly so. My endless years of transition, the pain and thousands of dollars of cosmetic surgery, are all erased in less than thirty minutes. I don a compression garment to flatten my breasts, and the belly padding from a Santa suit, then put on male jeans and a loose-fitting shirt. The final touch is a male wig and glue-on facial hair.

In the mirror, I look more like a man than I ever did a woman. The realization makes me sick at heart. It's a reality that has stalked me since I first played dolls and dress-up with the girl next door when we were seven. I was excoriated for being a sissy and a pervert, and didn't wear another female garment until I had my own apartment in college. But I never forgot the delirious thrill that came with donning Mary's dresses and I never quit longing for the day I could wear my hair long and later, wear heels and makeup and dance lightly on my tiny feet. Of course, my feet weren't tiny. My male body was a curse, even though it opened the door of privilege for me. I immersed myself in masculinity for as long as I could—through college, a stint in the army, and into marriage and a promising business career. It lasted until Tiffany was three and the walls of my lie crashed down around me and I could no longer pretend to be a man. It cost me everything—I had marriage, home, family, career, acceptance—but the alternative was worse. I could be an unwanted woman or a man who took his own life.

I take a last look at myself in the mirror to make sure there are no telltale gaffes in my disguise. I block all emotions at the sight of myself as a man. This is a means to an end. When Adolf started stalking me, the police told me they couldn't do anything about him until he commits a crime. When Tiffany arrived for her summer visitation, Adolf took a special interest in her and made sure I was aware of it. But the message from the cops was the same: we're on our own. A lot of my friends think the cops are part of the white nationalist movement. All I know is, keeping Tiffany and me safe is my problem now, and I'm going to take care of it myself. I'm not sure how, but it's going to start with me finding out where Adolf lives and what he does. He can't recognize me or he'd kill me. And however this ends, whoever sees me, whatever cameras record my comings and goings, it will be a paunchy, middle-aged man they see, a man who looks nothing like me.

I leave for the train station earlier than I should, too jumpy and nervous to wait any more. I promise myself I'll use the time to perfect my male walk, trying to undo years of practice to achieve a movement that is feminine without being prissy. I'm walking like a man by the time I near the L station, but I'm still too early. I stop at a café and order coffee. After a few sips, I remember coffee makes me need to pee, and the most obvious reveal of my male disguise is me having to sit to pee. This is the first moment I realize that my bowels are a serious threat to my plan. It's hard to think I can last hours without having to go. I erase the thought from my mind. I'll deal with it when I have to. I throw away the coffee and make my way to the train station.

Adolf stands at the far end of the commuter platform, his bearing equal parts sentinel and mobster intimidator. He's almost as large as the man in my dreams. He has buzz-cut hair and a fleshy face with a big nose and hooded eyes and thin lips that seem to naturally settle into a sneering position. His arms are covered in tattoos. Even from a distance, he exudes the arrogance of the master race and the intellect of a moron, though my impression of him might be colored by fear and resentment. He pays no attention to me, a nondescript, overweight male, as I get off the escalator. I go to the other end of the platform and sit on a bench and watch him watch for me. Eventually, he gives up. He boards a southbound train and I slip into the car just behind his. The mouse is now stalking the cat.

He gets off at a station on the fringe of the Loop and strolls west. His gait reminds me of a cocky gangster in one of the *Godfather* movies. He's oblivious to me, but I stay back and on the other side of the street anyway. He saunters into one of the city's transition zones, a neighborhood occupied by derelict factory and warehouse buildings, aging tenements, and sparkling rehabbed lofts and low-rise apartment buildings that represent the invasion of the Yuppie middle class. He turns into a shambling two-flat with peeling paint and dirty windows.

I wait two doors down and stare at the windows facing the street, looking for movement. I see a shadow pass over a window on the second floor, but I can't tell if it's Adolf. I circle around to the alley and count buildings as I walk west. The fourth building, Adolf's, looks even dingier from the rear, with patchy paint, a sagging roof, and a weedy lawn. There's a scraggly lilac bush at the back of the yard that has just enough foliage to provide cover for me. I risk pausing there for fifteen minutes, trying to ascertain which unit is Adolf's and whether or not there is anyone else in it with him. I'm not sure what happens if I find him alone, but I have to confront him sooner or later. I've dreamed of killing him, but that was in my slumbers when he was an invention of my imagination and I was in charge of the plot. I don't think I could actually kill him. In the army, they teach you how, but it doesn't mean anything until you actually do it, and I was a tech nerd, not a gladiator.

The cool morning air is giving way to rising temperatures and humidity. I can feel perspiration trickle down my face and body, and even though I try to focus on my objective, I can't help imagining myself in shorts and a tank top, spreading a towel on the beach, absorbing the heat. My mind drifts to Tiffany. Why haven't we gone to the beach together? What would she like to do with me on her birthday? How could I ever explain to her what I have to do here?

That's the one that gets me. I might have to kill a man this morning so that she can live a safe and happy life, and yet no one would condemn me more harshly than Tiffany for taking another life. Can I kill a man? I can't think of any other way to resolve this situation, but I've been dodging that question since I decided to stalk Adolf. As soon as the police told me they couldn't do anything, I just knew what I had to do, and I've always done what I had to do. Except live my life as a man.

My mind fills with pleasanter things. The memory of a new summer dress I bought, how its soft cotton fabric laid gently on my skin, me wearing it to dinner with Tiffany on her birthday, us smiling at each other across the candlelit table.

All my life I have wanted to be a woman, cultured, refined, civilized. My fulfillment of that ideal has always been plagued with self-doubts about my authenticity as a woman, but now I'm tormented by a new doubt. Can I really kill this Nazi if it comes to that? In my former life as a testosterone-fueled male, I might have been able to do it. But now, I'm a woman. I have painted nails and permed hair and I bake cookies and cakes for my friends. I can't imagine inflicting violence on another person, not even Adolf. It's too gruesome. I grope for alternatives but there aren't any. The police refuse to help, and negotiations with Adolf seem impossible. I try to envision striking a deal with him to leave us alone, but it's just not conceivable. The man is a terrorist who stalks us for pleasure. I try to envision blinding him, or smashing his kneecaps so he's too disabled to pursue us but that's as repulsive as killing. I banish those visions from my mind. Something will happen, I tell myself. It's as silly as a Christian putting everything in God's hands, but I'm too exhausted to think more about it.

Adolf emerges from the back door carrying a bag of garbage, barefoot and oblivious, his face fixed on a cell phone. I stay out of sight as he throws the bag in a dumpster near me, then I watch him go back to the house. He goes in the back door and starts climbing the stairs to the second floor. Seconds later, I see a body move in front of one of the upstairs windows.

I spend the next half hour checking the front and back windows of Adolf's place, trying to determine if anyone else is in there with him. And every minute I spend spying on him adds to the risk I'll be seen by a nosy neighbor who calls the cops or, worse, calls Adolf himself.

I'm wet with perspiration. My stomach burns with the acids of fear and my pulse has picked up. Angst has my whole body tingling with dread. I should go home. I should try the police again. I should follow him a few more times and establish his patterns, like he's done with me. But he's getting ready to release his demons on us. He could rape and murder Tiffany in that period of time. It's not really a choice.

Eventually, I walk to the front entry door and check the names on the two mailboxes. Apartment two has two names. He has a roommate. Another Nazi, no doubt. I curse silently to myself. I return to the back of the building, slip on vinyl gloves and try the back door. It's unlocked. I open it. My heart pounds against my ribs and small rivers of sweat trickle down my face. My baggy shirt has wet spots under the arms and my belly padding is getting heavy with moisture. I pad silently up the stairs, pulling my can of pepper spray from my pocket, just in case. I press my head to Adolf's door. It's completely silent inside. In fact, the whole building is completely silent.

My mind races with what-ifs. What if this is my one chance to catch Adolf alone? What if there are two goons in there instead of one? What if there are more in the first-floor apartment? What if they all come for me at once?

I'm on the verge of walking away, but my mind fills with the image of Tiffany, followed by the realization that I might not get another shot at this thug before he disposes of us. I have to act. Now.

The back door to Adolf's apartment has no peephole. It's an old building. It will have hardwood floors that squeak, and no sound insulation. Hardly ideal for my chat with Adolf, but I don't have other choices.

I take several deep breaths, partly to calm my nerves and partly to prepare for the athletic event in my immediate future. I uncap the pepper spray and then knock softly, three, four raps. Silence, then the sound of heavy footfalls coming for the door, just one person as best I can tell.

A gruff voice. "Who's there?"

"Lois from next door." I mumble the name softly, in my most feminine voice. I can hardly breathe. My body feels paralyzed. He'll kill me as soon as he opens the door, me watching, unable to move. I try to will my brain and body to action.

"Well, goddamn it," he curses while he opens the door. "Why didn't you—"

He's in midsentence when the door opens, his eyes frowning with irritation, his lips forming words but still sneering. I douse his face in pepper spray, an automatic reflex, a miracle I can't believe is happening even though I'm the prime mover. He recoils and steps back, hands to eyes, grunting and cursing, in shock, not sure what hit him. I deliver a massive kick to his groin and catch it perfectly, like I'd been assaulting behemoth Nazis all my life. He topples to the floor, writhing in pain. I step inside, close the door, and stop for a moment, looking and listening for signs of another person. None.

I'm still trembling with pent-up adrenaline, but I make myself focus on the things I have to do. I pull a length of 300-pound-test nylon line from my jacket pocket. It has a noose on one end, which I loop around one of his wrists. I try to pull it behind his back. He resists and he's as strong as a bull. I dance away from him while he kicks at me blindly, and then I deliver a kick to his liver. He cries out and reaches to the afflicted area with one hand. I hop to his front side and deliver a kick to his solar plexus. It freezes him. He can't breathe. He can't make a noise. He can't move.

I tie his wrists behind his back and use another length of line to fasten his ankles. When he's secured, I yank plastic ties out of my pants pocket and secure his wrists and ankles with them. He can beat the knots in the nylon cord eventually, but he'll need a knife to get out of the plastic bonds.

The gag is much harder. I try to pull it into his mouth but he closes down. I grasp his head with both hands and slam it on the floor. "Open your mouth or I'll splatter your brains all over this place," I whisper in his ear in my male voice. It's a loud whisper with a lot of vehemence. To my surprise, he opens his mouth. I slide the gag in and tie it behind his head.

I dash through the apartment to make sure it's empty, then sit on a chair at his kitchen table and stare at him. Close up, he's older than I thought. Maybe thirty. Not a dumb kid. A stud in his left earlobe bears the Nazi symbol. A devoted zealot. I'm not sure what comes next.

He makes some feeble attempts to yell and to writhe as the effects of the pepper spray and the kicks start to wear off. I wait for him to stop. His eyes flutter open and shut, red and swollen. He's angry enough to tear my limbs from my body, but maybe when he realizes how easy this has been for me he'll turn his aggression toward some other minority person. But that's neither a noble nor a realistic thought. The reality is, he won't stop until he destroys us, and as I consider his helpless form in front of me, I can't imagine killing him.

When he settles down I talk to him. "Keep your eyes shut and you might get out of this alive," I say in my most masculine voice. "I'm a messenger. You're messing with a protected community. Stop now or you are going to die badly."

I wait a beat. "Do you understand me?"

He nods his head and grunts. There's nothing sincere about his response. It's what he has to say.

"I'll have to kill you if you don't seem sincere," I tell him.

He doesn't move.

"Maybe I should take out one of your eyes so you know I'm serious," I say.

He shakes his head and grunts. I don't need to do that.

"Okay," I say. "How do I know you're telling the truth?"

He grunts and tries to make words. He's asking me to remove the gag. I shouldn't, but I do.

"You have my word as a Christian soldier," he rasps. He shows his sincerity by rounding his eyes, which are Aryan blue. But his thin lips are still taut and they always come back to a sneering position.

I almost laugh out loud. On my personal list of people most likely to lie, there's no daylight between right wing bigots and religious crazies. "You'll have to do better than that," I say. I'm so distracted by my inner thoughts, my voice travels back up to my feminine range.

He notices it. An ugly smile crosses his face. "You're the queer, aren't you." It's not a question.

I don't say anything. I can't.

"You're the tranny. You think you can scare me off?" He blinks his eyes open and looks at me. He blinks some more, trying to understand the potbellied man staring down at him.

I shake my head like a schoolteacher dealing with a second grader. "You people are so stupid," I say, too angry to keep up pretenses. I let my voice stay in the feminine range. I step over him and begin checking drawers in the kitchen while we talk.

"You think it takes balls to be cruel. You think only big, hairy men can be dangerous. You think queers like me will just accept your violence like passive little children." I come back to the chair, a knife with a six-inch blade in hand. He sees the knife and starts to scream. I leap to my feet and deliver a heel stomp to his face. My basic training instructor for hand-to-hand combat would be proud. Adolf's lips erupt in blood, two of his teeth dangle by their roots in his mouth. He whimpers. I choke back the urge to vomit.

"It's true that most transwomen are very civilized," I say. I'm overtaken by a sense of calm. I'm in charge here. "They'd be horrified at what I'm doing. They'd tell me to let you go, that you've learned your lesson."

He nods his head in agreement and whispers, "It's true. I'll leave you alone."

"If I cut you loose, can we stop all this?"

He nods, eagerly. "Yes. Yes." His *s* sounds aren't right be-cause of his teeth.

"You can forgive me for attacking you?"

He nods again. "Yes!"

"You'll stop stalking me and my daughter?"

He nods his head eagerly.

We establish eye contact. "I shouldn't trust you," I say. "You're much bigger and stronger than me. You might hurt me."

"No, no," he says. "I swear."

"Okay," I say, hesitantly. "I think I'm going to trust you. But on this condition. I'll cut your cuffs but you keep your hands behind your back until I leave, okay?"

He nods and tries to flash a reassuring smile. His bloody lips add a gruesome touch to the gesture.

I move behind him and slide the knife inside one of the plastic ties. "I have your word?" I ask. "You're not going to attack me?"

"No," he says. "It's over. I promise."

I cut the bond. As soon as it snaps free he rolls toward me and tries to grab me, a vicious snarl on his face. His move ends al-most as fast as it began. The nylon cord still tethers both wrists.

"Shit!" he curses, the *sh* sound coming out as mostly air be-cause of his missing teeth.

"You lied to me," I say. My voice is feminine and conversational, but a cold rage is building inside me.

He starts to scream but I put my foot on his crotch. "Are you in favor of enhanced interrogation techniques?" I ask. His sneer disappears. His fleshy face puckers in fear. For a fleeting moment he looks vulnerable. I almost feel sorry for him, but the rage comes back. I break into a torrent of furious obscenities, shocking even myself.

When the rage ebbs, I take a deep breath and try to collect myself. Adolf has his death face on, but I can still see his moment of vulnerability in my mind. That's what set off my fury. If he'd acted like a human being in the first place, he wouldn't be dying and I wouldn't be killing him. I don't have a choice anymore. I wish I did. I'd like to procrastinate. I'd like to go home and forget about the whole thing. But the only real choice I have is to act now. No hesitation, no doubts. The words of my old army drill instructor come back to me from bayonet training:

There are only two kinds of bayonet fighters, Bravo Company! The quick and the dead!

I descend the stairs on watery legs and let myself out. I remember to take off the gloves, then walk to the alley and make my way to the L station. I try to hide my shakes and trembles from the outside world and I think I'm succeeding, but internally my body and mind are a pitched sea of fear and loathing.

It's still early in the day. There's no one around my apartment building to see me when I get home. I go directly to my bedroom and peel off my disgusting outfit and step into the shower. In a few minutes I'll be wearing my beautiful new summer dress, my hair will be air-drying into highlighted waves, and I'll be applying just enough makeup to feminize my face. I hope to be able to breathe without the weight of the world on my chest by then.

When I collect Tiffany at six, I'll insist on going to dinner at a nice restaurant with tablecloths and candles and decent wines by the glass. Tiffany will be intent on expressing her disapproval of me and venting her adolescent angst. I will focus on enjoying my food and wine anyway. I doubt she will ever accept me, so it's an adaptation I have to make.

As for Adolf, yes, I murdered him. In cold blood. I could have waited until he attacked us and hoped we survived the assault and the police could make a case against him, but I couldn't take that chance. I chose to take the matter into my own hands. I suppose there's a chance I'll go to jail for it, but that possibility isn't going to keep me up nights. He was a cruel thug and a bully. I'm just another straw in the haystack of his enemies.

But Adolf will have his revenge every time I relive that moment of my life, which will be often. I'm already haunted by the memory of the knife slipping into his chest, how easily the blade penetrated his flesh, how the radiance in his eyes faded from hate to innocence. And just when my rage turned to guilt, his eyes turned to the glassy stare of death.

I'll replay that moment thousands of times in the years I have left on this planet. And I'll reconstruct the events that led up to it just as often, cursing myself for not having found another way. But when the nightmares pass, when my rational mind takes over, I'll know the truth: I couldn't take a chance with Tiffany's life, not after I've already taken her father from her.

CURRENTS

CONNIE JOHNSON HAMBLEY

I didn't know what to think when she washed up on my shore. Currents in this part of the Pacific capture garbage hurled from the container ships or mega yachts that cruise these international waters creating gyres of floating dumps. The trash vortex either flows past my island on its circular journey or snags in my craggy beach. Seeing the large red-and-white Igloo cooler bobbing in the waves didn't surprise me. Seeing a woman's body draped over it did.

She wasn't bluish-white or bloated. The pink skin of her arms put the distrustful part of my brain on hold as the scientist part kicked in. I scrambled down the cliff, keeping my eyes on her as storm-churned waves heaved her rag-doll body and makeshift buoy against rocks strewn with bits of multicolored plastics. I watched for the inevitable wave that could land her facedown to drown in a three-inch-deep tidal pool.

The gray-green clouds above me promised the building storm would scour away the flotsam and leave my island and me in refreshed peace. I reached the woman just as a receding wave wrapped itself around the cooler and tipped her body off. Faceup, she didn't sputter or cough away the foam. Still, I gaped. Bruises mottled her face forming a line that disappeared down her neck under her shirt.

She'd been through hell, and it wasn't simply the result of crashing against my rocks.

Long scratches welted her cheeks and arms. With her thick blond hair, full lips, and what used to be a great manicure, she had all the markings of a high-class trafficking victim favored by the wealthy. I figured she had had enough abuse and jumped.

The silver handcuff around her right wrist fit, too, but the other end of that cuff was clamped around a decidedly hairy and male wrist, the arm of which was severed just above the elbow. Bloodless, ragged flesh. Nicely buffed nails. No calluses. Skin firm and cold to the touch. They were cuffed right-hand-to-right-hand, a trick that meant one would have to walk backward or with their arm crossed in front, slowing any escape. Swimming would be impossible.

Solitary life on this rock provided little entertainment and this was as good as it gets.

I had to get the whole human out of the cove before the waves swept us both away. The handcuffs were high-end with a specialized lock that took precious time to undo. I took my all-in-one tool from my back pocket and pressed his fingertips against its blade to save whatever print ID I could. Then I hurled the arm into the waves, glad the cuffs would drag it to the depths and it wouldn't bob and drift back to my cove. I had no further use for it and doubted the fish would either.

She gave one gasp as I tossed her over my shoulder, climbed back up the rocks, and made my way back. That was good. It showed she was somewhat responsive.

The storm opened up full throttle about an hour after I had gotten us both into dry clothes. Wind yowled around the reinforced concrete structures that made up the bunkers I called home. I slept well in its solid embrace.

The remains of an ancient volcano that jut straight up from the depths is my chosen resting place between jobs. Without interference from the noises of modern living, it's a perfect listening post with my specialized equipment. And I hear plenty out on these high seas. The impervious veneer of mega wealth and these distant waters bring out the worst of human needs. Voices travel far along the water's surface. Screams even farther.

The awkward bump and bruising of her left ankle said she most likely had a fractured talus, the small bone that hinges the tibia to the foot, evidence of a jump and landing on a hard surface. The salt water had cleansed her cuts and the cold had kept the swelling down. White lines of older scars crisscrossed porcelain skin, many matching the size and shape of my own. Knobby circles or long ragged lines of healed tissue from burns, gunshots, or stab wounds each had a story. What were hers? What hell made her decide that jumping into the black churning ocean was better than staying onboard? Was it mad, crazy luck that the freak currents brought her here? Or fate.

In the life of an assassin, luck can never be trusted.

She looked Eastern European with a little Nordic goddess worked in. Language wasn't going to be a problem. I knew plenty of them.

At dawn, the horizon line where the sea and clouds met blended into one furious mass as the storm kept up its pace. I was on my second cup of coffee when I noticed her arm wasn't draped across her stomach where I had placed it after checking her vitals. Instead, it was tight against her side. I leaned closer and pressed the back of my fingers against her cheek.

She sprang up from the couch, clutching the blankets around her as if to make a shield. Terror widened her swollen eyes enough for me to see violet irises. She would have bolted for the door if her ankle didn't buckle underneath her.

I tried English with an American accent first. "Whoa. Easy. You're safe. I'm not going to hurt you."

She bobbed and swayed as her knees struggled to support her, responding only with rasping breaths. Her face didn't crease with pain as she surveyed the room like a cornered animal looking for escape. Terror subsided to fear and feral energy. Easing herself back down to the couch told me she understood my words even if she didn't completely trust them.

I stuck with English. "You're on an island. You saved yourself by clinging to a cooler. Do you remember that?" I figured I'd ask her about Hairy's arm when we got to know one another better.

I felt her eyes on me each time I walked past. She ate what I gave her only after she watched me eat some of it myself. I wondered how close to the edge of insanity she had been pushed— or if she'd already entered its looking-glass spiral. She seemed to live inside a fever dream, speaking in tongues during nightmares and clawing her way across the floors, never fully awake. The day after the storm—the second day she was here—I marveled that she scrabbled her way up the ladder to the observation deck and teetered over the edge, arms outstretched as if reaching for something only she could see. I wondered if she preferred death and hated me for saving her as I dragged her back from the brink.

On my island, I didn't have to worry about a laser dot on my temple or poison in my food. I could pursue my studies while I waited for a new contract: a prime minister ignoring the Paris Accord. A president ignoring a constitution. An industry titan inhaling wealth. They thought no laws would touch them. But I could. Death, accident, and disease are all natural and random events. It was my job to keep up those appearances as I rescued world orders from toppling without leaving damning evidence. Knowing the science behind investigations gave me an edge to plant confusing and conflicting facts. I could kill and incriminate with one act.

Sleep occupied most of her time, so I kept up with my routines of surveillance. I learned the mega yacht *Silhouette* was late to port without updates. Chatter of its presumed disappearance started. I logged transmissions, traffic, weather, water temperature, and anything else that would help me identify a pattern worth observing. I didn't search the fingerprints lifted from the blade. Doing so would begin a chain reaction if he was important. Who wanted to know? Where was the search coming from?

Inside, I listened. Outside, I walked to my favorite fishing spot looking for clues among the flotsam. The array of aging trash told me nothing more than it usually did—the Great Pacific Garbage Patch was alive and well, and served no greater purpose than giving me something to fight during my time off.

I cast my line as I considered the pieces of her appearance and was unsettled at her astonishing survival. I've kept myself alive this long by systematically weighing facts into theories.

The rod bent and reel spun. I hauled a bluefin tuna onto the rocks and clubbed its head. It was a beauty.

I wanted to examine its stomach contents under my microscope, so I didn't splay its guts along the rocks. Besides, I wanted to show off my trophy and headed back.

I froze when I saw her. What she did for my old T-shirt and sweats made me yearn for a different life. She was standing at the kitchen counter holding a knife in her fist, eyes pinwheels of panic and fury.

The tuna hit the floor with a slimy thud. "Don't." I held up my hands and walked toward her, placing my steps carefully, readying myself to lunge at her.

"Stay away from me." Those were the first words she had spoken. Heavily accented.

Ukrainian with a hint of something else. The blade hovered over her wrist, then up to her neck, then down.

I stepped toward her as if approaching a wild mustang. The blade of the knife disappeared into her upper inner arm. She stifled a scream as she gouged into her soft white flesh.

The knife clattered to the ground along with something else.

Bits of flesh and blood covered the smooth sides of the oval object about the size of a thumb. Tiny red-and-green lights flashed its life. A tracking device.

Red curled in from the edges of my vision. My oasis was discovered. My protective shell shattered. "Shit. Shit. Shit." I watched the color drain from her face as I felt it fill mine.

"I'm property. Too much value to lose." Blood dripped between her fingers clamped to her arm and she swayed on her feet. "Crush it," she said with a rolled *r*. She staggered a step forward.

I knew destroying it was too little too late even before I heard the deep rumble of a boat's engines.

Her eyes rolled back into her head. I scooped her up as she collapsed, carried her to my gear closet, and placed her limp body on the pile of old anoraks. I grabbed my pistol and two clips and shoved them in my belt. Then I shut the door and locked it.

I gathered up the fish, knife, and tracker and ran out the back door, away from the approaching boat.

The small ship that bobbed in the leeward side of my island was gunmetal gray and highly seaworthy. Its broad bow and reinforced bridge spoke to its seriousness just as the movements of its crew did.

Rubber skiffs emerged from the stern. One skipped away to circle my island. The other, carrying two no-nonsense men with buzz cuts, navigated between the rocks toward me.

"Hello! I don't get many visitors here!" I picked my way down the path from the direction of the windward cove, watching where I placed each step and balancing against the boulders knowing every step meant my life. I flashed my best aw-shucks smile and relaxed my body as much as I could to hide the threat my size would yield.

The bigger guy narrowed his eyes at me. "We received a distress signal from a vessel two days ago during the storm. We thought survivors might be here." The smaller guy darted a look that failed to engender my trust.

"Really? There was a problem in the shipping channel? I had no idea." I rounded my eyes in the way Anglo kids did when they tried to sell a lie. "The only things that wash up on my shore are soccer balls and sneakers from containers that break loose from cargo ships." I placed the bluefin tuna on a rock. They saw my knife and reached inside their orange life vests toward hidden holsters, revealing their military training. I kept my voice steady. "Nah. Storm churned up the flotilla of garbage. You never know what the fish think is food. Good tuna run, though." With that, I splayed the fish, spilling its guts on the ground.

I kept the smile on my face and my eyes on theirs. The small one nudged the big one, nodding toward the pile of fish guts. Bingo.

I didn't like how the big guy stared at me as if searching his brain for something familiar.

After a beat or two, he waded through surf and picked up the tracker.

"What the hell is that thing?" I asked as I reached for it, but he turned his body away.

"Some crew opt to have life beacons embedded in their arms to aid in rescue efforts in the event of sudden catastrophe, better guaranteeing their rescue." He held the two-inch capsule up to the sun. "At least, they think it will help."

"So, let me understand this. A ship disappeared during the last storm. You were hired to find survivors, and that tracker brought you here?"

"Yes."

I don't trigger easily, but his look almost made me shoot him right then. A fool's errand, I knew, as his boat would disgorge men and guns like clowns from a circus car. I'd be dead before he bled out. "You were expecting a human brought it here, or, at least, a part of one." I waited until that comment landed. Their mouths firmed in a way that hid what they knew, but they knew something. "Instead, the poor sap with that embedded bug got chopped up by the ship's propellers. Or maybe some shark got a tasty meal. Either way, that shiny bit of metal caught the attention of this tuna." I hacked off its head and tail and carried the body to the water's edge, washing the remaining guts from its insides.

"And brought us here." Little guy peered up to the bunker. "This island isn't on many maps and those that do show it say it's uninhabited."

"I never could understand those errors." Countries often paid me with favors as well as money. Hiding my island was one of them. I toned down the good ole boy vibes. "But this is the best place to be part of the Ocean Cleanup Project and observe current behavior and wind-wave surface interaction. I hope to find a way to corral the trash enough to scoop it up and recycle it back into a resource." I reached for the bug. Again, Mr. Big kept it away. "I guess you're done here, right?"

The other skiff returned. A man shook his head and circled back to the stern.

All covers are best if they hold elements of truth. If they suspected who I was, they didn't let on. If it was true I was just a loner scientist, they would know my specialized equipment would automatically record our encounter and register it with my sponsoring country. If they acted on their suspicions, killing me would put their asses in hot water and bring unwanted attention to their boss. After a few more pleasantries, they returned to the ship. The oversize binoculars and parabolic microphones exposed that they'd trust what they learned themselves, not what they heard from me. My story was just plausible enough to buy me the time I needed to flee.

My island sanctuary was history. But I had some questions to answer.

★ ★ ★

The throb of engines faded as I wondered how to keep myself alive, living up to the legend they'd no doubt expand on when they knew they were *this close* to the Assassin. I began my evacuation and imagined her listening for the crisp report of gunfire as she breathed in mildew and decaying rubber.

I didn't soften my steps as I strode to the closet. I slammed a clip into my pistol and raised it to head level, pressed my body to the wall, and yanked the door open.

The gaping circle of my flare gun was matched only by her rounded eyes. The barrel of the gun shook. The safety was off, index finger hovering over the trigger, chamber loaded. She was no amateur.

Neither was I. A click sounded as the pistol's hammer cocked. A flare would hurt like hell, but my bullet would kill.

"Your friends were looking for you." I softened my voice, hoping she believed my words.

"I don't want to be found. Don't let them find me!" She panted the words through a thick accent marked with inflections from different dialects while fumbling with the flare gun. The metallic smell of blood mixed with stale air of the closet.

"You can stop the crazy foreigner act now. They think you're dead."

She lowered her hand and slightly swayed on her feet. "I've been left for dead before," she said as she limped past me to sit on the couch. I could have snapped her neck right then, but she gave tantalizing clues to stoke my curiosity. Each move she made, each statement created a mystery. She seemed relaxed, knowing I wasn't done gathering facts.

"Who do you work for?"

"We are alike, you and I. The way you traced your fingers along my scars as you dressed my wounds was like you were reading Braille and absorbing all the ways we are the same." She put the flare gun down beside her and cradled her bleeding arm against her chest. The skin-deep wound looked serious, but the muscles were not impacted. "Did my scars tell you we share a fierce drive of duty and seek the higher good? Or that we share the ability to hide in plain sight because the human mind is a maze of bias? Few think the huge man like you can move like a lithe athlete, able to disappear into the crowd or shadows. Even fewer think the beautiful woman can kill with her bare hands or withstand the pain of combat."

"Did you use your bare hands to kill your friend, the hairy one with the missing arm?"

"He was a prisoner. Like me." Her pupils did not dilate when she lied.

"Doubtful that Raul Gianametti would be a prisoner on his own yacht. He's the third richest man in the world and the most opportunistic one. He was known to slash, burn, and churn his way to billions in profit."

"You finally ran his prints."

"Only minutes ago. I can almost hear the alarm bells ringing at Interpol when they pick up my search." I glanced at the clock on the wall. "I figure I have fifteen minutes to leave before your friends come back. Raul Gianametti has tried to kill me before." I kept my gun steady, watching for the telltale twitch just before she reached for the flare. "Why didn't you kill me when you had the chance?"

"I could ask you the same," she responded.

The energy in the room shifted as a truth shimmered between us. I needed to learn whose truth would live. I tested my hypothesis.

"You're the Ghost," I said.

The muscle beneath her eye twitched. "And you are the Assassin."

"I don't believe you cut the device from your arm," I challenged. "A hired killer of your stature would never allow such an implant. I was a fool not to find it hidden in your soft folds."

She did her best how-could-you-think-such-a-thing look. My mind raced over facts and re-examined her actions since washing up on my shore. She knew the puzzle of her existence would intrigue me. My heartbeat steadied as I realized she had let me live, but for different reasons than I had let her live.

She relaxed onto the couch as if it belonged to her. An uncharacteristic thrill went through me as her eyes moved along my body, taking in every detail. "You are bigger than I had heard. You're what? Six-foot-six? Massive chest and arms. Rock solid too." My blood warmed despite my discipline. She continued. "I was amazed at how nimble you are, moving with a predator's grace. People can't believe a demon like you exists."

"Some have tried to expose me."

"And died in their attempts. You're not the pure evil incubus I had expected. You didn't grope or explore my unconscious self, showing a vein of honor that shouldn't exist in our line of work."

Alluding to our unique skills snapped me back to the present. "The countries I work for support laws demanding corporate responsibility that cut into profits. He hired you to kill me, but something happened that changed the plan." A flat finality colored my words.

Her voice softened, lulling me. "Be happy. I have killed the man your countries hate for his theft and polluting corporations. I have done your job because I've seen the evil things men like Raul can do. They think they are untouchable. They use their money as a shield. I...I know why you choose the jobs you do." Emotion snagged her words. She sat forward on the edge of the couch, wincing with the movement.

Maybe she thought I wouldn't notice her hand feel between the cushions.

"You want me to believe you saved the women, killed their captor, and sank the *Silhouette*." Her pupils expanded to pools of black, inviting me in. "I would expect nothing less from the legendary Ghost."

"Only another assassin could possibly understand the choices a hired killer makes," she cooed. "We are one, you and I. Together we know the secrets of the world. Could we ever work together?"

She offered me something I had never contemplated. A partner. Someone to work with side-by-side. I let the thoughts telegraph across my brow, discordant facts challenging my assumptions and bias, demanding information. "What happened on that ship?"

Words tumbled out of her making her almost breathless. Her jugular notch pulsed in rhythm to her racing heartbeat. "Once aboard the *Silhouette*, I saw the abuses women endured at the hands of rich men. Raul made the mistake of thinking paying for your death gave him rights to my body. His attack made me see the world with fresh eyes. I couldn't continue the plan to kill you. He was a brutal fighter."

"Cuffing right hand to right hand would slow you down. He could drag you where he wanted you to go."

She nodded emphatically, and then quickly stopped. Her eyes widened as if the sudden head movement made the room spin. "It excited him, I killed him as he tried to chain me to the bed in his berth of horrors."

"You're right-handed and couldn't use your left to pick the lock."

"Yes! But my left was strong enough to saw through him."

"A feat only someone of your skills could achieve." My expression did not reveal my thoughts.

She smiled. "I found his implanted device and kept it. I threw Raul's body overboard, and planned my escape, but the crew soon realized what happened. I broke my ankle jumping off the bridge onto the deck below."

"And you floated here."

"I had to trust the currents of the trash gyre would bring me to you."

"Why do you want to partner with me?"

"I've studied your hits of world leaders and titans who deny global warming and pollute our earth. Eliminating those thought leaders is your guiding force when deciding to take a job. You need to know whether killing your mark will serve a greater good. Together we could force corporations and countries to clean the oceans."

Her purred vision filled my head, stunning me with an intimacy I never imagined. This was my joy, my sole passion in life was to right the environmental wrongs. "Men like Raul are not like you. They are weak in the face of pain and beg for mercy as they spill their secrets. I have money and you have knowledge. Together, we would be unstoppable."

I relaxed my shoulders. "You didn't kill me because you need me."

"Yes! Once I knew you weren't the brute I was sent to kill, I sensed another future for us." She paused, lowering her gaze. She nearly whispered, "Together."

"So, freeing yourself from your contract by killing Raul, you wanted to use me to help you disappear. I was not the monster Raul made me out to be. That's why you pretended to cut the bug from your arm. You wanted me to begin trusting you."

She cocked her head. "That...that was to explain why the men came," she sputtered.

I nodded slowly, grateful to know my sanctuary had been discovered before a seductress had been dropped into the sea. "Raul, a clever and worthy adversary, would have spared no expense to kill me or to find a way to access what I know. Sending the perfect woman to me was not an inconsequential cost."

Her eyebrow arched, habit keeping her in the game. "Am I the perfect woman for you?"

I let her comment settle in on me with a longing I didn't want. "What a waste to have me think the invincible Raul Gianametti was dead."

She swallowed. Pallor flattened her features to a waxy mask.

I was too intrigued with where her lies would take me to anticipate her attack. Her body slammed against mine, the momentum careening us to the floor. She had hoped for an advantage by using her injured arm to wield the knife she had retrieved from deep inside the couch, knowing my attention would be focused on her dominant, uninjured hand and the distraction of the flare gun. With sinuous movements, she writhed from my grip, and with battle-hardened force magnified by a will to live, she sliced the blade through my cheek and down my neck. Instincts and training overruled my surprise. The sharp crack of my pistol froze her. She gripped her side.

A mixture of anger and sadness filled me. Her vision of working with someone who understood my passions broke something loose inside of me that risked setting me adrift forever. I had been happy alone. Now, I could never be.

She pulled her hands away from her side, assessing the wound as I had. The bullet had passed through the flesh above her hip and out her back.

I felt an urge to press my palm against her cheek and tell her all was well. Instead, I stepped back and watched blood pool on the floor.

"When did you know?" Her voice told of a pain that was not a physical pain, but the lament of a mission lost.

"The moment I touched you."

"How?"

"Large and heavy objects float differently in the Subtropical Ocean Gyre, moved mostly by wind and not water currents. This would have forced you and the cooler into the Kuroshio Current, bringing you westward, away from my island. You used the tracking device as insurance in case your drop-off didn't go as planned."

"You said I was lucky."

"If it was truly luck that brought you here, the hours necessary to drift from the shipping channel to here would have severely puckered your skin. Plus, the wounds you arrived with were defensive wounds protecting yourself from inexperienced fighters. The trafficked women you said you saved turned against you and I can only imagine why. You became part of their hell."

"But they sank with that hell."

"No. The *Silhouette* is very much afloat. A lack of debris and no automated distress GPS signals proved that. Benetti Yachts, known for their unobtrusive security, manufactured the *Silhouette*. After dropping you into the currents, the *Silhouette* ran in dark mode to shield it from discovery, creating buzz among maritime traffic that a ship had gone missing. Doing so served the purpose of your mission, but it did not sink."

"You think you know it all. But you don't. I hacked Raul to death."

The corners of my mouth tucked into a grin. "No. Raul is intact and never had a tracking device implanted. A man of his stature employs other security measures and, like his ship, needs to be able to disappear when convenient."

"That's impossible!"

"What's more impossible is for his thumbprint to be on his index and middle fingers, too.

"Mis-imprinting fingerprints can happen in prosthetic manufacturing. The arm was his ego's calling card. He wanted to be sure I knew it was him. It was a fake, an excellent one that matched decomposition and water exposure, but a fake nonetheless."

In one fluid motion, I swept the flare gun and knife from her reach. She stood slowly, flinching with weight on her ankle.

I chuffed. "Jumping into the launch that would drag you and the cooler into position, you misjudged the swells and the currents of the ocean. You jumped lightly, but the launch rose quickly and snapped your ankle."

I grabbed my go-bag and extra food.

"He'll find you no matter where you go." Defiance creased her words.

Buzzes and pops sounded as timed detonators destroyed my radio and equipment. "Maybe. He's sloppy and arrogant. I'll find him first. The world needs less trash."

"You have to take me with you." Panic ringed her eyes as the reality of her situation dawned on her.

The prospect of a different future infused her words with an intoxicating brew. Our life's paths created an intimacy even before our bodies could. Her curves woke a dragon inside me that blurred my judgment with its heat. In the life of an assassin, trust was as fleeting as a calm ocean. Could I trust her?

"People lie. Currents never do."

WHAT THEY KNEW

GABINO IGLESIAS

Leonard Carrington knew many things. He knew the world belonged to those who already owned a lot. He knew talent and education were almost useless unless you had connections. He knew money made the world go round and worked as a trouble repellent. More importantly, he knew he had power. He sensed it. He could count the money in his pocket, feel his watch, run his fingers over his name, which had been hand-embroidered inside the pocket of his Valentino suit, or look at his bank accounts, but he couldn't touch his power. However, he knew it was there, and he knew it was far more important than anything he owned. When Leonard spoke, people listened. Orders that came from his mouth were absolute and unavoidable. When they weren't interpreted as such, he knew he had the authority to turn the event into devastating consequences that eloquently communicated his favorite message: Leonard Carrington was not a man you messed with.

Leonard also knew that he was desirable to the opposite sex. No, he wasn't tall and he didn't possess the chiseled jawline that

men like Brad Pitt had and women loved so much. In fact, he
even had a pudgy body because, when it came to the pleasures
of the flesh, Leonard was a firm believer in Oscar Wilde's beautiful words on temptation, which he had memorized in his late
twenties and kept in his bag of tools for those rare moments in
which his name, tailored suit, car, and watch didn't get the job
done with the opposite sex: *"The only way to get rid of a tempta-*
tion is to yield to it. Resist it, and your soul grows sick with longing for
the things it has forbidden to itself, with desire for what its monstrous
laws have made monstrous and unlawful."

Generally speaking, knowledge brought Leonard pleasure.
Knowledge is power, as everyone says, and Leonard knew he
possessed and craved both in equal measure. He wanted to know
things about everyone. He wanted to know what his competitors
liked to keep hidden. He wanted to know so that his power grew.
Unfortunately, not everything he knew made him happy. Leonard had recently found out that his wife, Amanda Carrington née
Mercado, was cheating on him with Eduardo Corral, her personal trainer. That made Leonard angry, but the infidelity itself
wasn't what got to him. He liked sleeping around—something
he constantly did with his never-ending roster of secretaries and
administrative assistants—and always suspected Amanda would
do so as well at some point. No, what got to Leonard was that
Amanda had cheated on him with a lowlife like Eduardo, an
absolute nobody who drove a fucking Yaris around and dressed
in shorts and T-shirts he probably bought online. If she'd done
it with a celebrity or a man on his level, he would have almost
understood, but a nobody? That was something he couldn't let
go. As far as he was concerned, Amanda had been another pretty
face until he made her someone, until he gave her standing by
allowing her to slap his last name to hers. He'd given her money,
cars, and a house, and she had repaid him with infidelity. That
made her feel like a walking stain in his home.

"Your office is what others see of you at work, so keep it tidy,"

Leonard's father, Willian Carrington, used to say. "Your house is the castle you build for yourself so you can enjoy what you earn at the office." Leonard had done just that. He loved his house. He loved the gigantic screen in front of the bed, the smell of his cigar room, the closet that housed his suits and shoes, the garage that protected his precious cars, and the pool in the back, which was perfect for enjoying drinks while staring at Amanda parading around in a microscopic bikini. Now it felt like someone had broken in and stayed there. He wanted Amanda out of his life and out of his house. She didn't deserve to be there.

Amanda Carrington knew her husband was an insufferable asshole. She knew the right thing to do would be to get a divorce, pack her bags, and start a life with Eduardo somewhere else, somewhere where no one recognized either of them. Ah, but that would mean walking away from her money and her house. She couldn't go back to an office after tasting the sweet nectar of wealth. Amanda also knew her husband knew about her new relationship. It wasn't the first one she'd had while married to him, but it was the only one she'd wanted him to know about. Why? Because men like Leonard Carrington are predictable beasts in tailored suits. Their anger is a weapon that can be easily turned against them with the right moves, and Amanda had all the right moves. That's why she left her phone around when he was home. That's why she met with Eduardo at her place a few times per week, where the nosy neighbors could see them kissing outside.

Amanda knew she'd married Leonard for his money. Money is a great thing, and Amanda had never had much of it until she met Leonard. She'd worked at a burger joint on Airport Boulevard for two years and then worked the phones at a life insurance company to get through college. Her mom had no education and had been stuck in poverty since birth. Her father was the ghost of a memory that sometimes showed up in one of her mother's sighs or a nasty comment about men in general.

After living her harsh reality all her life, the gig at Leonard's firm, and his subsequent courtship, felt like opportunities, like promises of a better future. Amanda had known back then that young, attractive women were always being hired, paid off, and fired after passing through Leonard's hands. She didn't want that. She played hard to get, and to a man that's never heard no, that was a new experience that made her irresistible.

Their prenup was solid, but it didn't have an infidelity clause. Amanda had emailed a version of it she'd scanned on her phone to her cousin Arturo, who worked as a lawyer out in LA. She wanted to know about what it all meant. He joked that Leonard hadn't included an infidelity clause because he was probably worried about what she'd do to him if she caught him cheating. That was a blessing.

Amanda knew Leonard would take care of her if she ever cheated on him with someone he felt was inferior to him, which was a lot of people. He had a taste for single malt—it had to be expensive, like Yamazaki or Pappy Van Winkle's—but he didn't hold his liquor well, which meant he talked a lot whenever he was hammered. When Amanda fell in love with Eduardo's sense of humor, easygoing attitude, and sweetness, she knew he was the one. He was her ticket out of a bland, loveless relationship and her future as the owner of everything she'd ever dreamed about. She would drop Leonard and keep the money. And she would keep her gorgeous house.

Pablo González knew evil wasn't as easy to identify as some people thought it was. He wasn't bad, just desperate. His friend Luis was bad, for example. He was in prison back home in Puerto Rico for killing two men in a deal gone wrong. Pablo knew Luis was evil the moment he caught him behind Doña Alina's house with his dick in a cat he'd just killed with a rock. Good people don't do that. Same went for Sebastián, a skinny kid who couldn't throw a punch, so he got good at pulling the trigger. He was also doing time, but he was in Florida, where so many of Pablo's friends from back home seemed to end up. Hell, he had more friends in prison in Florida than walking around back home.

No, Pablo knew he wasn't like Luis and Sebastián. He knew he was a good man. He'd always kept his kids' well-being at the top of his list of priorities. He always did whatever he needed to do to keep a roof over their heads and his pantry stocked. That Raiza had walked out on them wasn't part of the plan. A full cake is better than half a cake, especially if the cake is small, and small was exactly how Pablo felt after eight months of being the sole breadwinner in the house. The fruits of all his efforts amounted to a sad half of a tiny cake that wasn't enough to feed three people, keep the lights on, cover rent, make car payments, keep up with the insurance, buy stuff for school; the list went on and on. He was trying his best, and his best wasn't good enough. He worked eight hours a day at the HEB in Mueller, putting yogurt, frozen taquitos, eggs, milk, juice, and other things where they needed to be for folks who came looking for them. Then he went home, checked on the kids, and went to the big building at the corner of Lamar and 38th to clean the floors until 3:00 a.m. On lucky days, he was getting three hours of sleep per night. The money still wasn't enough. Also, going home was painful. His kids were always asleep when he came back from the cleaning gig, sure, but what hurt him more was not seeing Raiza there. His tiny bed was too big now. The bathroom smelled like her. Some of her clothes still hung in the closet next to his shirts. He knew Raiza had been the heart of the house, the person that made it feel like a home. Without her, the house was a corpse with two young, angry ghosts silently drifting inside it…and drifting away from him.

Pablo knew the man who owned the building where he worked at night, the chunky dude in the expensive suit with the TV-sized Rolex on his wrist, had more than enough money to solve all of Pablo's problems, so when he exited the elevator one night around midnight and called him over, Pablo went to the man with dreams of a promotion. After all, he was always there. Hell, he'd mopped two nights in a row while running a fever. The chunky man did have a gig for him, but not the kind Pablo had been expecting.

Leonard knew the man who cleaned the bathrooms and mopped the floors at night was the kind of man who would do anything for money. He literally went into the bathrooms on every floor and cleaned up shit and piss off the floor for a few dollars per hour every night of the week. Leonard knew people like that were desperate. He could see it in the man's eyes. The black circles around his eyes spoke of bad living and not enough sleep. Also, the man was brown. Leonard had thought he was Mexican, but the man with no name who got him information had told him otherwise. He was Puerto Rican, not Mexican. Same difference. Mexican, Puerto Rican, Colombian, Guatemalan, whatever; brown and poor is brown and poor. The only problem with this man—Pablo something—was that, as a Puerto Rican, he had a passport. Sure, he was a second-class citizen and his accent was atrocious, but citizenship wasn't a shiny lie Leonard could dangle in front of him…and deportation wasn't a viable threat. Despite that little shortcoming, the man with no name who got Leonard information had told him this man was better for the job than any of the other eight people he had in mind for it. His wife had left him, he had two kids at home, and his bank account at Bluegrass Credit Union had $363.49 in it. His rent was due in nine days. It was $700. He was behind on all utilities. He was a man ready to be bought. Leonard always thought about the same joke because it applied to all people: A man walks into a bar with a briefcase, walks up to a woman, places the briefcase in front of her, opens it, and politely asks her, "Madam, would you agree to spend the night with me for two million dollars?" She smiles and says yes. The man closes the briefcase and asks, "Madam, would you agree to spend the night with me for fifty dollars?" The woman opens her eyes wide and yells at him, "And what exactly do you think I am?" To this, the man calmly replies, "Oh, we already know what you are, now we're just negotiating the price."

When Leonard called out to the mop man, he dropped the mop in his yellow bucket and came running. His face betrayed the fact that he was surprised Leonard knew his name. That was all Leonard needed to push forward.

Leonard knew a lot about business and making proposals. The trick was to make his idea sound like a great offer, one the brown man couldn't refuse, but also to add a threat to it to ensure the man understood Leonard wasn't really asking. Plus, fifty grand was more money than that poor sap would make in a year mopping the floors and scraping shit off toilets. It was a lot of money for most people, but Leonard liked to keep a bit of cash out of the reach of the IRS and Amanda so he could indulge in some of his favorite pastimes without having to explain his spending to anyone.

Every business deal has its pros and cons. That was something Leonard knew well. In fact, he also knew this particular deal could be extremely dangerous for him, so he came prepared to his meeting with the mop man in the lobby. In his phone were two photos. The first one showed the outside of Pablo's house, his two kids walking away from it with backpacks strapped to their backs and serious faces. The second one showed Pablo in his car at HEB's parking lot, taking a power nap during his break. Leonard knew short threats worked better than long ones because they were easier to remember. "I know who you are, where you live, where you work, and where your children sleep. You get me dirty, I will bury all of you."

Pablo had learned the chubby rich guy was named Mr. Carrington. He'd spewed some tale about his "bitch" of a wife cheating on him with a "beaner" named Edward or something like that. The white sack of flab under his chin shook when he talked and

spittle flew out of his mouth when he said bitch. Pablo knew he
was angry. He understood. Men like him, always busy and whatnot, they always had a pretty wife at home that liked the money
but not the fact that their husbands were always at work, so they
cheated. Who wouldn't? In any case, the man wanted her gone.
All Pablo had to do was sneak into their house, kill her, and steal
some jewelry to make it look like a robbery. Mr. Carrington said
there were no cameras. He hated the idea of being spied on by
lenses in his own home. Also, he would show him signed sheets
from his supervisor for that night ahead of time, so he would have
a solid alibi. It sounded shady as fuck. However, he would also give
him $50,000 for the job, half up front and half after. Cash. That
sounded great. That was a lot of money. That was a new start for
him and the kids. That was a few fixes to his house.

Pablo knew killing was bad. He also knew that getting caught
and spending the rest of his life in prison while the world swallowed his children was his worst nightmare. However, he also
knew that, if he pulled it off, he'd be able to quit his second job
and spend all that time with Marta and Eugenio. That sounded
like paradise. The three of them at home, doing homework,
sharing meals, and healing. Together. He wanted that.

A voice in the back of Pablo's head kept telling him to never
show up at that stupid building again or to show up and politely
tell Mr. Carrington thanks but no thanks. The voice sounded
like his mom. He pushed the voice away. Pablo knew no one
was going to give him anything. He knew doing something bad
for all the right reasons didn't make it less bad, but it did take
away the guilt. He knew the woman had cheated, so it was easy
for him to take the hatred he felt for Raiza and put it on this
other woman. Mr. Carrington had said she was a bitch. That almost made it okay to kill her. Anyone would kill for their kids.
Assholes who said they wouldn't were lying...or were horrible
parents. All Pablo needed was some kind of guarantee that the
second half of the money would show up.

★ ★ ★

Amanda knew Leonard had everything set up. He walked around the house pretending to be normal, but his mood for the past three weeks had been like one of those black clouds that follow sad characters in cartoons. Then, his demeanor changed. He walked around with his back straight and she would catch him looking at her. And he hadn't grabbed her ass in days. He was different. She knew it was because he was sure he'd pulled it off. Unfortunately for him, there were things he didn't know.

The first thing Leonard ignored was that Amanda had installed a spy app on his phone two years ago, right after they came back from their honeymoon in Costa Rica. It was called mSpy and allowed her to see his incoming and outgoing texts and call history, look at the text messages he deleted, and let her track his phone using the app's GPS system. She knew of every tryst and fake long night at the office. She knew of every girl he'd paid off and even the guy he'd hired to get him information on competitors and women alike. She had gotten in touch with him as well. He wasn't cheap, but he was a good investment. He refused to give her his name, so Amanda called him Mr. Glasses. Mr. Glasses kept her posted on everything Leonard did. For a price, of course, but it was worth it. Amanda knew everything. Amanda's mother had been a hard, sad woman who'd gone through two marriages with abusive men and then raised Amanda by herself. She always told her the easiest way to keep trouble at bay was to know everything that happened in your house. Amanda had taken those words to heart.

Pablo knew Mr. Carrington was not a man he could trust. For starters, he was rich, and people usually don't get rich being decent. Also, he was a racist. Pablo could tell when someone was racist. They always changed their voice and slowed down when talking to him because they were sure a brown man with an accent was going to have a hard time keeping up. Mr. Carrington had done both, so Pablo knew he was probably plotting something to fuck him over. The second time they met, Pablo came to the meeting prepared. They talked about a place and a time for Pablo to pick up a gun and for him to show up at Mr. Carrington's house. They talked about the money and then Mr. Carrington talked about not getting dirty again. Pablo kept his mouth shut at first and then assured Mr. Carrington he was thankful for the opportunity and that he had been a lifesaver because he really needed the money. The asshole had smiled while handing Pablo the money and the gun, which was wrapped in a towel to keep his prints off of it. He surely felt he owned Pablo now. Pablo smiled back. He knew they both had reasons to smile, and neither of them were being honest about them.

Amanda knew all she had to do was wait. Men were predictable and knowledge made her safe. Leonard had gone through with it. When he said he had to stay late at the office, she knew it was because he wanted her to be alone. He was still there. The GPS told her so. The irony of him finally staying at the office for real only because he was sending someone to murder her wasn't lost on Amanda. She knew bringing him down would bring her a lot of joy. She also knew a lot about the thing that would truly keep her safe: the Glock 43 under her pillow. It was one of the smallest handguns ever produced by Glock, but it would get the job done. Amanda had gotten the gun from Leonard. He said criminals are attracted to people with money, and he wanted her to be safe. He even paid for the classes she took and went down to the shooting range with her once. She'd gone by herself many times since then. It worked better than Xanax to make her forget she was married to an asshole.

Amanda had built a routine in the preceding months. She knew how Leonard would react, so she wanted him to feel like he had a solid read on her and could plot accordingly. Every night, she watched TV in the living room. He called the living room her headquarters. Today, she wouldn't watch TV, and she wouldn't be in the living room. Too many windows there. She was in her room, listening. She knew what was coming.

Pablo left a note to his kids and walked out. He knew there was a small chance something would go wrong, so he wanted to cover his bases. He wanted to protect his kids and his home.

When he reached Mr. Carrington's place, he drove by, stopped two blocks down, and parked near some bushes before making his way back to the house. He looked around and then made his way to the back of the house. Mr. Carrington had told him he was going to leave the back door open. He knew his wife left it open from time to time so her lover could come in and out.

Pablo's heart was pounding against his rib cage when he opened the door. It was late, but not so late that everyone would be sleeping.

The back door led to a laundry room as big as his son's room. It was attached to a kitchen that looked like something pulled from a magazine. Pablo ignored it all. He knew he had to get the job done and vanish.

The lights were off downstairs, so he pulled out the gun he'd gotten from Mr. Carrington and slowly made his way upstairs. The only sound in the house was his heart. Pablo could hear his pulse punching his eardrums with the desperation of a wild animal.

The only light came from the room at the end of the hallway, the master bedroom. The door was halfway open. Pablo inhaled shakily and moved toward the door. He stopped in front of it. He wanted to be home. He wanted to be back on the island with his kids, enjoying a day at the beach. He would do that. He would do that because he was going to do this, the thing he came to do.

Pablo pushed the door open and raised his gun. He saw too much at once.

A woman standing next to a huge bed.

A gun.

A flash.

Pablo heard the gun go off and felt something hit his chest at the same time.

His gun thudded against the floor, a distant, muffled sound. He'd always thought a dream being shattered would make a loud sound, but this one didn't.

The pain came all at once. Pablo tried to inhale. The woman squeezed the trigger again. Pablo felt like his heart had exploded. The soft carpet ran up to meet his face. Pablo knew the darkness was bad news. He also knew he didn't have any power left to push that darkness away.

Marta woke up and went to the bathroom. After emptying her bladder and splashing cold water on her face—which a friend had told her was a trick to keeping wrinkles at bay—she walked into the kitchen. There was a piece of paper on the table.

Marta knew a note from her father was always important. He wasn't the type of dad to leave notes for his kids all the time. When he left a note, she knew Eugenio and her had to read it because it probably concerned them. She picked it up to read it and saw her dad's phone underneath it.

I love you both. That's it. If you get this, I'm not here and that's all you need to know. I love you both with all my heart. Sorry I never gave you all you two deserve. You know my passcode: 2004. Yeah, Marta's birth year. I have you in my laptop, Eugenio, so don't get jealous! There's an app on the last screen. It's a little icon with headphones on it. It's called VoiceRecord Pro. There is only one file in there. It's about six minutes long. It's my boss paying me to do something bad. I did it for us. I wanted to give you a better future, a better present, a better house. There's a towel in the fridge. The money inside is for you two. Take it and don't spend it all at once. Take the recording to the cops. Don't tell them about the money. I know you hate cops, but they will help you. I'm sorry. Please know I love you both. I love you with every ounce of my being, and that's all you need to know.

HAUNTED HOME ON THE RANGE

A.P. JAMISON

As an eleven-year-old cowboy-boot-wearing, pecan pie–loving cowgirl from the Great State of Texas, I was no Cinderella. Not at all. I didn't want to go to the ball. Instead, I was fixin' to hang out with my polka-dotted Appaloosa horse, Lonesome Dovey, and my golden retriever, Buddy Holly the Marshmallow, right here on our ranch two hours outside of San Antonio…that is until my neighbor's horse, Hennessey, went missing.

My name is Augusta DeWitt—my friends call me Gus—and I'm a private investigator. So, I had tried every dang thing to get out of wearing a fancy dress to a black-tie ball in honor of our upcoming VIP houseguest Jane Hetherington.

As a last resort, I had researched how Hollywood actors use a vegetable soup concoction to make their vomit scenes more authentic. That mixture was currently churning about in my belly while I lay on my four-poster bed staring out at my room filled with my favorite things: family photos, old saddles, new horseshoes, worn boots and bright bling—it's a cowgirl sort of thing.

But the high noon "dress rehearsal" was a comin', and I was ready as I'd ever be for the fashion makeover shoot-out. Even Marshmallow, who was on my bed resting next to me, barked as if he too was pawing for a showdown.

Suddenly, my bedroom door blew open. There stood my aunt, Miss Lemon Meringue Pie, who was normally the most delicious dessert of an aunt anyone could ask for—and no, silly, that isn't her real name, but in all my eleven years, it was the only thing I had ever called her. And, aside from always wearing white and yellow—Miss Lemon Meringue Pie was our very own ray of sunshine—she was so soft and sweet and beautiful, yet tart when she needed to be.

Miss Lemon held up a putrid dress that looked like it was spun from pink cotton candy into a silk, satin and tulle upside-down funnel. Worse, in her hand she also held a training bra. A training bra! What exactly does it train them to do?

"You're going to look so lovely, my dear Gus," Miss Lemon said, sweet as pie, but at that moment, she looked a lot more like an Eggs Benedict Arnold to me.

"I hate black-tie ball dry runs!" I huffed, staring at Marshmallow who put his two front paws over his eyes as if in agreement. I couldn't tell them I was working on a case 'cause I'd be grounded.

"You are going to be gorgeous!" Behind my aunt, I spied my twenty-one-year-old sister, Susana, carrying her makeup and hairstyling case. She was one of those Texas beauties whose lush black hair, large violet eyes, pale skin and petulant pout could start or stop a speeding bullet. "It's time to say goodbye to those pigtails and hello to some hairspray, lipstick and mascara."

Et tu, Susana? was the only thought going through my mind. Her dang dagger was a mascara wand!

"My denim blue jeans, boots and Stetson are sacred!" I yelled, jumping up and down on my bed while Marshmallow barked at all of us. See, unlike my aunt and my sister, I had thick blond hair that I always wore in pigtails, big adult teeth and wide-set green eyes. My sister, Susana, said I would grow into my face one day, but what the heck did that mean? I looked like a Tootsie Pop with boots, but I didn't care.

They grabbed me off my bed and went to work. I was being woman-handled into hair, makeup and fashion submission. Technically, I was being "family handled," so I did the only thing a cowgirl could do… I vomited that Hollywood-inspired vegetable soup onto Miss Lemon Meringue's beautiful yellow-and-white-dress. I had meant to hurl at her lemon-inspired designer shoes—it was a tactical error I regret.

I glanced at Miss Lemon's face—it was now the tartest I've ever seen it, so tart she looked madder than a snake finding out he was married to a garden hose. And that was my cue for Marshmallow and me to hightail it to my family cemetery, located on the edge of our ranch.

See, my parents died in a freak accident a few months ago and nothing had been the same in my world ever since. Their ghosts haunted me, but I couldn't tell my aunt or sister that I kept seeing them by the lake where they had died. There is "cra cra" and there is crazy. I knew I wasn't crazy…but this nagging pain felt like there was a five-hundred-pound saddle squishing my heart. Hanging out here in the family cemetery—surrounded by Southern live oak trees and bluebonnets—comforted Marshmallow and me.

The April Texas heat made it so dry out, I was worried our ducks would forget how to swim, and once I got close enough to my parents' cemetery plot, I could tell immediately something was amiss.

A stranger was resting on my parents' grave. And he was hanging out with Hennessey, the missing horse. What the heck?

It wasn't like our cemetery was Grand Central Station or something. My golden retriever might be a Marshmallow, but I expected him to growl. He was trained to protect me and had a four-paw sense about people. Instead, he raced up to what I could now see was a cowboy and his dog, a Golden Irish, (half golden retriever and half Irish setter)—who hung on to him like Velcro. This cowboy seemed to be talking to my dead parents. I was intrigued…he couldn't be all bad if he had two dogs and a horse that liked him. Or could he?

Once I got closer, I could see that this cowboy looked sad enough to bring a tear to a glass eye. I'd say he was about eighty-five years young. He wore a new Stetson hat, old boots, clean jeans and a stained vest.

The cowboy looked me in the eye and said, in a voice that sounded like it had been serenaded by some serious soul and scotch, "I'm Mustang and this here is Whiskey Kiss," pointing to his rhinestone-collar-wearing dog.

"Hiya. I'm Gus and this here is Marshmallow."

"Glad to meet you. Is everything okay with you, Gus?"

I couldn't tell a stranger I was running away because I didn't want to wear a pink dress to a ball; that I was worried that cowboys would make fun of me seeing me all dolled up; that I'd feel plain stupid; that I still looked like a toothpick who certainly had no need for an "over the shoulder boulder holder" yet; that I wanted their respect, not their teasing and taunting; and that Marshmallow and I were private investigators, but few adults took us seriously.

"You sure, cowgirl?" Mustang said.

"I just don't want to wear a dang pink dress to a black-tie ball." The words just fell out of my mouth.

Mustang slowly nodded. "I do understand your dilemma. That is one tough decision. Do you sacrifice your principles for your family and then face ridicule from your friends or do you remain true to your boots?"

"Yes, sir," I said. "That's it." Boom. Dang. Darn. He got me. The wise old cowboy was correct. "I just can't do it," I said, thinking about that pukey pink-tulle dress.

"Oh, child, life is made up of experiences that either inspire us or challenge us. It's how we grow. I know you prefer cowboy boots to ball gowns, but you should at least see what the dress feels like when you're wearing it before you judge it…" He lingered for a long moment like he was fixin' to pull out a harmonica from his jeans pocket and play a soulfully sad song I couldn't bear. "Gus, who cares about what the boys or anyone else thinks for that matter? Actions always speak louder than words when it comes to cowboys and cowgirls. Besides," Mustang said, "you never know, you might like to wear a dress every once in a while."

I dropped my head. We cow folk had a code: *Live Each Day With Courage*. Texas-sized salty tears started to burn my eyes. All my anger and grief were bundled up like a big, mad balloon just begging for the relief of a pin.

He handed me a clean, red-checked handkerchief and continued. "Now, I've heard great things about your detective skills, and I would like to hire you and Marshmallow."

"Us?" I wiped my eyes. "Most people think I'm just an odd eleven-year-old."

"I'm not most people. Word is…you two get results for your clients. I heard you and Marshmallow just solved the case of *The Nine Deaths In Hamlet* and caught the killer."

"You heard right." I clicked my cowboy boots. "How can we help?" I asked. I was all Stetson hat, cowboy boots and jack-rabbit ears…

"I had some jewelry stolen from me so I hid my big diamond and now I can't find it."

"Carbon placed under extreme pressure is so cool! I love Mother Earth. We'll need some information. What is the cut, color, clarity and carat weight?" I asked. I was a Texas girl. We started learning about diamonds as soon as we exited the womb!

"It's a three-carat round solitaire. Ideal Cut. H Color, VS2 Clarity."

"Whoo ah. That sounds like a $40,000 rock."

"It is. I love Mother Earth, too." Mustang grinned at me and I liked that sincere smile. It meant our investigation was off to a promising start. I had lots more questions, but Mustang seemed to be in some sort of discomfort. His breath was labored and raspy.

"Mustang, we need to get you back to the ranch and get you some sweet tea and Miss Lemon's perfect pecan pie."

Mustang nodded. "Can you do one more thing for me before we go?"

"Yup," I said. Even in a cemetery I always remembered my manners.

Mustang opened his leather vest to reveal two bloody gunshot wounds to his chest. I stepped back. Bullet holes are very small going in and very big coming out. He had been shot in the back.

As I reeled from this sickening feeling, Marshmallow raced to my side. "Gus," Mustang said, "could you also find out who murdered me?"

It was as if he could see the look of shock and confusion and heartbreak on my face. One didn't survive these types of bullet wounds…

Then Marshmallow stood up and barked at one of the trees. It was an urgent whiny bark. Boots on the ground now, I raced over to the live oak tree he had been pointing at with his nose.

There we found a very *dead* Mustang. He *had* been shot twice in the back. That's why his vest looked dirty. It was stained with blood. Marshmallow and I hurried back to my parents' plot, but the ghost of Mustang was gone…

Back in our bedroom, I had finally stopped sobbing buckets of sadness.

Mustang had been murdered right here on our ranch. This crime hit home. Only a greedy, dastardly coward would shoot a darling cowboy in the back!

Grief was a grim thing. In a short period of time, Mustang had become a trusted friend and a client. Now he was gone. I had to channel all my super sadness into finding out who had murdered Mustang, but first I had to talk to the two sheriffs assigned to the case. I had overheard them tell Miss Lemon and Susana that they were going to set up a sting at the hospital. I just knew Marshmallow, Whiskey Kiss and I had to be there.

Three hours later, Marshmallow, Whiskey Kiss and I were at the San Antonio General Hospital lobby speaking with Sheriffs Galleta and Leche. Sheriff Galleta looked like he worked out even in his sleep and ate iron for breakfast. He must have been over six feet, full of what seemed like all steel muscles and a cowboy hat. I bet he could strut sitting down. Really, I did.

Sheriff Leche reminded me of a thin Santa. He had a jovial laugh that put us at ease, a head full of silver hair, blue eyes that would make a blue jay jealous and he loved powdered donuts like I did. I could still see a little leftover powder on his silver beard.

"Please tell us what happened," I asked them.

Sheriff Galleta let out a big sigh. "Someone shot Mustang twice in the back and left him for dead. We think it was a robbery gone bad."

I had to play dumb to see what the sheriffs knew. "What were they trying to steal?" Through the hospital bay window I could see the full moon hanging out in the huge Texas sky.

"A diamond," replied Sheriff Leche.

"Did the thief take it?" I asked.

"We don't know yet. Can't find it." Sheriff Leche shook his head.

"What kind of gun did the killer use?" I asked.

The sheriffs looked at me for a long moment as if unsure what to say.

"You do know I live on a ranch?" I said. "Before I could walk, I had to learn gun safety. I know guns."

"A Smith and Wesson," Sheriff Galleta said like he was spitting bullets.

"Did they use a sound suppressor?" I asked. That's really what a silencer is called if you aren't watching crime TV shows.

Both their eyebrows almost hit the top of their foreheads. Then Sheriff Leche said, "Yes. We believe so. You didn't hear any shots, did you, on your way to the cemetery?"

"Nope. But, it doesn't matter what I heard, Marshmallow—who has the ears of Superman—didn't hear a dang thing, so the killer had to have used a sound suppressor. I bet it was an M&P 22 Compact."

Sheriff Galleta let out a long whistle. "Why?"

"Well, the Compact is a suppressor-ready pistol with a threaded barrel. Mustang had to have been shot no more than two hours before I found him as rigor hadn't set in."

Sheriff Leche just stared at me with that twinkle in his eye. "Did you really get a perfect score on your SATs when you were just ten years old?"

I nodded. It was as if they initially thought I was the Scarecrow and had just found out that I *did* have a brain. Adults! Then I saw Sheriff Galleta's brain wheels begin to move like a chuck wagon.

"Now little lady, despite that achievement, this is a murder investigation. You shouldn't even be here, so I want you to promise me that you will keep your ears wide-open and your mouth zipped shut."

Little lady? The nerve! I felt as welcome as a skunk at a dinner party, but I didn't care. Instead, I reached for my backpack to get some water and dog food for the pups and then glanced down at the Golden Irish doggy. I could tell he was upset about Mustang. "One more question," I said. "Was Whiskey Kiss there when Mustang was shot?"

"I have no idea," Sheriff Galleta said like his tongue was playing with a fake toothpick. "But we have a plan."

The sheriffs' plan was simple. They had put the word out that Mustang was still alive and asked friends to come to the hospital to pray for him so the sheriffs had arranged for one of our ranch hands—a cool cowboy named Canteen, who looked a bit like Mustang—to be tucked away in a sterile hospital bed, surrounded by get-well balloons and floral arrangements. The suspects could come and pray for him.

My plan was simple. The pups and I were going to sneak into the hospital room and find out who killed Mustang. The one advantage to being a kid is that adults ignore us or don't take us seriously and I was counting on both.

Fifteen minutes later, I was sitting in a very uncomfortable orange chair in the corner of "Mustang's" hospital room with Marshmallow and Whiskey Kiss by my side waiting.

The first visitor, a man of forty-something, came in and stood by "Mustang's" bed. Thanks to the ventilator it was impossible to see the patient's face. But this visitor seemed like a brown-nosed banker, who must've been raised on concrete he was so citified. I could just tell. He was what our family would call bad for business. All hat and no cattle, this dude was littered in monograms and he had slicked-back hair. Why did Mustang need a bedside visit from a banker? What was this banker up to? Why was he crying?

I gave him a tissue. "Here."

"Thank you."

"Are you a friend of Mustang's?" I asked. I could hear the rhythmic hissing sound of the ventilator.

"I'm his banker and his friend and his L—"

"Lover?" I asked.

Monogram man just stared at me. "No, I am his loan officer."

Now that surprised me. "But did you try and kill him?"

"No. Mustang is one of my best friends and I can't believe anyone would do this."

★ ★ ★

Ten minutes later, after Mr. Banker had left in tears, a mass of purple entered Mustang's hospital room. Wait. I had to blink again. I couldn't tell if my eyes were playing tricks on me.

Nope, she *did* look like a life-sized purple Popsicle in her scrubs. It was an outfit that personal caregivers often wear when tending to their patients. She must have been around twenty-five years young with a mop of hair tied up on top of her head and she was quietly weeping—like a leaky soda machine. In one hand, she held a big bag of vitamins, and in the other, was a bag of dog food. Dog food? Just how bad was the hospital food?

"Hiya," I said. "I'm Gus and this here is Marshmallow. You know Whiskey Kiss."

"Hi. I'm Velda. Mustang's caregiver."

"What kind of care do you give?" I asked. Whiskey Kiss wasn't running to her.

"I help around the house and make sure Mustang takes his meds and remembers to eat when the 'sundowning' begins."

Dang. Some elders get confused at night when the sun goes down so they are called "Sundowners."

That was bad and sad and scary. My granddad was a sundowner but he and his caregiver had developed a special bond.

"Who do you think shot Mustang?"

"I don't know," Velda said as my nose started rebelling against the antiseptic smell of the room.

"Why weren't you with him at the DeWitt Ranch?"

Velda sighed. "He said that the elder DeWitt had been a friend and he wanted to have a private conversation with him at the cemetery."

Mustang and my granddad were friends? Dang. Why the heck hadn't Mustang mentioned that? No wonder he was at the cemetery.

"I was supposed to pick Mustang up but I never heard back," Velda added.

I didn't like her but that didn't make her a murderer—or did it?

★ ★ ★

The third man who entered Mustang's bedroom was an elderly priest who had a ten-gallon mouth and kept nervously stroking his Bible as if it were a pet poodle. He must have been at least seventy—and his smile was so bright—his teeth might just be able to power all of the great state of Texas. Where were my sunglasses? Who smiled like this in a hospital? What was he up to? I just hoped he wasn't here to save my soul.

After he was done doing all his priest blessings over "Mustang," he turned to me. "May I pray for you too?"

"No, thank you." I had no idea what type of prayer he would be saying since he could be a killer. "I like talking directly to the big guy."

The priest smiled, but it wasn't a sincere smile.

"How do you know Mustang?" I asked very politely.

"I'm his priest."

"Who do you think tried to kill Mustang?"

"Mustang doesn't have an enemy in the world. So I don't know how they are going to come up with any suspects."

I knew of seven priests who had been convicted of murder, but I didn't think that would help move our conversation forward.

"I don't know who did it but let's pray for Mustang." The priest made the sign of the cross, we prayed and then he left the hospital room.

Once the priest had gone, Canteen popped up in bed and said. "Who did it—the banker, priest, or caregiver?"

"I need one more piece of the puzzle, Canteen, but I have eliminated one suspect. I'll meet you downstairs by the truck. I just have to say one more thing to the sheriffs on the way out."

Three minutes later, Marshmallow and I peeked out into the hallway. Sheriff Leche and Sheriff Galleta's bet was on the banker because suddenly, they read him his rights and put the banker in handcuffs.

Marshmallow and I hurried over to the sheriffs and I smiled my biggest smile, stopped, stood on the tiptoe of my cowgirl boots and whispered, "Sheriff Galleta and Sheriff Leche, you have arrested the wrong man."

The sheriffs were still staring at me. They looked as confused as two billy goats on Astroturf.

Two hours later, after Canteen drove Marshmallow and me home, we sat on the back patio by the firepit and listened to the crickets, coyotes and crackling sounds from burning logs. Then Whiskey Kiss, Mustang's brokenhearted dog lumbered over to me. It was as if he knew I needed proof for anyone to believe my theory. Staring out at the moon in the big Texas sky, I was missing Mustang and my parents.

"Howdy, Whiskey Kiss," I said. He was all awkward bones. But I knew by the way he hung his head, by the way saliva was slipping out the sides of his mouth and by the way he was arching his back that Whiskey Kiss wasn't feeling well. And it wasn't just grief. Then that marvelous dog howled at that moon and started shaking.

I sprang out of my chair to comfort him. He too was having a tough night and needed a hug. Talk about the magic of God's creatures. We humans could learn a lot from them if we just talked less and listened more. They have mad skills we don't have.

The next moment moved in slow motion. Whiskey Kiss finally threw up.

His skills so put my fake vomiting to shame and as a vomit expert I wasn't afraid of the stuff. His barf was something to behold. Then I saw something...

"Wait a minute." I spotted two brass shell casings in his puke and scooped them up in one of my evidence bags. Then I hugged that big, bony Golden Irish and gave him some water, dog food and treats. "Good boy, Whiskey Kiss. You are a very good boy." He put his big head back in my lap and I kissed the top of his sweet noggin.

★ ★ ★

Poor Whiskey Kiss, despite my lovin' on him, he still looked lonelier than a pine tree in a Texas stadium parking lot. He missed his Mustang...

"Gus?" a deep voice called out.

Dang. Suddenly, I spied Sheriffs Galleta and Leche standing in the corner of our backyard. What the heck? What were they doing here?

"Welcome." I didn't know what else to say.

Sheriffs Galleta and Leche walked over to Marshmallow, Whiskey Kiss and me with the three suspects—the banker, priest and caregiver—as well as the three San Antonio Police Department (SAPD) officers.

Then, Sheriff Galleta said four simple words that made my decade. "Gus, just tell us."

I could hear him very clearly, but shame on me; I pretended not to. "Sheriff Galleta," I said, "could you please repeat that?"

"Gus," Sheriff Leche whispered, "who murdered Mustang?"

"First, let's talk about Velda the caregiver, the purple Popsicle," I said bluntly. "She should *not* be allowed to look after humans or dogs."

"I beg your pardon," Velda, the caregiver, said in a haughty voice, her face now almost as purple as her outfit.

"Mustang deserved a caregiver who actually cared for him instead of stealing from him. You were supposed to bring the list of meds Mustang took, including his vitamins. Plus, you brought no photos or toiletries or change of clothes. And then there was that dog food. It was just enough to last for one meal. You were starving Whiskey Kiss."

Then Whiskey Kiss barked and wagged his tail as if agreeing with me.

Sheriff Galleta said, "That might be true, but it isn't enough to arrest her for murder."

"No, it isn't. She didn't kill Mustang but she did steal some of his jewelry and should be arrested for theft and elder abuse."

"How do you know that?" Sheriff Leche asked, intrigued.

"I got a list of what jewelry went missing and she is wearing one of the rings she stole."

Velda put her hands behind her back while Sheriff Leche headed over to her.

"Okay, but who killed Mustang?" Sheriff Galleta asked, looking from Velda to me.

"Here." I handed him the two shell casings wrapped in a plastic evidence bag. "I think this should be enough evidence to arrest Sheriff Leche for the murder of Mustang."

Sheriff Galleta's mouth opened but not a letter or a vowel fell out.

But Sheriff Leche pulled out his gun faster than a Texas Pronghorn who clocks in at a quick sixty-five miles an hour.

That was not the thing to do in front of Marshmallow. He lunged at Leche, and bit his ankle. Hard. Leche screamed in pain and dropped the gun. I kicked it away as the two SAPD police officers put him in handcuffs. No one messes with my Marshmallow.

"Why did Leche kill Mustang?" a shocked Sheriff Galleta asked.

"The white powder around his mouth wasn't from donuts, he had a burn mark on his lip and he doesn't look like a fat Santa anymore. I'm betting he needed the diamond to feed his cocaine habit."

"How do you know all that?" Sheriff Galleta asked, still stunned.

"I eavesdropped on Miss Lemon when she was giving Susana the 'don't do drugs' lesson. Plus, Leche got some powder on me when he shook my hand. Normally, Marshmallow licks it right up but not this time. Cocaine sure doesn't taste like sugar."

Sheriff Galleta, still looking like a deer in some serious Cotton Bowl Stadium–sized headlights, said, "I'm sorry that I underestimated you, Gus. I couldn't see what was right under my nose. Thank you, Gus."

Then Sheriff Galleta led Leche away in handcuffs. I would've preferred that he be hog-tied, but it wasn't my call. Following closely behind them were Velda in another set of handcuffs, the priest and the banker.

Once they were gone, Marshmallow and I stared at the stars saying hi from up in the big Texas sky. Suddenly to my surprise and delight, I saw the ghost of Mustang standing across from us on the patio, and he simply said to Marshmallow, Whiskey Kiss and me, "Hiya. Thank you for finding my murderer."

I grinned. Marshmallow wagged his plumed tail. Whiskey Kiss sprinted to the ghost of Mustang. "Oh, Whiskey Kiss," he said, like sorrow was dripping down his face. Then he looked at me. "Gus, you are my superhero cowgirl."

I beamed like the brightest Texas sun.

"Now do you know what happened to the diamond?" Mustang asked. "I still don't remember what I did with it."

"You were very clever indeed. I found the diamond in Whiskey Kiss's rhinestone collar."

Mustang laughed. "You Texas girls sure do know your diamonds."

I held up the diamond sparkler. "Who should this go to?"

"Whiskey Kiss, of course." Mustang glanced at his doggy with tender tears in his eyes. "You'll take good care of him?"

Tears were now forming in mine. "You betcha. He'll get butcher-grade bones and buckets of love every day," I said as Whiskey Kiss wagged his tail. "Besides, Marshmallow will be thrilled too. He suffers from horse envy. So he could use a friend his size."

Mustang let out a chuckle and winked at us. Then he put his hat back on and blew Whiskey Kiss, Marshmallow and me a final kiss goodbye and disappeared.

Another fat tear fell down my face as my aunt and sister

stepped out the patio doors. Miss Lemon looked like a sad Cheshire cat. "You don't have to wear that pink dress anymore."

"I don't?" I was now as confused as a moth in a mitten.

Miss Lemon and Susana had made such a big deal about it and after chatting with Mustang I was now sorta excited about the pink-ball-gown challenge. I should at least put on the dress and see if I liked it.

Susana shook her head. "After the tragic death of Mustang, there will be no black-tie ball."

"What!" I said, "I thought the ball was in honor of a woman named Jane Hetherington?"

Miss Lemon's smile was as wide as the state of Texas. "Jane was her given name but her friends got to call her Mustang..."

NOT EXIT

WALTER MOSLEY

1.

Tom Exit went to prison for yelling at two cops who were, in his opinion, inappropriately searching a young woman he later came to know as Patricia Neil. Because Tom was hollering and gesticulating at them Patrolman Hans Braun told him to lower his voice and then grabbed him by the wrist. Tom yanked his hand free from the cop's grasp. That was assault and so the police left off their search of Patricia Neil's person in order to batter Mr. Exit into submission.

When Tom's crime came to trial his mother testified that her son had learning disabilities that made him sometimes speak out when he experienced or saw what he thought of as an injustice.

"He loses control," she said. "But he doesn't mean anything."

She had medical papers documenting his condition but the court ruled her evidence inadmissible because she had highlighted in yellow those sections pertaining to the possible underlying causes of Tom's actions.

Patricia Neil swore under oath that the police, "had their hands all in my clothes and on my body and Mr. Exit was callin' out to them to respect my dignity."

But Patrolman Braun said that they had witnessed Miss Neil buying drugs from a known drug dealer and they needed to find the evidence in order to arrest her, and her connection.

The day before the case went to the jury Tom Exit, through his lawyer, Marcia Abraham, made a plea-bargain agreement to serve eighteen months for the class D felony.

During the first year of his incarceration at Rikers Island Tom was beaten, raped and otherwise sexually assaulted by multiple assailants, and placed in solitary confinement sixteen times. He was twenty-one years old.

The only bright light to Tom's imprisonment was the more or less biweekly visits by Patricia Neil.

"You know," she told Tom across the unobstructed desk that was available to visitors who could afford the forty dollars, "you saved my ass when you told them cops to leave me alone. I had enough chems on me to be called a dealer and I already got two felony convictions on my record. I'd'a been in jail till my ass was saggin' and wrinkled if they'da reached into my drawers."

Patricia had dark skin like Tom's and one of her front teeth was edged in gold. He wished like anything that he could go home with her just to sit on her couch and watch TV. He liked cartoons and shows about the animal kingdom. He could name every species of bird and most sharks, well over a thousand different dinosaurs, and mark many of the differences between mammals, reptiles, and fishes.

In his thirteenth month of incarceration Tom asked a nurse-intern for a drink of water. They were in the infirmary, where he'd been sent for a bloody nose received in an impromptu beating. The nurse-intern, whose name was Bernard Walters, denied the request and Tom said, "But I'm thirsty."

Walters said, "Then open up and I'll piss in your mouth."

Exit didn't remember attacking Walters but when he regained consciousness he was in a straitjacket, lashed to an aluminum framed cot. Lying there, bound to the metallic frame, Tom was thinking about a thick fog that had a pinkish hue.

"Mr. Exit struck and even bit Mr. Walters for no reason whatever," prosecutor Phil Hines told the judge presiding over the case.

The prosecution had convinced the court that Exit was a danger to others and so had him dragged into court in the straitjacket.

That day he got five years tagged on to his sentence.

Tom's mother, Deborah Marsh-Exit, remarried soon after her son's second conviction. Her new husband, Lance Ferragut, said he didn't like his wife going down to Rikers so often and from then on she only came to see her son on his birthday.

Patricia Neil decreased her visits to once a month because she kicked her habit and had taken a job in a small assembly factory in Queens. She told Tom that she and her fellow ex-con workers put together things like brushes and pails made from bright colored plastic fabricated and exported by a company in China somewhere.

Two years passed without official incident.

But along the way Tom experienced a whole raft of unofficial trouble. He was tasked by cell-block kingpin Billy Biggs to bring in drugs in order for Billy to put out the word that other inmates had to stop abusing and beating him. The only way he could achieve this goal was to ask Patricia to get one of her friends, who was still using, to smuggle a sachet of Oxycontin pills in to him.

Carellia Thorn, a light-skinned Black woman, took the job and visited Tom under the pretext that she was a distant cousin.

For the past year the guards had been allowing Tom open-desk visiting privileges due to his good record. To his surprise they put him at a station in the far corner where there was a modicum of privacy. Usually only the wealthier prisoners got that seat when their girlfriends or wives visited.

Carellia was large but not fat, what his mother called big-boned. Her face was beautiful and sensual and she had a smile that actually made the twenty-four-year-old convict's heart skip.

"Hi, baby," she said when they were alone. "Patricia says hi too."

"That's a pretty dress," Tom answered. The one-piece frock was peacock blue with serious décolletage.

"You like it?" she asked through a conspiratorial grin.

"A lot."

"I paid the visitin' manager to give us this desk because I wanted to be able to give you what I got without some stick-up-his-ass guard tryin' to mess with us."

With those words on her red, red lips she stood and walked around the wooden desk to where Tom sat. She handed him a package of ochre paper tightly bound with yards of scotch tape. He took the bundle, looking up at the woman, trying to remember how to breathe and talk at the same time.

Leaning down Carellia kissed Tom's lips running her tongue around them lightly.

"When's the last time?" she asked.

"Huh?"

"The last time you had a woman."

"Never yet," he said.

"You think you might be ready for me to sit on your lap?"

On that day, September 17, 1992, Tom Exit lost his virginity, was arrested in prison, and, ultimately, earned another eleven years of jail time. He found out later that Carellia had a brother in Rikers and that he started getting preferential treatment after his sister's visit to Tom and Tom's subsequent arrest for receiving contraband.

Maybe she set me up, Tom reasoned, but he couldn't help but feel grateful to the first woman that had ever loved him for real.

Tom stabbed Billy Biggs four days after the three-day trial that increased the length of his captivity by more than a decade. Billy had his men beat him three days in a row for failing to bring in the drugs.

The day of the attempted murder Tom had been talking to a new con named Jeff Fartheran. Jeff was white and had done many stints in New York state prisons as well as elsewhere.

"They give you two black eyes, huh, brother-man?" Jeff said. He and Tom were loitering in the recreation room waiting for a turn at the ping-pong table.

"They say they gonna beat on me every day until I finally die," Tom mourned.

Fartheran was of that select species of convict who believed in justice. He never complained about being arrested or convicted, sent to prison or even taking a beating if he deserved it. But Jeff could not brook an attack on a man when that man had done nothing wrong.

After Tom explained his circumstances Jeff shook his hand, passing the young prisoner a shard of sharpened metal that had a cardboard haft bound to it with dark green nylon twine.

Tom left Jeff, going out into the yard where he saw Billy and ran at him. It wasn't until sometime later he realized that the exceptionally short blade was meant for slashing and not stabbing. Tom knifed the cell-block boss thirty-two times without inflicting any serious damage when he could have cut Biggs's throat with a single swipe.

In the end he was happy that he hadn't killed Billy. He didn't think of himself as a killer. He didn't think of himself as a convict either but there he was.

★ ★ ★

This trial lasted longer. They kept Tom in a cell inside the courthouse in Brooklyn. There he glanced through picture magazines and started drawing mob scenes populated by dozens of stick-figure men. By the fifth week he had been found guilty. The last trial date was to be held on Friday of the seventh week. He wasn't really worried about the sentence, figuring that Billy and his friends would kill him long before he had any possibility of parole.

That Friday morning he was mildly surprised to see a man instead of the public defender, Charlotte Hampstead, sitting at the defense table. He shuffled up to the white man because he was chained, hand to foot.

"Art Cohen," the new lawyer said, patting Tom's shoulder. He wore a herringbone jacket, loud yellow pants, and a black shirt decorated by intersecting silvery white-line circles. He also sported an extraordinarily bushy mustache.

"Tom," Tom said. "Tom Exit."

"That's an odd name. I never heard it before."

"My great great great great grandfather exscaped in the Underground Railroad and took the name Exit because that's what he did from slavery."

"Well we're gonna try and get you on that train, my friend."

"What happened to Charlotte?" Tom asked.

"She had a heavy load and I've been following your case. Now that they found you guilty I thought I might try something. You game?"

"Uh. Okay...I guess."

The court was called to order and the judge, Vivian Mars, entered.

"Mr. Cohen," she said as she lowered into her chair, "what has you slumming with us today?"

"Justice is deserved by everyone, Your Honor."

"Justice is about to sentence your client."

"I understand that, Judge. My client has been found guilty but I believe that before he is sentenced I should bring a few extenuating circumstances to your attention."

"The trial is over, Art," Vivian Mars said.

"We do not dispute the guilty verdict but only wish to tell a brief story about how Tom Exit came to be here."

"How long will this story take?"

"Twelve minutes from start to finish. I timed it while trimming my mustache this morning."

"Go on then."

Art Cohen told about Tom's first arrest and conviction following up with the later convictions that now had him teetering on the brink of a life sentence.

"Tom Exit is standing before you today for no reason other than the fact that he believed a woman was being assaulted by two men," Cohen concluded. "Those detectives manhandling the woman were in plain clothes. His mother presented documents provided by a social worker that explained the young man's actions but the judge refused to allow them."

"I can feel the passion, Mr. Cohen," the judge said, "but Mr. Exit received fair trials in each incidence."

The sound of Mars's voice was somewhat sad, Tom thought.

"Not exactly," the flashy lawyer replied. "Because of the evidence that was suppressed Mr. Exit has never been given the proper psychological testing. The rush to judgment in every trial never took into account the prisoner's inability to deal with the world—untreated."

So on a rainy day in April Tom Exit was transferred from the Brooklyn courthouse to a minimum-security hospital where people suspected or convicted of crimes were examined, tested, and found either crazy or sane.

The facility was called Lorraine; just the name with no other adjective or appellation. It had four floors, a small, maze-like flower garden, good food with plastic cutlery, and real lighting—not that fluorescent bullshit they used in prison.

The second floor was for testing, interviews, group therapy, and one-on-one psychological analysis. The third floor contained the barracks where the women stayed in the corridor that went to the right while the men occupied the opposite side. The fourth floor was one big recreation room where the patients sat and spoke and sometimes smoked on a fairly large outside deck attached to the rec-area.

It was on the first afternoon on that very deck where Tom met Calhoun Dieterman. Calhoun was a biracial man born of a Black soldier and a white German man in Frankfurt. Calhoun and Tom hit it off right away because Art Cohen had given Tom three packs of unfiltered cigarettes before putting his client on the prison bus to Lorraine.

"Use these like you would money," Art had told Tom and Tom gave a pack to Calhoun when he asked for a cigarette.

"But if you waitin' for judgment on attempted murder then why they send you to minimum security?" the German-American asked his friend after the first group therapy meeting they both attended.

"My lawyer," Tom said. "He told how I attacked the head of a gang but it was because him and his friends beat me almost every day. He had infirmary records and the judge took pity on me."

"You lucky to have a lawyer like that. You rich or sumpin'?"

"Naw. It was just a lucky break, I guess."

A few weeks later Tom and Calhoun were in the flower garden looking into one of the therapist's windows because Calhoun knew that on Tuesdays at 4:45 in the afternoon Milla Thymeman visited with her therapist Morton Rawls. The doctor and patient never took off their clothes but they were vigorous in their athletics and now and then let slip the sight of a nipple or erect penis.

Only Calhoun knew about this regular assignation and he'd never told anyone other than Tom. The young men watched for a few minutes and then Tom began to rub himself. Calhoun joined in and soon they were both balls-out masturbating. That didn't last long and so the two wandered away from the high rosebushes where they could see without being seen.

"How come they got you in here?" Tom asked Calhoun when they were sitting on a heavy cast-iron bench which was painted pink and bolted to the concrete path that wound through the gardens.

"They think that there's a, a what they call a chemical imbalance in my brain that gets in the way of me being able to say no."

"You can't say no and that's why you in jail?"

"If my brain is tuned to that radio station and somebody ask me to help them move a bed, suck somebody dick, or rob some store I say, yeah."

"Even if you don't wanna do what they ask you?"

"I cain't explain it," Calhoun said. "They cain't neither, not really, but when you got a MD and a PhD and things like that people got to listen 'cause they know that they don't know."

"So nobody knows what's wrong with you?" Tom Exit asked his new friend.

"You ever think about Detroit?" Calhoun replied. He was well-known for changing the subject midconversation. That was one of the things Tom liked about him.

"Not really. I mean I know it's a city or maybe a state but probably not a state because I know all them. But anyway, I don't know nobody from there."

"Well," Calhoun said. "In Detroit, down on Tyler Street in Forest Park there's a, there's a real old buildin' called Miller's Mine—"

"Like a gold mine?"

"Like a diggin' in the ground kinda mine."

"Oh," Tom said, nodding his head though he didn't really understand.

"You got any talents?" Calhoun asked.

"What do you mean?"

"Can you do anything useful that most other people can't do?"

"Like what?"

"My buddy, Sharkie, used to have a girlfriend who had a brother and he lived at the Mine. Sharkie told me that there was a guy there called Gary Goodman," Calhoun said. "He forty-something and built like a brick shithouse. Gary stand behind the front door of the mine. He so strong that nobody, not even a professional football player could push past him."

"What if that somebody got a gun or a knife?" Tom asked Calhoun. It was a common question on Rikers when discussing superior strength, martial arts, or a big brain.

"Penta," Calhoun responded. "Penta Lively. Half Mexican half Black chick from Texas could shoot any gun or throw any blade an' hit the target just like she was reachin' out across to you with her fingertip. Her father was a hunter an' taught her everything he knew."

Tom thought that these were indeed good talents, especially if used together. Then he thought that he didn't have anything like that in his *bag of tricks*.

Tom's uncle, George Finez, would always ask his nephew, "What you got in your bag of tricks today, TE?"

Tom managed to most often have a pebble or some other found object in his back pocket to show Uncle George because if he had anything he would receive a quarter.

Calhoun was still talking but Tom had been distracted by the thought of his favorite uncle, who died of diabetes when Tom was almost fifteen.

"...and so if you use that door and can remember the name Miller's Mine on Tyler Street in Detroit you might just be able to do it," Calhoun was saying.

"Huh?" Tom said.

Calhoun grinned because he knew that Tom wasn't listening.

He knew and he was playing with him. Tom always thought that Calhoun had been a good friend.

"Hey, you two," the guard, Hardy Moore, called from one of the aisles of roses.

That call meant it was time to leave the garden and go in for dinner.

The dining room was large and usually pretty calm. Most of the eighty-two inmate/residents were medicated because of their possible conditions; and most of these were non-violent offenders. Tom was one of the rare exceptions. His doctor, Ferral Ericson, a psychiatrist from Denmark, was interested in his initial retention scores and wanted him free from chemical intervention until his testing could be completed.

Tom and Calhoun were sitting at opposite ends, and on opposite sides of the long dining table. It was a men's table and calm. A few of the patients babbled to themselves. Felix Todd was whispering jokes to no one then laughing quietly at them. Meat loaf, mashed potatoes, and wax beans were served and a window was open. Tom could feel the breeze on the back of his neck.

...there's a door behind the dark red rosebush like these ones here, Tom remembered Calhoun saying. He knew with recollecting that phrase that sooner or later he could put together every word Calhoun had said.

Thinking of his friend Tom looked up and saw it coming.

Big Bo Thigman from East St. Louis was walking with purpose toward their table. Bo's fists were clenched and his eyes set on Calhoun. Bo was big and brick colored and bald. His last name, Thigman, Tom thought, was something like his strong thick arms. When Tom told Calhoun what he thought about Bo's name and strength Calhoun began to call Bo "Thickman" as a kind of joke.

Bo, whose mental illness was a bad temper, was not amused.

Tom could see that the big man from East St. Louis intended to hurt his friend the same way Tom meant to hurt Billy Biggs.

That day stayed in Tom's mind for the rest of his life because it was the only time he experienced slow motion like in the movies. He put his left hand on Mills Tormé's right shoulder and pushed up until he was standing in the middle of the table. Then he ran to the opposite end just as Bo Thigman grabbed Calhoun's head with both hands. Tom leaped and, slipping on a mashed potatoes and gravy plate, went flying though the air at Bo. He heard, or thought he heard Calhoun's neck breaking just as he grabbed Bo by the left arm, pulling him away from the table and down to the floor.

The fight continued there but the security guards were already on them and so pulled Big Bo off of Tom.

By that time Calhoun was already dead.

2.

Calhoun's death stayed on Tom's mind like the crucifix, he thought, that was always in his paternal grandmother's, Ruth's thoughts.

"Jesus loved us so much that he died for us," Ruth would say. "I remember that every day."

"And what was in your mind when you jumped up on the table and started running?" Ferral Ericson, the forty-seven-year-old Scandinavian psychiatrist, asked. She had brown-and-gray hair with a face that Tom thought of as *sharp*.

"Um…" Tom said. "I, uh, was moving real slow."

"I don't understand what you mean," the doctor primed.

Outside the window there was a hummingbird darting from flower to flower. Tom loved birds, especially hummingbirds. Mrs. Crandel in tenth-grade remedial English had said that those birds were a *Met For*, something like that, hummingbirds and somehow that meant he wanted to be free like his ex-slave many-times-great grandsire that came up with his family name.

"It was like I was in a dream one time and this giant was chasing me and I was running but I couldn't get nowhere."

"Like slow motion on television?" Ericson suggested.

"Yeah," Tom said. He was listening to the doctor but he was thinking about something that he couldn't remember about the fast-winged bird.

"You felt that you couldn't get to your friend in time to save him," Ericson interpreted.

Turning to her Tom replied, "It's like that hummingbird. She's faster than anything but sometimes she's just stuck in place."

"You loved your friend," she said.

In prison you never said that you loved anybody but Jesus or your mother; that was more or less a hard-and-fast rule. Tom had been raped and forced to do other things dozens of times but no one ever told him they loved him.

They hurt him, they spit on him, they beat him like a dog but no one ever loved him, no one except for maybe…

"What do you think about that little bird?" Ericson said.

"That she loves red roses and that they like her too."

Dr. Ericson advised the guards at Lorraine that Tom was not a threat and he could be released from lockdown.

The next afternoon he went to the dark red rosebush and, when nobody else was looking he climbed in behind it coming to find the old, corroded copper door that Calhoun promised was there.

"If you make it through that door you could be free," Calhoun had said when Tom was thinking about his uncle. "And if you're free you could go to Detroit and find Miller's Mine. I'm gonna do that one day. You better believe it too."

Tom didn't want to leave Lorraine but Calhoun was his friend and he seemed to be telling him to run away for him; to run like he couldn't do on that table.

"Dr. Jericho," Tom said. He'd asked for a meeting with the director of Lorraine two weeks before.

"Mr. Exit," George Jericho acknowledged. "Please have a seat."

It was a big office with dark brown bookcases and hundreds of books. Tom liked books. He couldn't read hardly at all but some of the best times in his life were spent listening to books being read out loud.

"How have you been?" Jericho asked.

Sunlight from the large window seemed to be spilling across the director's desk. The shadows of windblown leaves made the green blotter look like a flowing stream.

"C-can I stay here, Doctor?" Tom asked.

"I don't know what you mean exactly."

"This is like the best place I've ever been in my life. When I was a kid in school the other kids all picked on me. And when I left school and got jobs I always got fired. Then in prison people did awful things and my mother hardly ever came and I'd always be in trouble even if I was just protectin' myself."

Jericho's skin was nearly paper white. He had a bald head and kind eyes behind rectangular-lensed glasses.

"No one ever showed you kindness," the director asked.

"Only my uncle George Finez but he died," Tom said. "And, and, and…"

"And what?"

"There was a Patricia Neil. I saved her from the cops and, and she said that she was my friend forever. Mine. But I'm in jail and she isn't and Lorraine is the best place I ever known."

"And so you want to stay here at Lorraine?" the doctor-director asked.

"Uh-huh. I'm really sorry about Calhoun gettin' killed and I feel bad that I couldn't save him. But instead of sending me to court and more prison you figured out that I was tryin' to do the right thing and didn't punish me."

A gentle smile on his lips the director said, "So you want to stay because it feels like a place you can live in harmony."

"I think so."

Peering through the glistening lenses Dr. Jericho smiled and looked sad at the same time.

"Part of the problem," Jericho said, "is that this place so fits your mood that it's hard to find that moment where you lose control. When you jumped up on the table to try and save your friend that was an example of your response to stimuli but no one would call trying to save a life aberrant."

"So you're gonna send me back to prison?" Tom Exit asked.

"Most probably. But Dr. Ericson and others feel that you have an innate ability to decipher information that forms your responses in a way you cannot control. It will take at least another five months of study to come to an understanding of this process."

"Most probably." Tom repeated the phrase as if it were a life sentence handed down from the court.

After his meeting with Dr. Jericho Tom visited the corroded copper door every chance he got. He took an awl from the leather-working workshop and used it to excavate around the lock. He enjoyed this work and did it diligently all the while thinking of his friend Calhoun.

"And so what did your uncle George say again?" Ferral Ericson asked Tom. It was a brilliant Saturday and most of the patients were off to nearby Lake Amedne for what they called the Lorraine Spring Picnic.

"He, um," Tom said. "He, um, said that this bright shiny green bug called the, called the cicada takes seventeen years or maybe thirteen sometimes to turn from a nip, a nip-m to a insect. They been around forty-seven million years and mostly live under the ground. Uncle George really liked bugs an' he liked to read about 'em."

"How long ago did he tell you about the cicada?"

"It was on July seventeen when I was stayin' with him an' his girlfriend Melba in St. George on Staten Island. I remember because it was funny that he was livin' in a place that had his name."

"And how old were you then?"

"I was, was seven. That was the year my mother and father broke up and she went home to her mother because she was so sad."

The Scandinavian psychiatrist spent the next few minutes reading a document while Tom stared out the window at the dark red rosebush that hid the old copper door.

"What you readin', Dr. Ericson?" Tom asked when looking at the rosebush began to make him nervous.

The woman looked up at Tom with soft, faded brown eyes.

"Your talent for verbal and mental retention is truly amazing," she said, a sense of awe in her voice. "In the past four weeks you have told me nineteen stories about things you learned, your family, and your experiences. Every description has been specific and when I ask you about them days later you remember it all word for word."

"Uh-huh. Does that mean that there's somethin' wrong with me?" Tom asked hopefully.

"Just the opposite," Ericson said. "Your mind is like a computer, taking data in and storing it perfectly. And what's more you don't remember this information until three to fourteen days after hearing it. It's like you have a built-in buffer that filters what you know before cataloging it."

"Mama used to ask me where things was that maybe she lost and I always knew. She used to say I was like a fortune-teller only I wasn't because I couldn't see the future."

"Your mind is truly amazing," the doctor said. "I've never seen anything like it."

"But I'm not sick?" Tom asked. "I still have to go back to Rikers?"

"We have to follow the rules as they exist," Ferral said. "And though your ability is extraordinary it cannot be classified as a disorder."

"But couldn't you just say that it is? You know, that the way I think makes me do things I don't know about or sumpin'?"

"No, Mr. Exit," she said. "No. Whenever we recommend that a patient be institutionalized the state demands corroboration."

"Huh?"

"They make you see other doctors to get their opinion."

"So you would get in trouble?"

"Yes, but the real problem is that you would be sent back into prison anyway."

Something like a red fog rose up in Tom's mind. He remembered then that the same mist appeared up when he beat the nurse-intern Bernard Walters and when he stabbed Billy Biggs. Tom felt lost and afraid at that moment. He remembered the years of being beaten and abused and made fun of by guards and prisoners. Even worse than those moments of pain and humiliation were the sounds in the night of men crying and hurting, screaming and begging. He was angry but there was no one to hit or stab. Dr. Ericson felt as bad as he did. And, like she said, she couldn't help it that his *talent for verbal and mental retention* wasn't a sickness.

Those few seconds in time, when the red fog mixed in with a memory of words, Tom felt something he'd never experienced before. He had a problem and the answer was in his mind. He knew how to maybe keep from going back to prison. He remembered what his good friend Calhoun Dieterman was saying about the copper door, the Mine in Detroit, and having, having...

"So my remembering things is a talent?" he asked the doctor.

"Yes," she said, "and something much, much more."

"You know what they gonna do to me if I go back to prison," Tom said. "Right?"

After a moment hesitating Ferral said, "Yes."

"And that's wrong, right?"

"Yes it is."

"So if I didn't go then it would be better than if I did," Tom Exit concluded.

"Yes. But why are you saying all this?"

"Can you give me a pass to make a telephone call, Doctor Ericson?"

3.

Sixteen days after a phone call to the Bronx, somewhere between 1:00 and 2:00 a.m., early on that Wednesday morning, Tom Exit slipped out of the third-floor window of the men's dormitory and shimmied down the ivy vines, slipping and sliding until he finally fell to the lawn below. From there he went to the dark red rosebush and finished the excavation of the locking mechanism securing the copper door. He pulled on the door grasping the hole where the lock had been and pulled with all his might. At first the portal did not budge. This was not part of Tom's plan. The door was supposed to open; that's what Calhoun had said. There was an odd animal sound in the air. It took Tom a minute before he realized that the sound was his own whimpering from the fear of failure, the dread of being sent back to prison. At that moment the red mist rose in his mind and he pulled as hard as he could for what felt like a very long time.

When the ancient hinges of the copper door gave they whined and groaned and a loud popping sound came from the breaking hinges.

"Who's there?" shouted Delmont Trextin, the nighttime guard at Lorraine.

Tom heard the late-night sentinel's fast footsteps coming toward the red bush and copper door. He slipped through the narrow space to the outside. There he found that he was on a steep hill dense with bushes.

He loped down the incline allowing the thick barrier of vines and branches to keep him from falling.

"Stop!" Delmont Trextin cried from somewhere above.

"I hear him down this way!" another man, whose voice Tom did not recognize, called out.

Tom ran faster, pressed harder against the wall of leaves and branches. Now and again he saw bright lights flashing through the foliage behind him. Other voices sounded. They were getting closer.

Then Tom broke through the thick hedges and went flying down the slope. He tumbled and fell down the hill that led up to Lorraine. His right ankle hurt and his hands stung from where dirt caked in them but he didn't care about the pain. Rising to his feet at the bottom of the hill he fell because his right foot couldn't support him. So then he crawled toward where he thought the road might be.

"He's down there!" a voice cried from up above. "We got him!"

Tom wanted to cry but he held back the tears in hopes that all was not lost.

"Tom!" she cried. "Tom!"

A moment later he felt her arms encircle him. He smelled the mild sweetness of the perfume she wore when she visited him in jail.

"Patricia," he gulped.

"Come on, baby," she said. "My car is just down here."

For the rest of his life Tom Exit remembered the acceleration of Patricia Neil's used Ford as he watched the electric torches of four guards, felt the agony of his swelling ankle, and the joy in his heart of finally being free.

"What did you say, baby?" Patricia Neil asked him as they turned onto the throughway going east.

"I will die before I go back there. I will die before that."

4.

Patricia brought Tom a change of clothes and old brown shoes that were a little tight, especially on his swollen right foot. She took him to a little motel outside of Syracuse. There he bathed and then luxuriated on one of the two single beds.

The emergency room doctor treated his cut hands, broken ankle, and the abrasions from the branches and thorns on his skin. Patricia explained to the admitting nurse that they had gone camping but then heard a growling they thought had to be a bear and ran down the hill.

"Tom went first," she explained to the medical receptionist, "and so he cleared a path for me."

He was lying in his bed half-asleep and happy that he was free for the first time in so long. Then he felt a weight next to him and hands—one on his chest and the other groping around between his legs.

"Does that feel good?" Patricia whispered.

"Uh-huh."

"When was your last time?"

"With your friend Carellia."

Patricia's grip on Tom's penis tightened and he moaned.

"Are you mad at Carry?" she asked.

"N-n-no."

"But why not? She tricked you."

"I, um, I, um, I...that was my first time so in a way I kinda, kinda loved her."

Patricia started pulling both softly and quickly on Tom's erection.

She pressed her lips next to his ear and whispered, "This feel good?"

"Uh-huh, yeah, uh-huh..."

"I'ma do it till almost and then I'm gonna stop and then I'ma do it again and again until you can't hold back."

"How, how come?"

"Because when you finally can't stand no more you'll relax and sleep good."

Halfway across the northern border of Ohio Patricia asked Tom, "So you don't hate Carellia because she fucked you?"

"I'm really shy around girls. I mean I really like the way they look and smell and smile and stuff. I like how nice they are but that makes me all the more scared."

"You scared of a girl?" Patricia said.

"How come you helped me get outta Lorraine?" Tom asked, using Calhoun's technique of changing the subject.

"You saved my ass from them cops," she said. "You been in prison for years because'a me. First because you stopped them cops from searchin' me and then because Carellia did you like she did."

"That was so great last night," Tom Exit said.

"It was like you hadn't come in a month'a Sundays."

"Does that mean you're my girlfriend now?"

"Uh-uh, baby. We just friends. I'ma let you off wherever it is you wanna be in Detroit and then I'm goin' back to the Bronx. You know my old man, Nathaniel, spects me back day after to-morrow."

"Was he mad that you came to help me?"

"I didn't tell him," she said. "That wasn't none'a his business."

"But what did he say when I called?"

"I told him that you needed some money in your canteen ac-count and I owed you that for savin' me."

"And what he say...?"

"Stop askin' me questions, Tom," Patricia Neil commanded. "I'm here, baby. That's all you have to know."

5.

After crossing the Michigan border they passed through Monroe and Dearborn, finally entering Detroit. It was a city of freeways and shattered streets; people that walked with a kind of dignity that convicts only pretended to in prison. There were a lot of Black and brown people and to Tom it seemed like another time like when in a television show people go through some kind of *energy door* that puts them in the past. He smiled at the thought of having slipped into yesterday.

"Nobody could find me if I wasn't even there no more."

"What did you say?" Patricia Neil, his best friend ever, asked.

"Nuthin'," Tom said for fear of breaking the spell.

"It's like a war zone," Patricia said when they finally made their way into the Forest Park neighborhood.

Whole blocks had been demolished and people moved around furtively behind rubble and into houses that looked as if they were soon to be gone.

"You think there's soldiers?" Tom asked, looking fearfully out of the passenger's side window.

"The soldiers done come and gone, looks like," Patricia said. "You sure you want me to leave you here?"

They were stopped at a traffic light that was turned green but there were no cars behind them. Both sides of the road had once been rows of small houses that were now just remnants of concrete foundations, stagnant ponds filling open cellars. Sapling trees and man-high wild weeds had taken ownership of the fertile devastation.

From behind the beginnings of a neighborhood forest a tall man emerged. He was walking straight for their car.

"We better get outta here," Patricia said. But before she could step on the gas the man reached the road.

He was tall and jet-black, maybe forty and strong from a life lived by his body alone. He had dreads, a straggly beard and wore only a loincloth that had once been white.

"Oh my God," Patricia uttered.

Tom noticed that her nostrils flared.

The man walked up to the passenger's side window. A wild smell assailed Tom's nose. It wasn't a bad odor but different than any scent he'd experienced coming from a man.

"Do you know where Miller's Mine is?" Tom asked. These were the only words he had.

"On Tyler Street."

Both Tom and the wild man seemed surprised by the exchange, as if words were a step down on the evolutionary ladder, unworthy of the grace that they had attained.

"We don't know where that is," Patricia said.

"Just keep on goin' the way that you goin' and you'll be there. It's a blue house on the corner and then you turn right for three."

"Three houses?" Tom asked.

The wild man nodded and then asked, "She yours?"

"She's my best friend."

At that the tall Black man leaned down and peered through Tom's window at Patricia.

"If you at Miller's I'll see you one day soon," he said. It came across like a promise. Patricia actually gasped.

"That man looked like a god come straight outta Africa," Patricia said when they were pulling up to the curb in front of their ramshackle destination.

"This is it," Tom said.

Miller's Mine was a big rambling building constructed solely from weathered wood that the paint had peeled from long ago. It was four stories and defied economic description. It might have been a mansion or apartments, an early twentieth-century factory of some sort or maybe even a hotel. But now its shattered windows and broken doors, a roof that had half blown off transformed the structure into the skeleton of a creature both extinct and nameless.

"How can you tell this is the right place?" Patricia asked.

"Calhoun described it. I wasn't listenin' at the time but after a while I remembered what he said. We go through the front door and walk all the way to the back. Then there's a basement door and steps that aren't very steady. You have to hold on to the rails but then, when you get three levels down there's a wall that was painted blue maybe ten years ago. You knock on that wall and shout out, 'Miller's Mine' while you do it and sooner or later somebody will answer."

"This is crazy," Patricia said. "I'm not goin'."

"Okay." Tom opened his door, more sure than he had ever been that he was doing the right thing.

"Tommy," Patricia Neil whined.

"What?"

"Nathaniel don't know I'm here. I didn't tell'im I was leavin' so I cain't go back there."

"But you said you were gonna leave me here."

"I was. But I'm scared. I thought I could go stay with Carellia in DC but Nate knows her and he's hella jealous."

"But why? Why would you take such a big chance if you were gonna get in so much trouble?" Tom didn't intend for his question to be mean but Patricia winced and looked like she was about to cry.

"Because when you were on trial I watched you and you seemed all right. You helped me and you still just sat there... ready to go where you had to for what you did. You're my best friend."

"But not your boyfriend?"

"Uh-uh. No. Never."

The subbasement was lit by maybe a dozen sixty-watt bulbs placed at no place in particular. The blue door was really just a wall. There were oil-stained planks, thick pine pillars, and a few holes that opened onto darkness. Tom banged his fist on the wall and yelled out, "Miller's Mine."

"We should go back," Patricia said. "You know I almost fell through those steps."

"Miller's Mine!" Tom yelled and then he kicked the wall.

"There ain't nobody there, Tommy."

"There's got to be. Calhoun said so."

"Maybe he was wrong."

"He was right about the rosebush and the door. He was right about the name. The naked man knew where it was. We here, Patricia. They got to be too."

"What the fuck you want!" a man shouted.

The voice came from behind them.

Patricia turned quickly, shoving a hand into her bright yellow calfskin purse.

Tom turned, twisting his ankles together and fell to the dusty, debris-strewn floor of the subbasement. When he looked up he saw a huge man of burnished skin, swollen with muscle and expressive of rage. A few steps behind him stood a petite, raspberry-brown young woman holding a long slender knife by the tip of its blade.

"That hand better come out empty, bitch," the woman said. "Cause if I see even a tissue with it you gonna have this here blade in yo' th'oat."

Tom scrambled to his feet.

"Gary Goodman and Penta Lively, right?" he said.

The angry man's face took on a stunned expression.

"And what's your name, Stumblefoot?" Penta asked, keeping her eyes on Patricia.

"I'm Tom. Tom Exit. My great great great great grandfather was a slave who excaped on the Underground Railroad and named hisself Exit because that's what he did from slavery."

The muscleman smiled slightly.

"What you doin' way down here, Stumblefoot Exit?" he asked.

Tom managed to stand up straight and tell everything from the time he fought with the police over Patricia to his escape from Lorraine.

"...I wanted to stay there but they had to send me back to prison," Tom said toward the end of his dialogue, "so I came here because my friend Calhoun said so."

What surprised Tom was that the sentinels of Miller's Mine listened to his whole story without complaint or derision. Usually people got upset with his long tales filled with details that meant nothing—to them.

"Where is this Calhoun?" Goodman asked.

"He got killed by a dude name of Big Bo Thigman. Big Bo was okay but he couldn't take a joke."

"We lost our comedian," Penta said. She was wearing a rainbow-colored dress that only came down over the middle of her powerful thighs. "Simtek was arrested for shoplifting and they got him on an old assault and battery charge."

"Why you here?" Gary Goodman asked.

"I wanna live here," Tom said. "Calhoun said that you might take me in."

"We never heard of no comedian name of Calhoun," Penta said. She took a step forward and it seemed to Tom that her eyes were the color of the kind of rainbow that appears in oil slicks. It wasn't until weeks later that he learned she wore rainbow-colored contact lenses.

"He told me that the only people they let in Miller's Mine had to have a talent that they could use down here. He said that he bet that I had what you wanted and that I should come ask."

"Did he tell you what we do with people who don't have what we need?"

"That you kill 'em and th'ow 'em in a lime pit under a lake they call Green Acres."

"What!" Patricia exclaimed. She turned to run but Gary, moving deceptively fast, caught her by the arm.

"Mothafuckah, let me go! Fuck you! Fuck you!"

Tom felt bad that his friend was so upset. He wasn't worried, just sad that she was so scared.

The Blue Door Guardians took Tom and Patricia down a long tunnel that led deeper and deeper into the soil beneath Detroit. For the first half hour or so Patricia shouted and screamed and tried to pull away. But after that she allowed them to drag her along.

There were electric lights here and there in the long tunnel. In places the passway bulged out to accommodate living quarters. They went by jury-rigged homes made from metal and bamboo, plastic containers, and boxes from all kinds of materials. There was even a home that looked like a castle fabricated from discarded car and truck tires. It was here that their journey came to an end.

"Go on in," Penta said. "Lamarelle in there with her seer—Blind Bob."

"This is crazy," Patricia said but she followed Tom beyond the pillars of tires.

There was no door to the used tire castle. It was a maze of pillars stacked as far as twelve feet high. Gary and Penta followed Tom and Patricia until they came to a large empty space where a beautiful woman of maybe fifty years sat behind a desk fashioned from the dashboard of an old American car. She had blond hair, fair skin, and wore a coral-colored T-shirt. When Tom and Patricia entered the largish space, she smiled.

"Hello. I am Lamarelle."

"Do you run this place?" Patricia asked. "Because you know I'm not even supposed to be here. I just gave Tom a ride and I got to be goin'."

Lamarelle studied Patricia for maybe ten seconds, then turned her attention to Tom.

"You seek refuge?" she asked.

"I want to live here," Tom said. "My friend told me I did before he died."

"And what is this friend's name?"

"Calhoun Dieterman."

"I don't know that name."

"But he told me to come here. He was planning to come himself but then he got killed."

"You realize that we are a secret place," Lamarelle said. "That we cannot let you out of here unless you become a part of us."

"So you gonna kill us?" Patricia cried.

"Bob," Lamarelle called.

From behind a double pillar of deep-tread tires came a man of maybe thirty years who wore a ruby-colored sarong and a silk, a soiled blue T-shirt, and an emerald-hued turban. A blind man in comfortable surroundings, he moved with confidence.

"Come forward, Tom Exit," Lamarelle offered kindly. "You can use that stack of tires to sit upon."

Tom sat staring into the corn-blue eyes of Lamarelle. Blind Bob sat between them.

"Do you have a talent useful for Miller's Mine?" the woman asked.

"If you tell me something, anything—I will remember it starting about fifteen days or so after I hear it. It doesn't matter what was said, I don't have to understand but I will remember exactly. And I never forget."

"What about what you've read?" Lamarelle asked.

"Maybe if I could read I would remember but I don't read too good and so that don't work too well."

A moment passed then Lamarelle said, "Bob?"

The blind man held his palms up and shrugged.

"Who is that guy?" Patricia asked.

"Be quiet, woman," Penta said.

"No," Lamarelle told the markswoman. Then to Patricia, "In most situations Bob can tell when a lie has been told. He says that there's a pulse in every word a person says and in that pulse is the barometer of truth."

"Is he ever wrong?" Tom asked. "'Cause you know I'm nervous but I'm not lyin'.'"

"He can't read you at all," Lamarelle said with a sad smile on her lips. "You confuse him."

"Then why don't you just ask 'im yourself?" Patricia said. "Why don't you just ask Tom?"

Lamarelle laughed and then stood up from the dashboard desk. Her coral T-shirt came down to the tops of her thighs and Tom could tell that she was pregnant. The bewilderment showed on the escaped convict's face.

"You think I'm too old to bear a child?" Lamarelle asked.

"Um."

"I have come to term twenty-one times in my life. All of those pregnancies have resulted in either twins or triplets—all except one."

"That's crazy," Patricia said.

"It is my talent," Lamarelle corrected. "Everyone here in Miller's Mine has something to offer; a talent that they were either born with or that they have learned."

"Do you know what the babies in your belly can do?" Patricia asked, unable to keep the sneer from her mouth.

Lamarelle laughed again and then said, "They will be educated by the people of the mine. They will be of us."

"Why havin' babies is a talent?" Tom asked.

"Twins and triplets often have unexplainable connections. They know each other better than most people can know one another. This knowledge, this connection makes them treasures amid the devastation of our world.

"This is our mission—to create a place of wonder built upon

the bones and minds, the souls and the magic that make us as rich as any millionaire or president, as powerful as any queen or army."

"Are you the leader here?" Tom asked.

"No. We have no single leader. There is the council of fourteen and the general elections."

For a moment there Lamarelle and Blind Bob, Gary and Penta, Tom and leery Patricia remained silent in the car tire palace.

"Tell me the history of the United States of America," the pregnant not-leader of Miller's Mine asked of Tom.

The request entered Exit's mind like a living thing, a fish or burrowing insect, a lightbulb illuminating some forgotten memory, memories. First came his second-grade teacher, Mrs. Reynolds, making all the kids learn the states in alphabetical order and the capitals of each state. Mr. Garner in eighth-grade Civics told about the structure of Congress, the Supreme Court, and the president who oversaw what he called the executive branch. There were dozens of teachers, relatives, TV shows, and radio programs—all of which held part of the answer to Lamarelle's request.

Tom was no longer underground, no longer in a room full of friends and strangers. He couldn't smell the rubber of the tires or see the motes of dust dancing in the electrical light.

For maybe a quarter of an hour the young man who had been abandoned by the schools, the government, the legal system, his own mother, and most everyone except for Patricia—who would never be his girlfriend—for that quarter of an hour he felt an ecstasy of organization, bringing every thought about the United States and its history into alignment.

When finally everything felt more or less in order he began to speak.

"To understand the history of the New World," he said, parroting Miss Chin, his eleventh-grade history teacher, "you must go all the way back to when Asia and North America were closer than they are now and the ocean between them froze sometimes and the Asians came and discovered a place that no human had ever seen before…"

He spoke for hours. During that time people wandered in and took up seats where they could listen to the lecture of a lifetime of study that Tom had never been aware of. The Louisiana Purchase and the Dredd Scott case, Thomas Jefferson and his slaves, slaves and their masters, the Civil War, and the War of 1812.

As more and more people came into the palace they began to move the tire-pillars aside so that they could all fit. After a while there were nearly a hundred people from the ages of maybe five to ninety. Some came and listened for a while and then left to be replaced by others. Some stayed the whole time, rapt in the tales where Tom changed his tone of voice to the teacher, announcer, or relative that related that part of the history.

He was in the middle of talking about the Harlem Renaissance when Lamarelle said, "I think that is probably enough for right now, Tom Exit."

The interruption manifested itself as a headache above Tom's eyes. There was so much more that wanted to get out.

"Excuse me," somebody said. It was a man. A white man.

"Uh-huh?" Tom replied. He looked out over the audience amazed at the number of people there.

"You said that the Chinese discovered America but they taught me in school that it was Christopher Columbus and my daddy was a eye-talian and he told me that it was true."

The speaker wore drab clothing and was missing a few teeth. He might have been thirty years old or sixty; Tom couldn't tell. But he recognized the anger in the man's voice.

"I don't know," Tom said.

"You don't know what?" the man asked, his voice rising on the tide of anger.

"I can only say what I remember. I don't know if it's all true.

All I know is what I heard, word for word. The only thing I can tell you is that somebody told me and now I'm tellin' you."

"What good is that?"

"I don't know," Tom said again.

"I have a question," another man said. A deep brown man. He was tall and wore a fancy off-white suit with a navy shirt and a perfectly knotted yellow-and-red tie. There seemed to be a flesh-covered horn, maybe nine inches long, protruding from the questioner's forehead.

"Okay," Tom replied, a little put off by the diabolical appearance of the strange man.

"My name is X and I have earned my place among the Chosen of Miller's Mine because of my particular affinity for evil."

"Uh-huh," Tom said, thinking that it would not take him fifteen days to remember the words this man had to say.

"You're a fountain of information," the horned man allowed. "But there's no way of telling what is truth or what is not. Your trove of knowledge is actually just a repository of misinformation."

"Um," Tom said. "I, uh, don't know what you're sayin'."

"I'm saying that we can't trust you and so you and your girl-friend should be sent to Green Acres."

"Listen, Dick Head," Patricia said. "Maybe you think you all special 'cause you got that bone implant but Tommy didn't come here to tell you a history class. He said what he said and maybe it was true and maybe it wasn't. But that's not what's important."

"No?" X asked, his smile revealing teeth most of which had been festooned with a bright jewel.

"No," Patricia replied. "History we could argue about. We could look it up. We could think about it. But what if Tommy was in a courtroom and the judge said this and the prosecutor said that? What if some witness said sumpin' that nobody re-membered but Tommy? Wouldn't you be glad if he remem-bered the one thing you needed to know? And what if there was some kinda contract or sumpin' he could remember. You know a insurance policy only need one thing wrong for them to turn you down."

"But your friend can't even read," X sneered.

"Cain't you read, Dick Head? All Tommy need is to hear sumpin' once and he know it forever."

The crowd murmured and X frowned.

6.

Miller's Mine was a series of subterranean tunnels that traveled for miles under the city of Detroit. When Tom Exit and Patricia Neil joined what the citizens of Miller's Mine called *the Sovereignty* there was a population of 857 citizens. Of these, 642 were adults or adolescents accepted because of their talents. There were lawyers and cat burglars, therapists and lie detectors, killers and soldiers, seducers and those that could change their voices and appearance so as to fool almost anyone. Miller's Mine had doctors and dentists, undertakers, tacticians, dancers, performers, jugglers, what they called a master librarian, and even a jail. There once was a comedian but he had been captured in the *Upper World*.

Over time the leadership of the Sovereignty had purchased and otherwise acquired houses all over the city. The underground tunnels connected these places so that it would always be easy to escape the nets of The Man.

Tom was accepted because he could attend trials, public speeches, classes, and even hang out around the cops when they were after some member of the Sovereignty. All he had to do was hear something spoken once and he never forgot—after two weeks. They accepted Patricia because she was one of the few people ever to outtalk the Devil, X.

"Why you even have a man like that down here?" Patricia asked Lamarelle a few days after she and Tom moved in.

"Evil is a part of life," the Great Mother replied. "If we don't know evil we are bound to be defeated by it."

★ ★ ★

The naked man that Tom and Patricia met on the way to Miller's Mine was also a member of the Sovereignty. His name was Survivor and he would be their last hope if The System ever got the upper hand. Patricia and Survivor married in the way of the mine and Tom cried for weeks. He still did his job; attending trials and public hearings, talking to librarians and community college teachers. He even learned how to read, after a fashion. But Tom was heartbroken for days and months and years over the loss of Patricia. He refused to talk to her or respond to Survivor. When the council of fourteen ordered him to settle his issues with his friend and her lover Tom replied, "Take me to Green Acres or shut the fuck up."

One night, a few months after Great Mother, Lamarelle, had delivered quadruplets, she and Tom were drinking spirits late at night in her tire palace. In the Upper World there had been instigated an investigation that Tommy and a young woman nicknamed Loga had discovered using his preponderance of knowledge and her ability to make sense of even the most abstract input. Loga and Exit came up with monthly reports identifying the Enemy and its likely moves.

"Dr. Hands told me that I'll never be pregnant again," Lamarelle was saying as she poured the golden-colored liquor that was unique to the Sovereignty into Tom's mug.

"How many kids you had?"

"Sixty-four that survived."

"You almost as bad as Genghis Khan."

"Are you ready for love, my friend?" Lamarelle asked.

"What do you mean?" the ex-con, honey-ant of knowledge asked.

"Patricia."

"I can't talk about that," Tom said. He shifted on his stack of tires as if maybe he was going to get up and walk away.

Lamarelle put a hand on Tom's wrist and said, "We all die.

And the only way to survive death is to forgive and feel and admit love into your heart."

Holding back his tears Tom said, "Patricia was the first ever in my life who was there for me, who stood up for me. I love her. I love her. And she out with Survivor with his big dick and strong arms. It hurts me all the way through my whole life because I know I'm not good enough to be with the woman I love."

"But she's your friend," the Great Mother argued.

"That's not enough."

"I've had twenty-four broods from twenty men," Lamarelle said. "I liked all of them. But the man closest to me is Blind Bob. He reads my heart. He knows my soul."

"But does he want your body along with your heart?" Tom asked.

"Probably, yes."

"Then," Tom said. "If you understood him you would know the pain he suffers every time you call his name."

"But we all have a duty," the Great Mother said. "Our lives are owed to the future."

"Maybe," Tom allowed. "But for a guy like I am love only comes around once."

Three weeks later the Detroit police invaded the Sovereignty. Sixteen citizens were killed. One hundred and forty-eight were arrested. But eleven hundred and seven escaped into the properties bought by the Central Committee of the Sovereignty.

Now aboveground these foreign citizens began to make a political society that could one day control the out-of-control city of Detroit.

Years passed.

Romulus Exodus, nee Tom Exit, personal secretary of Laverne Mamman, sat at his post in her city council office on a Thursday when Patricia Neil appeared.

"Tom Exit!" she exclaimed.

"Not Exit anymore," he said.

"I miss you so much, baby," she said sadly.

Tom Exit heard her, understood what she was saying, believed that her words were true. He thought about his dead father and absentee mother, about prison and the 94 times he was raped. He imagined Patricia coming to see him every week when she was on heroin and then once a month when she was clean. He thought about the seven years underground with the Citizens of the Sovereignty and then the invasion of the Detroit PD.

He thought about Loga, now called Mary Smart, and their children Marcus and Stellar.

"You saved me and then you left me," Tom Exit said. "Can't we just leave it at that?"

Patricia waited a moment before rising.

"Can't you forgive me, Tommy?"

"There's nothing to forgive," he said. "You haven't done anything wrong."

"Then why can't we be friends?"

"Because," Tom said and then paused. "Because I hurt before you came to see me in prison and the pain came back after you were gone."

"Then you'll never be free," she said.

"No," he said. "Probably not."

MISSING ON KAUA'I

TORI ELDRIDGE

Makalani braked for the rooster strutting across the road. The feral chickens ruled the island of Kaua'i with prideful indifference. This one was no exception. Crowned in red and caped in gold, this bird's brilliant teal plumes arched up and over from its rump like a cresting wave. It cocked its head toward Makalani then pecked at the asphalt, twice, before moving on its way.

Hawaiian time.

One of many reasons Makalani had flown the coop before the ink on her high school diploma had dried. She'd been away for ten years, four at the University of Colorado and six more in Los Angeles and Portland, with brief visits sprinkled in between. Not much had changed since she lived at home.

Makalani drove up Highway 56—a generous name for a two-lane road—and passed the offshoot toward the preschool she had attended and the Ko'olau Hui'ila Protestant Church, where her family worshipped.

How long had it been since she prayed in a church? Christmas? Christmas before that? Makalani preferred communing with God on mountain trails and ocean shores. Although, the cozy structure and pastoral setting of the hale pule did inspire peace and community. The best kalua pig she'd ever eaten had come from an imu dug into that sacred earth.

Would someone dig a pit in the rich homestead land for Tutu's birthday celebration?

Makalani gave thanks that someone in her family could. Unlike the Habitat for Humanity homes she was passing now—stilt-foundation structures on barren land—the Department of Hawaiian Home Lands had awarded her grandparents a fertile plot from road to ocean-bound stream. On this land, leased at a dollar a year to natives with a Hawaiian blood quantum of 50 percent or more, her grandparents had built a sprawling home with wings for their children and children's children over the last fifty years.

The pyramid-capped stilt-houses along Highway 56 stood like sentries to the economic poverty of her native people—no crops, no flowers, just bitter grass clutching to hard, red dirt.

Makalani turned away from the sight and onto the narrow road tunneling through a jungle of jacaranda, monkeypod, and banyan. The lush foliage eased her heart and lightened her spirits.

Would Solomon be home?

Of all her cousins, she missed him the most.

She turned onto the dirt road and slowed beside a tree.

"Ho, look what the trade winds blew in," Uncle Eric said, from his beach chair wedged between the roots of a banyan. He slipped off a rubber zori, nudged open the cooler with his foot, and retrieved a fresh can of beer.

Makalani turned off the engine and hung out the open window. "Howzit, Uncle?"

"Eh, Makalani. You back for Tutu's birthday?"

"That's the plan. Solomon around?"

"Nah. Not since yesterday. Try wait, yeah? Bumbai, he come

back." He nodded toward the cooler and scoffed. "If fo' nothin' else, fo' da beer."

Makalani jutted her head in goodbye and restarted the engine. Was her cousin doing as badly as everybody said?

When Makalani had babysat him as a child, he'd been active and bright, scholastically challenged, to be sure, but intelligent all the same. If he'd had better grades in high school, he might have thrived at UH. But without the football scholarship, he couldn't stay. He had blown out his knee during the first season and returned home, canceled scholarship in hand, a failure—just like his "good-for-nothing" father.

Makalani shook her head. She knew better than to buy into family judgment. Still, Solomon's father had less ambition than the breadfruit hanging from Tutu's trees. If not for the apartment built onto the far wing of her house, he and Auntie Kaulana would be living under a hala tree on the beach.

Makalani continued down the road through the family's grove. Before her Hawaiian-Chinese grandfather had passed away, he had cultivated a wide variety of fruit and nut-bearing trees—breadfruit, mango, papaya, banana, avocado, macadamia nut, even a mountain apple—enough to sustain the family with surplus to sell. Other fruits and vegetables grew in plots closer to the house with a sizable taro patch near the stream. All of this, combined with the pigs, chickens, and okolehau fermenting behind the farming shed, made the Pahukula family nearly self-sustaining. Everything else they needed they either bartered for or bought with the proceeds from their homesteading crops. The biggest challenge was labor.

Would that change now that Solomon had returned home?

Her beefy cousin would never survive another tackle or be able to sprint across a football field for the winning catch, but he was still strong and disciplined. Or he had been before depression had steered him to drink.

Makalani parked under a shade tree and hefted her travel

backpack onto her shoulders just as her two aunties stormed out the front door and down the steps.

Tutu's youngest daughter whirled on the elder, hands on hips and nostrils flared. "Shame on you, Maile. How you let your son spread dis junk about mine? Solomon would nevah hurt one child. Nevah."

"Oh, yeah?" Auntie Maile said, challenging her heavier sister like a terrier nips at a boar. "The police say otherwise. Your precious Solomon is a drunk and a degenerate."

"No throw big words at me, tita. Your Japanee husband and haole daughter-in-law no make you bettah than us. Your mo'opuna barely got any Hawaiian left in her. She just a skinny, stuck-up slut."

"Whoa," Makalani said, stepping between her aunties. "What's going on?"

Auntie Kaulana swatted her hand aside. "You nevah heard? Dis one's granddaughter wen missing. Runaway more like."

"Or taken by your son," Auntie Maile snapped.

Makalani gasped. "Solomon? What are you saying, auntie? The police think he abducted her? That's crazy. Solomon adores Becky."

Auntie Maile scoffed. "Exactly my point."

"You lolo or what?" Auntie Kaulana said. "Everybody knows your girl's crushing on my son. Been lidat since junior high. Every time she come fo' one visit, she stick on his skin like sweat."

Auntie Maile crossed her arms. "And now they're gone."

"Not together. My Solomon's twenty-two and full grown. He can go where he like. Dis trouble is about your Becky."

Makalani's father yelled for them to "Knock it off, already," as he walked up the side of the house, carrying fishing gear and a string of papio. The jack fish looked tiny and pale swinging alongside Papa's powerful sun-blackened legs. "Eh, little girl. When you get home?"

"Just now." She hurried to give him a hug, reaching her long arms around his massive chest. Although a tall and sturdy woman, Makalani felt tiny in her father's arms. When he bent down for a kiss, she whispered in his ear. "What's going on with Solomon and Becky? Auntie Maile said something about the police."

"Auwe. Things are so messed up, I had to get away just to think. Those kids been gone since yesterday."

"Together?"

Papa shrugged. "Nobody knows. But your aunties aren't the only ones fighting. People talking stink about Solomon all ovah town."

Inside the house was just as bad.

Becky's mother had faced off with Makalani's mama in the kitchen. "Why are you defending him? He's not even your blood. You married into this family same as me. You should be sticking up for Becky, not Solomon." Linda's pale skin had turned lobster red with anger, like the haole tourists who fell asleep on the beach.

Mama shrugged. "Becky's my grandniece, Solomon's my nephew, both ohana to me. What's the difference?"

"Because Becky's hapa-haole like us. You know how it is in this family. She's less than 50 percent."

Makalani hid on the other side of the doorway, unwilling to enter the fray.

Auntie Linda was referring to the blood quantum required to apply for a cheap lease through the Hawaiian Homes Commission Act of 1920. Although the eligibility rules discounted Becky's 3/8 as Native Hawaiian, the family never did. All of them were hapa in the truest sense—part Hawaiian and part something else—with Makalani's *half* Hawaiian adhering to the original meaning of the word.

Despite the arguments for a blood quantum of 1/16 by Prince Kuhio—who became a representative for the Hawaiian Territories after the monarchy had been overthrown—the US Congress had insisted on 50 percent. It was this rule—and not Auntie Linda's accusation of bigotry—that set Becky, her sister, and her half-Japanese father apart from the rest.

None of this made any practical difference in the Pahukula ohana since Tutu would pass the dollar-per-year lease to one of her three 3/4 Hawaiian children. But the fact that the Muramoto branch of the family couldn't even be *considered* made a difference. Not only had Auntie Maile married a full-blooded Japanese husband, her son James had married a pure haole wife.

"Enough already," Tutu said, throwing up her hands from the dough and sending a puff of ulu flour into the air. "Both da kids Pahukula. I no like fight in our ohana. We all need fo' come together to find Becky and bring her home safe."

Makalani peeked around the doorway to the kitchen. "Hey, everyone, I'm home."

"E komo mai, mo'opuna," Tutu said, waving her into the kitchen as Mama descended with a hug.

Auntie Linda muttered, "the favorite child," just loud enough for everyone to hear.

"You just get in?" Mama asked, smoothing Makalani's thick, unruly hair. The moment Makalani had stepped off the airplane, her formerly blow-dried tresses had tripled in volume and rebellion. Nothing would contain her hair in the islands short of tying it into a knot on top of her head.

"I came straight from the airport. Glad to be home but sorry about all this trouble. Any more news about Becky, Auntie Linda?"

The skinny woman crossed her arms and huffed, her pale skin sticking out in this family like a puka shell on a black sand beach.

"I'm sure your *ohana* will fill you in," she said bitterly, and left.

"Nevah mind her," Tutu said. "How you stay?"

Tutu Kahilina was a rarity, a true Kanaka Maoli, one of the last remaining pure-blooded Hawaiians.

"I'm good. But what's going on with Solomon?"

Tutu sighed. "O ia mau nō. Same as usual, drink too much, do too little. No one happy wit him dis days."

"Did he really run off with Becky?"

"Of course not," Mama interrupted. "Probably drinking with his old high school football buddies, talking story about the old times and sleeping off a keg of beer."

When Makalani had seen Solomon at Christmas, he'd been relatively sober and only mildly depressed. They had talked deeply, and Makalani had hoped he would turn his life around.

"Why would anyone even suspect him of abducting Becky?"

Mama shrugged. "He got into a fight with Kimo last month."

"The cop?"

Mama nodded. "You know how it was, best friends as kids, rivals in high school. Want the truth? I think Kimo's happy to see Solomon brought low."

Tutu pounded her dough and muttered something in Hawaiian about kuleana. Although Makalani had forgotten much of the language during her years on the mainland, the concept of a reciprocal responsibility was deeply ingrained. Living off the land was a prime example of this reciprocity. The Pahukula family cared for and protected the 'aina, which in turn, provided food, water, and shelter for them. The same applied to people. Without kuleana, there could be no harmony, balance, and respect.

As the eldest daughter of Tutu's eldest son, Makalani accepted this responsibility for her cousins' safety and reputation. She would find them both and restore peace in her family.

After changing into shorts and slippers, Makalani drove to Kanuikapono Charter School where Becky's younger sister attended sixth grade. Since the school taught kindergarten through twelfth, Makalani hoped Lisa might be harboring secrets about her fifteen-year-old sister's whereabouts and know where Becky's friends hung out on campus.

All Makalani found was more bitterness.

"I'm sick of her," said Lisa. "Even when she's gone she gets all the attention. I'm the one with the good grades. Does anyone care about me? No."

"Aren't you worried about her?"

"What for? Becky's cut school plenty time."

"But she went missing *yesterday*."

"And when she comes back, she won't even get in trouble. Mom will let her skate just like she does with Dad."

"What are you talking about?"

"Guess you been away too long to hear. Dad lost his store. He wants us to move back to Tutu Nui's homestead in that shack where Becky and me grew up."

"I thought Solomon had moved in there."

"Not for long."

She gave Makalani a world-class stink eye and walked away.

"Wait. What about Becky's friends? Where would I find them?"

"The Queen Bees?" Lisa pointed across campus at a green-roofed building. "They hang out at the big tree. Better hurry, though, lunchtime almost pau."

What had happened to Makalani's family? Each relative was doing worse than the last. Envy, alcoholism, depression, bickering. Only Makalani's branch of the family tree appeared to still be growing strong.

The Queen Bees, as Lisa had tagged them, turned out to be the Kaua'i version of *Mean Girls*. Each of them had Hapa looks, trendy shorts, and serious attitude.

"She ditched school, so what?" the first girl said, with a toss of her long black hair.

Makalani sighed. "She hasn't come home."

The other girls giggled.

"Why are you laughing? Is she with a guy?"

"If she's lucky," the second girl said.

The third girl elbowed her in the side then turned to Makalani. "Don't listen to Kimi. She's in love with Becky's cousin."

"Is that who you think she's with?" Makalani asked.

The first girl shrugged. "If Becky wore him down. She's pretty and all, but Solomon treats her like a kid."

"Wore him down how?"

"You know, asking him to take her da movies, da beach, hiking up Pihea Trail."

"Where?"

"Kōke'e State Park, on the other side of the island. The trail starts at Pu'u O Kila Lookout and goes through the Alakai Swamp to Kilohana. Becky's been wanting to hike that trail fo' evah, but nobody will take her. Maybe Solomon finally agreed."

Armed with a plausible explanation, Makalani zipped home for her hiking pack and basic supplies—water, snacks, jacket, first aid, and sunscreen. The wimpy mainland sun had lightened her normally dark skin to an ashen brown. She'd tan quick if she didn't burn first.

"Where you go?" Mama asked.

"I thought I'd stretch my legs with a hike over in Kōke'e Park."

"Why you go all da way ovah dere?" Papa asked. "The Moloa'a trail ovah here mo' bettah."

Makalani checked to make sure her aunties weren't around to give her a hard time then whispered to her parents. "I went to Becky's school and spoke with her friends. They thought she might have convinced Solomon to drive her to the other side of the island to hike the Pihea Trail."

Papa laughed. "No way. Dat boy too moloā to hike up one mountain." Lazy? The Solomon she knew would run to Hanalei just for fun.

Makalani shook her head. "I spoke with Lisa at school. She told me Uncle James lost the store. She said they wanted to move back here."

"Auwe. Bumbai, everybody come back, but nobody want work. Your mama and Tutu bust their okole while my sistahs bicker all da time. And their husbands? Your uncle Eric drink mo' dan his son even, and Maile's husband wastes time talking story with his Japanee friends. Everybody wants the land, but nobody shows it respect." He heaved a sigh. "Listen to me, squawking like one myna bird, when I got work to do."

"You're not going to search for Solomon and Becky?"

He shook his head. "I ask already, but her parents don't want my kōkua. They got their own ways. Same wit your cousin Solomon. Maybe he come back. Maybe da police catch him. Make no nevah mind. He stay lost either way."

"He's not a criminal, Papa."

"I hope not, but you nevah know. Your cousin change a lot since you been gone."

Makalani considered her options: stay and help Papa, Mama, and Tutu with the chores for tomorrow's lu'au; confront Officer Kimo Kalaniana'ole and try to smooth the waters between him and her cousin and convince him of Solomon's innocence; visit Uncle James and Auntie Linda to get a feel for their true intentions and if moving back to the homestead is dependent upon disgracing Solomon; or hike up the Pihea Trail and search for her missing cousins.

"Wanna come hike with me?" she asked her father.

"Nah. I gotta fish for Tutu's lu'au. But be careful, yeah? After all da kine rain, dat trail gon' be hamajang."

As Makalani drove around the island and up to the Pu'u O Kila Lookout, she noted the deep color of the earth and the pungent scent of growth and decay. Papa wasn't kidding—the trails would be a slippery mess.

She parked in the lot and checked out the other cars. There were only three, but one of them looked like Solomon's beat-up Explorer. She noted the UH football sticker as she peered into the rear window at a pink hibiscus backpack.

Becky's?

Definitely not Solomon's.

But why had they camped out overnight?

Makalani pushed away her doubt: no matter how low he had sunk or how desperate for attention and affirmation he had become, Solomon would never... She shook her head. She couldn't even think the words. Becky was their cousin, their *underage* cousin.

Makalani sighed. How much did she really know about Solomon as an adult? She had left the islands when he was twelve. As the years had passed, he had made less and less time to visit with her when she came home. In the two years since he dropped out of UH, she'd hardly seen him at all.

Becky, on the other hand, had always rubbed Makalani the wrong way. Favoring her haole mother in appearance and attitude, Becky looked down her straight, narrow nose at the rest of the family as if they were a bunch of lazy, dumb locals. Auntie Kaulana had not been entirely wrong when she said Becky was stuck-up and that she clung to Solomon like sweat. Even on Makalani's short visits home, she had noticed that.

None of this explained why Solomon would take Becky hiking without permission—or, if they had intended to spend the night, why they hadn't parked near a campsite.

Makalani tightened the straps of her backpack and hiked up the initial hill and down what had originally been intended as a road to Hanalei. Although rutted, the wide trail was gravelly enough to run at a cross-country pace—something she did often where she lived in Oregon, near the Columbia River Gorge.

A mile in, the would-be road ended and the narrow trail became too slick for the ambitious pace she had set. She tried to slow, but the mud and momentum propelled her forward. She flailed her arms, reaching for something to grab, as her feet shot out from under her. She landed hard and slid down the muddy chute, spinning on her okole before hitting a bump and sprawling on the trail.

She crawled onto her knees and massaged her hands. Her

wrists hurt from breaking her fall, but not as much as where she landed on her butt. She had underestimated the local terrain just as mainlanders frequently underestimated her people. Makalani had been away from home too long.

She stood and wiped her hands on the back of her shirt and shorts, the only part of her clothing not stained with the iron-rich mud. From here on in, she'd have to hike smarter and watch the terrain for signs of other sliding accidents.

Could this be why her cousins hadn't returned home?

When she reached the intersection with the Alakai Swamp Trail, she paused. If she continued in the same general direction, she'd head toward a distant campsite. If she took a hard left, the new trail would lead her through the Alakai Swamp up to the Kilohana Lookout Becky's friends had mentioned. Before she could decide, she heard crying.

"Becky?" she yelled. "It's Makalani. Can you hear me? Becky, is that you?"

The crying stopped and a girl shouted back. "I'm down here."

Makalani looked through the trees and saw her bedraggled cousin slumped in the mud. "Are you hurt?"

Becky shook her head and sobbed.

"Can you make it up here?"

"I keep slipping," she whined, clearly exhausted and at her wit's end.

"Okay. I got you."

Makalani took her jacket out of her pack, held onto a cuff, and tossed the other sleeve to Becky. "Grab that and try again. I'll pull you up."

When the girl made it back to the trail, she fell into Makalani's embrace. When she finally calmed down, Makalani lifted her chin. "Where's Solomon?"

Becky burst into tears. "He's dead."

"What?"

"He slid off the cliff."

"Where?"

"Kilohana Lookout."

"Oh, my God. Come on. We have to find him."

"I can't."

Makalani shook her cousin hard. "You can, and you will."

They hurried as fast as Becky's shaky limbs would allow, over the wooden boardwalk and through the first bog, and the second, and the third. Before the rangers put in the double-plank pathway through the swampy forest, hikers would wander off the trail after flowers, birds, and Venus flytraps. It was easy to get lost in the fog or stuck in deep mud. Makalani's mother had been lost for hours, once, when she was a kid.

"Why did you guys come up in the rain?" Makalani asked.

"It had stopped already."

"And what were you thinking wearing Vans up here?"

"I didn't want to go home and change my shoes."

"You didn't want to get busted more like."

When they reached the other side, Makalani dragged her exhausted cousin up the slippery trail to the soggy wooden slats anchored onto the eroded muddy peak. Ferns, grasses, trees, and plants grew on the slopes and clung to the rocks making it hard to tell where the edge dropped away.

"Where did he slide off?"

"Over there," Becky said, pointing to a waterlogged board, slick with mud.

"Stay back, okay?" Makalani laid on her belly and crawled toward the edge.

"Do you see him?" Becky asked.

"Not yet."

"Told you. He's dead. It's all my fault. I never should have guilted him into this."

"Guilted?"

"He promised to take me for the last two years, but he's been so messed up since he got kicked out of UH I honestly thought the exercise would do him good."

Did Becky really mean that? Or was she justifying her selfish manipulation? Makalani grabbed onto a sturdy root and inched farther over the edge.

"I see him!"

A hundred feet down the ravine, her strong, athletic cousin was caught like a rag doll in the dense branches of a tree.

"Solomon," she yelled. "Can you hear me?"

He looked up in surprise. "Makalani?"

By the time Kaua'i firefighters had rescued Solomon from the cliff and airlifted him and Becky to the hospital, the entire Pahukula ohana and Officer Kimo Kalaniana'ole were waiting. All of them descended on Makalani as soon as she walked in the door.

"What happened?"

"Why were they hiking?"

"How did he fall?"

"Was she fighting him off?"

Makalani whipped her head toward Becky's mother. "Are you serious? Becky begged him to take her hiking, hounded him for months...years. The only reason he finally agreed was because she burst into tears about getting disinvited from some stupid party. Solomon was trying to cheer her up."

Auntie Linda opened her mouth to argue, but her husband beat her to it.

Makalani shut him down, as well. "I'm sorry your store closed down, Uncle James, but you can't kick Solomon out of the guesthouse just because you want to run back to Anahola."

"See?" Auntie Kaulana said, smirking with satisfaction.

Makalani turned on Solomon's mother. "Becky may be skinny and a little uppity sometimes, but she's a good kid. Maybe if you cut her some slack, she might feel more welcome in this family." Makalani glanced at Becky's younger sister. "Lisa, too."

"Eh, no be lidat," Uncle Eric said, stepping forward to stick up for his wife.

"No, Uncle, don't *you* be like that. Your son needs encouragement and motivation, not cases of beer. You and Solomon should be helping Papa with the fishing and farming."

Makalani took in the shocked expressions of her ohana and nodded. "I know. I'm just as bad, living on the mainland and pursuing my life. But you're all here, living off this land. The least you can do is pull your own weight and support each other."

She turned her ire onto Officer Kalaniana'ole. "The only crime committed by Solomon or anyone else in this family is the crime of failed kuleana."

He held up his hands in surrender. "Hey, leave me out of this. Glad it all worked out. Tell Solomon, give me a call some time, we go surf or whatever. Catch up on good times."

Everyone else was too shamefaced to speak.

Tutu leaned forward in her seat and swept her gaze from one family member to the next. "Sounds like we all got work to do."

She settled on Makalani. "You been away long time."

"I know, Tutu. I have no right…"

She shook her head. "We all gotta speak up. Make sure everybody get the kōkua they need. And remember Akahai, Lōkahi, Olu'olu, Ha'aha'a, Ahonui. You remember what dat means?"

Makalani nodded. "Kindness, unity, agreeableness, humility, patience—five aspects of the true meaning of aloha."

Tutu laughed. "Well, I don't know what *aspect* mean, but I tink you got it right."

And just lidat, the tension eased.

Tutu nodded at Makalani and smiled. "It's good to have you home."

CALLING MR. SMITH

ELLEN HART

Late October, 1987

When I tell people I grew up in Hollywood, I often get amusing reactions. Most think it must have been super cool, that I sat around swimming pools rubbing elbows with the kids of rich Hollywood greats. While that would have been amazing, the truth is, I did grow up in Hollywood…just not that one.

My Hollywood is located in northern Minnesota. It's small, rural and conservative. The biggest celebrity was Salty the Chef, a seven-foot-tall carved wooden bear wearing a red apron and matching oven mitts. Salty stood in front of Salty's Pie Shoppe, one paw waving toward the door. I loved Salty. I love pie. I am, therefore, a true citizen of my hometown.

That said, I hated growing up there. Every time I've ever heard someone repeat the title of that Tom Wolfe novel, *You Can't Go Home Again*, their eyes downcast, their expression glum, my reaction is a fist pump and a hearty, "Right on."

Having fled the town nineteen years before vowing never to return, I do admit to a strange mixture of emotions as I pulled my borrowed Volvo into my parents' driveway late one Saturday afternoon. I rolled down the window and sat for a moment to take in the scene. My eyes roamed over the house and the lawn that sloped gently down to the dock. The air outside was filled with the itchy scent of drying leaves. Everything looked so much smaller, older and somehow sadder than I remembered. Indeed, my first reactions were so jumbled and messy, I figured it would be pointless to try to untangle them. Instead, I slid out of the front seat, grabbed my overnight bag from the trunk and headed up the walk to the front door.

My dad, Lou Ahlness, built the place a few years after his return from the war in Europe. His parents owned a small construction company, which, in time, he inherited and expanded. He died when I was ten. My mother ran the company from then on. After I'd escaped to Chicago, Mom remarried a man I'd never met and sold the business for a tidy sum. She moved with the new guy to St. Cloud. Now, having outlived, or perhaps the word is "exhausted," two husbands, she was still going strong, according to my brother, Ivor. Mom and I aren't exactly estranged. We do send an occasional Christmas or birthday card. But Ivor, not Mom, was the reason I was here.

When my brother called to invite me up to our old family home to celebrate Gloria's—that's how we both referred to our mother—seventy-fifth birthday, my first instinct was to run screaming in the other direction. And yet the longer we talked, the more it became clear to me that something seemed to be amiss in Ivor's generally charmed life. If I'd asked him about it directly, I knew he wouldn't answer.

Ivor and I might be brother and sister, but we don't have a close, confiding kind of relationship. In fact, we'd only started talking again a few years ago. Mostly, on our occasional late-night, often alcohol-infused conversations, we discussed movies and books. Ivor is six years older than me. As kids, we didn't have all that much to do with each other. I suppose we were both attempting to navigate our mother's rules and expectations, many that pitted us against each other. The fact that we'd managed a rapprochement with some semblance of affection still intact seemed to me a minor miracle.

The reason the old house was still available for the birthday party was because, instead of selling, Gloria had been renting it out. The last tenant had left in August, and since nobody was breaking down the door begging to rent it, Gloria had asked Ivor to travel north and give her his opinion about necessary repairs. He ended up making some of them himself, driving up on weekends from his home in Minneapolis, which was simply further proof that my brother was a saint.

"Astrid, you made great time," he said, grinning as he pushed the screened door open and motioned me inside. "How was the trip? Are you cold? I've got a fire going. Come into the living room." He took my bag and walked ahead of me.

No, we didn't hug. I come from a family of non-huggers.

Ivor would turn forty-five in December. He'd been a thin, bookish-looking kid who'd grown into a thin, bookish-looking adult. Ivor M. Ahlness was an attorney-at-law, a man who normally took great care with his appearance. The stubble on his cheeks, dust on his jeans and paint on his ratty old sweatshirt suggested he'd spent the day working. "Where's the rest of your family?" I asked, unable to keep my eyes from ricocheting around the room.

"Yeah, it takes a minute to absorb," he said, turning to face me. "You look healthy. Fit. How goes the battle?"

The reference was to my cancer diagnosis and the brutal rounds of chemo I'd undergone. I'd been in remission now for a full two years. I hadn't mentioned to him that I'd just undergone another battery of tests last week to confirm my healthy

status. I'd been feeling unusually tired again and, though I kept
it to myself, was pretty nervous. "Everything's good, thanks."

"I've got your old bedroom all made up. Clean sheets and
towels. As for the family," he said, easing down on a tired-
looking recliner, "it's just me. Jake's back at Northwestern and
Billy couldn't possibly miss homecoming weekend. Did I tell
you he's got a new girlfriend?"

"What happened to the old one?"

"You think he'd tell me?"

We both laughed, which, thankfully, eased the tension in
my stomach. "How's Darla?" It seemed unfriendly not to mention his wife.

He glanced out the picture window facing the lake. "She's
good. So, you hungry? I made chili. Or we could eat out."

"I feel kind of jangled. Got anything to drink around here?"

"Come with me."

I followed him into the kitchen, where he opened a bottle
of Cabernet and then filled two juice glasses. We moved over
to the stove so he could stir the chili. I continued to feel a little
dazed, as if I'd entered a time warp.

"How's Annie and Rose?" he asked.

I'd been together with Annie for almost nine years. Rose was
from her marriage, which had ended in divorce the year before
we met. Ivor and I never discussed the reality of my relationship. He treated my living with Annie as if we were roommates.
I figured he didn't want to pry or didn't want to know. Either
way, our brother/sister truce still seemed tenuous enough that I
didn't want to rock the boat. I'd eventually tell him I was gay,
but for now, I kept things casual and superficial, and Ivor, for
his own reasons, did the same.

Unlike our mother, whose religious intolerance would have
set off a Richter scale, Ivor occasionally expressed a liberal view,
though it was hard to tell where he stood on most social issues.
Gloria kept in weekly contact with her brilliant lawyer son, the

one who'd done her proud, unlike the daughter she'd never really wanted and who never failed to disappoint. I knew she made an effort to keep her finger on me through him. I hated the idea of putting him in the middle of some family crisis, which coming out to Gloria would prompt. Secrets create barriers. The one between my mom and me was inevitable and even necessary for my mental health. With Ivor, it was a different story.

We talked nonstop all through dinner. I tried my best to ask leading questions, hoping he'd open up about whatever might be wrong in Ivor-world, but he seemed completely normal, even upbeat. I began to think I'd misread him. We laugh a lot when we're together, which I love. Growing up, our lives couldn't have been more different. He was the golden child, the one my mother had prayed her heart out for. After a stillbirth and two miscarriages, she'd all but given up on having a child when Ivor came along. She wanted to give her beautiful, miracle boy everything. To that end, my parents set aside money every month to ensure that he could go to college, something they never even tried to do for me. If I sound bitter, I am.

My appearance on the family scene had been an unwelcome accident for my mother. My dad, for his part, seemed to really enjoy having a little kid around again. While Ivor was off overachieving, I was there to throw a ball or go fishing. When I lost my dad, all the care and comfort in my home life seeped away. I miss him every day of my life.

"I would imagine Gloria will be here by one tomorrow," said Ivor. "The party starts at four."

"Why so late?" I'd been hoping to get back on the road before dark.

"Her cousins are driving up from Rochester after church. They go to the late service. Come on, Astrid. They're old. I figured we should cut them some slack. It'll be a good crowd. Aunt Laverne's coming from Grand Rapids. That should make you happy."

I adored my aunt, and was never able to understand how Gloria and her younger sister could have come from the same family.

"I'd say there will be at least thirty people, not counting us. I had a cake made at Finstadt's Bakery and I ordered some cheese and meat trays from the Piggly Wiggly. Oh, and I bought a case of champagne—not the expensive stuff."

I sat up straight. "Gloria's drinking again?"

"It doesn't seem to be the problem it used to be."

I'd believe that when I saw it. The idea of watching her get slowly hammered while she grew ever louder and more sarcastic was nothing I wanted any part of. On the other hand, it might provide me with an excuse to leave early. "Tell me," I said, raking my hair off my forehead, "whose idea was the party?"

"Idea?"

"Gloria's?"

"Well, yeah, I suppose. She wanted to take a look at the house, so this provided her with an opportunity. Thing is, I've suggested more repairs than she wants to make."

"She's not thinking of selling, is she?"

The house was the one asset I knew I would inherit after she was gone. I'd already made a will stating that my half of the property would go to Annie in the event of my demise. You have to understand. Ivor is a wealthy man. I, on the other hand, am part owner of a struggling bar in Chicago, which I also manage. Annie is a fifth-grade teacher at Hamilton Elementary. Her deadbeat ex rarely pays any child support. We have bad health care, which means we're deeply in debt because of my insanely expensive medical bills, which also means we have no savings. You get the picture. If I outlived Gloria, I might—and this was a big if—inherit some money from the rest of her estate, though with my potential health issues, the "outliving" part of the equation was beginning to look like another big if.

Annie and I had done the commitment ceremony thing. We would gladly have married if that had been an option, but because it wasn't, Annie was legally nobody. She would continue to be nobody if I came out to Gloria because my mother would never accept her as a legitimate heir. The idea that Annie and Rose would get nothing if I died before my mom had been eating at me for years. With my latest health scare, it had risen from indignation to outrage.

"Here's the thing, Astrid," said my brother, adjusting his glasses. "I'm planning to offer to buy the place from her. I'll give her a fair price."

"You're...*what*?" I tried not to gasp.

"I love this house. It would make a great summer cabin. It's already on a lake with a good dock. And it's only a couple hours from the cities."

I gripped my napkin and tried to slow my breathing. I had no actual claim to the house until Mom died. Ivor had every right to buy it. I doubted he'd ever given much thought to the disparity between his lifestyle and mine. And that made me want to scream at him, tell him he was a selfish, entitled SOB.

"Anyway," he said, rising from the table and walking his dishes over to the sink, "I'm beat. There's a college game on tonight. Should be a good one. Any interest in watching it with me?"

I forced my anger away. I needed time to think. "Let me take care of the dishes. You made the meal. Seems only fair."

"Hey, much appreciated." He kissed the top of my head. "I'll be in the den when you're done."

I sat at the table for a few more minutes. Beyond my anger, I was mystified by the idea that Ivor would want any part of this house. He'd left for college when I was twelve, and was only home sporadically after that. He'd escaped most of the fun with Gloria, the worst of her drinking years.

For me, it was all still so heavy and vivid, especially the constant slurred ragging on what I chose to wear and my utter lack of interest in dating, dances and the opposite sex. She loathed my hippie friends—it was the sixties, after all—and my general tomboy ways. Most important to her was my refusal to go to church with her so I could hear the minister preach me into hell. By the time my brother left, I wasn't just the inconvenient child. No, Gloria had finally nailed it. She never said it out loud, but in her bones, she knew my "inclinations" would make me a stain on the family name. In a small town, that was nothing short of infamy.

After finishing the dishes and putting the leftovers away, I wandered into the den, only to find Ivor asleep. Instead of sticking around, I decided to take a drive. I left a note on the kitchen table, telling him I'd gone out and not to wait up.

After driving around town, doing a short walk down memory lane, I ended up at the Anchor Bar. Once upon a time, I'd worked at the Anchor. I was fifteen when I was hired, which meant I couldn't bartend because I was underage. But I could stock, cut garnishes, bus dishes, wash glasses, wipe down tables and sweep floors. Eventually I was allowed to heat up the crap frozen pizza that was served to the desperate. From the moment I stepped inside the Anchor all those years ago, I felt at home. The people I saw sitting at the bar or at one of the booths or tables weren't making good choices either. It was dark inside, even during the day, and there was always music playing on the jukebox. It became my refuge, my hiding place and the place where I finally grew up.

The interior of the building had aged rather badly in my absence. Everything looked threadbare and even a bit derelict. There were a couple dozen people sitting around, mostly on stools at the counter. A few guys were playing darts at a board hanging on the back wall. The Notre Dame game was on, so I approached the bartender and asked what rail bourbon they served. Ten High came his answer. Since I found the brand borderline tolerable and didn't want to spend an arm and a leg to lighten my mood, I ordered a shot with a beer back, carried the glasses over to an empty booth and sat down, turning sideways and leaning against the wall so I could watch the TV. I didn't recognize anyone, which was kind of surprising.

An hour or so later, after finishing off two more shots and a basket of popcorn, I saw a figure looming directly front of me.

"Hey," came a deep voice. "I know you."

"Yeah?" I was feeling no pain as I looked up.

"You're Astrid Ahlness, right?"

"And you would be?"

He grinned. "You don't recognize me?"

"Can't say I do."

"Chandler Dix. We graduated high school together in sixty-seven."

The use of the word *together* struck me as a bit of a stretch. Chandler Dix had been a fat kid with flaming red hair. This dude was cue-ball bald and, for want of a better term, ripped.

"I'm gonna grab a beer. Mind if I join you? What are you drinking? I'll get you another—on me."

I'd spent a seriously tense week worrying about my cancer roaring back and now I was about to lose the only family inheritance I could count on. "A shot of Ten High would be lovely."

"You're a cheap date."

He wasn't wearing a wedding ring. If he thought I was going to be an easy pickup, he was mistaken. "I'm married," I said, wiggling my fingers at him. I keep a gold band in my wallet and put it on whenever I'm in a bar, socializing or working. It saves a lot of time and unnecessary grief. "Happily married," I added.

"Sure, whatever," he said. "I'm not hitting on you."

Right.

I'm hardly bragging here. I mean, I'm not model material, though I do seem to attract my share of guys, especially in dark bars—which, when you think about it, isn't saying much. But I'm friendly. Approachable. I like to laugh. Underneath my misanthropic cloak of darkness, I do genuinely like people. Beyond that, I enjoy a good conversation when I'm drinking. So if he could keep from hitting on me or boring me to death, I welcomed the company.

While Chandler placed the order, I slipped out of the booth and grabbed another basket of popcorn. As I resumed my seat, he reappeared and dropped down across from me. He was holding four shot glasses and pushed two across the table. I was surprised, but didn't object.

"How come you're back in town?" he asked, making himself comfortable.

"For a birthday party. My mom's."

He eyed me a moment. "You don't look too happy about it. I remember your mom. Always dressed up, wearing high heels, like she was going to church. I don't think she liked me very much."

He was probably right. She wouldn't have had much time for a fat kid with acne. The fact that he *was* fat in a fat-phobic high-school culture made me think his youth hadn't been a piece of cake either. I immediately felt a certain solidarity. "Yeah, my mom has what they call a 'difficult personality.'"

"Know what you mean," he said, throwing back one of his shots. "Mine had one of those, too. But your mom, I mean, she was a force to be reckoned with."

"In what way?"

"Oh, you know, a local mover and shaker. For instance, she was always pushing these weird nutrition ideas on the ladies who worked in the school kitchen. My mom had a job there for a while so I know. She thought your mom was…kind of—" He twirled a finger next to his ear.

"She was." I tossed a popcorn kernel in the air and caught it in my mouth. I've had years of practice. "She has a bunch of seriously psychotic obsessions. Sort of a…serial obsessionist."

"Huh?"

I held up three fingers. "God, health food and her Norwegian heritage. That last one is why she named my brother Ivor and me Astrid. It could have been worse, I suppose. She could have named me Borghild and him Woden." I downed one of the shots. A second later, I felt a stab of pain in my gut. Not a good sign.

We spent a while swapping childhood war stories. He had a bunch of his own, mostly about his crazy uncle. He reacted most strongly to my story about Mr. Smith, the threat my mother would trot out whenever I refused to take orders. "She'd say, 'You know, Astrid, if you don't start listening, I'll have to call Mr. Smith. You know who he is, don't you? He's the man who comes to take away bad little girls.' I would beg her not to. Once, she actually did it—called him. Let me tell you, I spent a whole lot of my grade school years standing at my bedroom window waiting for his car to arrive. I was absolutely terrified. All Mom had to do to get me to knuckle under was let her hand hover over the phone."

"Bitch."

He had a way with words.

"Jeez," he continued. "Stories like that make my blood boil. I may be down with a lot of super twisted shit, but you don't do that to a kid."

To lighten the mood, I moved the conversation to school memories, the teachers we loved and hated. We used our last shots to drink a toast to Mr. Miller, everyone's favorite. As soon as the alcohol hit my stomach, I felt another stab of pain. "Damn it all," I muttered, my mood instantly souring.

"You okay?" he asked.

"I've been better." I glanced down at the wedding ring on my left hand.

"What is it?"

"Oh, you no, nothing important. Just my life."

"What about your life?"

I leaned forward. I probably shouldn't have, but I gave him an abbreviated version of my situation, my illness and all the ramifications for my family if I died before my mother did.

"She hates your husband and daughter, huh?"

"Everything will go to my brother. It's just not fair. I mean, do you ever think that…if you could just change one thing, that everything would—"

He held my eyes. "Finish the sentence."

"It's just…if my mother simply disappeared—you know, got erased—" I laughed at the absurdity "—that the sun would finally come out and life would be a whole lot better."

He studied me for a few seconds, then grabbed another handful of popcorn.

"Anyway, let's change the subject. Tell me more about you."

He shrugged. "Did a couple tours in 'Nam. Worked as a security guard in Fargo. I came home last year to take care of my mom. She was diagnosed with Alzheimer's."

"I'm sorry. You're a good son."

"I like to think of myself as a helpful kind of guy."

I felt another jab of pain in my stomach. This one nearly doubled me over.

"You okay?" he asked, reaching across the table.

"Just give me a minute." When I was finally able to straighten up, I said, "I think it's time I get home."

"Sure," he said. "You need a ride? Your house is over on Deer Lake, right?"

I told him I had a car. He walked me out to the parking lot, where, feeling a slap of cold air hit me as I reentered the real world, I realized I was more tipsy than I'd thought. Even so, I figured I could make it home on back streets.

"A Volvo," Chandler said, whistling as I unlocked the driver's door. "Nice."

"It belongs to a friend. Had to borrow it because my piece-of-shit Taurus is on its last legs." I got in and pressed the key into the ignition. The motor refused to turn over. "What the hell?"

"Let me try," he said. After cranking it a few more times, he gave up.

I kicked the front tire so hard I hurt my foot. "I'm supposed to head back home tomorrow. Is there a garage in town where I could get it fixed in the morning?"

"On a Sunday? I doubt it. I mean, maybe you could find a mechanic who'd look at it, but a Volvo? Not many of those around these parts. Gonna be a problem."

I cursed a blue streak as he led me to his truck. Closing my eyes, I leaned my head against the side window. The cold glass felt good. All the way home he kept peppering me with stupid questions, mostly about the birthday party, when it would start, if my mom was already in town. I was relieved when we finally made it to my parents' driveway.

"Do you need help?" he asked.

He was right. I was pretty tight. But help? "Nah."

I waved him away as he backed up and drove off, and then I dragged myself in through the unlocked front door, made it to my bedroom and fell face-first into a pillow.

I woke to the sound of a ringing phone. It took a moment to remember where I was, and a moment more to recall why I was still fully dressed. As I swung my legs out of bed, it occurred to me that my headache wasn't as bad as expected. It was going on eleven-thirty. "Whatever will my brother think of me," I mumbled. At least I was still capable of snark.

I showered and dressed in my new jeans and a favorite ski sweater—I had to impress Gloria after all—then made my way downstairs. My brother was in the kitchen, clean-shaven, and sitting at the table reading the newspaper.

"Afternoon," he said, emphasizing the word with a smirk.

I poured myself a mug of coffee. "You know any local mechanics?" I asked, offering him an edited version of last night's visit to the Anchor.

"That's too bad," he said. "Why don't you look through the local phonebook?" He nodded to the one on the end of the counter.

It sounded like way too much work. "I heard the phone ring a while ago."

"That was a weird one." He lowered the newspaper. "It was Chandler Dix. He wanted me to give you a message."

I lifted my eyebrows.

"He said that he might have a fix for your problem."

"A mechanic? Fabulous. Did he give you a name?"

"Said he'd be in touch."

My heart sank. It looked more and more like I would be stuck in Hollywood for at least another night. And then there was the cost of repairs to worry about. The day had just started and already it was headed south.

"That was sad what happened to his mom," continued Ivor.

"You mean the dementia?"

"Well, yeah, but also the way she died. Apparently she wandered away from her home sometime last February. It was after midnight. Chandler told the cops she only had on a thin cotton nightie and slippers. A farmer discovered her body in a field a week or so later, dead of exposure. Thing is, she was found a good three miles from her house. Nobody could figure out how she got that far."

"Huh."

Taking a last sip of Coke, he rose and said, "I suppose we better get busy. There's a lot to do before the party."

While I waited for Chandler's call, I did the vacuuming and Ivor drove into town to pick up the food.

"Where's Gloria?" he asked when he came in the back door a while later.

I shrugged. I'd just finished sweeping the kitchen floor and was sick of the entire enterprise.

By three thirty, we were even more concerned. Having completed all our tasks, Ivor cracked a couple Dr. Peppers, our child-hood favorite. We took the cans into the living room and each took a seat.

"Astrid?" my brother said after staring out the window for a couple of minutes. "I need to tell you something."

"Yeah?"

"Darla and I...we're divorcing."

I was stunned. So I had heard something in his voice. "Oh, Ivor, I'm so sorry."

"As a divorce lawyer, I've always known that marriages come apart in stages. And yet, I was still surprised, you know? She's found someone new, a guy in her doctoral program. I knew we weren't getting along. It's why I want to buy this house. I need a place I can get away to. I might even live up here full-time."

"But your practice? Billy?"

"I haven't made any final decisions." He hesitated, shifting in his chair. "There's something else I need to say, something I should have said a long time ago. The way Mom treated you when you were a kid, that wasn't right. You think I didn't notice, but I did. I never understood where that meanness came from."

I felt a shiver. And then the words just flew out. "I think she's always known I was gay."

He looked down, then back up at me. "Yeah, you're prob-ably right."

"You knew?"

"I'm not a total moron. I figured you'd tell me if you wanted to. If not, well, that was your business."

I'm rarely at a loss for words, but I was right then. But before I could form a response, I heard the front door open and a voice call, "Yoo-hoo. Anyone here?"

"Thank God," said Ivor, jumping up and rushing out of the room.

A few seconds later, Gloria hobbled in leaning on a cane.

The cane was new. And she looked so old and wizened that the sight of her almost took my breath away.

"Astrid," she said, somewhat coolly.

"Gloria."

She raised an eyebrow and gave me the once-over. "I'm not the only one who's aged, you know."

I smiled. She'd read my mind. "I wore my new jeans specially for your birthday party. Do you like them?" I wanted to ask if she'd invited Mr. Smith, but decided it was too snarky, even for me.

"Let me take your coat," offered Ivor, moving in between us.

"My luggage is in the trunk. Be a good boy."

"Of course," he said, giving me a stern look as he steamed off.

Almost immediately, people began arriving, bringing presents, offering congratulations. Ivor put on some music my mother liked and I poured champagne. I wanted to continue the conversation I'd begun with him, but that would have to wait.

Gloria eyed me as I moved among the guests. I figured we'd tangle properly, I mean *talk*, after everyone had left.

As the sun faded over the lake, more lights were turned on. I'd been tasked with answering the front door. While I stood waiting for people to come up the walk, an idea occurred. Annie calls these my *Magnum, P.I.* moments. I began to wonder how on earth Chandler's poor mother could have made it all the way out to a farmer's field in freezing cold weather with virtually nothing on. Had her death really been an accident or could it have been something more sinister? Was I seriously contemplating using the word *murder*? Could Chandler have been involved?

Okay, so I admit I can be pretty thick sometimes. It took a while, but it finally penetrated my consciousness that there could be another meaning to Chandler's phone message. He wanted me to know that he might have a solution to my problem, but that begged a significant question. Which problem had he been referring to?

That's as far as my thinking had progressed when the front bell chimed just after six. As I walked into the hall, I saw Chandler standing just inside the screened door, a box under his arm.

"Hey," he said, reaching into his pocket and pulling out what looked like my keys. "I didn't give these back to you last night. Thought maybe I could find someone to look at your car."

I hadn't even realized they were gone.

"So, turns out I have a buddy whose dad used to own a Volvo. He came over to the parking lot and did a little tinkering. It's working now." He dropped the keys into my hand.

"That's incredible. What do I owe him?"

"Nothing," he said. "It wasn't a big deal. You gonna invite me in?"

"Um," I said, not sure why he had any interest in an old lady's birthday.

"I bought her a gift."

"You did?"

"Yup." He grinned as he pushed past me and disappeared into the crowd.

I felt a bit embarrassed for thinking so ill of him. After saying goodbye to an older couple who thanked me profusely for the wonderful party, I returned to the living room. By then, Chandler had found Gloria in the back by the fireplace. She'd already opened the box. The gift appeared to be some kind of liqueur. I watched while he found a glass and then filled it with a dark brown liquid.

You know how, when something terrible happens, time seems to stand still? That's what happened next. My mother sniffed the liquid. Chandler looked around the room until he found me, and then he winked. In that moment, I knew what was about to go down. I'd been such a fool. How could a simple conversation in a bar end like this?

"No," I screamed. The scream coincided with swelling trumpets in a big band tune. "Mom!"

I could see her lift the glass to her lips.

I flung myself forward. It felt as if every warm body in that room moved to bar my way. I saw Ivor glance at me, looking startled. Chandler appeared surprised. He held up his hands as if to suggest innocence, but I saw right through him. He wasn't innocent any more than I was. "Mom, no," I yelled again, blocked by some aging linebacker. I began to jump up and down, waving to get her attention.

That's when she handed the glass back to Chandler and turned to face me.

And she glared.

Had I saved her life? Maybe, though I never found out. Chandler slunk away before I could talk to him. I eventually managed to dump the contents of the bottle down the bathroom sink. Should I have saved it and had the contents tested? Magnum P.I. would have, but I didn't have the stomach for it.

Gloria, of course, demanded a reason for my outburst, but how could I explain that I'd sort of told a stranger in a dive bar that my life would be oh so much better if only my mother would get fitted for a couple of cement shoes? I let her—and everyone else—think my actions were the result of too much champagne. What did I care? It was just one more nail in my coffin.

So, there you have it. My trip home to Hollywood, Minnesota, had pretty much been the train wreck I'd expected. All I can say is, by the end of the evening, I'd decided that *I* should be the one to call Mr. Smith to come get me. It seemed only fair.

FOREVER UNCONQUERED

G. MIKI HAYDEN

Watching a yellow-legged white heron wading in the water, Billie Sua, proprietor of Seminole Billie's Airboat Rides, prepared to allow himself to snooze. Seconds later, however, the sound of a car on the packed-dirt road off the Tamiami Trail caught his attention. Could be friends come round for a visit, or might be pleasure-seeking tourists carrying cash.

But when two men parked and got out of their SUV, Billie knew the pair of them weren't his friends, or even sightseers of any kind—only trouble.

Billie, an Army Ranger who had experienced enough combat to last him the rest of his days, had returned to the Big Cypress reservation from Afghanistan a while back with a busted knee. And after two years of war, he had a good idea of what deep-down, serious trouble looked like.

In this case, trouble looked like two men in hunting khakis, muscular men who carried with them their own atmosphere of tension, mistrust, and obvious danger.

This was not good.

For a brief moment as the two approached, Billie switched his gaze toward his sister and mother at their sewing machines near the family chickee, where they made colorful patchwork skirts and shirts to sell. Billie's sister had come back home once Billie returned, and after her no-good husband had disappeared. Billie's lips tightened, and his gut contracted. Without his family, a man was nothing, and Billie would handle whatever he must to protect his plump, brown mama and his long-suffering sister.

The darker, taller man with a livid scar across his left cheek took the lead when he arrived at the plastic-webbed lounger from which Billie had quickly stood.

"We want to hunt wild pigs in the Everglades," the bigger man announced, making no effort at casual conversation.

Billie searched the scarred man's face and that of the smaller, bearded man but didn't answer. His intention was to reply with a "no." He didn't take people hunting, except with cameras.

Scarface then pushed a map under Billie's nose and pointed at one of the hammocks of trees and stable land. "We want to go there."

"That's in the national park," Billie answered finally, sure of himself. "They don't allow hunting inside the park."

"Okay," agreed the man without hesitation. "Then we won't hunt. But that's where we want to go."

Billie shook his head in refusal. "Can't take you there. They don't allow airboats in the park."

Both men stared at Billie as if evaluating whether he was lying.

"I can tell you where to go for a wild boar hunt, but they may be booked," Billie went on. The idea of getting rid of these two lightened the heaviness he'd begun to feel.

His sense of relief lasted no longer than it takes to exhale once. "Look here," said the leader, the man with the scar. And he directed Billie's attention to the semiautomatic pistol he carried in a short holster on his waist. "Can you take us where we want to go?"

Billie's heart sped into overdrive, and he made a sound indicating acquiescence. These men didn't understand the Indian people, however, or the Muskoki, as Billie's tribe was actually called. The Muskoki, the Seminoles, had not been conquered despite three wars with the US Army. Billie's people had hidden in the swamps and had never surrendered.

The time had not yet come for a defeat, and Billie wouldn't let himself be taken down.

But as the ex-Ranger began to limp toward the seven-passenger airboat Billie'd bought secondhand for seventy thousand bucks, the man with the scar put out his hand to detain the Indian. "We want the girl to go with us, too," Scarface said. "As a kind of insurance against your misbehaving."

That statement stopped Billie's scurrying brain midstream, delivering a further and still more horrid blow. His sister, whom he loved dearly and had protected all her life, shouldn't be a pawn in this high-stakes game.

"Call her over," Scarface ordered.

Billie realized that was his only choice. Because you don't argue when the other guy holds a gun on you. And if Billie balked, he would only get all three Suas killed.

Because this was the rainy season, Billie had wide sloughs of open water to fly the boat over. In his seat above the passengers and in front of the rotor spitting out a constant grating noise, Billie looked down at the two thugs—with Mary Jane next to the bearded one on a double-seat bench. If they touched her, if either of them touched her... The burning heat of anger flushed through his body.

Mary Jane hadn't protested when he'd said to join them. She was smart and capable in her own right, but very used to following Billie's lead. Still, he'd seen the tension in her jawline

when she'd come along, as he saw it in the back of her neck right
now. She'd been through too much in her twenty years of life,
and he grieved at her having to endure this present situation.

One thing that Billie wasn't, and that was stupid. In fact, he
was usually the opposite—and cool under pressure. Such was
the part he'd almost liked about engaging in combat. He could
think clearly in the midst of the shooting, and strategize. But
having his sister with him made him more emotional. He wasn't
quite sure what he might do.

Right now, Billie understood that the men he was carrying
onto federal land were criminals of some kind—and they were
ignorant. Didn't they know these swamps were heavily patrolled
by air for signs of cocaine and illegal-immigrant smuggling?

The man with the scar turned and called up something Billie didn't catch at all.

He was already half-deaf from the gunfire of battle; in another few years, the grinding of the engines of *The Unconquered*
would leave him completely without the ability to hear.

Supposing, of course, he lived that long.

But Billie could see what the man was driving at: a park
ranger in uniform paddled toward them in a fiberglass canoe—
Billie's old schoolmate, Eddie Gordon, a white guy. Billie decided to do the ranger a favor and save his life. He veered the
airboat in the other direction, away from the park.

"Hey, Billie. Your mother phoned," yelled Eddie over his
battery-powered megaphone. Billie waved in response to show
he'd heard. He smiled at the thought of his mother on the cell
phone—which she hated—insisting someone find her kids.

The man with the scar got out of his seat and looked ready
to approach the airboat captain. Scarface really shouted this
time, and his intense volume showed a temper. "What...trying
to do?...arrested?"

Billie couldn't hear every word, but he caught the gist and

shook his head in the negative. "No problem," he yelled back. "I know him." He smiled.

If he had stopped for Eddie, and Eddie had warned the airboat away from the park, Scarface might well have just shot the ranger where he sat, paddle in hand.

What now? Billie could hardly turn around and cross over onto federal land while the ranger watched. And, of course, only Billie, and not even his sister, knew where they were and where he was headed.

Entering one of the narrow channels of sawgrass for which the Everglades had been named a "river of grass"—Pa-Hay-Okee—Billie slowed. During the dry season sometimes the sawgrass burned, but this was the wet season in which the alligators enjoyed their wallow, and the mosquitoes bloomed.

Below Billie, the two men swatted at their arms and necks. Mary Jane and Billie with long-sleeved garments and perpetually drenched in natural repellents did no such dance.

Mary Jane had married her husband, Joe Osceola, while Billie was away. The first time he'd come home after that, he'd seen her with a red-and-black swollen eye from where Joe had punched her. The once cheerful girl appeared subdued. Joe didn't let her out to see her friends and didn't even want her to spend time with her brother.

Billie had smoldered, but Mary Jane had tried to calm him down. "I can dispose of him for you," Billie had said.

His sister had given him a wary look. "It hasn't come to that," she told him. And by the way she spoke, he'd known she might sooner rather than later arrive at that point.

Thereafter, he'd spent a couple weeks at home one more time before coming back again with his knee busted in a Humvee accident. On that visit, his sister looked haggard and ten years older, but once more she'd restrained Billie from taking action. He supposed that the killing of a civilian in the civilian world might not be wise, but Joe was a Seminole though he lived like a white man—drinking, and treating his wife like a dog.

The traditional Seminole husband went to live with his wife's family after marriage, surely the solution to any possible abuse. The Seminole way—the native way—had always been one of respect for women. Women tilled the soil, made their own money from the sale of their crops and crafts, participated in governing the tribe, and owned their own property.

This ill-treatment of women was an aberration, a sickness that came from alcohol, drugs, and the white form of society.

But why should Billy kid himself? The native culture, which had developed during a span of 12,000 or more years, had disintegrated quickly over a mere couple of hundred. Like the whites' favorite foodstuff—sugar—the white style of living had its sweet attractions, ones that often led to devastating results.

The way Mary Jane looked at her brother when he'd come back, a crutch under one arm—he'd seen an explosive emotion smoldering in her eyes. And neither of them had questioned Billie's willingness to do absolutely anything for her.

Billie spent a while trolling the swamps for nothing at all. Scarface came up to him once and glared, carefully gripping onto the railing so that Billie couldn't have just gunned the engine and raised a wave big enough to throw the thug off. Billie simply nodded to indicate he knew what he was doing.

What Billie was doing was wasting time—plus thinking—which *itself* really was a waste of time since he was able to form no clear tactic or clever plan. He frittered away a half-hour or so in the hope that Eddie would be gone by then, in order for the airboat to have a clear shot into the park.

Billie ran his hand down his right leg, the wounded one. He wasn't trying to soothe the knee, he simply wanted to reassure himself that his Ranger assault knife was there as always—reachable through the hole in his jeans. You'd have to be crazy to go into the glades without a knife as a tool or as a weapon. A man, a soldier, would have to be nuts to go anywhere these days unarmed. And, see: he was right.

Then while Billie motored through the swampland, he thought of the pricey fuel he was burning up. Filling the tank these days cost between four thousand and five thousand dollars at a gulp. These gangsters hadn't paid him one copper cent.

In fact, that line of thought rang an alarm bell in his mind. If they were picking up a cocaine delivery at Gumbo-Limbo Hammock, which they had pointed to, where was their suitcase full of cash in exchange? They didn't have one. Maybe drug smugglers in the twenty-first century took bank checks from the local distributors? Billie didn't think so.

So, could they be dealing in something else? Illegal immigrants? No, not these men. They were too…killer…too aggressive. Men like these weren't sent to pick up fearful day workers. That was a job for low-level bullies.

Maybe they were supposed to collect one important illegal immigrant such as a higher-up mob boss or major drug lord? That, too, didn't make sense—why the Everglades, and not a regular flight with a falsified passport?

As for terrorism, these thugs were thoroughly red, white, and blue—even if Scarface was Latino. So what? He was obviously not a traitor to this country, just a professional criminal scumbag.

Billie played it the way he usually dealt with risky situations. He leaned into them. That approach struck him as sort of Seminole, the strategy of using what the enemy did and turning it against them, instead of chancing a hotheaded, stick-your-neckout frontal attack.

Plus he was curious. Billie wanted to see what happened next. He knew for sure his passengers weren't going to shoot him right now. They had to return to where they had started from to pick up their car. And Mary Jane was the hostage to make Billie behave. After they returned to Billie's chickee, then they would kill him, his sister, and his mother. So he had time.

This was a beautiful season in the Everglades if you didn't mind the heat or the mosquitoes. Billy didn't. The summer heat had been a whole lot worse over in the Middle East.

Anyway, he was used to this. He loved the wading heron, egrets, spoonbills, and ibis. He liked to watch the pelicans swoop directly onto their prey. He had seen every kind of animal here, from the elusive Florida panther, to the deer, to manatee, to rabbits, to foxes, to frogs twice the size of his hand, to crocs sunning in the salty marshes.

And he couldn't list all the plant life here or the fish, from bass to bluegills, he caught for dinner right near the family chickee. In the wet season. The dry season could be problematic, with alligators crawling underneath the house, fish dying in droves, and the airboat having limited waters through which to navigate.

Luckily, the three Suas received tribal money—which was how they'd built their somewhat modern chickee, tithed to the Seminole Baptist church, paid their electric bills, and bought necessities. White money spent gambling on their land meant Billie could handle the loan for *The Unconquered*.

Although navigating with his eye on the scenery, Billie remained watchful for any activity below him, and a flash of motion caught his attention. Scarface had seized Mary Jane's arm and now pulled the resisting girl directly toward him.

Billie cut the engine, and, boiling mad, descended the steps to the passenger level. His knee hurt, and though he was aware of the pain, it wasn't at the forefront of his mind.

Scarface, of course, was ready with the gun in his hand.

Some emotions rise up more strongly than the drive for survival, however, and Billie felt pushed into a state beyond rationality or caution.

"Let her alone," he insisted, as if he himself were the one with the gun.

"Oh, hey there, man. Is this your girl? Your wife, maybe?" Scarface continued to tug the girl toward him.

"Do you want to get out of the Everglades?" Billie asked in turn. "Leave her alone."

Scarface must have believed him, and for good reason. The thug released the girl and Billie took her hand then had her sit down in the double seat on the other side of the bearded one. "Look around you," he said to the second man. "If either one of you touches her, this is the last place on earth you'll ever see."

Not that he intended to take them back alive, anyway.

He hove around to the Gumbo-Limbo Hammock, a well-known stand of red-barked gumbo-limbo trees. Unlike some of the other named hammocks, this onetime shell mound of the Calusa tribe remained unconnected to land by bridge or path.

Whoever had chosen the spot was either a good reader of maps or knew the park intimately.

Billie drove the front end of the airboat onto the elevation of land and shut off the motor. Not only had he torn up some of the sawgrass on his journey here, but he now threatened the fragile limestone underlayer, two of the reasons why airboats were unwelcome in this environment.

Billie nodded solemnly at Scarface, who scratched at his arms in response. "Here we are," said Billie, glad not to be in competition with the whine of the rotor for the moment. "What do we do now?"

"Shut up," answered Scarface. "Now we wait."

And so they waited, the two thugs scratching and dipping into the marsh for water to soothe their itchy bites. Billie watched for the snout of an alligator attracted by the splashing, which might make for an attention-grabbing interaction. But after minutes of tense quietude, the first message to Billie's senses wasn't a sight, it was a sound—the buzzing of something overhead.

Then Billie looked up to see a light, two-seater plane, maybe made from a kit, circle around. Shortly after an elegant dive, it landed like a dragonfly on top of the water.

In other circumstances, Billie might have jumped up at once to offer to trade his earthbound *Unconquered* for the sexy little waterskiing bird. But he restrained his enthusiasm as Scarface got out of the boat and walked onto the hammock. Billie would love to see the man crash through the porous limestone and maybe break his leg.

No such luck.

The second thug, Blackbeard, didn't follow, but kept his eyes on Mary Jane, glancing up occasionally at Billie.

Scarface stepped over to meet a man in a blue shirt who had exited the plane.

Then, before Billie had even a second to prepare himself, Scarface brought his gun out of nowhere, placed it against the man's torso and shot.

Instantly, Scarface turned and shot directly into the plane through the windshield, catching not only Billie off-guard but the pilot as well. The flier's expression turned to wide-eyed astonishment, and in that very second, he slumped over the instrument panel.

Despite being a man who had regularly seen other men blown to pieces by bombs and mortar, Billie was stunned. Scarface had positioned himself precisely right to shoot his victims.

So much for long-term business partnerships. And that explained their not needing cash to pay for a shipment.

"Bring the girl and come help me," Scarface called to the bearded man still in Billie's boat. Scarface waded the few feet out to the plane and looked as if he was making sure the pilot was dead.

Billie also disembarked. He caught up with Mary Jane, gripped her hand and squeezed out a reassurance. He felt her body shaking. Well, of course.

Although he hadn't been summoned, Billie helped Blackbeard check a couple of small suitcases for bags of powder and then take them from the plane while Scarface stood on shore holding the gun on the girl. Scarface smiled at the sight of the haul.

"Let's get rid of the plane now," Scarface said to the bearded one.

"Set the gas tank on fire," Mary Jane advised.

Billie understood that she wanted to attract law enforcement attention, but he didn't see that as being wise. *Hostages Killed in Shootout with Officers* was something you heard about all the time. Besides which, when Billie fell in love, he fell hard, and he had a hard-on for the little seaplane. "Not good," he said, quickly disagreeing with his sister. "A fire will be seen for miles around. Just leave it."

Without pausing to find out if Scarface agreed, he led the way back to *The Unconquered* then clambered on. The others followed.

Stepping up to the captain's chair, Billie worked to disengage his mind from the situation. Thought would bring him no advantage now, only action would, and not his brain, but his body, had to choose the moment.

Billie hadn't buried Joe Osceola, but had taken him out to a gator hole he knew, an efficient way to dispose of unwanted dead meat. Somewhere a gator held a swallowed bullet in its belly, unless it had already excreted it. Driving the airboat in that direction, Billy wondered about the bones.

Signs all over the Everglades told tourists not to feed the alligators. Yet Billie had trained one or more to eat human flesh.

Joe Osceola—gone but not forgotten, neither by his wife nor by Billie. Nor by the predator that had had its fill of him.

Trust his body? Billie thought with an inner laugh. He must have twisted his knee just the slightest bit at the hammock and now it pulsed with pain. A few years before, he would have jumped on Scarface from above with confidence in his body to do the deed. Today, his ability to perform what a young man should be able to had vanished. And he was one of the lucky ones. He had come back from the war without some limb completely missing or his brains permanently scrambled like they showed on TV. That was what he got for fighting in a white man's war.

Push was coming closer to shove. On the way to Gumbo-Limbo Hammock, Billie had felt he could take his time. Now, their time was running out.

Back in his seat, tooling along, Billie began to feel anger at his failure to kill the two thugs, and he tried to calm himself. Could he have taken the initiative at any moment so far? He wanted to tell himself that he could have done something if he'd been in better shape, but he really didn't think he could have. The gun had been right there, between the two of them, all along. Billie was a trained fighter despite his bum knee, but he wasn't Chuck Norris. Plus the fight hadn't been planned out for him by some choreographer on a movie set. This was the real world, with real stakes.

Now, Scarface looked back at Billie from time to time—with a smile as if he were amused. But Billie didn't believe he was amused at all. Scarface simply had in mind how he was going to kill Billie and rape and kill Billie's sister. The man's mind was small and shallow and easy to read.

Right now, all Billie wanted to do was lull Scarface into thinking everything was A-OK. Though if he thought that after seeing Billie's true nature earlier, he was even stupider than Billie thought.

All of a sudden, Billie took a deep breath and made the engine stutter—on and off, on and off. The boat jerked, and upset one of the drug cases so it slid across the deck. Billie shut off the engine at once, his heart pounding in his ears. "Sorry," he shouted, or he hoped it came out that way because he could barely even hear himself. "Not enough gas. I'll get it for you."

He hurried down the two steps again awkwardly, and reached to the deck for the case. He steadied himself once or twice as he bent and held onto his leg.

"Listen," said Mary Jane. "I have an idea."

Billie could feel the drug dealers' attention turn to her.

Clever girl. In that moment of cover, he slipped the knife out of its sewn-in sheath and pulled it through the slit in his jeans. He picked up the case and turned back to Scarface.

"We'll help you get away," she said. "We'll give you our pickup in case they're looking for your SUV." She was babbling.

Sweat dripped off Billie's forehead into his eyes. His knee throbbed. Scarface's gun was his primary target—then, Scarface. After that, he'd disable Blackbeard.

Billie held out the case to Scarface, and behind it came the knife in his hand.

Next, he used the case to crack Scarface across the delicate small bones that connected to the fingers, taking the drug dealer by surprise.

The gun hit the aluminum hull with a clunk.

At the same time, Billie shoved his knife into the man's soft guts, the easiest target. Sure, the heart was potentially more deadly, but much better protected by a cage of ribs.

One deep cut into Scarface's abdomen with an upward twist was all he had time for. He had to get rid of the bearded guy quickly.

While Billie held Scarface at bay as the man bled out, a glance showed Billie his sister had sprawled on the deck, going after the gun. Blood gushed over Billie's right hand, and he pulled the knife from the dying gangster.

Billie had been fast, but not fast enough. Blackbeard already held his gun in hand.

One shot and Billie would be dead. Two shots and his sister would be gone as well.

"Hold it," shouted Blackbeard. "Hold it. Hold it." His Beretta was steady on Billie though half his attention focused on Mary Jane.

Billie had taken a risk and he had lost. He hadn't been quick enough. That would have been next to impossible. The good news was that Blackbeard still needed Billie to pilot him over to his SUV.

Okay, okay. One down; one to go. Billie's only question was whether Blackbeard was a greater or lesser danger than Scarface had been. Billie feared the second man might be even worse.

"Let's calm down," said Blackbeard. His face streamed with sweat and his breathing came hard and heavy though he had done nothing physical as of yet. The man's adrenaline must be through the roof. Did that mean his brain might short-circuit and his trigger finger jump? Or did he understand he needed the airboat pilot?

Still, Billie felt like his old self for the moment. With his own excitement pumping through his system, he felt good. And having killed Scarface, the dirtbag, he felt victorious. He felt like a soldier. He felt like a Seminole. He didn't feel like a has-been.

For the time being.

"I'm DEA Special Agent Dennis Cole," said the thug.

Billie's knee gave way as much from surprise as fatigue and pain, and he sat without wanting to on the blood-and-gut-spattered deck. Billie had killed someone with a federal agent as his witness. That was bad, potentially very bad.

Billie's plan had been to feed Scarface to the gators. Blackbeard—Cole—too.

Billie would have driven the SUV out of the area and taken a bus back.

He could still do that. He could still kill the DEA agent, and killing Cole might in fact be wise.

"Get up, young lady, and take the seat below me," said Blackbeard, who maybe wasn't a thug at all.

Mary Jane did get up, but her expression was a cynical one. "Why are we supposed to believe you?" she asked.

That's what Billie could always say if he was caught. *We didn't believe him. I didn't believe him.* And he knew he would be caught, that Cole would have told the feds where he and Scarface were going, for sure, or he had a government tracking device on him.

Billie sighed. He didn't want to kill the damn DEA guy, anyway. Not really.

Blackbeard retrieved Scarface's gun and pushed it into his waistband. Then he stuck his own gun into a shoulder holster. "You'll believe me, because it's true." He took out his cell phone. "I'm part of the High Intensity Drug Trafficking Interagency Taskforce, and I'm going to get some of our team in here now."

Billie had been in the US Army, and he knew how the white government operated. These people did what they wanted to. Their rules were meant to be bent and broken. But what was the reality behind what Billie had done? Could his killing Scarface be seen as self-defense? Or would they prefer to try him for murder? He looked around, got up, went back to the captain's seat, turned on the engine and drove the airboat forward.

Cole looked at Billie as if he was crazy, but the DEA agent didn't do anything.

Billie wasn't crazy in the slightest, however. He was cautious.

What was self-defense in the white man's world, anyway? Billie figured it depended on whether they wanted to get you or not. Billie didn't matter—only the feds' take on the situation did.

With the rotor squealing, Billie couldn't hear a thing, but Cole pointed out at the water as Scarface had done earlier in the day. US Park Ranger Eddie Gordon. At least this time the ranger's life probably wasn't in danger. Billie glanced around and cut the motor. He had a way to handle this.

He walked down the steps and came to the railing. "What's up?" he shouted down at Eddie. Mary Jane and Cole came to the railing, too.

"Where's your other passenger?" asked Eddie.

Billie pointed. He doubted if Eddie could see the body from his canoe. "Dead," he told the park ranger coolly. He didn't elaborate.

"Does he need medical attention?" shouted back Billie's old schoolmate.

The Seminole resisted his natural inclination to be sarcastic. He shook his head.

"If he died in the park..." began the ranger.

This was exactly the signal Billie had waited for.

"You're trespassing on sovereign territory," he yelled out. "You're on waters belonging to the Seminole Nation." He had to smile.

Could be that he'd killed Scarface in the national park. The moment had become a blur to him now. He'd moved the boat along to be further into Seminole territory, but he couldn't be sure where he'd killed the man. At any rate, he couldn't be arrested here—not by the ranger and not by the DEA special agent. Only by the tribal police.

He would be brought before the tribal council, and that was fine. They'd give Billie Sua a commendation for handling a threat. He was home free. And they'd never find out about Joe Osceola. That Osceola had been shot in the head, and that Billie had brought him out to the gator hole to get rid of the body.

What would they do to Mary Jane if they knew? Probably do nothing to her, either. Because they all understood the nature of Joe Osceola and how he'd treated the vivacious, smart, and capable young girl.

"…reward for capture of drug smugglers…" Eddie was saying. "What about him?" Overhead, Billie noticed a helicopter. It swooped in and swooped away.

"DEA Special Agent Dennis Cole," called out Blackbeard. "I'll vouch for the young man's reward."

A reward? They were going to make a hero of him? That might put a different spin on things.

"That little plane the drug dealers came in, the seaplane. Will they put it on auction?" Billie asked Cole. "Can I get her?" Only true love could conquer the Seminole.

Cole seemed to sort of laugh, though Billie couldn't hear him above the first and second copters and the speedboat. Cole nodded his head yes.

"I'll follow you into the park," Billie shouted down at Eddie. "Can't have the feds on Seminole land. Stop the speedboat, Ranger, and don't let it in. We Seminole don't want intruders here."

Billie looked at Mary Jane, and she looked strong. Just as she had after she'd killed her husband.

PRIVATE DANCER

JONATHAN SANTLOFER

It was like a drive-in movie, her body shimmering in a rectangle of light two stories above the dark street, and me, wrapped in my winter coat and privilege, watching. Everything else irrelevant—the time, my long workday, the fact that my wife was home waiting—everything but this incandescent woman dancing, just for me. When the window went dark, I tugged my coat tighter and got into the car. "Home," I said, and my driver took off, though the girl in the rectangle of light continued dancing behind my lids.

The next night it was crisp but not too cold and I decided to walk, something my dear wife, Cora, had been urging me to do, get more exercise. I had no destination in mind until I was there and saw the girl in the window, dancing, this time noting the small neon sign, GALLO DANCE STUDIO, and was once again hypnotized until a cold wind hit me like a slap. I checked the time and was surprised to see I had been there almost an hour.

I hurried down the street trying to shake off the absurdity of it, of *me*, a prosperous man standing in the street like a homeless beggar. I shivered, tugged on fur-lined leather gloves I'd purchased in a little shop off the Corso Venezia in Milan less than a year ago, and searched for a taxi, the streets of the financial district quiet and practically deserted at this hour. It was nearly twenty minutes before I found one, slumped into the back seat, and called my wife. I told her I'd been trapped in an endless meeting, and that I'd be home soon.

"I'll wait and have dinner with you," she said, always sweet, never demanding and surely not suspicious. Why should she be?

Cora and I ate alone in our Sutton Place penthouse. It was late and the cook and maid had both gone home. We chatted about my day at the office, hers organizing a charity ball, our two grown sons, one working at the Swiss National Bank in Bern, an obvious asset for me, the other a forest ranger in Oregon, not something I had taken to easily but had come to see as a noble occupation and I was proud of him. Proud of them all. My boys. My wife. The wonderful family I had created, the homes I had acquired, New York, Palm Beach, Palm Springs, the ranch in Jackson Hole. But still, this thing called home felt elusive, as if on loan and not really mine to keep.

I took in the wall of windows, the dark swath of river and the glittering lights along the East Side Drive, but it was another view, of a girl swaying in a rectangle of light, that sparked in my mind.

"Have you spoken to your partners about purchasing a table for the gala?" Cora's voice cut through my reverie.

"I don't have to *ask*," I said. "After all, it is my business."

"Of course," she said, and smiled, never one to criticize me even when I recognized I was being a bit pompous.

That night I had trouble sleeping, the girl in the window playing on an endless loop, and in the morning, I was tired and impatient with myself for being so reckless.

Cora, always attuned to my moods, asked if I was okay and I told her I was fine but wanted to get out, skipped breakfast and made it to the office early, my day filled with the usual calls, meetings, emails, texts, stock prices rolling on a screen opposite my desk. Several times I thought about the girl in the window but vowed I would not go back and was sticking to it.

That night, I headed downtown, telling myself I just needed to see if she was real.

She was. Dancing in the window, short black dress flapping above her knees, arms fluttering around her face. I guessed she was in her twenties, and tall, though my sidewalk view possibly skewed and elongated her figure. Her hair was long and red, like a flame, and I the moth. I knew what happened to moths and didn't stay long, pleased that I was able to tear myself away.

The next night I had dinner with a business associate at the Metropolitan Club. Founded by J. Pierpont Morgan in the late nineteenth century it still maintained its old-world glamour and dignity, men in jackets and ties, women (a much later and dubious addition), in dresses, skirts or what was referred to in the House Rules as "dressy pantsuits." The Fifth Avenue mansion was as quiet and comforting as ever though my mind wandered. After dinner I took a cab and found myself staring up at the dance studio window, tonight a garish rainbow of colored lights painting the girl's body blue then red then purple. She was dancing to a beat I couldn't hear, but something fast judging by the way she moved, quick-stepping in high heels, hips shaking, head whipping, and after a while I could hear the music muffled through the glass and the noise of the city, some kind of rock with a pulsing beat that coiled inside me like a snake, and though I didn't move it was as if I were dancing too.

Cora didn't ask why I was late, and I offered no excuse. *Why should I?* I had done nothing wrong. She got into bed early complaining of a headache and I made the appropriate *too-bad* face and kissed her forehead. Then I sat in my book-lined study gazing down at the river. I thought about slipping out to see if the girl was still there, but at one in the morning it was doubtful, and I didn't really need to see it, she was still dancing in my mind. When I finally went to bed, I imagined the two of us dancing, and the colored lights, warm and rhythmic, rocked me to sleep.

In the morning, I recognized my folly, this weakness in me, once again. What I was doing was not only absurd but dangerous, the idea of jeopardizing my home and family, my reputation, and resolved to do better. I was on my game at work, stayed in my office even later than usual, then took a walk. I asked my driver to follow me, an escape if I needed one. When I found myself on that familiar street, I looked up to see the window was dark and took it as a sign. It was over and I was glad, relieved.

I was walking toward my car when I felt the splash of light and turned to see her in the window, dancing as sinuously as a snake charmer, drawing me in.

Could I chance it? Did I dare? I took a deep breath and headed toward the door then stopped and quickly backtracked into my waiting car. "Drive!" I said. I had to get away fast. The idea that I'd almost acted on my impulses yet again, risking everything, my wife, my home, had me trembling.

I stared through the car's tinted windows, the city lights streaking and blurring. This was not the man I had become, in control, sensible, responsible—to my business, the people who worked for me, the clients who entrusted me with their money, and especially to my wife and family.

I could barely look at Cora when I got home.

"Are you all right, Arthur?" she asked with typical concern.

"Of course!" I said too loud. Then softer, "Just tired, dear."

"You're working too hard. Late every night. It's not good for you."

"No," I said, and touched her cheek. Cora, kind, still lovely, I had no complaints after thirty-two years of marriage, not with her. We were a devoted couple, a power couple, Cora always behind me, supporting me.

"Is it really necessary to keep working this hard at your age?"

She had a point, though it irked me: I did not feel old nor enjoy being reminded of my age.

I took a pill that night, I needed to sleep, but the girl in the window would not rest, dancing in my head, red hair whipping around her face like flames, but it was *me* who was on fire.

I kept telling myself not to go back, but I did. One night blowing off a client, the next arriving an hour late to Cora's charity gala.

"Where have you been?" she asked. "I was so worried."

Cora, always concerned, how could I deceive her?

I vowed to stay away. And this time I kept my vow.

For five long days.

On the sixth, I called home to say there was a complication at work, once again gave my driver the night off, then headed over to the dance studio the whole time telling myself to turn around.

The window was lit but the girl wasn't in it. Couples skittered across the light-filled rectangle, dipping and whirling.

Where was she?

I felt empty, bereft, as if I had lost something I'd never had.

I was just reaching for the knob when the door swung open. I stumbled back, almost falling, but the man caught hold of my arm.

"You okay?" I nodded, anxious to get away. "Hey, I seen you here the other night, and the night before that."

I couldn't miss the outer-borough accent or the cheap, flashy clothes. Tall and thin with slicked-back hair, and young, no more than midthirties. I could see he was sizing me up too.

"It's...on my way home," I said, which it wasn't.

"You like watching the dancers?"

"Sure, why not?" I forced a laugh.

"But you can't hear no music out here. C'mon," he said, taking hold of my arm again.

"Where?"

"Upstairs. To the studio. To dance with the girls."

I tugged out of his grip. "I don't dance."

"Anyone can dance," he said and laughed, high-pitched and nasal. He pointed up at the building, to the small neon sign. "That's me, Gallo, Sal Gallo. This is my place, five years now. I live above the studio."

I was torn between running and the idea he had just planted in my mind: dancing with the girls, one in particular.

"I got three older sisters who taught me how to dance and now I teach it, salsa, rumba, jitterbug, cha cha cha." He did a little cha-cha right there on the sidewalk, swiveling his hips in a way that embarrassed me. "C'mon," he said again. "Live a little."

His hand back on my arm, I let him lead me inside and up a narrow staircase.

The music was pulsing and percussive, colored lights bouncing off mirrored walls and the shiny floor which reflected the dancers.

"Cost me a small fortune," Sal said, stamping his tap shoes on the floor and shouting over the din. "Non-slip vinyl, but worth it. You can't have people falling on their keisters, right?" He leaned in close and I caught a whiff of store-bought cologne and cigarettes. "I got ballet, jazz twice a week, modern, everything, and real pros working here, not just your everyday Joes, not that I got anything against amateurs. They pay the rent."

I nodded but had stopped listening because I saw her, across the room, dancing alone, eyes closed and rippling to the music. I started walking toward her, couples cutting across my path, raking their shoulders and rolling their hips, colored lights turning them into abstract paintings. Halfway there, she opened her eyes, angled a smile at me and I knew it was too late, that the switch had been flipped, one that I was unable to turn off.

Arms stretched out, she beckoned to me.

I took a step, then stopped because I had caught my reflection in a mirror, tall older man in a topcoat, stiff and comical among the nubile young crowd. *What was I doing here?* I turned to go, but Sal laid a hand on my back and urged me forward until I was in front of her, standing there, no idea what to do. But she knew. She took hold of my hands, pulled me toward her, and I let her guide me, gently leading me one way then the other. When the music slowed, she did too, and we were finally together, my arms around her back, her perfume in my nose. She stripped off my topcoat and tossed it to a chair, then my hat, all without missing a step, then her hands were on my hips rotating them while she shimmied to the music and I felt something open up inside me, something adolescent and yearning. When the music sped up, we spun and twirled and laughed until I was dizzy and had to let go and sagged into a chair, the colored lights throbbing, and me breathing hard but still watching her, shimmering and gorgeous, my private dancer.

She gave me a few minutes to catch my breath then had me up again for an old-fashioned foxtrot, but I insisted we sit out the jitterbug, watching others kick up their heels, Sal the best of the bunch, a hot-wire of rhythm, slicked-back hair the only part of him that wasn't moving.

"Sal is something, isn't he?" she breathed into my ear and I felt a kind of envy I hadn't felt in years.

"He your boyfriend?"

"Sal?" She tossed her head back and laughed. "No way."

When the music slowed again, she tugged me out of the chair. I was self-conscious and sweaty, feeling clumsy again, but she held me close and we danced like that, her heart beating against mine. I didn't want it to end but then the lights came on, bright and harsh, and Sal announced it was closing time and people started to leave and I let go of her to get my coat and when I turned around, she was gone.

I grabbed hold of Sal, tried hard to keep the desperation out of my voice when I asked, "Where did she go?"

"Amber?"

"Is that her name?"

"Your dance partner?" Sal winked. "Yeah, that's Amber."

Amber, like a flame.

"Did you see her leave?"

Sal shrugged while I scanned the room, ugly in the cold glare of fluorescent light, the shiny floor scuffed, mirrors scratched, almost empty now. I headed quickly downstairs and outside, but Amber was nowhere, just a few tired dancers inching down the street like caterpillars.

I had to find her but where to start, and when I looked at my cell phone and saw it was nearly 2:00 a.m. I hailed a cab, the whole way home thinking up excuses.

Cora was asleep when I slipped into bed.

"What time is it?" she asked, her voice thick with dreams.

"Shh," I said, and pecked her cheek.

"Everything okay?"

"Just work," I whispered, then rolled away from her unable to turn off the music thrumming in my head and the heat of Amber in my arms.

The next day I was all resolve again. It was enough. I was through, finished with it, with her. No more risking home and family.

A week passed. I took lunches at the Manhattan and Core Clubs with men I'd known for years who talked of bear and bull markets, multimillion-dollar artworks bought at auction, Alpine ski trips, the excellent cigars at my favorite gentlemen's club, Cercle de Lorraine, in Brussels. In the office by six and home by seven, each day I renewed my vows to stay away, happy to have gotten myself under control this time. Though the image of Amber, dancing, flickered in my brain more than once, I fought it the way you would any addiction. Mind over matter, I told myself. *You're better than this.*

On the weekend Cora and I went to a performance in the East Village, a young dance troupe she was supporting, no scenery, atonal music, only one dancer who caught my attention, a sinewy redhead, nothing at all like Amber except for the color of her hair, but enough to set my mind in motion so that I found it difficult to stay in my seat. When I couldn't take it any longer, I slid my cell phone out, pretended to read a text then whispered my usual excuse, "Work crisis—the Asian market," a cunning detail as it was Sunday. Cora sighed and I kissed her cheek. "I'll leave the car for you," I said, then excused myself down the row, my pulse already moving faster than the rest of me.

The studio window was lit with dancer's silhouettes, but no Amber.

Fine, leave, go home, the words in my head as I mounted the stairs.

Inside, a class was in session, women in leotards and tap shoes, a few men in shorts and sneakers, but no sign of Amber.

A part of me was relieved, enough of this madness. *Go home!*

Sal was outside, smoking a cigarette. "Hey, man, where you been?"

I was surprised and less than happy he remembered me.

"Just passing by," I said.

"You looking for Amber?" he asked, smoke snaking into his eyes. "I told her you'd be back."

I didn't like the idea that Sal thought he knew something about me, and worse, that he'd been talking about me. I told him to give Amber my regards and turned to go.

"Tell her yourself," he said. "She's close by. Got a place over on Pearl Street, near the water."

I kept walking, trying not to hear him.

"Twenty-six Pearl," he called after me. "Top floor, apartment eight."

★ ★ ★

The streets around Pearl were quiet and mostly deserted, tall ships anchored in the seaport like a movie set.

Twenty-six was an old brownstone, the entrance to the building beside a dive bar, The Far East, the door covered with graffiti half hiding the names and buzzers, but I could make out number eight: *A. Loomis.*

I hadn't known her last name.

I stepped back to look up at the building, then leaned in and pressed the buzzer and the front door clicked opened.

The vestibule was lit by a bare bulb, and claustrophobic. A moment's hesitation before I took the stairs, steep and uneven. By the third floor I was breathing hard, huffing by four. A door on each end of the landing, one slightly ajar before it swung open and there she was. Amber. Naked. Seconds later, in my arms, her mouth pressed against mine and we stumbled backward into her apartment. She pushed my coat off and undid my tie as we moved down a hallway into a dim, blue-lighted room, music playing softly. I tugged off my shoes and pants and then we were rolling together, my arms around her, kissing her, losing myself in the taste and smell of her.

Later, with Amber crushed beside me half asleep, I took in the room, the blinking neon light from the bar downstairs playing over a dresser covered with cosmetics and jewelry, an open closet, blouses, skirts and shoes spilling out, pantyhose draped over a chair, the clothes we'd shed on the floor. Not exactly my scene. No Hermès cashmere blankets, no Egyptian cotton sheets. Amber's linens were threadbare and worn. Everything a bit too real. I was ready to go. I reached over for my pants and Amber stirred.

"You okay?" she asked.

"Fine," I said, fighting an impulse to run.

She reached up and stroked my cheek, the sheet falling from

her breasts, and I settled back, asked how she saw anything in the murky blue light.

"There's an overhead, a standard hundred–watt. This is for *mood*, and just for you."

It got me thinking: Had she been waiting for me, blue light on, music playing?

"How did you know it was me?"

"What do you mean?" She sat up and her bare breasts brushed my arm, which almost but not quite knocked the question out of my mind.

"You buzzed me in without asking who it was."

"I looked out the window, silly. I saw you."

"I thought maybe Sal had called you."

"Why would he do that?"

"He told me where you lived."

"He knew I wanted to see you again. You're not sorry you came, are you?" She leaned in to me, and if I was sorry, I could no longer remember.

"So, you and Sal are friends?"

"Yes. I teach dance at his studio."

"You make a living at it?"

"Why? Big finance guy like you can't imagine I could?"

"How did you know I was in finance?"

"You said you worked in the neighborhood. What else could it be?"

"When did I say I worked in the neighborhood?"

Amber lay back against the pillows and sighed. "I dunno. Maybe it was just the pinstripe suit and suspenders."

I had to laugh, outed by my Wall Street costume. Then I relaxed enough to tell her my story.

How I had been working forever: paper route at ten, packing bags at the grocery as a teen, dishing out food in the school cafeteria, a job that came along with the full scholarship that had paid for my four years at Harvard. The long nights as a parale-

gal that took me through grad school and the internship at the
Wall Street firm before creating my own.

"A self-made man," Amber said.

"Totally," I said and explained how growing up an orphan I'd
never had a home, had long dreamed of having one, and how
I'd made the dream come true.

"Wow," she said. "That's like, inspiring."

I nodded then checked my Rolex. "It's late. I've got to go."

"The wife?"

"How do you know I'm married?"

"You mean, other than the band of gold on your finger? It's
okay. I don't mind."

"No?"

"No." She got up but made no attempt to get dressed. "Married or not, I think you're *swell*."

"I'm too old for you," I said, a thought in my head I hadn't
meant to say out loud.

"You're not *old*. You're handsome and *vital*. You just proved
that."

I felt my face go hot but liked it. "You're not like other
women," I said.

"Oh. Were there others?"

I shook my head and she stood back and swayed to the music.
"You like to watch me dance?"

"You're my private dancer."

"Happy to be," she said. "But you should go. I don't want to
get you in trouble."

At the door, she took my cell phone, punched in her number
and handed it back. "It's up to you if you want to call me," she
said, caressing my cheek. "But I hope you do."

The seaport streets were cold and damp, but I needed to walk,
needed to pull myself together before I got home, before I saw
Cora. Away from Amber, my guilt was kicking in: *What was
I doing here risking my family, the home I had built?* By the time I

caught a cab and it dropped me at my building, I had promised myself I would not go back.

Three nights later I did.

And the next night. And the one after that.

I couldn't stay away, couldn't get enough. I missed business meetings, dinners, events with Cora, who was always understanding. "You're working too hard," she'd say. "Exhausting yourself."

And I *was* exhausted. But exhilarated too. I was building a new home with Amber. Outfitting it with Frette sheets and Eliasa silk down pillows, soaps from Floris of London, Oribe shampoo and La Mer moisturizers, products my tribe took for granted and ones Amber got used to. As she did the expensive gifts, an antique ring with her birthstone, an opal, a platinum bracelet studded with diamonds, which I had purchased for Cora, at Cartier, for her upcoming birthday. It was easy enough to get Cora something else, and she was happy with the gold chain I had my secretary pick out, elegant and plain, and more like Cora.

The weeks passed and it was all going well. The market was up, my clients were happy, and I was in a good mood. I actually whistled on my way over to Amber's, something I rarely did; an act I considered common. I used the keys to her building and apartment and let myself in. Before I could say a word, Amber collapsed into my arms.

"I'm sorry," she said.

"About what?"

"It's not what I wanted... I never intended... Please forgive me..."

I calmed her down and she explained that the landlord had more than doubled her rent, she had no savings and would be out on the street.

I didn't see the problem. I told her I'd find her a new apartment and would pay the rent.

She was quiet a moment. Then, "I'm going to need more."

I should have seen this coming. No fool like an old fool, and a rich one. "How much?" I asked, not bothering to filter the bitterness in my tone.

"It's not what you think," she said.

"If it's not a shakedown, then what?" I was hurt and disappointed, angry too.

"Forget it," she said. "I don't want your money. I'll deal with it."

"Deal with *what*?"

Amber took a breath. "It's Sal. He put me up to this. His place, the dance studio, is going under. He's the one who needs money. He said I had to convince you, blackmail you, threaten to go to your wife."

"And you would?"

"No. Never. But…"

"But what?"

"Sal has pictures of us, of you and me, from the studio."

I tried to imagine them, Amber in my arms, her hands on my hips, my lips on her neck.

"How much does he want?"

"A lot."

"How much?"

"Two hundred and fifty *thousand*."

I had to stop myself from saying, *Is that all?* What a piker Sal was. I could have wired that much out of my account without blinking an eye, but I was still suspicious and not ready to be a patsy. "Have you and Sal been playing me all along, planning this?"

"No! I swear. But…" Amber swallowed. "He's got something on me."

"What?"

"A place where I worked, a long time ago, a law firm. I was a secretary, a temp for a few months and I…" She let out a breath. "I stole some money. I knew it was wrong, but I was very young and very broke. I promised myself I'd pay it back one day but..."

"How does Sal know about it?"

"I told him one night after too many drinks. I thought we were friends. Now he's using it against me. Says he'll turn me in if I don't get the money out of you."

"How much did you steal?"

"Ten thousand."

"I'll pay the law firm back."

"No. They'd still prosecute. I could go to jail!"

"Maybe," I said. I still wasn't sure I believed her. "Sal's pretty *certain* you can get money out of me. Did you tell him that you could?"

"Of course not!" Amber's eyes flashed. "Look, just forget it. Let him go to the law firm, to the police. I don't care. I don't want your money. It made me sick to ask."

She turned away, but when I drew her back, she fell against me, crying, and I held her, wanting to believe her, and so I told her I'd handle it.

"How?"

"I'll go to Sal. He doesn't scare me."

"That's not a good idea. Sal's family is...connected."

"Connected? As in the mob?" I laughed.

"I'm not kidding. Stay away from him. He's dangerous. You don't know him. Forget I ever asked. I'll be fine." Then she kissed me and led me to her bed where we made love.

Afterward, I told her I'd wire ten thousand dollars into her bank account and would continue to do so as long as she needed it. She insisted she didn't want my money, then she was up, dancing, swaying her body and rippling her hips, my private dancer.

I told her I would make it go away, the law firm theft, Sal, all of it, and I believed I could. I had made plenty of things go away in my lifetime, plenty of transgressions kept secret, plenty of wrongs made right. And no way I was giving Sal any money. I didn't believe he was connected, and he didn't scare me. He was just a small-time hood, a nobody, scaring Amber and now trying to scare me, the rich guy, the fool. Or so he thought. But he was wrong.

I called a guy I used to work with, a shady character, who knew a guy, who put me in touch with another guy who gave me a number, told me to use a burner phone, and I called. The man I spoke to said that for a thousand dollars he would hurt Sal. For five thousand, he'd kill him. I opted for the first. I would teach him a lesson, that was enough. The guy explained how to pay him in untraceable bitcoin through the dark web, a new experience for me, and intriguing.

I wired 10-K into Amber's account and though she said she didn't want my money, she kept it. I let her know there would be the same amount coming next month.

You could say I was blackmailing myself, but the cynic in me believed that Amber would not go to my wife if I had her on the payroll. I was controlling the situation, something I was used to.

A few days later the guy called to say he'd taken care of the "situation," that a certain someone had been "gone over" and would not be bothering me again.

The rest of the day was taken up with meetings and conference calls. When it was finally over, I called Cora to tell her I'd be working late, gave my driver the night off and took a cab to Amber's. I let myself in and hurried up the stairs, excited as a kid to tell her she would no longer have to worry about Sal.

Music was coming from the back of the apartment. I saw the familiar blue light under the bedroom door and pushed it open.

At first, I wasn't sure what I was seeing, everything bathed in blue so that the blood appeared purple, almost black.

Then it snapped into focus: Amber's nude body angled across the bed, the expensive sheets stained with blood, her arms spread wide, and when I dared look closer, I saw jagged cuts on her wrists.

Tiny flashbulbs popped behind my eyes, a chill shook my body. I swallowed hard and leaned down to see if she was breathing, then stumbled backward out of the room, bile rising in my throat. I made it to the bathroom just in time.

For a while, I sat on the cold tiles trying to think. *Amber, take her own life?*

Then my instinct for self-preservation kicked in. *What had I touched?*

I found a pair of latex gloves and a bottle of Lysol and went through the apartment spraying and wiping, telling myself it would be okay, there was no way to link me to Amber, no one knew about our affair.

No one but Sal.

I went back to look at Amber, the pose, her arms stretched out, eyes open staring at the ceiling, no grimace, no signs of convulsing with pain, and surely there would have been. It was all too perfect. Too staged. And she had no reason to kill herself. She was happy. She had money.

My money.

Money easily traced back to me.

I tried to breathe. To think. What would I say? That she had invested with me? No one would believe that; I didn't take clients with less than five million.

So who had killed her?

The same name sounded in my mind: *Sal.* Who had a reason: he'd come to Amber with a plan to get money out of me and she had betrayed him. And so, he or someone in his *connected* family—if that unlikely factoid was true—had killed her as payback for the beating.

My fault. And a message to me? My mind was firing off theories faster than JFK conspiracies. *Would Sal try to implicate me? Or had I already implicated myself?*

I went through the apartment again, looking for anything that could link me to Amber, one item in particular, the bracelet. Which was not in her jewelry box, nor the dresser drawers, not in the fringed pocketbook of hers I knew well, nor the fake leather one I found dangling on a clothes hanger. I went through the pockets of her coats and slacks and found nothing but loose change and used tissues.

I looked again at Amber. No bracelet on her wrist but rings on every finger, including the antique opal I had given her. My fingers brushed against hers. I reeled back. Couldn't do it. But had to. I took a deep breath, got a grip on the ring, closed my eyes and tugged. Her body jerked but I had the ring.

But where was the bracelet? Had Amber hocked it?

Or had the killer taken it?

If it was Sal, I would get it back. Later. Right now, I had to erase all traces of my existence in Amber's life.

I found her cell phone and deleted my number but when I saw how many texts and calls of mine had been recorded, I slipped the phone into my pocket. Then, one last look around the apartment before I used my coat sleeve to wipe off the doorknob and make my way down the stairs.

Outside, hat on and collar up, I forced myself to walk at a normal pace. I decided against a cab—too easy to trace—and took the subway. Got off earlier than my stop, retrieved a crumpled McDonald's bag out of a trash bin, put Amber's cell inside it, along with what may have been a half-eaten Big Mac and dropped it back into the trash. Another block, another trash can where I deposited the plastic gloves. Then, I walked home.

The doormen greeted me, and I did my best to act natural.

Cora was in the living room, feet up on an ottoman, book in one hand, drink in the other. "You look awful, dear."

"Thanks," I said, trying to sound casual and flip. I made a pit stop in the bathroom where I scrubbed my hands until they stung, then came back into the living room, poured myself a scotch and kissed Cora on the cheek.

"You smell funny," she said.

"Do I?" I made a show of sniffing my armpits.

"Not like that," she said. "Like...cleanser or bleach or...something."

"Odd," I said, sniffing the arm of my shirt. "Maybe it's from the dry cleaners."

Cora shrugged. "Have you eaten? Fran made a very good couscous. It's in the fridge."

"Maybe later." I sipped my drink and stared out the windows as if the glittering city view was something I needed to memorize.

Cora asked again if I was okay and I said I was tired, drank my scotch and poured another. Then I told her I was going to sleep.

I stripped off my clothes, rolled them into a ball and hid them in the back of my bedroom closet. Tomorrow, I would throw them away.

That night I slept fitfully, dreaming of my homes collapsing one by one, and Amber, standing in the wreckage.

In the morning, I slipped out of bed early, showered and ran an electric razor over my face. Then, I put last night's bundled clothes into a shopping bag to drop into another city trash can and tiptoed out of the apartment so as not to wake Cora.

My workday dragged on, but when it finally ended, I went looking for Sal. He was easy to find. He answered the door to his apartment above the dance studio with an ice pack pressed against his bruised cheek, a gash on the bridge of his nose.

"Amber," was all I said, and pushed past him.

"What about her?"

"She's dead."

"*What?*" he said, dropping the ice pack.

"And don't tell me she killed herself."

"I don't know what you're talking about. Amber, *dead*?" He

shook a cigarette out of a pack and lit it with shaking fingers. *"Jesus. When? How?"*

"Oh, come on. She told me all about you, how you held that law firm theft over her head unless she got money out of me."

"Law firm? Theft? What the fuck are you talking about?"

I moved in close enough to smell his cheap cologne, his sweat and his fear. "You want me to believe you weren't blackmailing her about the money she stole when she worked at the law firm?"

For a few seconds Sal gave me a blank stare then he laughed. *"Amber?* Working at a *law firm?* Doing *what?* Servicing the lawyers during their lunch break? Sorry, man, but if Amber ever worked at a law firm then I ran Goldman Sachs! She never made it past junior high, she ever tell you *that?"*

No, she hadn't. She had not told me much about herself because I had never asked.

"Look, Amber was a player, and if she played you, I'm sorry, but I had nothing to do with it."

"She told me you had connections to the mob."

Sal sputtered a laugh through his bruised nose. "Mob connected? You mean like the Sopranos? Hey, my old man's a plumber and my mom cleans houses. If we got mob connections how come they live in a shithole on Staten Island, and I'm in a one-bedroom above my shop?"

"Amber said you were about to lose this place, the studio, the building, all of it."

"News to me, pal. The dance classes cover my mortgage and taxes, and I got a little left to live on. Not all that well, but I manage."

"If you didn't kill Amber, who did?"

"Amber's got more boyfriends than Snow White's got dwarfs. Maybe one caught her two-timing and got sick of it. I'm sorry, man, but you're just one of many." He raised the ice pack to his cheek. "You arrange this beating because of what Amber told you?"

I didn't answer his question and he didn't answer mine. I left him to lick his wounds. Then I headed home.

★ ★ ★

The detectives met me in the lobby. They took me to the station and questioned me though I refused to say a word. They'd already searched my penthouse, had taken a custom-made shirt they found "balled up and hidden" in the back of my closet, my initials monogrammed on the pocket and stained with Amber's blood. They showed me the Hommage Damascene straight razor and a Kent handmade comb taken from Amber's medicine cabinet—both mine—and now "at the lab." And they had the bracelet, found among the tangled sheets of her bed and my credit card receipt from Cartier and copies of my 10-K wire transfer into Amber's account.

My lawyers requested bail but were denied; I was a flight risk, rich enough to go anywhere and disappear.

The trial was swift, the DA's case simple and solid: I was having an affair with Amber, she blackmailed me for money, so I killed her. And they had the evidence: her blood on my shirt, my DNA on the straight razor and comb taken from her apartment, the wire transfer. They found drugs in Amber's system, enough to keep her quiet while her wrists were slit.

They had no other suspects and never looked for one. I was it.

Sal testified that he'd seen me "stalking" Amber from the street, and "dancing, practically having *sex* with her in the studio," the whole time preening as he hammered the nails into my coffin, and other dancers verified what he said.

I was the last to speak, though my lawyers advised against it.

Hand on the Bible, I swore to tell the truth, the whole truth and nothing but the truth, but even as I spoke, even as I gave my account of the truth, it sounded like a lie. I admitted to the affair and the wired money, but swore it wasn't blackmail. I could not explain the bloody shirt in my closet (I knew I'd thrown the clothes away, but obviously couldn't say *that*), nor could I say I had never brought my razor or comb to Amber's apartment (I hadn't, but what was the point of denying it?). As for the drugs, I guessed Amber could have been using though she never had in my presence. In the end, my lawyers advised that I take a deal, twenty-to-life, and the judge went along with it as this was my first offense and a nod to my age, though I would spend the rest of my days in prison.

Cora sat behind me throughout the trial, though we did not speak until she visited me four months later at the Coxsackie Correctional Facility in upstate New York.

Behind the glass she was perfectly made up, her hair a new shade of blond, and looking fresher and younger than she had in years. Surely a lot younger than me with my gray pallor and new gray beard.

"You look well," I said.

"You don't," she snapped, then quietly, "You think I'm a fool, Arthur?"

"Of course not."

"All those women, all these years, the humiliation and suffering I put up with for so long."

"Cora, I—" There was nothing to say. Because it was true. I had not only lied to Cora but to myself, lying was part of the game.

"Did you give this last one your poor little orphan story?"

The other lie. One I had told so many times I almost believed it.

"I know you told the others, at least the ones I paid to disappear. Did you wonder where they went? I suppose not. You replaced them so quickly. Really, Arthur, the idea of you, born with a silver spoon in your mouth, taken into your father's financial firm at twenty-one, full partner at twenty-six. *You*, an *orphan!*" She scoffed a laugh then sobered. "I took it as long as I could, but it was finally too much. There was always going to be another girl, and another. I had to stop it, had to do *something.*"

I watched her through the glass the way I had once watched Amber through the window. "You..."

"I've sold Sutton Place," she said. "Too many bad memories. Sotheby's took the art and antiques, but I'm afraid your clothes didn't have much resale value, though Goodwill was happy to have them. I gave them everything of yours." She came closer to the glass, whispering into the phone. "Except for the shirt I'd already given the police. That, and your handmade comb and expensive razor. I didn't think you'd need them in here."

"You…" I said, trying to take it in, the idea of Cora being capable of such a thing. "My God, Cora. What did you do?"

"*You* did this Arthur, not me. You shattered everything, our marriage, our family, our home." She took a deep breath and let it out slowly.

I stared at her, really looked at her for the first time in years.

"I hope you enjoy your new *home*," she said, "your *cell*." Then she dropped the phone, stood up, and I watched her walk away, a lightness in her step, almost as if she were dancing.

THE RELENTLESS
FLOW OF THE AMAZON

JONATHAN STONE

"What'd you order?"

"Nothing. The usual. What'd *you* order?"

It's the time of boxes. Everything delivered. Everyone's domestic consumption dropped off in cardboard stacks on front porches, by back doors and garages. Online groceries, toiletries, cleaning and sanitizing products, upgraded electronics, new exercise gear, cartons of wine, anything and everything to ride out Armageddon.

It's still early in the pandemic, when everyone's still terrified about surface transmission, so Annie and Tom always leave the cartons in the garage to let the virus "cool" for a day or two, then nevertheless wipe down the contents just to be sure. Annie's asthma leaves her especially vulnerable to bronchial infections, so they're pretty much locked down, which is fine by them. They can both work remotely (he's in digital marketing; she's in HR), and neither really minds being home. Never leaving. Totally isolated. Ordering everything online. Which it turns out, you can. The invasion of the boxes—to prevent the invasion of the virus.

But the latest stack of cartons has now made it into the kitchen, and the online grocery carton is obvious, as is the bag from Lands' End, and the new responsibly-sourced "tree-free" toilet paper from Who Gives A Crap.

Plus this Amazon box—which is something one or the other of them will no doubt remember ordering the moment they open it—but inside it Tom finds another box, unlabeled—obviously just extra, wasteful packing for whatever this is—and he tears open the inside box, expecting socks, underwear, replacement batteries…

"Shit."

"Whoa."

They both stare silently.

It's not the heavy, gleaming black-and-chrome firearm of a thousand cop shows.

This one is white. Very lightweight, efficient looking. Wait—is it actually *made* of plastic? Boxy barrel, primitive handgrip, its white panels smooth and unadorned. Function over form. A little toylike, oddly—but so clearly not a toy. No-nonsense. All business.

He's not sure he's ever been this close to a gun. They're afraid to even touch it—at first.

"What are you *doing*?" she says, as he begins to lift it out. "Jesus, just leave it alone."

"Relax, I'm keeping it in the packing. It's just…there's something else underneath."

A second gun, it turns out. Identical. Packed directly under the first one. As if reproducing there in the carton.

"His and hers," Tom observes.

"How thoughtful," Annie says.

No card or note inside.

They double-check the address on the Amazon box.

Their own address—12057 Waverly. On a printed label. No mistake there.

Return address? Same one as a half-million boxes delivered across America that day: Amazon Fulfillment Services. The carton says nothing more—insuring privacy, presumably.

They immediately consult Siri and Alexa and the internet, who are all in clear agreement: yes, it's illegal to ship guns and no, USPS and Amazon and FedEx don't and can't scan all packages, only suspicious ones.

Maybe the extra interior packaging hid the contents somehow? Maybe the fact that it's plastic means it avoids scanning detection? But there's no way Amazon sells guns online anyway, right? (Which they assume, but double-check to be sure.) So it's gotta be some third-party seller that Amazon does the shipping for. They're way out of their depth here. Way over their skis.

"Okay, obviously a mistake," Tom says.

"I'll contact Amazon. They'll pick it up," she says.

"Well, no, they won't," Tom says. "Not if they know what it is. They can't. You heard Siri and Alexa, you can't ship firearms if you're not a registered dealer." He looks at her with a gentle smirk. "And when's the last time you tried to get someone from Amazon on the phone?"

"I'm sure they've got an online customer service chat."

"Yeah, but firearms? That's gonna get upgraded to some supervisor, and maybe have to go beyond that," Tom says. "I can just feel it, Annie. It's gonna eat up hours of time—if we even get to a human to begin with. And all the extra volume they're dealing with right now, pandemic-wise?"

They're both in the middle of intense projects at the moment. Can't be losing hours to this shipping mistake.

"And if we do get someone and explain what happened, it might be contractual that they have to loop in law enforcement. I mean, interstate transportation of weapons or something."

"So maybe our local police can tell us what to do with them."

"Well, wait a second," Tom says.

"What do you mean, wait a second?"

"I mean, what's the big deal, Annie? Everyone in America has guns. What is it, 300 million firearms in this country, some crazy thing like that? What's two more?"

She narrows her eyes. She knows him. "What are you afraid of?"

"Frankly, everything. Someone official having to come to the house and pick up the guns and talk to us. Or us having to go somewhere, to an official dealer or the police station to drop them off, and our names get registered somewhere. And either way, more contact and risk of the virus, right? And we won't be able to say no because it's gun laws." He closes the flaps on the package. "Look, it's obviously an isolated error of some sort. Wrong address somehow. Isn't it easier to just leave it alone? Just—I don't know—stow the box in the basement and forget about it?"

But he opens the flaps again, now lifts the packaging beneath the second gun to search the rest of the carton.

"What are you doing *now*?"

He looks up at her, smiling. "No ammunition in the box, okay? So the guns are totally useless. Let's at least think about what to do with them. I mean, thirty-day return policy, right? Let's just let our brains Covid-cool on it a little."

A few days later, they're still discussing which of them is willing to dive into it with Amazon. Enough time has passed for another Covid-cool and wipedown, so they open a new pile of packages.

The little space heater she ordered for their bathroom. (The tile floor is so cold on winter mornings.)

A new delivery of supplements to keep her immune system boosted. (Vitamins A, D, B_{12}, zinc, fish oil, CoQ10, glucosamine.)

Vermont Country Store candy from her parents in Ohio.

And—opening one last Amazon package—several boxes of ammunition. Again addressed to 12057 Waverly.

Again, no card or note.

"Oh, goody," she says sarcastically. "The missing ammo. Looks like enough to wipe out the neighborhood."

★ ★ ★

A neighborhood they were just getting to know, before the pandemic shut everyone in. A discussion comes back to him: a discussion with a neighbor across the street, when Tom and Annie had first moved into the housing development a few months ago. The development's houses looked generally, oppressively, laughably the same, sure, but over time, here and there, individual touches had been added—a new bay window, a front portico, a small side porch. Distinguishing features, if you looked closely. Much like the people inside them, he'd thought. Case in point, their neighbor Phil.

Phil and Evie had stayed after at the open house that Tom and Annie threw themselves (the best way to meet the neighbors, they figured). Phil, standing in Tom's little backyard, had gestured with a wave of his beer to all the oppressively similar houses in the neighborhood—"you know, every home is a crime scene," he'd declared—clearly, intentionally provocative.

"Say what?"

"Every home is a crime scene," Phil repeats. "Doesn't need yellow police tape. Or bodies buried in the yard. Although there could be some." He shrugs, gesturing to Tom's little green manicured patch of grass and two spindly lemon trees.

"Okay," says Tom cautiously. With little choice but to humor this neighbor he's just met. Who lives right across the street. "Okay, you've got my attention."

"Show me any home, anywhere," says Phil. "It's on land that was taken from native Americans. Or it's developers selling swampland that shouldn't be built on in the first place. Or it's a slumlord overcharging tenants every month before forcing them out. Or brokers manipulating closing costs to pocket illegal commissions."

He was just getting started. "Whole communities, whole towns, are crime scenes, when you think about it. Planned communities from Long Island New York to Orange County California, keeping out the Blacks and the Jews. Decades of housing discrimination. And mansions? Forget it. Built with bootlegging money a century ago, or with Oxy fortunes or laundered money today. Add in subprime mortgage and foreclosure scams. Whole neighborhoods built on toxic dump sites. Neighborhoods with cancer clusters from high-voltage wires. I'm telling you, every home is a crime scene, somewhere, somehow."

Tom had nodded politely. But when Phil paused, Tom suddenly smiled. "Come on, Phil," he'd said, gesturing behind him, "even my dumb three-bedroom, two-and-a-half-bath, with a plain vanilla thirty-year fixed?"

Phil had relented. Smiling back at his host. "Well, okay, neighbor—hopefully not *your* house." Lifting what was left of his beer in a silent toast. *Sorry about the rant. Welcome to the neighborhood.*

Tom smiles now remembering the discussion—because with the arrival of the guns, his dumb little three-bedroom suddenly kind of qualifies too. *Every home is a crime scene.*

Interesting guy, Phil. Tom wanted to get to know him better—resident socialist here in a massive housing development stretched over several hillsides—arguably capitalist-consumerism's beating heart. But for now, they're all locked down. The housing development's streets and cul-de-sacs are empty and quiet, except for the darting UPS and FedEx trucks and Amazon vans, like drone bees in a frenzied dance of delivery; busy insects humming and circling in an otherwise heightened, sunny silence.

He'd love to tell Phil the anecdote about the guns and ammo. *Every home is a crime scene—Phil, you were right!* But Annie wouldn't want him mentioning the guns to anyone. He'll have to keep it to himself.

An anonymous gift? Someone being *thoughtful*?

They think through all Tom's crazy Florida cousins. All Annie's distant, fundamentalist-alarmist relatives in Arizona. "A national lockdown, a huge political divide, crazy times, the threat of civil unrest—maybe somebody's just trying to protect us?"

"Then wouldn't there be a note?"

"Maybe no note because they know how we feel about guns, Annie. That we'd never keep them if we knew who they came from, but they just want us to be safe."

"I just want to return them. Be done with them," says Annie.

"Done with them is putting them aside and forgetting about them," Tom says.

A week later, more toiletries. (Toothpaste, deodorant, shaving cream, floss: this was so much easier and cheaper; no standing anxiously masked in the CVS checkout line.)

Jigsaw puzzles. (Something to do in the long locked-down coming winter; puzzles of vacation spots they wouldn't be going to anytime soon.)

Seed packets. (She'll grow some plants indoors this winter, good spot under the bay window.)

New doormat. (The old one is totally shot.)

And these must be the pillar candles she ordered. (To make their unvarying pandemic dinners a little more special.)

She opens the carton to find the candles still in individually wrapped boxes. What a waste of packaging, but she's already anticipating the nice scent as she opens the first box to find inside it—inside all of these small, unmarked boxes, in fact—stacks of cash.

"Oh my God."

"For Christ's sake," Tom says, looking over the carton of cash she presents him with. Dirty bills, he notices. Stacks of tens and twenties. Not crisp and sorted by some bank machine but bundled roughly with rubber bands. Street cash, thinks Tom.

Again, no note or return address beyond Amazon's. Tom goes quiet, looking at it.

Obviously, a mistake, he'd said about the guns. But now, probably not.

"So?" Annie says. "Someone sending us the cash they think we'll need along with guns when society collapses? Could still be your crazy relatives, I guess."

"Could still be yours."

But they both know it's not. Not cash like this. Not this much. "How much is it, you think?" she asks.

"No idea." Like the guns, he's never seen stacks of cash like this. Fifty thousand? A hundred? "Enough for me to stop working on this stupid marketing deck," he jokes thinly. But they're not about to count it. Dirty, haphazard stacks of cash. They both sense it strongly: it's not theirs to count.

"What now?" she says, annoyed. "Put it in the basement next to the guns?"

Still trying to thread together these delivery mistakes into one non-mistake—and thinking about the timing of the gun carton and now the cash—something occurs to Tom.

"The guns might have been a test, Annie."

"What?"

"To see if we'd try to return them, or call someone, or just leave them in the carton."

"What are you saying?"

"To see if we can be trusted. To see if we're going to call law enforcement, or just kind of stay quiet about it." He looks up at her. "And we stayed quiet, and this cash shows up next."

Cash that would normally generate fantasies of escape, vacations, a fresh start—but it's doing the very opposite now—making them feel imprisoned, stuck, cornered. Annie is experiencing respiratory constriction that has nothing to do with the virus.

"What if it *is* a test?" she says. "A test that we passed. We've got to say something. Tell someone."

"Oh, I see. Complain to Amazon that they delivered us a box of cash? You don't think *that* triggers some kind of investigation?" He looks at her. "And they're not gonna tell us to just box it up and send it back, any more than they would the guns." He looks at her, pleading. "Bad idea to tell anyone about the guns. Worse idea to mention this much cash."

"What the hell is going on, Tom? Where did our address come from?"

"Who knows?"

"Who is this, Tom?"

He can only shrug. No idea.

Whether it is some kind of "test" as they now grimly speculate, or just a darkly compounding mistake, the fact of a pattern forming seems undeniable.

Annie narrows her eyes at him. Squinting into the pattern's future. "Don't you understand, the more we don't say anything, the more they're gonna send," she says.

"But the more they send, the more we can't say anything," Tom says.

Both listening to the circular argument. A circle tightening, closing in on them.

Now they're careful with each package, of course. Keeping close track of everything they've ordered.

Making sure they recognize everything they're about to open. No more surprises. The carton of replacement lightbulbs—yes, exactly the ones they clicked on.

The meal kit from HelloFresh. (They'll give it a try.)

Grapefruits and oranges from his aunt in Coral Gables—an *uncrazy* one—that she sends every year.

New patio furniture covers. (The old ones leak.)

New towels at 50 percent discount. (A deal too good to pass up.)

And inside the soft plastic packaging where Annie is fully expecting to find the new discounted towels—to feel their soft fresh terry cloth—six sealed bags of white powder.

Annie screams.

"For god's sake, don't touch it!" says Tom. "Seal the carton again."

Which she does. Tapes it up.

Maybe this explains the guns, thinks Tom. *So we can defend ourselves.* "Cocaine? Heroin?" she asks, voice trembling.

"How the hell would I know?" *Fentanyl? Meth?* Whatever it is, it's not baby powder.

"We have to tell someone now, right?"

They look at each other, silently. Each weighing the fact: *Guns, cash, and now heroin or coke? Isn't it getting a little too late to tell?*

He's thinking through the logic flow, how one package has led to the next, what the sequence might mean.

"Well now we've got a problem," Tom says, looking at the package.

"Now?" she says sarcastically.

"I mean, a bigger problem."

"Bigger?"

He shuts his eyes for a moment, as if not wanting to even look at what he's now realizing. "Guns and cash, Annie, those can be stored. But heroin or coke or whatever this is, it's not for storing. Someone's *invested* in this...in order to sell it." He looks at her. "Meaning someone's gonna be coming for it."

While Tom and Annie absorb the cold logic of this, he looks more closely at the box she's just sealed again.

"Holy shit," he says quietly.

"What now?" *What more?*

He lifts the carton to eye level. Examining the tape that Annie had just used to seal it, and the tape beneath it.

Several layers of tape, he sees now. Neatly applied.

"It would have done no good to call Amazon," he says, his voice flat, deadened. "They'd have no record of the delivery."

"Why's that?"

"These boxes aren't coming to us from Amazon." He can see she half understands already.

"They're being slipped into our pile of deliveries, by hand, I'm guessing—" he looks at her "—somewhere along the way."

Neither of them has to say it: *maybe from somewhere close.* A physical shudder goes through Annie.

"A Trojan horse," says Tom, quietly. Sneaking inside the walled city of their dumb little three-bedroom.

"Pandora's box," says Annie. Unleashing new chaos, every time they lift a lid.

The invasion of the boxes. Meant to combat the invasion of the virus—but for Tom and Annie, the infection has mutated. Their fear of what the boxes carry is no longer about pathogens.

She looks at the package. "You think I should put it in the freezer?" Tom immediately understands her comment. *To keep it safe. Take care of the merchandise. Cooperate. So we don't get in trouble with…whoever will be coming for it.*

The next arrival at 12057 Waverly—the next intrusion—is perhaps the only one that could be worse than the white powder.

Squad cars and unmarked black Suburbans pull screaming and screeching to the curb. A dozen cops—uniformed and plain-clothes—jump out.

Annie starts to weep.

Tom takes a deep breath. Half expects to hear a lieutenant's bullhorn instructions to them. His arms are already half-up in surrender.

The cops swarm the sidewalk in front of 12057 Waverly.

Adjusting their helmets. Positioning their shields and gun belts. And Covid masks, Annie notices. How considerate, she thinks fleetingly.

The cops crouch. Begin to trot. Toward the house across the street. Phil and Evie's.

Tom and Annie watch through their front bay window, as

the cops knock loudly, wait crouched, poised, and when Phil and Evie don't open their front door after a minute or so—*Jesus, why not?* Tom is wondering—the cops bust it in.

The police are in there for over an hour, during which Phil and Evie, emerging as if in a daze, wait at the curb, between two uniforms. Phil and Evie are both smoking. Shaking their heads. Looking upset, distraught. But also, Tom can't help but notice—annoyed.

It's the first time he's seen Phil, Tom realizes, since the discussion. *Every home is a crime scene.* And look what's happened to Phil. Jesus.

A number of the neighbors come drifting out, assembling on the sidewalk to see what's going on. So Tom feels it's safe to join them. He won't be noticed. Maybe he's less noticeable anyway if he's out there with everyone else.

"Jesus, Phil," Serge, another neighbor, is saying. "What the hell?"

"Hell if I know." Phil shrugs. "So sorry for the commotion. Really embarrassing. Really upsetting. It's just some big mistake. Cops make mistakes, you know."

Sure enough, the cops begin to exit.

"What about my door?" Phil demands loudly, accusingly.

Jesus, Phil, you don't talk to cops like that! Tom thinks—even when they bust in your front door.

"Take it easy," says the detective lieutenant in charge. "Locksmith is on his way."

"What do you think they were looking for?" Serge asks Phil.

"Who knows?" Phil shrugs again. "Guns? Cash? Drugs?" He catches Tom's eye. "Whatever it was, they've got the wrong house, don't they?" Looking at Tom a few more seconds before shifting his gaze away.

They've got the wrong house, don't they? Jesus, Phil knows about the packages.

How could he possibly know?

But it's instantaneously clear how Phil knows. *Every house is a crime scene.*

The cops have the right house, Tom realizes. But the goods aren't there.

Because Phil has stored his goods across the street, at Tom's.

And at how many other houses in the neighborhood? Where the neighbors are afraid to say anything? Where Phil similarly tested them first? Stowing goods with fearful, baffled couples all over the neighborhood? Because you don't run a criminal enterprise on just three boxes.

Unless it's a small enterprise? Careful. Focused. One illicit deal at a time. Just enough narcotics and cash flow to not risk too much? Yeah—some socialist.

12057 Waverly is a storage unit, Tom realizes. The storage unit Phil and Evie don't have to lease. The attractive storage unit right across the street, where Phil can keep an eye on it, and whether the cops suddenly pull up to Phil's home or up to 12057 across the street, Phil can plead ignorance, disavow any knowledge, have no connection to any evidence, either way.

But there's no way for Tom to really know. And you can't exactly bring up the idea with other neighbors. *Hey, are you hiding guns or drugs or packets of cash at your house too?*

"Get in the back of the squad car," the detective lieutenant instructs Phil.

Phil shakes his head, annoyed, yet almost comfortable, Tom sees—*wait, has he been through this before? Maybe the cops did find something in his house?*—and Tom and the neighbors watch the squad car pull away.

Two hours later, another squad car drops Phil back at home. Tom watches through the bay window.

Released for lack of evidence?

Evidence that's hidden across the street, at Tom's?

★ ★ ★

Sitting down to dinner. Annie has just lit two of her new pillar candles—with her hands shaking.

They're deciding on a plan at last, finally committing to the long, ugly interaction with Amazon—the long, ugly interaction suddenly useful. The longer and uglier the better.

"We call Amazon. We online chat with everyone. We talk to supervisors. Create a paper trail, a record, of our complaints about all these mistakes. Complain loudly, bitterly."

"But the boxes didn't come from Amazon."

"But as far as we know, they did," Tom says firmly, resolutely. Looking at her. "Amazon is our best alibi, Annie. Big, bad Amazon—it's now our best friend." He's thought more about those Amazon boxes, so clearly addressed to 12057 Waverly. A label-printing device, to print fake labels? Simple enough, probably. But some part of him, some little stirring and tapping at the back of his brain, suspects something even simpler. And potentially more problematic for them: that it was their own old Amazon boxes. Taken from their own trash, repurposed, repacked and delivered to them again.

He doesn't know what stings more—the ingenuity or the irony. Foiled by their own rabid consumption. Victims of the plague—without ever getting sick.

But creating an Amazon complaint record will take time. So they're now weighing the merits and risks of something much more direct. Taking a cue from the simplicity of what fooled them. "What if we just head out right after dinner, as soon as it's dark," says Tom, "and toss the weird plastic guns and the ammo and the white powder into the trash—"

"—Someone *else's* trash," says Annie.

"Exactly," says Tom. "And just drop the cash anonymously with some local charity."

Sounds like a plan.

A firm plan at last.

As firm as the knock on the door.

Tom opens it to find three uniformed cops and three plainclothes—including the same detective lieutenant—all wearing masks.

The detective lieutenant is holding up a search warrant.

Behind them, Tom catches a glimpse of his neighbor Phil standing across the street.

Looking over at Tom with—*What's this? A quick thin smile? A little nod?*—before turning and shutting his newly repaired front door behind him.

Phil, Tom figures.

Phil, interrogated at the police station. Phil who, judging by his impatience and annoyance—*"What about my door?"*—has dealt with the police before. Phil, weaving a story, finding a way, apparently, to give up one of his "storage units" to save his others.

Tom and Annie stand outside while the police search. It takes only a few minutes. Not even long enough for Tom and Annie to decide whether to tell them where everything is. Not even long enough for any curious neighbors to wander out.

Two of the uniformed cops bring out the carton of guns, the carton of cash, the carton of white powder.

You see, Detective, they just arrived without our knowledge and kept arriving. We didn't know what to do, we didn't want to waste hours dealing with Amazon, so we just kept putting the stuff aside. We're being used by someone. A bunch of us, here in the development, being used like that. It's a way for them to store their contraband and not get caught. Why was the heroin in the freezer? Oh, just 'cause my wife didn't want it to go bad.

It's just a mistaken delivery, Detective. Well, two deliveries. Well, okay, three deliveries. But they're not real Amazon boxes. Well okay, they are real Amazon boxes. Well, yes, they are addressed to us.

I'm telling you, contraband stored in houses all over this development. Well, okay, maybe just mine.

What evidence do I have?

None, Tom realizes. No evidence at all.

My neighbor Phil's smile as he closed his front door? Will that launch an investigation, Detective? A house-to-house search?

Guns, cash and drugs found in a basement. That's evidence. A thin smile from across the street? Not so much.

It's the time of boxes. Everything delivered. Everyone's domestic consumption dropped off in cardboard stacks on front porches, by back doors and garages. Online groceries, toiletries, cleaning and sanitizing products, upgraded electronics, new exercise gear, cartons of wine…and one more box.

The one that Tom and Annie have gotten themselves into.

They won't be riding out Armageddon the way they thought.

LIVE PAWNS

OVIDIA YU

"Get the fuck away from me!" Lina Jo Lanam said to me. "Go the fuck home!"

Lina Jo Lanam, Ryan Lanam's mom, stood blocking the entrance to the Queens Supreme Court. She grabbed the arm of Jacob Rubinek, Mikkel's father.

"My boy Ryan never meant any harm to your son. It's those Chinese gangsters he was after. Your son shouldn't have been there at all!

"Get your son to tell the judge to go easy on my boy, tell him to forgive like a Christian. My Ryan was only trying to protect him from those damn Chinese!"

Jacob Rubinek, a tall, gray-haired man with deep lines on his face, removed her hand. He saw me standing off to one side and looked away.

"She's the manipulating bitch. Pam Phan's the one who got all those people killed!"

I knew she was right.

★ ★ ★

My home growing up was two rooms above the Lucky Panda restaurant on Mott Street, between Worth and Hester Streets. My family migrated from China to Vietnam generations ago, then more recently from Vietnam to the United States of America where I was born.

My father and his elder brother put everything they could scrape together into the Lucky Panda restaurant. The restaurant opened the same month as I was born. When my mother left the hospital with me, she went straight to the restaurant kitchen with me tied to her chest with a cloth sling.

Before I started school, it was my job to watch the entrance during the afternoon lull and call a grown-up if anyone came. Mostly I just sat. I envied my older cousin Sara, who had the job of writing prices on plastic lids for takeaway. Sara had also written the Live Pawns sign outside the restaurant.

Even spelled correctly that was a lie. All our seafood came dead on ice. But when I started winning chess tournaments, Uncle Meng claimed that sign helped make it happen.

I taught myself to read during those long afternoons.

Chinese kids are never told they're smart though we're expected to ace all the tests in school. But I knew I was clever because my older brother and cousins came to me for help with their math and physics homework in exchange for letting me read their textbooks.

It was also thanks to them that I learned to play chess.

Danny and Sara found a discarded chess table with brown and green squares while scavenging and dragged it back to the restaurant. It was used for takeaway menus till Mikkel Rubinek, Danny's high school friend, brought over his old chess set and chess strategy books.

"I used to be in my school chess club," he explained.

Those chess books changed my life. I played chess every chance I got and when no one would play with me, I replayed classic games from the books: Kasparov vs. Portisch with double bishop sacrifice, Fischer vs. Spassky with Queen's Gambit Declined.

Word went around about Pigtail Pam, the tiny Chinese girl who played chess in front of the Lucky Panda restaurant. People started coming to challenge me to games. Uncle Meng didn't mind because these impromptu matches drew observers who bought drinks and food.

In fact he offered free egg rolls to anyone who could beat me. As I got better, he upped this to vouchers for a four-person crispy chicken dinner. Always looking for the next small advantage, Uncle Meng played life like a chess game and I was one of his pawns.

I don't mean that in a bad way. In the right position, a pawn can become the most powerful piece on the board. I loved chess because on the chessboard I could be a general, an emperor, the god of war, controller of my own destiny. I had no trouble ignoring onlookers with their comments and jokes.

Some of the regulars liked to bet out-of-towners they couldn't beat a ten-year-old who didn't even speak English. After a long game (especially when customers had spent a lot of money), Uncle Meng would give me two egg custard tarts and hand my mother five dollars for my savings.

The first time I met Ryan Lanam was at the finals of a district-level schools competition. He was one of the highest-ranked players and it was my first tournament, so I was unranked.

Ryan's parents were there. His dad sat quietly with the other parents, but his mom walked around talking loudly. "My son's a genius, the next Bobby Fischer."

When people asked her to lower her voice or move, she yelled at them.

I recognized her once she started yelling. Lina Jo Lanam and another woman had come to the Lucky Panda last week, right after I'd made it to the tournament final.

"That's not real chess," she said, watching the regulars taking bets on me winning despite starting with a two-bishop handicap. "That kid's just a gimmick. But hey, at least the food's free!"

She'd interrupted the game, yelling and throwing her plate so it cracked one windowpane. When another customer called the police, Lina Jo Lanam told them there'd been a huge cockroach in her food.

Uncle Meng was mad because of the cockroach story.

I was mad because I *was* playing real chess.

Neither of us said anything because we were Hoa—Chinese Vietnamese whose ancestors had never been fully accepted in Vietnam, had no place or connections in China and knew we could only survive in America, our now and only home, by keeping quiet.

Ryan Lanam didn't play by the rules. He kicked me under the table and whispered, "You know what's the difference between garbage and Chinese girls? Garbage gets picked up!"

His behavior probably upset other kids he played against, but I was used to playing in a noisy restaurant, translating orders and bussing tables between moves. Distractions were part of my game.

Ryan played White. He was one of those players who came to tournaments armed with opening trap variations leading to early advantages, so his opponents often came out of the opening down a piece or two—and off balance and demoralized.

All I had to do was counter his attacks while moving in on every tiny advantage. Sometimes the best thing you can do is let your opponents tire themselves out while you keep your mind on the bigger picture.

Ryan's mother came to stand by our table, which was against the rules. "I'm Mrs. Lanam—Ryan's mother," she told the room monitor who asked her to leave. "Ryan may need his inhaler and his medications. No, I can't leave them on the table. It's not safe."

She got louder and ruder when she saw she wasn't upsetting me. "You need to disqualify that sly slitty-eyed girl, she's cheating!"

"Cheating? How?" The official stopped our time clocks.

"Come on, isn't it obvious? Chinese children are crammed into chess schools and injected full of steroids so they play like computers. This little freak shouldn't be allowed to play against normal children. She's probably got a brain implant or an info chip or something. How else can she play chess? She can't even speak English!"

In the end I think she distracted her son more than me. That was the first official tournament I won and I got a trophy and a $20 voucher for Jimmy Joe's Burgers.

Another reason I loved chess was the same rules applied across the board. Even if you start out a pawn, you can become a queen.

Later, waiting for my brother to collect me on his electric bicycle, I saw Ryan Lanam and his dad outside an old white van in the trash collection area. What caught my attention was the sound of his dad slapping him. Ryan's head jerked left and right with each blow. He was sobbing so hard his whole body shook, but he didn't make a sound. All I heard were the rhythmic slaps; left, right, left, right.

Our eyes met for an instant and I turned away.

I never again wished my family took my chess more seriously. When Danny picked me up, I was so shaken he thought I'd lost and he sneaked me a whole carton of shrimp wontons to comfort me.

"Ryan is smart, but he could never be bothered to apply himself at school," Vince Lanam, Ryan's father, told the press later. "He was smarter than all his teachers so he got bored and acted up. When I tried to straighten him out, he reported me for assault, and his mom backed him up. She said she would home-school him. That meant he pretty much did what he liked."

Ryan Lanam had a half sister, a half brother and four step-siblings but he was the only child who lived consistently with Lina Jo Lanam after she divorced his father. It was her third divorce. Court records show the two of them were evicted at least three times for not paying rent, but still Ryan played chess. It was never proved that Lina Jo was running bets on Ryan's chess victories to support them but between that and a little part-time prostitution, she managed to keep them going.

I could understand her resentment of people she felt were squeezing her into the cracks of her own country. But we had nowhere else to go home to either.

Last March was only the second time I played Ryan Lanam. This was at the playoffs for the Dutton Energy Drink Youth Brainiac Challenge for Under-18s. This was a big thing. There was a $100,000 prize up for grabs.

There had been some talk of canceling the event, or having us play online from different rooms in the same center, but Lina Jo Lanam started a petition objecting to that. "If they're not playing face-to-face then it's not a real competition."

Maybe for her "real" competition included all her pushing and distracting. Whatever they decided was okay with me. For me it was just a part of the whole "real life" competition.

The Lucky Panda restaurant was closed because of Covid-19. I knew my family could really use the money.

In the end we played in the same room, on touch pads. Our moves appeared on an electronic board fixed into the Plexiglas shield between us and were automatically recorded, so we could focus totally on the game.

I liked it.

Lina Jo didn't.

I found my table early and sat down to breathe deep and center myself before my opponent arrived. But the seat opposite remained empty. Just before the clocks were started, one of the tournament officials came to tell me there had been complaints about me. "You're making the other competitors uncomfortable. Talking Chinese loudly and spitting germs all over the place."

I had arrived with two other Ochs Perry Middle School students (neither of them Chinese speaking), but they were far away at their respective tables and I had not spoken to anyone since getting my table number.

I looked around, confused. A Japanese girl and a Filipino boy were at their nearby—socially distanced—tables. Then I recognized Ryan Lanam and his mother. They were watching me with a sly smugness that told me our match had already started, no waiting for the tournament director's signal.

Another thing I love about chess is that it's acceptable to put everything you have into destroying your opponent.

"Weeall," I said with Oriental earnestness and my best New York drawl. "Who heah would I tawk Chinese to?"

"Well, you've been warned, so just watch it, young lady." The official tugged one of my plaits gently and waved Lina Jo off as she protested his not removing me. Ryan took his seat.

Ryan kicked me under the table. I ignored him. He kicked again, harder. I raised my feet and sat cross-legged.

I heard Lina Jo Lanam complaining about how I was sitting. But the officials ignoring Ryan's humming, gum popping and table rapping ignored that too.

Ryan leaned around the Plexiglas and said, "Do you know why Chinese people have Chinese babies? Because two Wongs don't make a white!" His jerky, rasping giggle sounded halfway to an asthma wheeze.

It was the perfect moment.

I sacrificed a pawn, pushing it carelessly forward as though irritated by Ryan's fidgeting. Then, as soon as he took it, I looked upset and pushed a second pawn forward rashly, as though in a knee-jerk reaction.

Smirking at me, Ryan grabbed my second pawn sacrifice then tapped the clock, leaned back and stretched before yawning.

But the game was not over, just his dominance of the board.

I moved up my knight and threatened his bishop.

From the start of the game, I'd hunched over my touch pad as though intimidated. Now I sat up straight and smiled at Ryan as I tapped the clock. It threw him. Reacting to counter my confidence he moved fast, recklessly, to save his bishop—and my knight moved again and pinned his queen.

I had got him.

"Wow!" Ryan said.

"Yeah!" I said.

We grinned at each other, connecting in that moment to the brilliant, beautiful dance of chess that flows in timeless and eternal patterns beneath superficial individuals playing to win ranking games. And I saw that beneath his bravado, Ryan Lanam saw chess the way I did. It was like suddenly encountering another human who speaks your language after a lifetime surrounded by deaf, dumb and blind sea slugs.

Ryan leaned right around the Plexiglas shield again. "Did you report my dad?"

I remembered his dad beating him up the last time he lost a game to me. Ryan's dad looked like the kind of man who cuts the ears off dogs for losing races. Ryan had looked like a beaten dog. I'd gone in and told one of the chess officials what I saw.

I nodded.

"Let's call it a draw and ditch this place."

His voice was low and urgent.

"You know one of us is going to win this. We'll split it 50-50, whichever of us gets it."

The thing was, I wanted to get away from all of that too. I felt a connection with Ryan Lanam that went beyond chess games in smelly high school gyms.

He stood up and held out his hand over the top of the shield.

People were watching us. We were the two highest-ranked players in the tournament.

I'd got him away from his abusive dad. But was he really better off? Gossip in the chess community said Ryan and his mom lived in the beat-up old Subaru they drove to tournaments. And I knew she barely understood chess. Last time we played she'd argued, "Ryan should've won because he had more pieces left on the board, I demand a recount!"

I started to stand up to take his hand. Half of $100,000 was still a lot of money.

"Ryan! I swear I'll never talk to you again if you take the hand of that chink bitch!" Lina Jo tore off her mask and slapped the hall monitor trying to hold her back.

"Well?" The longing in Ryan's eyes matched what I felt. My family didn't understand chess any better than Ryan's mom.

"I want to but I can't. My brother needs the money for his restaurant. All of it."

My brother Danny had just come out to our parents.

He'd had no choice once Season 19 of *Chop Shop* aired with fan favorite Danny "Dan the Pan" Phan making it to the final cook-down and talking about his dream of running a restaurant with his partner, Mikkel.

I don't know what hit Ma and Ba hardest; that Danny was gay and wanted to marry a man or that he wanted to be a chef and had dropped out of medical school to take part in *Chop Shop*. "Mikkel and I found this perfect space. If I win, we'll get married and start The Orient Express." I was meanly glad when he lost to a molecular gastronomist from Chicago. But that meant he would need money for the restaurant even more.

"Your brother's Dan the Pan? Why doesn't he get the money from his fag lover? The guy's OG rich!"

I hadn't seen Ryan as the type to follow reality cooking competitions like *Chop Shop*.

"Mikkel's covering rent and renovations. Anything I win will go into their new restaurant. It's the way my family does things."

I sat back down.

Ryan swore and jerked the table viciously, ripping the tape securing the wiring. He tipped it over, scattering board, clocks and pieces across the floor.

The tournament director and chief arbiter hurried toward us, along with all the room monitors. But Lina Jo Lanam reached our table first.

"The Chinese bitch did it. That's the kind of thing they do when they're losing. I already warned you about her but you still let her play. Get rid of her and all the Chinese before it's too late and everything'll be fine."

I didn't have to act to look scared. But inside I was confident. I even felt sorry for Ryan Lanam.

"She's a monster, an evil piece of trash! Look at her! My boy should be able to beat her like he beats everybody else, but she's using her Chinese voodoo on him!"

"Will you shut up?" Ryan screamed over his mom's noise. "Just shut up! Shut up for once!" We were all relieved (and surprised) when she did.

"My fault. I got a cramp in my leg," Ryan said. "We were discussing a draw." He offered his hand to me again and lowered his voice. "We'll work out the family stuff."

Lina Jo batted his arm down, "You cowardly little shit! No son of mine surrenders to—"

"Will you shut the fuck up!"

"You're just like your dad!"

I thought he was going to hit her. She thought so too.

This time I was the higher-ranked player. Meaning, if we agreed to a draw, Ryan would go through to the next round. There was no way his mom would let him split the prize money.

"No."

I've wondered many times how things would have turned out if I'd given Ryan Lanam a draw that day. My family wouldn't have got the prize money. But they might still be alive.

Of course the prize money went toward kitchen equipment for the new restaurant.

"This is a lousy time to open up a restaurant. Everything's closed."

"That's what makes it the perfect time. Everyone's down and broke and hurting. We're starting on par with everyone else."

"It's not easy making money in the restaurant business."

"Probably easier than making money from playing chess!"

My brother, the eternal optimist. But even if he didn't play himself, Danny had always supported my passion for chess. He was the one who'd transported me to and from training sessions and tournaments in between making food deliveries and he'd always managed to find money to "lend" me for coaching sessions and books. I figured I was finally paying him back for some of that.

Danny and Mikkel decided on a soft opening for The Orient Express. They would start with deliveries only. Of course, now there was money at stake, my whole family flocked in to support the new business.

I didn't see Ryan Lanam again till the night before The Orient Express opened for deliveries.

That evening, my relations laughed and gossiped as they set out the plates and bowls and spoons and chopsticks. All the tables were pushed together so everyone could sit together. We were going to sample the entire takeaway menu.

Court records show that around the same time, Ryan Lanam bought eighty-eight hollow-point bullets at a Walmart on Long Island. He then went to Vince Lanam's place (he was staying with his dad again because Lina Jo was locked up for assaulting a policewoman) where he took the Glock 17 from the glove compartment of his father's car.

According to a news report:

Ryan's stepbrother, Franklin Bell, 19, said Ryan asked him to "come along for some fun." Bell refused because his girlfriend, Emily West, 32, was with him and Lanam left alone.

"I was surprised," Franklin Bell said, "Ryan gets pretty worked up when he doesn't get his way. But that day he just said something like, 'It's not meant to be' and left."

Emily West agreed. "One time Ryan hit Frank with a bottle just because we went bowling without telling him. But this time he was just very Zen about it. I remember saying that that Chinese girl he was hung up on was doing him good."

"What Chinese girl?"

"Lina Jo—Ryan's mom—told us some Chinese girl put a hex on Ryan. He was obsessed with her. He wouldn't go to tournaments if she wasn't playing. But if she was playing, he wouldn't play against her."

After leaving his father's house, Ryan Lanam drove to The Orient Express Restaurant on Johnson Street in his dad's car, arriving around 6:15 p.m. and parking illegally at the curb.

Security cameras from across the street show he stayed in his car for almost ten minutes. Then he walked into the restaurant. The closed sign was clearly visible, but there were lights on inside.

We were waiting for the first course: creamy sweet corn and shrimp soup (even the mention of shark-fin was banned by eco-warrior Danny) when the front door rattled. It was locked, because the family had all come in through the back door via the kitchen. The closed sign was up, but the banging went on.

Uncle Meng went and unlocked it because Danny and Mikkel were both in the kitchen.

"Sorry, sorry, we are closed," Uncle Meng said. "Official

opening tomorrow morning. Sorry, sorry, this is private function. Sorry, sorry. Please come back next time."

"I'm looking for Pam Phan."

"Oh, you are Pam's friend?" Uncle Meng said loudly. He turned and winked at me. "Sorry, sorry, please come in. Come in, Pam is over there. Come in and sit down."

My mother glared at me, "Who is that?" she hissed. "You are not old enough to have boyfriends!"

Ah Ma craned her neck to see better, "Pammy got boyfriend ah? At least not so big as Sara's one."

My grandmother had threatened to die of a heart attack when Sara announced she was marrying a blond giant named Charles Blomquist. For the first two years, she refused to talk to or even look at poor Charles. Then one day she dropped one of her gold rings down the toilet. Charles wrapped his hand in a plastic bag and groped around in the shit till he retrieved her ring. From then on he was her favorite grandchild.

Right then, all six foot two inches of Charles was folded onto a child-sized stool beside Patti, their little girl. Sara, in her eighth month, was taking photographs of them.

"Next year there will be two of them to feed," Sara said, a hand on her swollen middle.

"*Choy!*" Ah Ma scolded her. It was bad luck to count on children before they were born.

Sara raised her camera and pointed it at Ryan as he came toward us. He stopped and grinned at the camera. "Shoot," he said. He giggled like it was a huge joke.

Somehow leaked to the press, those photographs show a scrawny, fair-haired young man wearing a hoodie over a dark T-shirt and jeans. He has a backpack hanging from one shoulder and looks harmless and geeky.

Ryan put down his backpack and rummaged around in it.

"Why didn't you tell me you were seeing someone?" Sara leaned across to jab my arm. "I would've kept your secret. He's cute." She was so large she almost overbalanced and Ah Ma had to ease her back on her seat.

Danny pushed open the kitchen doors and came out wheeling the huge soup tureen. "Soup's up!"

My father, following with a ladle sang out, "Everybody! Time to eat!"

As my family cheered, Ryan took a gun out of his backpack and fired at my father. His first shot struck the tureen. Then he shot my father. Then my brother, Danny, rushing to our father. Then Uncle Meng who still stood, gaping, by the front door.

"You all just stay right where you are."

Ryan took his time. He took careful aim and shot my cousin Jack. Then he shot my cousin Joe. He paused at Sara.

"Please! Please don't shoot!" Sara begged. "I'm having a baby— Look, I'll go with you. I'll do whatever you want. You can kill me after my baby is born. Please!"

"Is it going to be a boy or girl? Do you know?" Ryan's thin reedy voice sounded like he was making polite conversation.

"It's a boy. Please don't shoot. Please!"

My grandmother's throat made a small involuntary sound. The pattern of rice grains scattered before my late grandfather's altar had foretold a grandson, but Sara and Charles refused to confirm it.

"Stay calm, Bubala," Charles called from where he was hunched over their daughter, protecting her with his body. "It's going to be all right. Just stay calm."

"Sorry," Ryan said. "If it was a girl then, maybe, I guess. But there are already too many Chinese men around. And they're all full of germs because they eat dogs and bats and rape white women—"

He came right up close and fired three times into Sara's swollen stomach.

For an eternity of a moment Sara remained upright in her chair, bloody finger fragments clawing at the shredded chaos of cotton smock, flesh and fetus in her middle. Then she gurgled blood and crumpled.

In the silence that followed, Ryan giggled again.

I remembered that rusty, jerky laugh. He reloaded his gun before turning to me. Meeting my eyes, he gave a little shrug, "It had to be done," he said. I knew what he meant.

Again, I felt that connection we'd shared across the chess board. I knew Ryan was going to kill me and then himself. And it was the right thing to do.

Ah Ma pulled my hand, trying to get me to crouch down beside her, but I stayed where I was and looked back at Ryan. Beneath the brittle sheen of fear, I was glad. I would finally escape the game I'd been born into.

Mikkel came out of the kitchen carrying the deep fryer basket full of wontons. He dropped them and howled on seeing Danny lying on top of our father covered in a sludge of blood and sweet corn soup. Ryan started to turn his gun on him but Charles left his daughter and charged Ryan, so Ryan shot him instead. Patti was screaming on the floor. He shot her too.

Then Mikkel reached him. Ryan's shot hit Mikkel in the shoulder and spun him round and down but didn't stop him. He grabbed Ryan's knees and brought him down. He grabbed Ryan's hair and pounded his head into the floor.

"It wasn't Ryan's fault," Lina Jo Lanam was quoted as saying. "My boy's like me. He's got mental health issues. I have medications for bipolar disorder and depression and anxiety. I tried to get Ryan to take my medications but he wouldn't. This isn't his fault. If those people didn't keep coming here, he couldn't have killed them. They should all just go home."

Ryan Lanam got seven consecutive life sentences.

I got a bedroom in the Rubinek penthouse on the northwest corner of Madison Square Park.

Jacob Rubinek (Mikkel's insanely rich father) got himself appointed my guardian. He told me he would take care of me till I turned seventeen, on the condition that I took over Danny's share of The Orient Express and "ran" it with Mikkel.

What he really wanted was for me to be Mikkel's suicide watch.

Mikkel wouldn't talk and wouldn't leave home for any place except The Orient Express. When he was at the restaurant he sat and cried, same as he did in the apartment. The disaster recovery cleaning service had gone over the place, but there was no question of opening for business.

Mikkel wouldn't talk to any of the expensive therapists his dad hired. He wouldn't let anyone near him except for me, wouldn't even eat unless I sat there and fed him.

I got texts from Ryan.

Want to play chess? You didn't screw me over like my mom thinks. You freed me. Thanks.

Prison's not so bad compared to living with my mom. Or my dad. Want to play chess?

I'm in holding till the appeal comes up. My mom's sleeping with Garbin, the cop who got me this phone. Want to play chess?

I ignored the messages. Till, Mom's planning on doing something to your restaurant tonight. Watch out.

Just watch out. Stay away from restaurant.

And, two hours later, just after 7:00 p.m. from the same number, Top secret. Urgent. Meet me at Orente Expres 8pm, don't tell anyone.

"Want to go to The Orient Express?" I asked Mikkel.

Of course he didn't answer. But when I stood up he followed me as usual, like a loyal codependent bloodhound.

Once, when I'd spent too long in the shower and Mikkel couldn't find me, he'd had a panic attack and tried to climb over the railings his dad installed around the rooftop garden.

I found the housekeeper, two gardeners and his driver/bodyguard all struggling to hold on to him.

"Mikkel! Get down here!"

Once Mikkel heard and saw me he stopped fighting and let them get him down from the railings. I suspect that's where the stories about me controlling people with black magic started. The gardeners were from the landscape agency and hadn't signed nondisclosures.

At The Orient Express we went round to the back entrance as usual. The back door was standing open. Someone had smashed the window next to it and reached through the grill to unlock the door. The endgame was on.

"Fix it so no one can get in or out," I told Mikkel, "then go back to the car and stay there."

The good thing about a guy who doesn't talk is that he doesn't ask questions.

Lina Jo Lanam was in the front room, where her son had wiped out my family and Mikkel's reason for living. She had a gun in her hand. I saw and smelled the gasoline she had doused the room with.

"I'm calling the police." I held up my phone.

"The police won't listen to you. Put that phone down. Now!" She pointed the gun at me. I wondered where these people got their guns from. The trouble Danny had gone through just to find one good caramelizing blowtorch.

I put my phone down on the counter next to Danny's dusty chef's knives.

"I know you used your black magic on my boy. You're not

so smart as you think! I'm going to burn it out of you. That's the only way to deal with witches like you."

Had Ryan wanted to warn me or to set me up? I didn't really care, either way.

Just then Mikkel came in through the kitchen.

Lina Jo looked startled to see him. She turned her gun on him.

I wasn't going to let her hurt the only family I had left.

"Hey! Look out!" I grabbed and threw a steak knife in a high arc, making Lina Jo look up and sneer, "Missed by a mile—"

She staggered backward when the heavy mortar hit her somewhere between her chest and throat. She skidded on the oil-slick floor and, flailing, landed heavily on her bum.

"Come on." I grabbed Mikkel and dragged him to the front door. Outside, I handed him over to Darren, the driver/bodyguard on duty who was smoking by the car.

"Can I borrow that? And give me one minute."

I locked the door when I was done. Then Darren drove us back to the Rubinek apartment.

"Can we see your phone?"

I hadn't been surprised when the police came. After all, we were the joint owners of The Panda Express.

It was only when I reached into my fanny pack and found my phone wasn't there that I knew they had found it at the restaurant. I froze.

"I must have left it somewhere."

"A kid these days loses her phone and doesn't know it?"

Jacob Rubinek came into the room in time to hear Mikkel say, "You couldn't find your phone last night. Remember? I said maybe somebody pinched it but you thought you left it at the restaurant."

Mikkel was talking? When was the last time Mikkel had said a word?

I stared at him. I saw his dad was gaping at him too, tears in his eyes.

The police didn't realize what a huge moment that was. Though on the downside for me, if Mikkel was recovering, that meant they wouldn't need me around anymore.

The policeman looked put out. The policewoman looked smug. They'd clearly had a discussion, maybe even a bet riding on my phone being evidence.

The policeman turned to Jacob Rubinek. "Mr. Rubinek? Officer Garbin and Officer Richards. There's been some trouble at one of your son's properties."

Officer Garbin?

Was this the cop Ryan's mom was sleeping with? *Had been* sleeping with?

"At the restaurant? What happened?" I saw the old man didn't really care. He came and stood next to Mikkel and squeezed his arm, like he was welcoming him home.

"We believe it's arson. And murder. We're here to take her in for questioning." Garbin jerked his head at me.

"Murder? Who's dead?"

"Lina Jo Lanam." Officer Richards glared at Officer Garbin, who was too busy evil eyeing me to notice. "She was found on the premises. We aren't saying it's arson or murder. We just came to inform you there was a fire at the restaurant property you own—"

"And bring this one in for questioning. Sorry to bother you and your son. It's nothing to do with you good people, except she's moved in on you here. We'll take it from here. Come on."

Officer Garbin twisted my arm to clip a handcuff round my wrist.

"Ow!"

"Let her go," Mikkel said.

"It's nothing to do with you."

"Why does it have anything to do with my ward?" Jacob Rubinek asked.

"We have evidence."

"What evidence?"

"Lina Jo Lanam posted on Twitter that she was ending it once and for all where it all started."

"Why does it have anything to do with my ward?" Jacob Rubinek asked again.

"Well, her phone was found at the site."

"As my son has said," Jacob Rubinek paused to smile at Mikkel, "as we all just heard my son say, Pam left her phone at the restaurant yesterday. Why does it have anything to do with my ward Pam Phan?"

"Did you give Lina Jo Lanam a gun? Just like you gave her son a phone?" I asked Officer Garbin.

That finished it for Officer Ace Garbin. He smacked me on the side of my head, yelling that he knew Lina Jo was coming after me so I must have killed her.

Jacob Rubinek called in a whole armored division of lawyers and by the time they were done, I didn't need charity from anyone. The Rubineks said I would always have a home with them.

You learn from chess that the true home of a pawn is not the side of the board it starts out from but the other side, farthest away, that it's heading for.

So what happens when you reach it?

You get crowned queen, game over and your whole world dies around you. Most pawns don't want to win. We just want the game to go on.

Why did you warn me?

Did I?

Anyway, thanks.

What you say we call it a draw?

This time I accepted. I still don't know if he was setting me up or setting his mother up.

That's why I still play chess with Ryan Lanam online.

It's always interesting.

THE HAPPY BIRTHDAY SONG

BONNIE HEARN HILL

I didn't want to come out stealing today, not with Mercury in retrograde. But Brownie makes all the decisions in our family, and he only pays attention to what he calls that astro mumbo jumbo when I tell him about good things. Mercury could mess up everything with its mechanical failures and its throwing up long-lost people and old problems in your face. It can also make you lose things like your glasses and your car keys. *Please, Brownie,* I think. *Don't lose the keys to the van.* Today, we're going for that fancy bottle of Patrón, all $5,999 of it, and then, we're leaving here.

I look younger than my age, especially in the backpack and the pink T-shirt with PRINCESS printed out in clear stones across the front. Not my real name, thank goodness. I'm Lilith, a fierce independent spirit, and I can do anything. Astrologers say your Black Moon Lilith is the part of yourself you cannot repress, your hidden strength. I'm going to have to depend on mine today, and not just because of Mercury.

I've never talked about astrology or anything else in any of the schools I've been to. Brownie and Gran warned us about the teachers, the way they get points for how many families they can turn in. The kids at those schools are just as bad. They get points too. At least we'll be out of here soon.

The customers in the front of the store look past me, staring at the big-screen TVs. That's where Costco keeps its computers, jewelry, and other high-priced stuff and where the security people hang out. Gran and I head straight for the liquor department over on the left side. If anyone notices, they probably see only another skinny kid wearing an old backpack and standing in front of a case full of expensive liquor, her hand in her jacket pocket. No one sees the tiny key I'm clutching as I back up against the glass door.

"Who spends six grand for tequila?" That's what Brownie had demanded when Gran came up with the plan.

We were watching Christmas movies in the living room of our apartment, the twins Heather and Joey sharing the couch, Elise and I on the carpet, close to the TV so Elise could see without her glasses, which had gotten broken the day before.

Last year, Brownie spliced together the endings of his favorite Hallmark films, so that all he has left is a lot of endings. He knows all the stories by heart, and this way, he doesn't have to go through the whole thing to get to what he calls the best part. Those movies are all he ever watches, never the news, never the reality shows Elise sneaks to see.

That night, he stretched back in the butter-yellow recliner we managed to carry out from a busy store in Pasadena and load on the rental truck with so much confidence that no one questioned us.

The foot lift was so high that, as we watched the movies, I could see the pink bottoms of Brownie's bare feet from my place next to Elise on the floor.

Gran had cooked macaroni and cheese that night, the way she

does when it's cold outside, and she made the breadcrumbs on top extra crisp the way Brownie likes them. Before she adopted me, she used to work in a school cafeteria. That's where she got the nick marks on her hands, from the sharp knives she used.

"He's got the looks, and I've got the brains," she always says, when she's trying to talk him into another adventure. That's her word for what we do.

That night, while we sat watching the end of a film about two single parents getting brought together by their dogs at Christmas, Gran stood in the doorway in her cutoffs and T-shirt, pointing to the Costco website on her phone.

"This is our new adventure," she said, and tapped the photo of a liquor display. "We can sell that baby and get out of here before everything catches up with us. We just have to figure out how."

At first, Brownie wasn't sure. Then, he glanced down at me. Brownie's not a big man. In fact, he's on the skinny side, but when his face is focused on you, that's all you can see, no matter how big the room is. Those bushy raised eyebrows and quick-to-nail-you blue eyes always remind me of the times I got the belt. That's how Brownie was raised, Gran says, and if we misbehave, especially if we talk back the way Elise does, we just have to take the punishment.

That night, though, he looked at me the way he did the TV when he was really interested in something on the screen.

"You know, Princess," he said slowly. "You're the smartest of all the kids. You're the only one who can take that bottle and get away with it."

"He's right," Gran said, and I could feel as much as hear the nervous edge to their laughter.

Now, I look over at Gran and hope this will be quick. She stands nearby, shopping tote open in that accidental way only perfect planning can achieve. No one would ever guess there's a gun in there. But as Gran says, you've got to take care of your own.

The baseball cap hides most of her gray-streaked blond hair. Her eyes appear even larger behind the pink-tinted glasses she picked up a couple of months ago. She looks at me blankly. Part of it is the show we're putting on for anyone who might be trying to catch us. Part of it is that she doesn't like any hint of celebration until we're out of here and back in the van with Brownie.

This store is my second home. I like how the furniture displays look like real rooms and how no one yells at you if you sit on one of the black leather sofas or stand on the shag area rug. I also like the way the people who work here greet their regular customers like us with smiles and how they don't pay much attention to what you do, even though it's right under their noses. That's what we're counting on now.

Once I get the bottle out of the case, I'll put it in Gran's tote. Then, we'll head to the bathroom and hide the bottle in this *Jurassic World* backpack of mine that used to be Elise's. No, not Elise. I can't think about her right now.

When we were in here yesterday, Gran asked one of the clerks to open the case to get her a bottle of pinot grigio. While she distracted him, asking about the sale on Keystone Beer, I reached up and yanked out the key, grasped it in my sweaty fingers, and headed for the front of the store. Now, I'm hoping Brownie was right, that the case locks itself, and they haven't noticed the key is missing.

My hands behind me, I back up against the door and move the key across it, searching for the lock. I'm good at this, the best in the family, Brownie says. "Nerves of steel," he tells the others when he's happy with me. "That's Princess."

There. I find it. Carefully, I move the key over the raised surface until it touches the opening. I press. Nothing happens. *Don't panic. Turn it the other way. Press again.* Yes! The key slides inside. I turn it, tug slightly, and feel the door open.

Gran inches closer. Just as I turn toward the case, I get the feeling that someone is watching me.

The tall, bald man across the aisle gives me a casual glance that stops me. Something about this guy is familiar. His jacket is way too formal for this place and his tie way too shiny. Everything about him screams *security guard*. No uniform, of course, because he's looking for shoplifters.

I begin to hum the Happy Birthday song.

On cue, Gran asks in a loud voice, "Whatcha doing there, hon?"

"That wine you like?" I gesture toward the glass shelves and try to keep my voice from shaking. "Didn't you say you wanted some?"

She pretends to decide and then shakes her head.

"Not today."

I give her a fake smile. Then, I turn away from our prize, hoping the guy hasn't noticed the case and its open door.

The Happy Birthday song was my idea, and it's saved us more than once. Gran and I push our cart down the crowded aisle, heading for the housewares department.

"Don't worry," she says under her breath. "We'll come back for this. But, Princess, that guy's trouble. Stay away from him."

"I'll try," I tell her.

I'm pretty sure I know where I've seen him. School, that last time when I got called to the office. I never made it there because we had to leave, but there was someone who looked like him, pacing up and down the corridor.

Our family has moved a lot. I stopped counting at six times because I didn't want those numbers in my head. We never left a place as fast as we're leaving this one, though. Tonight, we're going up north, close to San Francisco, a place where there's a harbor and some people who live on boats. Brownie says we might even rent a houseboat of our own. But for now, we've got to get that bottle.

Joey and Heather are here to distract from what I'm doing. If someone in security gets too close, I'll text Joey, and he and

Heather will cause a disturbance on the other side of the store. In the meantime, they're supposed to steal stuff like shavers and supplements that will tide us over in case I don't get the Patrón. But I will get it.

We work together but separately, and if somebody questions us, it's my job to do the talking. As Brownie says, I lie better than anyone.

Heather's fake maternity top bulges, and I wonder what's in there. The girl can walk down an aisle of electronic gadgets and fitness watches, and the displays will disappear off the shelves. She looks the way I wish I did, with shiny blond curls and eyes such a clear blue you believe there's nothing but truth there. Her sharp tongue has gotten her almost as many beatings as Elise, but she cares about the family. I know she'd never do what Elise did.

"Nice espresso machines," Gran says, as she checks out the display.

"Not today." Joey never stands up to Gran unless he knows something's impossible. "We're maxed out."

"Princess?" Gran asks.

"I can do it." Heather moves in front of me, competing as always, as if I don't already have enough on my mind.

Before I can tell her to back off, I see that same security guard along the aisle behind us. Something's wrong. Security people have their stations. They don't follow you all over the store. This one is though, watching me, trying to get closer.

I begin humming again. The Happy Birthday song. Gran stops and glares at Heather.

"Not now," she says, and puts her hand on my arm in a warning way.

"I said I can handle it." Heather uses that tone that's gotten her in trouble with Brownie before.

"And I said not now."

The guard heads toward us. I turn and face a display of coffee-makers and K-Cups, but I can still sense him approaching, past

Gran, who turns her back on him, past Joey, past Heather, who is really going to be in trouble tonight for all her spouting off.

But I'm the one the guard is coming for, as if he knows my special talent for lying, as if he wants to challenge it.

"You ladies need help?" he asks me.

I turn slowly and look up at him, forcing myself to meet his lie-detector eyes.

"Sure do." I shoot it back at him in a friendly kid voice, like I think it's normal for a security guard to wait on customers. "My gran, she's looking for a slow cooker we saw on one of those infomercials?"

I say it like a question. Brownie would be proud.

"What kind of slow cooker?" His voice is low, almost musical, like he's trying not to scare me. No worries. I could lie my way past a dozen security people.

"Well," I begin. "It was really big, know what I mean? You could cook a four-pound chuck roast in it."

He looks down at me in an arrogant way, almost daring me to continue.

"That's not exactly a detailed description."

"What's not detailed about a four-pound chuck roast?" I ask.

"Princess," Gran calls out. "Come on. We're going to get some lunch."

"I need to catch up with my family," I tell the guard.

"See you later," he says.

That makes me shiver.

"Princess," Gran shouts again, and I run to her.

The aisle is bordered by women in hairnets who look like different versions of my elementary schoolteachers. They offer samples of pizza, pasta, and those fruit drinks Elise used to love.

"You ditched him," Gran whispers. "Are you okay?"

"I'm fine," I lie. "And I wish you wouldn't call me Princess."

"It's your name, hon."

"No, it's not." I'm scared enough to talk back the way I never would at the house. "I told you my name is Lilith."

"That's just something you read in some astronomy book," she says.

"Astrology."

"Whatever. Come on. Joey's ordering for us. Hot dogs today."

We all eat the same thing. It's the way we've always done it.

"I wanted tacos today."

"Don't complain." Even through her glasses, Gran's eyes are hard. "We had them on Monday."

Monday. When Elise was still here.

"I just hoped we could have them again today." I look down at her scarred hands and fight tears.

"No, hon. It's not good for you to eat just one kind of food all the time."

"Hot dogs will be all right." I can't help but remember Monday, the way I knew something was wrong even before Elise told me what she was going to do, and I had begged her not to.

Last year, after I got on one of the computers at school, I started reading about astrology on the internet. That was the same time I learned about Black Moon Lilith, about how every Sun sign has one.

Lilith. The name hooked me the moment I saw it. She was who I wanted to be. As I told Heather and Elise, most people try to ignore the darkness in their lives. Doing so doesn't get rid of your fears, though. It only manifests them. If you don't step up to your demons, they own you.

My sisters weren't interested in any of that. All they cared about was what their signs meant and when they'd find true love. At night, in our bunks, I explained to them what traits made them special, and I warned them about what situations they should avoid. Right now, I wish I'd tried harder to stop Elise.

Gran's staring at me, and I know she's worried about whether

I'm going to crack under the pressure. I distract her by going up to a lady who's giving away samples of pasta salad.

"Get back here, Princess."

Funny thing about Gran. She'll help us steal a store to the ground, but never once have I seen her take any of the free food. Heather says it's because she thinks she's too good, but I'm not so sure. Gran says it's because she'll never accept another hand-out, and maybe the reason is as simple as that.

I think about the time I watched her lift three cases of champagne from a hotel room before a wedding. Not to drink it, of course. Gran hates any kind of addiction. If she has one, it's what she's doing right now, and Brownie, of course. They've been together a long time, since before my own folks died, and Gran took me in.

We pass the free mini-burritos and cheese wedges, the paper cups of berry yogurt, the stiff, stir-fried chicken strips in teriyaki sauce.

"No, thanks," Gran replies to every offer.

Once more, we return close to the inside entrance to the store and stake out a table near the food stand.

"I told Brownie that Mercury is in retrograde," I say to Gran. "Not a good time for new projects. Lots of potential for mechanical failure."

"You're making that up." Heather pats the bulge beneath the top. "You're just saying it because you're afraid."

"I'm saying it because I hope Brownie got the van checked out," I tell her. "You know I'm right about this stuff."

Heather looks down and seems to shrink, almost disappearing the way I've seen her do when Brownie gets mad.

"Whatever."

I suspect that she's thinking about Elise too, and that's the real reason she's been extra snippy.

"Take it easy, will you?" Gran toys with a squeeze bottle of relish. "Just remember what we're here for. Let's have lunch like a normal family. Then, we'll finish here."

Behind the tinted lens of her glasses, she looks like she might have the pink eye. The thought of that makes me break out in chills.

Gran notices me and demands, "What's wrong?"

"Did I ever have something wrong with my eyes when I was young?"

"You're still young," she says. "And no. You were fine."

"I never had the pink eye?" As I say the words, I feel the cool sting of medication and hear a male doctor voice calling me a name that is swallowed by a roaring in my ears.

"I told you no. Don't start getting weird on me, Princess, especially not now. You know what we've got to do."

She's right. I know it all, including the part she doesn't have to say. What we have to do to save our family.

Joey comes back with the hot dogs and iced tea. Behind him, that same guard leans against the food booth, a cup of coffee in one hand. He's about Brownie's age, fifty, maybe fifty-five, but taller, and he's too far away for me to tell about his expression. I wonder if he has kids. When he comes home at night and takes off that pale gray jacket and expensive-looking tie, do they talk about how many shoplifters he busted at work that day?

"He's watching us," I say.

"Watching you." Heather picks up the mustard and squeezes it along her hot dog in a determined yellow line. "He looks like that other guy, the one who stopped me outside that school in Gilroy."

"Better call Brownie," I tell Gran.

"I'll call him once you take care of business."

"Just be sure he's out there," I say. "Anything could go wrong. We might need to leave in a hurry."

"You read too much of that astronomy, Princess."

"Astrology," I tell her again.

She knows the right way to say it, but I can tell she's more worried about that guy than she lets on. She taps out a text on her phone, and I know it's to Brownie.

Astrology has done things for me that no person has. It's told me why Brownie can be so mean sometimes, and why Gran stays. It even warned me about Elise. Thinking about her makes me want to cry again. I bite into my hot dog and pretend it is the sharp whiff of the mustard that causes me to blink.

We eat lunch in a hurry, but the guard is still hanging around. He leans against the food bar and stares at us.

"We need to finish here right away." Gran pushes out of her plastic chair and stands up next to me. In the bright light, the lines in her leathery skin seem to deepen. "If we upset Brownie today, I can't stop whatever happens."

Like she couldn't stop what happened to Elise.

I dump my plate and cup into the trash can. "Then, I guess we'd better go back for the you-know-what."

"That's more like it." She touches my arm in that soft way she does sometimes, just to let me know she's there for me. "Why don't you and I head through this side of the store, Princess. And Heather and Joey, you go the other way, and we can meet up in front."

Elise told me that if I screamed the way she always did, Brownie would stop sooner. But I couldn't, probably because I never believed it was true. Brownie stopped when he got tired, and the rage in his eyes dimmed and burned out the way a fire does. I never made a sound when he hit me. Now, all the screams I bit back and bottled up are ready to explode inside me.

"Please call him," I ask Gran.

"I sent a text." For a moment, something like fear flashes in her eyes. "You've got to get yourself together, Princess. Come on now."

We walk through the gift area. The mingled scents of candles make me want to sneeze. I turn toward a display of fountains, and there he is. The guard.

"Keep going," Gran says. "That creep can't prove anything."

My flesh tingles. He won't stop looking at me.

Gran pauses and picks up a candle the color and scent of fresh pine.

"No need for us to stay together," she says. "You head back where you need to be. I'll walk straight through the gifts and meet you there."

"What if he follows me?" I'm really getting scared now, and all of those screams are swelling up inside me.

"You know what you have to do." She sneaks a glance at me. "Brownie will be proud of you."

The moment she takes off, I realize that my eyes are burning. I walk blindly through this store that's supposed to help launch our new life in a new place. I hate every step, and yes, I hate myself. I'm not sure why. It must be because of what happened to Elise. Did she really do it to herself, or did Brownie? Please don't let it be true because if it is, I know he'll hurt me too. No, not hurt. Kill. Might as well be honest about it. Brownie could kill me too.

I enter the liquor department from the back, past the shrimp plates, fried chicken, and other prepared food. Sure enough, the glass door of the fancy liquor case is slightly open. No one's around. *Gran, where are you?*

I take a breath and realize this might be the only chance I have all day. Without thinking about what might happen if I fail, I grab an empty shopping cart in front of a cheese display and put my open backpack in it. Then, I head across the space between the cabinet and me. Finally there, I look in every direction, grab that bottle by its neck, and shove it in my backpack. My legs go weak as if they can no longer hold me up. I push the cart down the nearest aisle and try to slow my breathing. Then, as quickly as possible, I put on the backpack, which feels like it's holding a boulder.

Got it. I text Gran.

She shoots back a text. Meet me in front.

Then, I hear his voice.

"Where are you heading?"

I look up into the face of the guard and clutch the handle of my cart.

"Leave me alone, will you?"

"I just asked where you're going next."

If he's a cop, I'm dead.

"To meet my gran. I'm not supposed to talk to strangers."

The stuffed-full shelves of crackers and cookies seem to close in on me, and I wonder if I should try to make a run for the door.

"Don't be afraid," he says.

"Why are you following me?" I stand up straighter, acting like I don't feel the weight of the bottle in my backpack. "Are you some kind of perv?"

"You know better." He takes a step closer, like I'm something wild he's trying to tame. "I'm here to help."

So, he's not just a security guard. He's one of those people Brownie and Gran warned us about. I need to hum the Happy Birthday song, but there's no one around. What a dumb idea that song was. I should have realized that it doesn't work unless the people who care about you are close enough to hear.

"If you take one more step toward me, I'll yell my head off," I tell him.

"Calm down," he says. "Tell me your name."

"None of your business." I keep pushing the cart, faster now, past the crackers, past the chips, past the people crowding the aisles.

"You don't remember it, do you?"

I can't look at him anymore. His questions are coming too fast.

"Princess." I keep my voice low and steady.

"Your real name," he says.

"I haven't done anything wrong." That's such a complete lie. I've done everything wrong, everything. Right now, if I'm not careful, I'm going to destroy my family's chance for a new life.

"You'll be all right," he says. "You're strong, like Elise." He speaks as if he knows her, as if he knows me.

"Elise?" I say, and then stop myself and reach for my phone. "Get away. I'm calling my gran."

"She's not your grandmother." He shakes his head, but his smile is friendly. "She takes children no one else wants. Every now and then, she and her boyfriend take the wrong kid, and all hell breaks loose."

"You're not a security guard, are you?" My voice is shaking. "You don't even work here, do you? You're that guy who came to my school."

"I'm a friend," he says. "Families hire people like me to help kids remember. My approach is different than some. I think the remembering should come first."

First? I wonder. *Before what?*

Memories flash through my head. A stuffed rabbit. Muffled voices. The pink eye. It's just Mercury trying to mess with me. Mercury and fear.

"You saw Jay Brown beat Elise, didn't you?" he asks.

"No." My face is on fire.

"She said he tried to kill her because she was going to tell what he and his girlfriend are doing to you kids."

"Elise is alive?" I blurt out before I can stop myself.

He nods. "If the police don't have Brown by now, they will shortly. You need to come with me."

"You're lying." My eyes fill with tears. I'm the one who's supposed to be the liar, the one who can talk my way out of any situation, the one with nerves of steel.

"You deserve better than the streets," he says. "There are people who care about you, people who love you."

I start to tell him that this isn't the streets. This is my home. But I can't speak. The people-who-love-you part has hit me like a fist.

Gran stands at the entrance in front of the large-screen TVs. All the other people in the store, walking past me, lined up at the registers, seem to dim. Gran shoots me a look that's a combination of *hurry up* and something else I can't define, something I've never before seen on her face. She speaks into her phone and mouths my name. I watch the angry twist of her lips.

"Princess," she calls to me. "Let's get out of here."

"Come with me," the man says. "I promise you'll be safe."

"Princess," Gran calls out again. "Hurry up, or we're leaving without you."

"I can't."

I am saying it to both of them now and to myself. "I just can't."

"All right, then." He starts to turn away, and the look Gran gives me tells me we've done it again. I can almost hear her sigh.

Brownie will be pleased with us, and when he's pleased with us, he's pleased with her. We can go north, maybe live on a houseboat, be a family.

Without Elise.

My feet won't move.

"I can't," I say again.

The man pauses, turns, and stares back at me.

"If you won't let me help, there's nothing else I can do," he says. Then, he starts for the back of the store. With each step, he's farther away, my decision more permanent.

Before I know it, I am taking off my backpack, slamming it in the empty cart, and moving toward him.

"Wait," I call out, and he stops.

"Princess," Gran shouts. "Don't be crazy."

He turns as if just noticing me.

"Lily?" he asks.

The word chases me and echoes in my eardrums.

Not Lilith. Not Princess. Not the many lies I've told to others and myself, layer upon layer, so many times that they buried anything I'd once known as the truth.

I stop.

The man puts out his hand.

"Lily?"

His voice is soft now.

Lily?

It is my name, mine, and at this moment, it is all I have in the world.

Slowly, I put out my hand too.

JACK IN THE BOX

STEVE LISKOW

Sometimes the voices get real loud, but I ignore them, mostly. They get me into trouble. That makes sense because sometimes they sound like my ex-wife. Wives. I try to leave everyone alone and if they leave me alone too, everything is fine.

I got a new house two weeks ago. Rafferty Brothers got a new shipment in, and when they unloaded the furniture from the van, they tossed some of the boxes in back near the dumpster and I took the biggest one, a couch. Now there's room if Dasha and Molly and Leo want to hang out, too.

Nobody bothers me, mostly. My box is behind a mini-mall, an ice cream place at one end, Rafferty Brothers, a jewelry store, a shoe outlet, a computer repair place, a chiropractor and Mario's Pizza at the far end. I get most of my meals from that dumpster. So do the others and we share. Mostly. Leo needs a lot 'cause he's bigger.

Now that it's warmer weather, I like a bigger box 'cause I can leave my other clothes there. I can leave my cart in there, too, and the rain won't get at it. Nobody's going to steal anything because nobody knows I live there. Well, except Dasha and Molly and Leo.

Last week I was in the parking lot looking for bottles and cans I could recycle when a little girl looked at me.

"Mister?" She pointed at me and her mother tried to shush her. She—the little girl—had hair the color of honey and big blue eyes. She was missing one of her top front teeth, so her esses whistled.

"Are you a homeless man?"

Be nice, Beverly warned me. Bev was my first wife. We got married a week before I shipped out for basic, and I got wounded in Desert Storm. When I came back, she complained a lot more than she used to. I never did anything right, she said, and I forgot stuff. Somedays I forgot to go to work because I couldn't remember where it was. Somedays, I didn't even remember *what* it was. When I didn't show up, they called and that got Bev even more upset.

Next thing I knew, she wanted a divorce.

Yeah, Bev. Be nice. But I didn't have any problem with the kid. She was little. How was she going to learn stuff if she didn't ask questions? Molly told me that once and it makes sense. "Nope," I told her. "I've got a nice place to live. Big enough so my friends can visit, too."

"Where is it?" the little girl asked.

"Jackie," her mother snapped. "That's rude."

"No," I said. "It's fine. How will she learn anything if she doesn't ask about it?" I almost heard Molly saying it again. I pointed back toward the stores.

"It's back there, the other side of the stores."

They both looked back and up the hill. There were some nice houses up there, with big garages and cars and green grass. Some of them had trees, too. They got red and orange and yellow in the fall and I liked to walk up there and kick my feet through the leaves like big cornflakes. They aren't very friendly up there, though. Once when I was kicking leaves in someone's yard a police car came up.

"What are you doing here?" the policeman asked. He looked younger than me, but he had eyes that looked mean, like Leo's when someone tries to take his food.

"Kicking the leaves." He must have been pretty dumb if he couldn't see that. I thought policemen were smart.

"You can't do that around here. People don't want you kicking their leaves."

"They can come out and kick them, too, can't they?" I said. "After all, they're *their* leaves."

"That's not the point." He looked at me funny. Lots of people look at me that way, though, so I'm used to it.

"You need me to take you somewhere?"

I thought he meant jail, so I shook my head.

"I'll go somewhere else," I said. "I'll find other leaves to kick."

He nodded. "That's a good idea. But not around here, okay?"

"Not around here."

You are such an idiot, Bev whispered. I walked away without looking at the policeman again. Or at Bev. She wasn't really there, anyway. "Jackie," I said. "Do you like dogs?"

"That's enough." Her mother looked at me and her hair turned into snakes, their forked tongues flicking at me like flames. "You should go somewhere else."

"I just got here," I told her. "Didn't you, too?"

She looked at me like my mother used to do. "Are you all right?"

"Sure," I said. "Actually, I can't get my meds anymore, but it's okay. I don't need them." The snakes in her hair moved and settled again when they saw me watching.

"Why do you need them?"

"It was the war," I told her. "I was wounded in Vietnam and I needed it for a while to get rid of the nightmares and...other weird stuff."

You got that right. Beverly's voice had a sharper edge than usual.

One of the snakes peeked out behind the mother's ear. "You look awfully young to have been in Vietnam."

"I stay out of the sun," I told her. "It ages your skin like you wouldn't believe. I had a hat once, but I lost it somewhere. Maybe I'll get another one."

She backed up and led the little girl into the shoe place. They walked fast like it was raining, but the sun was shining so it was hot. Maybe they'd go in the ice cream place later. I thought about going in there, too, but I didn't have any money and they don't like me to stay in their air-conditioning if I don't buy anything.

I got a better idea and walked farther down the road. Cars went by me and some of the people looked at me. Maybe they talked about me, too. I walked off the pavement so nobody hit me, though.

The Angels Rest Motel had plump green bushes on both sides of the driveway and a big sign that said Hourly Rates X-rated Video Wifi. They had a big swimming pool, too, behind a chain-link fence, and hardly nobody ever used it. Well, at night once I saw two people in it. They didn't have bathing suits. If I couldn't use the air-conditioning in the ice cream place, maybe I could swim in that pool. I didn't have a bathing suit, either, but that didn't bother those people I saw, so I figured it would be all right.

There were only three cars in the lot and they were down at the other end. I walked over to the chain-link fence. I couldn't find a gate, and finally saw that you had to come out a door on the building.

I had one foot on top of the fence when a man dashed toward me. "You. Hey, you. What the hell are you doing?"

He looked mad as a big dog when you steal his food and his voice barked like one, too. He had an accent. He had black shiny hair and dark skin.

I looked down at him and the wire fence hurt my hands. "I wanted to swim. You know, in your pool."

"That's for guests, you bum. Get out of here before I call the cops."

"I was just going to visit," I told him. "Doesn't that make me a guest?"

"Get the hell out of here." His teeth got real big like Leo's when he's mad. I shifted my weight and dropped back down on the cement. He reached into his pocket and pulled out a cell phone.

"Keep moving, mister. If I call the cops, they will put your ass in jail."

"That's no way to get company," I told him.

You are such an idiot.

That was Kate, my second wife. We met after I got out of the VA hospital. Or maybe at the employment agency. Maybe it was somewhere else. I'm not sure. She was young and pretty like a magazine and she liked to dance. We went driving a few times until I lost my license.

I told her about the war and being wounded in Afghanistan and she was really sorry about it. She and I went back to her place and she held me and made me feel better. We got married, but I started losing track of where I worked when Beverly started talking to me again. She told me Kate didn't really love me and just wanted to steal my checks. I told Kate and she got real mad and we argued. She told the police that I hit her, but I would never hit a woman. Especially not my wife. Especially not Kate. Maybe Beverly was just jealous and lied to me because Kate was prettier than she was.

Anyway, after Kate divorced me, I told myself I wouldn't listen to the voices anymore.

I walked back down the road toward the mini-mall. Across the street I saw the pharmacy where I used to get my Haldol. Or one like it. There are a lot of them around. The VA told me there was something wrong with my papers and they wouldn't give me medicine anymore. I think it was because of when I was in combat.

When I got back, lots of cars filled the parking lot and the smell of spicy tomato sauce and hot pizza from Mario's made my nose run. Jackie and the snake woman were probably gone by then. Or maybe getting ice cream. I wanted some ice cream on a warm day, but I didn't have any money. They don't throw ice cream in the dumpster in back like Mario's does with some of their food. Or if they do, I never see it. Maybe it melts, or maybe Molly and Dasha find it first.

I had a garbage bag in my pocket and I walked around the parking lot picking up bottles and cans people threw away.

What are you doing? Bev sounded like she did whenever I did something she thought was stupid.

"These are valuable," I told her. "People don't even think. They just throw them anywhere and they mess up the parking lot. It's like weeds in grass. They look bad."

You are something else, Bev said.

"Yeah," I said. "I should be a housewife, picking things up all the time." *That's what I did all the time, pick up after you.*

I stopped listening. When I couldn't find any more cans or bottles, I carried my bag down the road to a supermarket. They had a machine in the front and I fed the bottles into the hole, one at a time. It was like feeding a little kid. Give them time to chew what they've got in their mouths before you give them more. When my bag was empty, I pushed the button and got my receipt.

The lady at the cash register wrinkled her nose when I got in her line, but I smiled at her and showed her my paper. She took it and gave me enough money for a small ice cream cone.

I went back and got a small cone, coffee with sprinkles, and took it back to my box. I licked the sprinkles off onto my tongue. It was cool in the shade.

You're a lazy bum. That was Kate again. She was really sweet and kind when we met, but after we got married nothing I did was good enough.

"I worked for this ice cream," I told her. "I picked up a whole bunch of trash around the parking lot."

Speaking of trash…

I stopped listening to her.

When it got dark, the cars went away and the big light on a pole behind the box went on. It turned the whole area behind the buildings bluish gray like a full moon, but there was only a sliver of a moon that night. It was warm and the breeze over the dumpster smelled like tomato sauce and cheese and garlic.

When I went over, Dasha was there, too, with some of her friends. So was Leo. I climbed up the side of the dumpster and looked inside. I found a partly-eaten grinder and a few slices of pizza that were only a little soggy, and a couple of rolls and some bread. I brought everything out and spread it on the ground for my friends and they came over and started munching. I kept the piece of grinder for myself. It was okay, but I like pepperoni better than salami.

Leo and Molly and one of her friends followed me home and we stretched out in my box.

Traffic went by on the road, but the stores were closed and nobody came back to bother us. Molly climbed on my chest. I stroked her chin and she purred.

"Who's your friend?" I asked.

"Lucinda," the other cat said, "but you can call me Lucy."

Lucy was a tortoiseshell with white whiskers. Even in the dark, her eyes were a soft mossy green. Neither of my wives had eyes half as beautiful. They didn't purr like Lucy, either. I stroked her forehead and she cuddled into my side.

"You're a nice man," she said. She licked my fingers like a Popsicle.

"Do cats like Popsicles?" I asked her.

"In hot weather," she said. "Who doesn't?"

Leo finished his roast beef. I don't give him spicy meat because it gives him heartburn. Believe me, you don't want to be in a box with him when he's got heartburn.

"Tomorrow they empty the dumpster," he said. He stretched, his butt in the air and his head sticking out the end of the box. "Who's that?"

"Who?" I said. I started to sit up but Molly was still on my chest.

"There's a man outside," Leo said.

Maybe a policeman was out there. If he was, I'd have to be real quiet. We'd eaten all the food, though, so he wouldn't smell it.

I said, "Come back inside."

Leo stuck his head farther out of the box.

"He's doing something to one of the back doors."

Molly eased off my chest and Lucy followed her up next to Leo. "The stone store," Molly said. "Why doesn't he go in the front?"

"They're closed now," Lucy said. "Maybe you use the back door at night."

"No, that's wrong."

I crept up to join them. A man in dark jeans and a hoodie crouched by the back door, the light on the pole turning him into a dark smudge on the wall. He opened the door and slid something back into his pocket, then he closed that door behind himself again.

You should do something. Bev sounded stern, like my mother telling me to clean up a mess, but there wasn't a mess. Leo and the others ate everything I put out for them, and I wiped the floor with an old rag. Actually, it isn't a floor, it's the bottom of the box, so I'm careful. If cardboard gets wet, it gets soggy. When we had a heavy rain, I'd have to find another box. So far, I'd been lucky. We'd had this box for over two weeks with only a few sprinkles.

"Like what?" I said to Bev.

Molly looked back at me. "What do you mean?"

"Nothing," I said. "I was talking to someone else."

"We're the only ones here, Jack."

"Never mind," I said. Leo stepped out of the box and his ears flattened back on his head. The light on the post made his shadow real big and long, and he moved closer without making any sound at all.

"Leo," Molly said. "It's none of our business."

"I'm just wondering about it," Leo said. "Nobody's ever done that before, so I want to see what happens next."

Lucy sat with her tail wrapped around her four paws, and Molly did the same. They were like cookie jars at the edge of the box, one black-and-white and the other a mix of black, brown and orange. I lowered myself from hands and knees to my stomach, the way I lay in combat when I had my rifle. I almost wished I had it back, but it didn't do me any good then, or I wouldn't have been shot.

"Why would he go into the stones store?" Molly asked. "He should go into the ice cream store and get something to eat. If he got a lot, he could bring it back here and we could all share it."

"The stones in the store are valuable," I said. "They've got nice things people can wear. Rings, watches, necklaces…"

"What's a watch?" Lucy asked. "We're watching now. How can you sell what we're doing?"

"No, a watch. You wear it on your wrist." I tapped her front paw. "Here. And it helps you tell time."

"Time?"

"Like day and night. When to eat. Things like that." Sometimes I'm so smart I wonder how I got here.

"I don't need a watch," Molly said. "My stomach tells me when to eat, doesn't yours?"

"Watches are pretty, though," I said. "People like them like for…decoration. You know?"

"I know what a necklace is," Leo said. "That's like a collar. Like mine."

Voices I hadn't heard in a long time talked louder and I clamped my teeth tight to shut them out, but it didn't work. A whole bunch of voices talking over each other, telling each other I was down and take cover and where was the SOB and someone calling "Medic, Medic, over here," and someone else calling for air cover and then Bev's voice asking me if I was all right and if it hurt.

"Stay here," I said. Then I stepped out into the cold gray light. I might as well have stood on a bull's-eye 'cause there was no cover. The dumpster loomed off to my left, so big it probably didn't come in a box. If I had a box that big, Leo and Molly and the others could stay with me all the time and we could have our own rooms until it rained. That would be nice. But now they all went somewhere else and came back. I never thought to ask if they had boxes of their own. If they did, we could all hang out at their boxes, too, instead of mine all the time.

I crouched and hustled over near the back door, cupping my rifle in my hands. Then I looked down and it wasn't there. Why was I going into a firefight without my weapon? My sergeant's voice hissed in my ears.

"Jack, you section-8 fool, get your ass back here."

Something was wrong, though, and I had to check it out for the other guys, Leo and Molly and Lucy and…the others. The wall scratched against my hands and I smelled the dumpster. The light hummed against my back and my shadow fell across the door. That was wrong. I had to get to the other side so the man wouldn't see my shadow. If he even came out again. But why would he stay in there at night? Leo saw him too, so he was real, not something I made up when I was lying in a hospital bed with those tubes in my arms.

I looked both ways. Leo and Molly and Lucy sat alert, ready to give me cover. I scuttled to the other side of the door and hunkered down. My pulse beat in my ears, even louder than the voices. Now I was looking toward the light, though. I put my hand above my eyes like a cap so I could see. Sarge whispered even louder and Bev told me to be careful. Kate called me an asshole. Yeah, that was Kate, all right.

The door moved and I held my breath. It opened wider and the man stuck his head out. Then his whole body. He eased the door shut and his shadow spread over me. A key clicked in the lock and he stepped back holding something about the size of a big book in his other hand.

He saw me.

"What the—?" His eyes turned to flames.

I tackled him and we fell together, the blacktop scraping my hands when he landed on them. The book thing flew out of his hands and burst open so stones rattled on the ground. I tried to pull my hands free, but he punched me in the cheek. The *whump* of his fist filled my head. My cheek hurt, but I butted him with my forehead. I wanted to move up on top of him, but he punched me again and I saw a flash brighter than the flames in his eyes.

"Knee him, knee him," Sarge yelled. I tried to spread his legs, but he kneed me in the stomach first. My breath whistled out and he slammed me in the throat with his forearm. I rolled off him, choking and gasping for breath, and he jumped to his feet. Stones dug into my back before I rolled to my hands and knees.

He kicked me. The salami grinder taste filled my mouth again. I clamped my teeth tight and rolled away. When I stood up, my hands burned and my stomach hurt. I danced so my shadow fell over him again and his eyes flamed even brighter.

He tried to kick me again, but I moved away and punched him in the ear. He stumbled against the wall, then bounced off faster than I expected.

"Look out," the voices shouted. Sarge, Bev, Kate, Leo, Molly, Lucy, all of them, but too late.

He kicked me between my legs. I fell to my hands and knees, my ears ringing and my stomach clenching. This time I threw up and my grinder splatted on the blacktop. I rolled away from it and tried to stand, but my legs wouldn't work. The center of my body felt like shattered glass.

"All right, buddy."

The man picked up a board lying near the back door and held it in both hands. I tried to get to my hands and knees so I could tackle him, but something wet ran in my pants and my legs could hardly move. He raised that board over his head and stepped closer.

Leo jumped on his back. The man staggered and tripped over my feet. The board rattled on the ground next to my head, and Leo pushed him facedown, his mouth open wide, his teeth glittering like the stones on the ground, and then he dug his snout into the man's neck.

The man screamed, but he bucked Leo off and rolled to his feet. Leo rushed and the man kicked him. Leo howled and flew off to my right. But the board was in my hands now, heavy and solid, and it swung at the man, crunching against his temple so the impact vibrated up my arms, all the way to my shoulders. The *thud* drowned out the voices cheering me on and the man spun and fell on his face.

I held the board like a baseball bat and moved closer, but he didn't move. Leo limped over and sniffed at him, but he still didn't move. The flame in his eyes went dark.

My heart pounded between my legs and I had to lie down again. The light got dimmer then brighter a few times. Breathing hurt. Molly licked my face.

"Are you all right?"

I nodded, even though I couldn't talk. I unwrapped my fingers from the board and slivers burned my fingers. Leo was panting for breath, too. Lucy went over to him.

"What now?" she asked.

Molly watched me struggle to my knees. I felt hot, then cold, and dizzy, like I was going to be sick again, but I wasn't. Molly came over and licked my face and I stood up and leaned against the wall.

"We can't leave him here."

I walked around until my legs worked again, then rolled the man onto his back. His head flopped loosely and he wasn't breathing. Light spilled across a dark shiny spot on his forehead. I took his arm and pulled him to a sitting position, then dragged him onto my back. My legs wobbled, but I carried him to the dumpster. I got his head over the top and lifted his torso up until his legs tumbled over the edge. Everything rustled and crunched until he settled.

I picked up the board and tossed it after him.

Lucy and Molly examined the glittering stones scattered on the ground.

"Pretty." Lucy's soft green eyes reflected the light. "But you can't eat them, can you?"

"People wear them for decoration," I said again. How could I get them back into the store? I'd have to open the door again. The man had a key so he didn't set off the alarm, but I wasn't going to climb into that dumpster to find it.

I knelt and picked up all the stones and put them back into the box. Molly and Lucy helped me find the ones that rolled away, but they were mostly bracelets and rings so they didn't roll far. There was a necklace, too, and I thought it was diamonds.

When we couldn't find any more stones, we went back to my box. Leo was walking better by then and his breathing was okay.

I put the box back in the corner with my clothes and we all huddled together and fell asleep. When I woke up in the morning, Molly and Leo were gone, but Lucy was still there.

Hours later, police cars appeared in the parking lot in front of the jewelry store. I heard one of the people from the store say one of their employees didn't show up that morning. The police asked what he looked like. He didn't wear jeans and a hoodie.

When I walked back behind the buildings, the big truck grumbled near the dumpster. It slid its forks into the slots on the side and lifted the whole thing up to dump the papers and boxes and food and bottles and board into its big bed. And the man in the jeans and hoodie. It put the empty dumpster down and growled away.

Molly and Lucy and Dasha all stayed over that night and I went back to the dumpster for more food. I wanted ice cream, too, but I didn't have any money.

Two days later, we opened the box for the first time. It held some pretty rings, a few bracelets and a necklace.

"I should give these back," I said. Bev's voice drowned out the others.

Are you crazy? Then she laughed. *Of course you are. But don't try to give them back.*

You'll get yourself into even more trouble.

Sarge said pretty much the same thing.

Leo looked at the necklace. "It looks like my collar, only nicer."

"You want to try it on?" I asked.

I put it around his neck and found the catch. It fitted perfectly. The bracelets fitted the cats, too. Lucy wore green stones that matched her eyes, and Molly wore pearls.

A few days later, a policeman found me picking up bottles in the parking lot.

"Jack," he said. "You know the jewelry store over there was robbed last week, right?"

"Yes, sir." I'm polite to other men in uniform. Besides, this officer was nice to me whenever we talked. He bought me an ice cream once.

"Well, we're pretty sure we know who did it, but we can't find the guy. That's just a matter of time." He pushed back his hat and wiped his forehead.

"You might be able to help me with something else, though."
"Sir?"

"Well, a few people have called us. Their pets have shown

up at home wearing jewelry. Seriously expensive things. The stuff that was stolen."

"Pets?" I said. "You mean like dogs and cats?"

"Yeah. A golden retriever mix, a few cats. They live with people close by, but they run free. I was wondering if you've seen anything like that?"

"A dog wearing jewelry."

"Yeah. Or a cat."

"A dog with jewelry sounds kind of sissy, doesn't it?"

"It does," he agreed. He looked at my bag of bottles and cans. "It's a warm day. You need an ice cream cone?"

"Are you buying, sir?"

"Sure."

I took my bag of bottles and my chocolate ice cream cone back to my big box and licked slowly. Leo wandered in while I was eating and he didn't have his necklace.

"Molly and Lucy don't have theirs, either," he said.

"I talked to a policeman a little while ago," I told him. "He got me the ice cream. You want a taste?"

"Is that chocolate? I'd better not."

Molly and Lucy both came by later, and Leo was right, they didn't have their collars, either. We hung out and talked about the jewelry store and the robbery and how the police wouldn't find the man they were looking for.

When everyone else left, I stretched out and looked at my ceiling. One of these days, we'd have a heavy rain that would soak this box and I'd have to find another place to live, but for now, it was home sweet home.

There was even enough room for all the voices.

PLAYING FOR KEEPS

S.J. ROZAN

"Jews can't play! Girls can't play! And Jew-girls specially can't play!"

Petey Conner's blue eyes narrowed on Hilda as he chanted, "Jew-girls can't play! Jew-girls can't play!"

The other boys didn't join the chant, but they stood in a silent semicircle behind him.

Hilda and Jacob being taken out of school for transport to the camps. The other children watching wordlessly.

"You let my brother play."

"Her brudda! We let her brudda play! Listen to the Jew-girl, listen to her talk funny!"

Hilda flushed. English was harder for her than for Jacob. The war had been over for three years but they'd barely been in America for one. Jacob was ten, Hilda eleven, when they were brought by a cousin of their mother's to live in this Ohio town.

Jacob was better able to forget his Polish and his Yiddish and to mold his tongue around the strange new sounds. Hilda didn't find it as easy to forget.

"Attention, Jews and Romanis! None of your dog-languages! Polish only! Children speaking dog-languages will be punished."

"You let my brother play yesterday. After the game you kept the marbles. You took them."

"We were playing keepsies. Jew-boy lost. Tough on him."

"No, you weren't. He asked at the beginning the rules. You told him give-backs."

"Ve veren't! He esked the rules! Do you hear this?" Laughing, Petey Conner turned to the other boys. He spun back to Hilda and the laugh stopped abruptly. "If he says we were playing give-backs he's lying."

Hilda stepped forward. "My brother doesn't lie."

A boy with curly black hair shifted apprehensively. "Petey, we were, though. We said, give-backs—"

"Shut up!"

The Romani boy, Andrezj, glancing at the guard and then stepping in to help Hilda pull a heavy stone out of the earth and carry it to the pile across the field.

"I want to play you. Now. We can play keepsies. But you must use the marbles you took from my brother."

"Is det so? Vich marbles is doze? Det I took from your brudda?"

"The ones in the blue bag, Petey," said the black-haired boy. "You said they were Jew marbles and you were keeping them separate."

"I told you to shut *up!*" Petey turned savagely on the boy.

He had disappeared, Andrezj, a week later. No one saw him again.

"I will play with these." Hilda poured yesterday's purchase into her palm. She'd gone without lunch at school today, and would again tomorrow and the next day, to pay for them, but she was used to hunger.

"One of you has stolen an apple from the Commandant's kitchen. No one will eat tonight."
"One of you has stolen a loaf of bread from the Commandant's kitchen. No one will eat tonight."
"One of you has..."

Petey Conner had his mouth open to speak when Hilda spilled out the marbles. He stopped and she watched the contempt on his face melt into greed. Her shooter was a steelie, a large, shiny stainless steel sphere. None of the boys had one. It was heavy enough to knock anything out of the circle. It had already turned her thumbnail a painful purple after yesterday afternoon's long practice session.

"Keepsies?" Petey said, still staring at the marble. "You know that means shooters, too?"

"Of course, shooters, too." Though Hilda knew it didn't always mean that. Jacob had explained the rules. Even playing for keeps, players almost always kept their shooters. But rulers can change the rules.

"Why are you over there? Stupid children, so stupid. Today boys line up on that side and girls on that side. Run!"

Petey's face crinkled in a mean smile. "Okay," he said. "Okay, Jew-girl, I'll play you." He reached into his pocket for the blue bag and poured the marbles out. "I'll use your brudda's Jew marbles. But I'm not using his Jew shooter. I'm using this." From a different bag he took out a large glass sphere.

The boys crowded around. Hilda didn't move. "Wow," a freckled boy said. "What's that?"

"It's German," Petey answered. "German!" He thrust the marble in Hilda's face. "It's called a sulphide cause it has sulphide in it. Do you know what that is? It makes shapes. In the marble. Animals and people and stuff. They have dogs and cows and chickens and this one's a *pig!*"

"The soup is made from the bones of a pig. You'll get nothing else. Go ahead, Jew-children, eat. Eat!" Some of the children got sick. Hilda forced the soup down by telling herself the guard was lying. She told Jacob the same.

The pig inside the marble was fat and pink and unmistakable. Hilda's stomach turned over. She swallowed bile as she watched Petey draw the circle in the dirt.

"Go ahead, Jew-girl, put your marbles down," Petey said after he'd placed his. Hilda crouched in the dirt, steeling herself automatically against a blow from behind.

"Jew-children, Romani children, so lazy! Here there is no coddling from your mamas and papas! They are gone now. Here you must work!"

No blow came and Hilda placed her marbles to complete the X.

One of the boys drew another line a few feet away. Petey stepped to it, knelt, and shot the pig marble toward the circle. Hilda did the same with the steelie. A murmur, both apprehensive and appreciative, went up from the boys as the steelie rolled close to the edge of the circle, closer than Petey's pig shooter had.

Petey's lip curled but he didn't dispute Hilda's right to go first.

Hilda placed the steelie on the circle and knelt beside it, knuckles down as Jacob had showed her. She took aim. Her eye was good and her hand was steady.

Anna, or sometimes Vadoma—the smallest girls—climbing through the scullery window Hilda held open while she watched for the guard. The girls with instructions on what to take that wouldn't be missed—scraps, slops. Those nights, no one got caught, and every girl ate a tiny bit more. Hilda saved her share to give to Jacob in the morning.

She shot, ignoring the pain in her thumbnail. The steelie clinked against glass and one of Jacob's marbles rolled out of the circle. Hilda moved inside the circle to where the steelie had stopped. She shot it toward a second marble. That one rolled out of the circle also. The third shot was more painful and the marble she hit didn't roll far. She stood, pocketed the two she'd knocked out, and waited for Petey to take his turn. She didn't look at her aching thumb or try to shake the pain out.

Rachel, newly arrived and afraid of everything, falling, gashing her leg. Hilda hissing, "Don't cry. They don't know you hurt yourself but if they see you crying they'll hurt you on purpose. Just keep digging!"

Petey, crouching at the line, didn't even look at the marbles Hilda had put down, or at Jacob's, either, that he had placed. He gave Hilda a nasty grin and aimed his pig shooter directly at the steelie.

Hilda stood perfectly still. The steelie was far away from the pig shooter's place on the line, but near the edge on the other side of the circle. If he hit it he might knock it out, but it would be hard to hit. The sensible thing for Petey to do would be to shoot at a nearby marble, as she had.

But that would mean they were actually playing. Even if he won, he'd have played a game with her. That wasn't what he wanted, she knew that. He wanted the steelie and he wanted her gone.

The guard coming into the stable where the girls slept. Looking at Elsa. "Around your neck. What is that?"

"My mama—"

"Your mama's gone. She's dead! Give that to me."

"No, my—"

Hilda, stepping to Elsa, ripping the chain from her neck, holding the locket up for the guard. Until the day the soldiers came to liberate them, Elsa never said a word to Hilda again.

But she lived.

Hilda didn't know if Petey had the strength in his thumb to get his shooter all the way across the circle, but if he did and knocked the steelie out, the game would end. Except for the two marbles she'd already won, Petey Conner would keep everything.

The boys fell silent. Petey shut one eye and squinted the other. He moved his hand slightly, to improve his angle, and shot.

The pig shooter sped across the dirt. Just before it collided with the steelie it skipped over a tiny stone. That little jump made it wobble, and it didn't hit the steelie full-on, glancing off it instead. The steelie rolled but came to rest still inside the circle, and the pig shooter stopped a few feet away.

Petey yelled, "Hey! No fairs! It hit a pebble! Do-overs!" Looking at the other boys, he started to reach for his shooter. The black-haired boy scowled and stepped forward and the boy with the freckles frowned. Another boy frowned, too. Slowly, Petey withdrew his hand.

Hilda, heart pounding, walked to the other side of the circle and crouched by the steelie. Knocking the pig shooter out from here would take a good deal of force. She'd have to send it spinning into another marble or even two on the way. But she might not get another chance.

Her thumb had started throbbing but she told it *just one more*.

A guard beating Hilda for not replying fast enough to a question she hadn't heard. With each blow, Hilda telling herself just one more, until it was finally true.

She bit her lip to stifle the cry that would try to escape when her thumb hit the steelie. One chance, she thought.

To escape the camp, there had never been a chance. To save her friends, to stop the beatings, to prevent the deaths, never.

Hilda shot her thumb into the steelie. Pain stabbed as far as her elbow. The steelie hit the pig shooter hard. The pig shooter sped away, caromed off a tiger's eye and then off a blue aggie. The aggie rolled out of the circle.

And so did the pig shooter.

Silence.

Hilda didn't look at Petey Conner. Standing, she crossed the circle, picked up the glass globe, examined the pig inside. She scanned the dirt for a stone. She found one that just fit her palm and placed the pig shooter in the center of the circle.

With all her strength, all the memories of her parents and her friends, with Andrezj and Anna and Vadoma, with the cold and the hunger and the savagery of the guards, she smashed the stone down on the pig shooter.

Shouts and gasps from the boys. A wail from Petey. Hilda lifted the stone to expose shards and chips and powder. Some fragments were clear. Some were pink.

Hilda threw down the stone, scooped up the steelie, and walked away.

Half a block later the dark-haired boy jogged up beside her. Silently, he opened his hand and held out Jacob's marbles.

ABOUT THE CONTRIBUTORS

Naomi Hirahara is an Edgar Award–winning author of multiple traditional mystery series and noir short stories. Her Mas Arai mysteries have been published in Japanese, Korean and French, and feature a Los Angeles gardener and Hiroshima survivor who solves crimes. Her first historical mystery is *Clark and Division*, which follows a Japanese American family's move to Chicago in 1944 after being released from a California wartime detention center. Her second Leilani Santiago Hawai'i mystery, *An Eternal Lei*, is scheduled to be released in spring of 2022. A former journalist with *The Rafu Shimpo* newspaper, Naomi has also written numerous nonfiction history books and curated exhibitions. She has also written a middle-grade novel, *1001 Cranes*. For updated information, go to www.naomihirahara.com.

David Bart has been published many times in *Alfred Hitchcock's Mystery Magazine*, *Ellery Queen's Mystery Magazine* and *Mystery Magazine*. This is the fourth Mystery Writers of America anthology to include one of his short stories. He is currently working on a novel based on his story, "Brothers Out of Time," first published in *Alfred Hitchcock's Mystery Magazine*, May/June 2021 issue. David and his wife, Linda, live in New Mexico with their rescued cat, Ripley.

Sara Paretsky and her acclaimed PI V.I. Warshawski helped transform the role of women in contemporary crime fiction, beginning with the publication of her first novel, *Indemnity Only*, in 1982. Sisters in Crime, the advocacy organization she founded in 1986, has supported a new generation of crime writers. She has published twenty-three novels, two collections of short stories, and edited a number of anthologies. Her memoir, *Writing in an Age of Silence*, was a finalist for the National Book Critics Circle award. Among other awards, Paretsky holds the Cartier Diamond Dagger, MWA's Grand Master and *Ms. Magazine*'s Woman of the Year. Paretsky is vain about the quality of her cappuccinos. Visit her at www.saraparetsky.com.

Susan Breen is the author of the Maggie Dove mystery series. Her first novel, *The Fiction Class*, won the Westchester Library Association's Washington Irving Award. Her short stories have been published in a number of venues, among them *Best American NonRequired Reading*, *Ellery Queen's Mystery Magazine*, *Alfred Hitchcock's Mystery Magazine* and two Malice Domestic anthologies. She teaches novel-writing for Gotham Writers and is on the staff of the New York Pitch Conference. She lives in the Hudson Valley with her husband and two sweet little dogs and two aggressive cats.

Gary Phillips is the son of a mechanic and a librarian. He's published novels, comics, novellas and short stories, and edited or co-edited several anthologies including the Anthony-winning *The*

Obama Inheritance: Fifteen Stories of Conspiracy Noir. He was also a staff writer on *Snowfall*, an FX show about crack and the CIA in 1980s South Central L.A. where he grew up. *Violent Spring*, his debut mystery from nearly thirty years ago was named in 2020 one of the essential crime novels of Los Angeles. His latest book is *One-Shot Harry*, set in 1963.

Neil S. Plakcy is the author of over fifty mystery and romance novels, including the best-selling golden retriever mysteries and the highly acclaimed Mahu series, a three-time finalist for the Lambda Literary Awards. His stories have been featured in numerous venues, including the Bouchercon anthology *Florida Happens* and Malice Domestic's *Murder Most Conventional* and several Happy Homicides collections. He is a professor of English at Broward College in South Florida, where he lives with his husband and their rambunctious golden retrievers. His website is www.mahubooks.com.

Renee James is a confessed English major and out transgender author who is also a spouse, parent, grandparent and Vietnam veteran. She took up fiction writing after a long career in magazines. She has published six novels and a biography along with short stories under various bylines. Her novels include the Bobbi Logan trilogy (*Coming Out Can Be Murder*, *A Kind of Justice* and *Seven Suspects*) which depicts the life and times of a Chicago transwoman after gender transition in the early 2000s.

Connie Johnson Hambley horrified her parents by using her law degree to write high-concept thrillers rather than pursue gainful employment. She's written for *Bloomberg BusinessWeek*, *Nature*, *Financial Advisor Magazine* and other journals, but her passion is writing great suspense. Her high-concept thrillers weave fact and legal fiction into tales of modern-day crimes. Two of Connie's novels in *The Jessica Trilogy* won the Best English Fiction literary award at the EQUUS International Film Festival.

Her short stories appear in *New England's Best Crime Stories, Mystery Magazine* and *Running Wild Anthology of Stories.*

Gabino Iglesias is a writer, editor and literary critic living in Austin, TX. He is the author of *Zero Saints* and *Coyote Songs* and the editor of *Both Sides* and *Halldark Holidays.* His work has been nominated to the Bram Stoker Award, the Locus Award and won the Wonderland Book Award in 2019. His editing work has been nominated to the Anthony Award and the International Latino Book Awards. He teaches creative writing at SNHU's online MFA program. You can find him on Twitter at @Gabino_Iglesias.

A.P. Jamison is a former investment banker who then received her MFA from Columbia University. Her short story, "The Nine Deaths in Hamlet?" starring detectives Gus and Marshmallow appeared in the Malice Domestic 2020 Anthology—*Mystery Most Theatrical.* Her first short story, "Death of the Hollywood Sign Girl," appeared in the Sisters in Crime/LA's 2019 Anthology—*Fatally Haunted.* In 2018, A.P. won the Sisters in Crime-LA/Mystery Writers of America twelve-word short story contest. She recently completed her first novel featuring the fearless and fun detectives Gus and Marshmallow.

Walter Mosley is the author of more than sixty critically-acclaimed books of fiction, nonfiction, memoir and plays. His work has been translated into twenty-five languages. His books have been adapted for film and TV and his short fiction and nonfiction essays have been published in a wide range of outlets from *The New York Times* to *The Nation.* He has won numerous awards, including an O. Henry Award, MWA's Grand Master Award, a Grammy®, NAACP Image awards, PEN America's Lifetime Achievement Award, the 2020 Robert Kirsch Award and the National Book Award's Distinguished Contribution to American Letters.

Tori Eldridge is the Honolulu-born and Anthony, Lefty and Macavity Awards–nominated author of the Lily Wong mystery thriller series—*The Ninja Daughter, The Ninja's Blade, The Ninja Betrayed*—and the upcoming dark Brazilian fantasy, *Dance Among the Flames* (out May 2022). She is of Hawaiian, Chinese, Norwegian descent and was born and raised on Oʻahu where she graduated from Punahou School with classmate Barack Obama. Her shorter works appear in horror, dystopian and other literary anthologies, including the inaugural reboot of *Weird Tales* magazine. Her screenplay *The Gift* was a Nicholl Fellowship semifinalist. Tori holds a fifth-degree black belt in To-Shin Do ninja martial arts and has performed as an actress, singer and dancer on Broadway, television and film.

Ellen Hart is the author of thirty-five crime novels. She has won numerous awards, including the Lambda Literary Award for Best Lesbian Mystery and the GCLS Trailblazer Award for lifetime achievement in the field of lesbian literature. In 2017, Ellen was named a Grand Master by Mystery Writers of America. This award was established to acknowledge important contributions to the genre, as well as for a body of work that is both significant and of consistent high quality. Ellen lives in Minneapolis with her partner of forty-four years.

G. Miki Hayden is a short story Edgar winner—the story, "The Maids," having appeared in an MWA anthology, much like this one. Her *Pacific Empire* (an alternate history), won a rave in the *New York Times*. Other novels of hers in print have ranged from mystery to science fiction/fantasy. She has had many stories published, including in *Alfred Hitchcock* and *Ellery Queen*, and has two writing instructionals in print. Miki has taught at Writer's Digest university online for more than twenty years.

Jonathan Santlofer is the author of *The Last Mona Lisa* and six other novels. His memoir *The Widower's Notebook* appeared on over a dozen "best books of 2018" lists. Santlofer is the editor of seven anthologies, including the *New York Times* Notable Book *It Occurs to Me That I Am America*. His short stories have appeared in magazines and anthologies. Also an artist, Santlofer's work is in major private and public collections, including the Metropolitan Museum of Art, the Art Institute of Chicago and Tokyo's Institute of Contemporary Art. He is the recipient of two National Endowment for the Arts grants, has been a Visiting Artist at the American Academy in Rome, and serves on the board of Yaddo, the oldest arts community in the US. He lives in NYC where he is at work on a new novel.

Jonathan Stone has published nine mystery and suspense novels, including *Die Next*, *Days of Night*, *The Teller*, *Parting Shot* and the bestseller *Moving Day*. Several of his books have been optioned to Hollywood, and *Moving Day* is set up as a film at Lionsgate Entertainment. His short stories have appeared in *Best American Mystery Stories 2016*, *New Haven Noir* and three previous MWA anthologies: *The Mystery Box* (ed. Brad Meltzer); *Ice Cold: Tales of Intrigue from the Cold War* (ed. Jeffery Deaver); and *When A Stranger Comes to Town* (ed. Michael Koryta).

Ovidia Yu writes short stories and mystery novels set in Singapore where she was born, lives and writes. In addition to novels and short stories, she has written plays and a children's book. Awards include: First prize, Asiaweek Short Story Competition; Scotsman Fringe First Award, Edinburgh Fringe Festival; Japanese Chamber of Commerce and Industry Singapore Foundation Culture Award; National Arts Council Young Artist Award; Singapore Youth Award (Arts and Culture); Southeast Asian Writers Award. She believes many crimes and most wars are sparked by people trying to impose their idea of what "home" should be on others.

Bonnie Hearn Hill has published more than a dozen novels as well as short fiction in *Ellery Queen's Mystery Magazine* and other publications. She was a 2019 Harlequin Creator Fund Re-